Lestrade and the sawdust ring

Walk up! Walk up! This way for the greatest show on earth!

It is 1879. Disraeli is at Number Ten. The Zulu are being perfectly beastly to Lord Chelmsford. And Captain Boycott is having his old trouble again.

What has all this to do with the young Detective-Sergeant Sholto Lestrade? Absolutely nothing. Or has it? He has his work cut out investigating mysterious goings-on at 'Lord' George Sanger's Circus. First, the best juggler in Europe is shot in full view of a thousand people. Then Huge Hughie the dwarf dies an agonising death under the Ether Trick. Finally the Great Bolus dies by swallowing the wrong sword. And all of this *after* two bodies have been found with multiple slashes . . .

And what is the link with Mr Howard Vincent, founder of the CID? And has the Prince Imperial *really* been caught by the Impis? A trail of murder is laid among the llama droppings as the World's Second Greatest Detective goes undercover to solve the Case of the Sawdust Ring.

LESTRADE AND THE SAWDUST RING

M. J. Trow

Constable · London

First published in Great Britain 1993
by Constable & Company Limited
3 The Lanchesters, 162 Fulham Palace Road
London W6 9ER
Copyright © 1993 M. J. Trow
ISBN 0 09 472170 X
The right of M. J. Trow to be
identified as the author of this work
has been asserted by him in accordance
with the Copyright, Designs and Patents Act 1988
Set in Linotron Palatino 10/12pt and
printed in Great Britain by
Redwood Press Limited
Melksham, Wiltshire

A CIP catalogue record for this book
is available from the British Library

1

'Gone?' the Prime Minister repeated. And again, for good effect, 'gone?'

There was a nod from the crimson face across the room.

'A curiously simple word,' the Prime Minister observed. Well, he had, a long time ago, written the best political novels in the English language. 'Yet I don't like the way it rolls out. When the Commander-in-Chief of the British Army comes to me on Shabbas . . . er . . . Saturday . . . and says "Gone", then I know there's trouble in the wind.'

He leaned back on the ottoman, named for the Empire he had always backed through thick and thin – the sick furniture of Europe.

'Perhaps you'd better tell me all about it, Your Royal Highness.'

His Royal Highness always knew when the Prime Minister was furious. His little goatee would twitch, his eyes would narrow and he would always use people's full titles. So what, he thought to himself and felt his aiguillette tauten as his chest puffed. He was Commander-in-Chief of the British Army, for God's sake. Duke of Cambridge, for God's sake. Cousin to the Queen . . . .

'For God's sake, George, he was under your care!' the Prime Minister had exploded rather earlier than usual. 'Having him doing tricks at Woolwich is one thing, but how could you have lost the little abortion?'

'Well, you know he gave an interview at Windsor?'

'Yes, I read it.'

'And another one at Woolwich?'

The Prime Minister nodded. 'Yes, I read that too.'

'And a few little impromptu words at the Army and Navy

5

Club, at which nearly one hundred Gentlemen of the Press happened to be present?'

'On all those occasions, no doubt, with his hand tucked firmly into his waistcoat, like his great uncle?'

Cambridge nodded. 'I'm afraid so.'

The Prime Minister's eyes rolled in his head so that he looked even more like a gargoyle than ever.

'Well, anyway, Napier saw him to the station.'

'Old Whiskerandos? He must be nearly three hundred. You'd think the Conqueror of Scinde would have something better to do with his time.'

'Gaga, I'm afraid,' Cambridge said.

Takes one to know one, mused the Prime Minister, arranging the tassle of his smoking cap. 'Then what?'

'Instead of saying his customary few words, he darted for another platform. Last seen waving from the quarter past eight from Victoria.'

'How's she taking it?' the Prime Minister asked.

'Who?'

'The Queen, God Bless Her,' the Prime Minister explained, as though to the regimental goat. 'Your cousin by the Grace of God.'

'Oh, God, she doesn't know,' Cambridge fiddled with his Mameluke hilt and wiped his rheumy eyes with the bullion tassels of his sash, 'and I'm not going to be the one to tell her.'

The Prime Minister looked at the Commander-in-Chief. Sixty, if he was a day. Old soldiers never die, he reflected – they just become Commanders-in-Chief. Odd, though, how the family likeness had come out. Cambridge had the same waist measurement as his cousin and the same red-rimmed, poppy eyes. Only the fluffy sidewhiskers were fuller.

'Did no one stop the train?'

'Mrs Cambridge could stop a clock. But you can't stop a train . . . can you?'

'There are such things as stations in life, Your Royal Highness. Such is my intimate knowledge of the Southern and Kent Railway network that I can tell you he should have stopped at Bromley.'

'I had a man waiting there,' Cambridge said, clearly proud of himself. After all, he had had a horse shot from under him at Inkerman. He was not a nincompoop. 'Sent ahead a telegram.'

'And?'

'Cow on the line at Penge East. He must have got off there.'

'What was he wearing?'

'Undress RA,' Cambridge told him.

'If my encyclopaedic knowledge of the British army serves me aright, that's a natty little blue number, narrow red stripes on the trousers, fetching little pillbox and Austrian knots to the cuffs.'

'That's the ticket.'

'Not exactly everyday wear at Penge East, I wouldn't have thought.'

'Mr Disraeli,' the Duke of Cambridge leaned forward as far as his girth and gilt decorations would allow, 'we must assume that His Highness the Prince Imperial had been planning this little disappearance for a while. Had it orchestrated to a tee, honed to a whisker. It's my belief he'd bribed an employee of the Southern and Kent Railway Company to have a civilian suit stashed aboard at Victoria. As I believe one of your predecessors is reputed to have said, "Every man has his price".'

'Let's leave Lord Derby out of this equation, shall we?' Disraeli snapped. 'You don't have to live with his choice of wallpaper in the bathroom – quite gives Lady B the staggers, I can tell you.'

'I just felt you ought to know, that's all,' Cambridge shrugged.

Disraeli rolled upright on the ottoman, as sprightly as a man can be at seventy-five with more than his fair share of gout. 'And I feel you ought to know, Your Royal Highness, that I disapproved from the start of the prince being here in the first place. I know his dad was a Special Constable in Chartist days and I know he had a house in Leamington, but good God! The man is a poseur, a charlatan. You only have to look at the way he waxes his moustache!' The Prime Minister struggled to his feet and staggered around the study with the aid of various pieces of furniture. 'It was, was it not, the machinations of the little abortion's ghastly mother that got him a commission?'

'Er . . . only my cousin can grant commissions, Lord Beaconsfield,' Cambridge said. 'You know that.'

Disraeli spun on his good leg, his dark eyes smouldering, his rococo curl flashing in the morning lamplight. He looked at the silver trowel on the sideboard and the little bunch of primroses beside it. 'The Empress Eugenie was responsible,' he said, mindful of the loyalty he owed to Her Majesty. He rather liked being Prime Minister. He rather liked being Earl of Beaconsfield. He rather liked his eighty-two-roomed mansion at Hughenden. And he didn't want to lose any of them. True, the country chose its leaders nowadays, not the monarch, but the monarch's enmity could be fatal – look at Gladstone. He'd never be resting his dubious backside on this ottoman again because it was common knowledge that the Queen detested him. True, Disraeli had the Queen around his little finger; but his little finger was giving him gyp these days.

'And you,' Disraeli pointed at the rotundity before him, 'you acquiesced, nay, you make acquiescence into a fine art.' The Prime Minister sat down in his desk chair. 'God help us if that bastard Gladstone ever finds out.'

There was a knock at the study door and a rather pompous flunkey entered. 'That bastard Gladstone to see you, sir.'

'Not now, Thatcher. Tell him I'm busy. Affairs of state. When am I free next?'

The pompous flunkey consulted a pocket diary. 'May 1884, sir,' he said.

'Five years,' Disraeli's grasp of mental arithmetic was legendary. 'Yes, that should do it.'

The study door crashed back and a seventy-year-old politician stood there, top hat firmly on his head, collar awry around his scrawny, chelonian neck.

'Gladdy!' Disraeli extended a hand, 'My dear fellow, why wasn't I told you were here? Thatcher,' he caught the flunkey a nasty one around the side of the head with his cane, 'you're fired.'

'Very good, sir,' and the flunkey exited.

'Dizzy, my dear fellow. Brother in Christ,' and Gladstone shook the Prime Minister's hand warmly.

'You know the Duke of Cambridge,' Disraeli motioned the Leader of the Opposition to a seat.

'Of course,' Gladstone shook the man's hand with the sinews of a keen axe-man. 'Can I apologize in advance for the cuts.'

'The cuts?' Cambridge rattled his sabre.

'That I intend to make in the army next year.'

There was silence.

'You know,' Gladstone explained in his melodious Lowland Scots accent, 'after the election, when I move in here. I hope you haven't changed that lovely wallpaper in the bathroom, Dizzy. Mrs G does so adore it.'

'What is it, Gladdy?' Disraeli flipped open his cheque-book, an object of virtue few living men had ever seen. 'A contribution to the Destitute Liberal Politicians' Fund or perhaps a token for your excellent work as founder of the Church Penitentiary Association for the Reclamation of Fallen Women?'

'Ah, generous as always,' Gladstone's thin lips snaked into the icy smile for which he was famous. 'By the way, did you ever pay dear old George Bentinck back for buying your country estate for you?'

Cambridge cleared his throat. 'Good Lord, is that the time? I must be away. Mrs Cambridge will have ratafias.'

'No, no,' Gladstone held his arm, 'it's rather fortuitous your being here this morning, Your Royal Highness, with Dizzy. Two birds with one stone, so to speak.'

'If it's Afghanistan . . .' Disraeli began.

'No, no,' Gladstone grinned, 'it isn't Afghanistan.'

'Well, if it's the Egyptian matter, I assure you that the Khedive . . .'

'No,' Gladstone beamed, enjoying the rattle of his Nemesis across the desk from him, 'not the Khedive.'

'Don't tell me there's been another Bulgarian Atrocity?' Disraeli widened his eyes. 'I don't think any of us have recovered from the last one.'

'Neither did some twelve thousand Christian souls butchered in the most barbarous way imaginable. Unspeakable tortures, Cambridge. Fates worse than a fate worse than death.'

'Fancy that,' was all the Commander-in-Chief could think of to say. He didn't like the blaze in Gladstone's eyes or the whitening of his knuckles, even the missing one covered by the black finger stall.

'What then?' Disraeli was prepared to risk the worst rather than hear *another* speech on the subject. At the *very* worst, he'd quickly reinstate Thatcher and get him to kick Gladstone out of his study, bag and baggage.

'The Prince Imperial,' Gladstone's anger had subsided and the veins ceased to bulge and throb in his forehead.

Cambridge squeaked.

'A brave, bright lad,' Disraeli nodded, stroking his not inconsiderable nose. 'He has, I gather, won golden opinions from all, both officers, professors and comrades, with whom he has been brought into contact in his Woolwich training and during the manoeuvres in which he has taken part.'

'Yes, thank you for that,' Gladstone said, crossing his obsolutely-trousered legs. 'I read that bit in the *Charivari* too. It failed to convince, I feel.'

'Well . . .' Disraeli wasn't often lost for words.

'The point is, he's gone to Zululand.'

'Er . . . he has? Cambridge, why wasn't I informed?'

'Um . . .' the Commander-in-Chief hadn't thought on his feet for nearly thirty-seven years. He'd rather lost the habit by now.

'No, no,' Disraeli assessed the man's incompetence at a glance. It was the way the colour had drained from his cheeks, 'just joking.'

Cambridge grinned like a rat in a trap. Gladstone's face remained the Lowland granite it usually was.

'You know, Gladdy, that the Prince Imperial is a Buonaparte. He has the blood of genius coursing through his veins. Oh, a different genius from my own, of course. More of the military type. He received his baptism of fire at Saarbruck against the Prussians. But he longs to taste steel again – the roar of musketry, the lines of bayonets . . .'

'Beaconsfieldism!' bellowed Gladstone.

'I beg your pardon?'

'Beaconsfieldism,' he repeated. 'It's my wee little word for military adventuring, Lord Beaconsfield. Rather akin to piracy.'

'Now, now, Gladdy,' Disraeli waved his ringed fingers to placate his old enemy, 'I have every confidence in Bartle Frere . . .'

'As you had every confidence in Lord Chelmsford, no doubt,' the Leader of the Opposition snapped, 'and his defeat at Isandlwhana is the most disastrous in recent history. As for Bartle Frere, the sooner you stop appointing people with silly names to the Foreign Office . . .'

'The Zulu attacked our forces,' Disraeli explained.

'The Zulu are a fine and magnificent people,' Gladstone had found his underdog again. 'King Cetewayo is worthy to hold court at Windsor itself.'

'I say, steady on,' Cambridge broke in, but the cold eyes of the two greatest politicians of their day stopped him dead.

'They merely responded to Chelmsford's presence,' Gladstone swept on, his blood up. 'A presence spearheaded by the 17th Lancers, I believe. The 17th Duke of Cambridge's Own Lancers. *Your* regiment, Your Royal Highness.'

'Er . . . is it? Er . . . are they? Oh, yes. Yes, I'll have a word with Colonel . . . Thing.'

'We are discussing Lieutenant Thing at the moment,' Gladstone reminded him, 'to be precise, Lieutenant Napoleon Eugene Louis Buonaparte, Royal Artillery seconded. You know what this is, Disraeli, don't you?' He leaned forward, his eyes smouldering.

'No, Gladstone,' Disraeli leaned forward too, 'but I'm sure you'll tell me.'

'It's murder.'

'It is?' Disraeli blinked.

'The Prince hasn't any of his own natives to kill, now that, for the moment, all is quiet on the Algerian Front, and so he's asked if he can come over to kill a few of ours. And you've let him. I call that murder.'

'And I call it international diplomacy,' Disraeli thundered, his goatee wagging, his brows beetling. 'And as long as I'm this side of this desk, and you're over there, that's how it'll stay. Was there anything else?'

Only the shaking of Cambridge's medals broke the silence. Gladstone smiled, stood up, bowed to the two men and crossed to the door.

'I shall watch the Prince Imperial's adventures with interest,' he said. He looked beyond Disraeli to the window and the bleak weather outside. 'Snow in the wind,' he said. 'I'll give you a year, Lord Beaconsfield. Then we'll see who's on which side of the desk. Don't get too comfy, will you?' And he left.

Cambridge crumpled like a bag of sugar, mopping his bald brow with his gauntlet-cuffs. 'Good God,' he mumbled, 'that man is terrifying.'

Disraeli dismissed him with a flutter of rings, 'Lukewarm,' he said. 'Usually after a visit from old Gladeye, the walls are awash with blood.'

'What shall we do?' Cambridge flustered, 'What shall we do?'

'Get a grip on yourself, man,' Disraeli ordered. 'The first thing we do is to thank whatever God we pray to that Gladstone's spies are clearly not aware of the Prince's little disappearing act this morning. They think he's in Zululand. That's all to the good. Gives us a breather, already. How long will it – would it – have taken him to get there?'

'Er . . . three weeks, if the engines don't pack up.'

'Three weeks. That makes it 24 March,' he rang the bell cord and a rather downhearted, but still pompous, flunkey appeared in hat, coat and bag.

'You rang, my lord?'

'Take that expression off your face, Thatcher – and that coat off your back. Who's that hack on the party payroll? Writes, for want of a better word, on the *Graphic*?'

'Andrew Burns, sir,' a glimmer of relief flitted across the strong features of the flunkey.

'Right. Get him here. Now. You'll find him at the Waysgoose in Fleet Street. You'd better brief him in advance. He'll need time to assimilate the situation. He is to take ship from the Port of London today and paddle like Hell to Natal Colony, having put in at the Cape to buy a huge supply of pencils and a cholera belt. There he will report on every breath the Prince Imperial takes. Got it?'

'Every word, sir.'

'If His Highness breaks wind, I want to read about it in the *Graphic* three or four days later. Understand? We'll tackle the Association Against Rabelaisian Sentences in Editions as and when they cause a rumpus. Well, don't just stand there, Thatcher; you're supposed to be one of us.'

'Very good, sir,' and the flunkey was gone, delighted to be reinstated.

'But, Lord Beaconsfield . . . the Prince Imperial has not gone to Natal.'

Disraeli sighed and closed his rococo eyelids. 'Oy vay,' he whispered, '*you* know that, Your Royal Highness. *I* know that. Probably the Prince Imperial knows that. We can safely add Thatcher to that small but unhappy band – the man has a degree in listening at keyholes. And by eleven o'clock, journalist Burns of the *Graphic* will know it too. But Gladstone, the Queen, the Empress of the French and the great British public? They are as ignorant as shit. And that is how I'd like it to stay. Tell me, you must have had a man with the little abortion. An aide or something?'

'Yes indeed. Captain Jaheel Carey, 98th Foot. He's a good man. Passed the Staff College.'

'Yes, I did that once,' Disraeli was unimpressed, 'on a whistle-stop tour of the Home Counties. I have also been known to pass water. This Carey is clearly an idiot.'

'Oh, yes,' Cambridge changed front, 'I'll have him cashiered.'

'No,' Disraeli was thinking aloud, 'that's too easy.'

'You're right, of course, Lord Beaconsfield. I'll have him shot as well, although of course, we'll have to make it look like an accident – Martini-Henry jamming or something like that.'

'All in good time,' the Prime Minister said. 'Heads can roll later in as much abundance as we think fit. In the meantime, get this Carey out of his uniform and on to the road. It is his job to find the Prince Imperial at all costs, before he does something daft and attention-seeking.'

'But, how . . . ?'

'How,' glowered Disraeli, 'is not a question worthy of an Englishman. It does not exist, any more than the Irish Question does. The little abortion was last seen on a train tooting its way through Kent. That's where Carey's task starts. And he'd better make a better job of it than he has so far. The problem of course is that the man speaks six languages, including English, like a native and as for his appearance, he is Mister Average. If he chooses to become incognito, we're all buggered. This Carey, presumably, knows him well?'

'Er . . . no. Only met him half an hour earlier. Shouldn't we call in the police, Prime Minister? Scotland Yard?'

Disraeli shuddered. 'Two years ago, Your Royal Highness, the bowels of the Yard were ripped open in the Trial of the Detectives, exposing a number of Yard officers as guilty of corruption the likes of which would cause steam to pour forth from the ears of Mr Gladstone and his ilk. We haven't come very far from the Thief-takers, have we really? It's well known that the Yard runs on the policy of this new – and I shudder to note, French – system of Mr Howard Vincent; the CID. Do you know what that stands for?'

'Er . . . no,' Cambridge was the first to admit.

'Corruption, Incompetence and Drunkenness. Rather than

hand this wretched business over to the Yard, I'd consider becoming a Liberal.'

Cambridge's mouth gaped open.

'Well, there you are,' Disraeli said. 'Now, if you don't mind buggering off, Your Royal Highness, I have two wars to run and your Cousin's horse is running in the two-thirty. Good morning.'

The body lay in the morning mist, the chest ripped open to the sky. Black-feathered rooks cawed and flapped, pecking suddenly at clothes and flesh. Two of them, braver, more tenacious than the rest, ripped harder and flew to the high elms, each with its dripping trophy – the right eye and the left.

2

The reptile lay across the armchair, its long tail sliding from side to side across the carpet. Other than that, there was no movement in its green and brown body. Only its eye swivelled to take in the view. And the view was blocked by an extraordinary sight. A man with skin the colour of parchment, the eyes sad and dark-circled, the moustache like a tropical caterpillar of frightening proportions. The hair was carefully macassared, the parting central, highly unfashionable at this end of the '70s. He was wearing a Donegal, the collar of which he had unbuttoned against the roaring intensity of the open fire. He was bending down, peering at the lizard, when a voice broke the sanctity of the moment.

'Lestrade!'

The man jerked upright and the reptile's hackles rose, only to fall again at the approach of its master.

'What are you doing there? You are aware that there is a law against carnal relations with *Iguana Tuberculata* – 6th of William IV, I think.'

'I . . .'

The master had swept the cold-blooded thing into his arms and it rolled on its side, toes pawing the air in a slow-motion paroxysm of delight. 'Was the horrid man hurting you, Ignatius?' and he ran a finger the length of the creature's belly. 'Sergeant Abernethy in Accounts says they purr, you know, but what with his short sight and his tragic lack of a brain, I think he's thinking of another animal entirely. No, Iggie,' he rubbed noses with the reptile, 'it's not time for w-a-l-k-i-e-s yet. Do you mind, Lestrade,' he pushed the man aside, 'you're blocking Ignatius' view of the fire. The Central American climate, you see, is vastly different from our own.'

He laid the beast down gently on the armchair again and threw it an apple. Then a thought occurred. 'You don't have any Mexican blood in you, Lestrade?' he asked, scrutinizing the dark features.

'I don't believe so, sir.'

'Just as well,' Sir said, 'Mexicans eat them, you know,' his voice had fallen to a whisper, 'and their eggs. Their flesh is white and delicate, apparently.'

'Mexicans?'

'Iguanae, Lestrade. Oh dear, this doesn't bode too well.'

'What doesn't, sir?'

'I've got to put you to work with a new Inspector this morning, sergeant. And you don't know what day it is.'

'It's Thursday, sir,' Lestrade was at pains to establish his integrity and professionalism.

'How old are you, Lestrade?' the master peered at him from behind his opulent desk, 'forty-three? Forty-four?'

The Detective-Sergeant bridled. 'I have recently celebrated my twenty-fifth birthday, sir.'

'Good God. Really?' Sir looked askance. 'Nothing much to celebrate there, I wouldn't have thought. Well, there it is.'

A powerful pair of knuckles rapped on the glass-panelled door.

'Come!' Sir bellowed.

A tall man, a little older than Lestrade, swept in wearing an astrakhan coat and topper.

'Ah, Inspector Hastings Heneage, may I introduce Sergeant Sholto Lestrade, your number two.'

'*Enchanté*,' the Inspector smiled, shaking his man's hand firmly, 'Now, don't tell me . . . er . . . Eton.'

'Mr Poulson's Academy for the Sons of Nearly Respectable Gentlefolk, Blackheath, sir,' Lestrade said.

'Oh, really,' Heneage's face fell. 'Good God!' he suddenly

15

recoiled in horror, 'Director, there's a ... thing ... on your armchair.' He twirled a gold-topped cane upright with both hands. 'I'll get it.'

'Heneage!' the Director screamed, but it was too late. Ignatius had clearly learned the dictum of Frederick the Great – an iguana awaiting attack will be cashiered – and he went for the Inspector in no small way, gripping his gonads with powerful jaws. Heneage's eyes crossed and cane and man toppled to the carpet, the reptile rolling with them both.

'Heel, Ignatius!' the Director commanded. Nothing. The beast did not move, clearly finding his current mouthful far more succulent than a heel. The Director shook his head. 'He's quite inoffensive usually – apart from the smell, I mean – but get him roused...'

Lestrade shuffled uncomfortably, 'Oughtn't we to ... rescue the Inspector, sir. Perhaps if I ...' and he bravely put out a tentative toe, steel-shod as it was.

'No, no,' the Director tapped his leg away, 'Iggie will let go in an hour or so. It doesn't look as though the Inspector is going anywhere.' He checked his eyelids, 'Out like a light. I'm not sure I like that in an Inspector of Scotland Yard. Well, Lestrade, to cases. Sit down, man. I'll have to brief you alone. You can pass the word to the Inspector when he comes to.'

'Very good, sir,' and Lestrade sat gingerly on the upright chair as far away as he could from the beast and its kill.

'How long have we known each other, Lestrade?' the Director asked.

'Er ... nearly two years, sir.'

'Quite. The Trial of the Detectives, wasn't it? You grassed on Palmer, Druscovitch and Co.'

'I was asked to report by Mr Williamson, sir,' Lestrade corrected him, 'and I didn't enjoy doing it.'

'Quite, quite. I know, Lestrade, I know. There's honour among coppers. But they were bastards, sergeant. Gave the whole Force a bad name. Their removal marked the end of one era and the start of another. As the Attorney-General said, the Scotland Yard scandal came as a thunderclap to the community and spread over England the greatest possible alarm.'

'Did it, sir?'

'Of course it did, Lestrade. If the Attorney-General says so,

16

then it certainly did. Which is where Inspector Heneage comes in. His credentials – despite a certain lack of understanding of *tuberculata* – are impeccable. Harrow, Balliol. First Class Honours in Jurisprudence.'

To Lestrade, prudence seemed the last thing that Heneage had a degree in, but it wasn't his place to say so. 'Which Division is he from, sir?' he asked.

'Division?' the Director frowned, 'Oh no, Lestrade. Mr Heneage has no divisional experience.'

'Another Force, then?'

'No.'

'But . . .'

'It's an experiment, Lestrade,' the Director said. 'To add tone to what would otherwise be a vulgar brawl. We need a few nobs on the Force. Mr Heneage is a gentleman,' he closed to Lestrade, 'His father was at school with Palmerston.'

'Oh, good,' said Lestrade without smiling, 'Mr Vincent,' he leaned forward too, 'are you telling me that this man is already an Inspector and he has no police experience whatever?'

Vincent sat back in his chair, tutting by the firelight, 'Tsk, Lestrade – and again I say, tsk – that is the politics of envy. You haven't read any Marx, have you?'

'I've had a few black ones against me in my time, sir. I'm not anxious to gain more.'

'Ah, yes,' Vincent's eyes narrowed above the aquiline nose, between the large, drooping ears and even further above the monstrous moustache that totally eclipsed his mouth, 'Your career. Let me see,' he opened a ledger on his desk. 'A slim volume. Police Constable, City Force, 1873. Detective-Constable, H Division, Metropolitan Police, 1875. Detective-Sergeant, attached Headquarters, 1877. Your rise has been that rare phenomenon – meteorically unspectacular.'

'Thank you, sir.'

'The point is this, Lestrade. You know Detective-Inspector Blake?'

'Yessir.'

'Of marginally greater intellect than a turnip. Inspector Bryden?'

'Yessir.'

'Likewise. Chief-Inspector O'Donnell?'

17

'Indeed.'

'Can't – and I don't want this noised abroad, Lestrade – tie his own bootlaces.'

Lestrade blinked and glanced down to check on his.

'A disastrous lack of the old grey matter,' Vincent tapped his temple. 'We just aren't attracting men of the right calibre. All the bright ones – like Palmer, Druscovitch et al – are bent. The honest ones are no doubt straight as pokers, but they have similar intellects to those household implements. Heneage there has a huge intelligence quotient.'

They looked down, the Director of Criminal Investigation and the Detective-Sergeant, at the elegant, astrakhan-covered heap on the floor. Ignatius showed no signs of relinquishing his prey, but rolled an eyelid at Vincent.

'Look at him,' the Director smiled indulgently, 'like the cat that's got the cream. Your rôle in all this, Lestrade,' he sat upright, 'is to provide experience. You've pounded the beat where Heneage has not. You know what it is to wear the helmet, to twirl the rattle. You know a tipstaff from a set of handcuffs. With your street-wise qualities and his brilliance, you'll knock 'em dead in Ilkley.'

'Where, sir?' Lestrade's eyebrows rose.

Vincent sighed. 'Well, there you are. Heneage would know instinctively where that is.'

'Where?' Inspector Heneage asked squeakily, walking a little gingerly along C corridor.

'Ilkley, sir,' Lestrade told him, supporting his guv'nor's tottering bulk. 'It's a spa in the West Riding of Yorkshire, on the River Wharfe, near Bradford.'

'Good God. And there's been a murder there, you say? Well, well. How do we get there?'

'By train, sir.'

'Train? Oh, marvellous. I love trains. How long are we going for?'

'That depends, sir.'

'Does it? Oh, yes, of course. On the inquiries, I suppose. Right. Only I need to tell my man how many shirts to pack. Any ideas? What do you tell your man?'

'I don't have a man, sir.'

'Really? Good Lord. My dear fellow, how ever do you manage?'

'With difficulty, sir,' sighed Lestrade.

'Ah, well. Buck up. Lisbon is a capital fellow. He'll do for us both.'

'Yes,' muttered Lestrade, reaching for his battered Gladstone, 'I'm sure he will.'

Up a bit on the Great Northern. Across a bit on the North Western. For the first time in his life, Detective-Sergeant Lestrade rode first class. He dozed in the snug compartment, with the blinds down against the inclement face of Disraeli's England. March it may have been, but north of Watford the slush lay brown and treacherous and north of Headingley the snow white and unrelenting. Inside, his head nodding against the Chinese flock and his socks steaming nicely over the portable Silber and Fleming stove, Lestrade's dreams were less tranquil than they ought to have been. Not six months earlier, the rubber-faced Charlie Peace, facing a train window not very far from where Lestrade dozed fitfully now, had unfastened his fly buttons to answer the call of nature and had taken the opportunity to kick his way free of the guards who held him. For a while the piercing eyes flashed in the sunken skull in Lestrade's dream, the silver whiskers bristled. Then the jaw clicked sideways, the white hood was hauled over his head and the hemp noose slipped into place. There was a jarring sound as the lever was hauled back, the doors crashed down and the thud of the dead man's shoes as they hit the floor woke the Detective-Sergeant up.

'You for coffee, Mr Lestrade?' Lisbon was standing over him, beaming like a hangman.

A chaise took them through the blackness of the watering place, past the little churchyard of All Saints with its three Saxon crosses, over the old packhorse bridge that still crossed the darkling waters of the Wharfe. They stood at last below the sheer precipice of the Cow Rock, the great crag that with its child, the Calf, towered over the little town of Ilkley. The Romans had camped here in the early days, when it was called Olicana and dotted here and there were the great, grey mills that gave the North its satanic gloom. But in the centre, where Inspector Heneage had found the only decent hotel, the new hydropathic establishments were springing up, threatening to rival Buxton in their opulence.

Inspector Bosomworth of the West Riding Constabulary stood ankle deep in snow with his knot of blue-caped men.

'Doesn't care for t'weather, then, your Inspector,' he observed in the stentorian tones of those parts, 'seeing as 'ow 'e's not actually up 'ere wi' us?'

'It's been rather a tiring journey, sir,' Lestrade told him, 'what with an oyster shortage on the Great Northern.'

'Aye,' Bosomworth looked at his own sergeant, 'life's a bugger all round, in't it? Any road up, 'e were found 'ere.'

''Ere?'

'Precisely where you're stood standin' now.'

'Who found him?'

'You know, I don't want t' pull rank at all. But I speak as I find. Call a spade a spade, that's my motto. You're a bloody sergeant, aren't you?'

'Yes.'

'Right. Well, I'm a bloody Inspector. Thirteen years, man an' tyke. I don't believe in standin' on t'dignity, but a little "sir" now and again wouldn't come amiss.'

'Yessir,' said Lestrade, 'Of course, sir. My pleasure, sir.'

'All right. All right. No need t' overdo it. Now, what was yer askin'?'

'Who found the body, sir?'

'Oh aye. Some bloke called Haythornthwaite. Local shepherd. 'E were out checkin' 'is lambs – it bein' t'season an' all. An' 'e stumbled over 'im.'

'Had he fallen . . . sir?' Lestrade shielded his eyes from the glare of the leaden sky. The great grey crag loomed over him so that he felt for a moment as if the ground was leaving his feet and he would topple backwards.

'It's possible. But that's what you're supposed t' be tellin' us. That's why we called you buggers from t'Yard in. Not, mind you, that that were my idea. Oh, dear me, nay. It were t'Mayor.'

'The dead man?'

'Nay. It were t'Mayor who insisted on calling in t'Yard. Buggered if I know why, lookin' at you. 'E's worried, y'see, abowt t'tourists. Afraid no bugger will come to take t'waters if there's bodies all over t'shop.'

'There's more than one . . . sir?' Lestrade frowned.

'Nay, lad,' Bosomworth explained, 'It were just a figure of speech – an idiot, you might say. But the Mayor, 'e wants this business cleared up right away. I don't see 'ow seeing t'murder site is going to 'elp you at all. I've got my man.'

Lestrade looked at the Inspector. 'You've made an arrest?'

'Eighteen of 'em.'

'What?'

'What, sir?' Bosomworth reminded him. 'I said,' he raised his voice against the east wind and stamped his feet in the drifting snow, 'I've made eighteen arrests.'

'On what grounds?'

'Grounds? Grounds?' Bosomworth closed to his man, 'This is my patch, is this,' he said. 'This isn't bloody London town. We've got ways, y' know. There's been a police force in Ilkley since I were a tyke – and that's going back a few years, I can tell yer.'

He spun round suddenly to silence the sniggers at his back. It was pretty effective. 'I've picked out eighteen buggers I reckon 'ad every reason to do fer whoever it is was done fer up 'ere.'

'Such as?'

'Such as? Such as? Well,' he raised a stubby left thumb, 'Joe Arkwright for a start.'

'Did he have a grudge against the dead man?'

''Ow should I know? I don't even friggin' know who t'dead man is, do I? But Joe Arkwright's been poachin' across t'moor for bloody donkey's years. I'll settle 'is 'ash.'

'Anybody else?' Lestrade was incredulous.

'Aye. Seventeen other buggers. Thieves, confidence tricksters, malingerers and layabouts. Oh, and one army deserter. One of 'em must 'ave done it.'

'Why?'

'Stands to reason,' Bosomworth shrugged, 'Most of 'em 'ave no fixed abode. You show me a man wi'out an abode that's fixed an' I'll show you a scallywag of t'worst water.'

'Bit of a difference between scallywagging and murder, sir,' Lestrade observed.

Bosomworth's northern lip curled into a snarl. His southern one stayed where it was. ' 'E were found 'ere,' he growled, 'Right where your feet are. Now unless you'd like us all t' join 'im by freezin' t' bloody death, let's bloody go. Resnick?'

'Inspector?' a uniformed constable piped up.

'Your turn for t'cocoa.'

T'cocoa was just what the Detective-Sergeant ordered. Or rather, he didn't, but he got it anyway. As Bosomworth's man reminded him as he slammed the chipped, handleless mug down on the table, Ilkley was famous for its bloody 'ospitality. Still, chipped and handleless was what Lestrade was used to. Home from home, really.

Inspector Heneage had risen by this time and Lisbon had helped him dress. Mufflered against the vicious afternoon nip, he crossed the Wharfe in a pony and trap and arrived at the Pump Rooms basement as Lestrade and Bosomworth approached from the station yard.

The basement of the Pump Rooms did stalwart service as a makeshift morgue. On the very slab where in the season, retired colonels let their flab hang out amid swirling mists of steam, the cold, white-blue body lay naked before the policemen's gaze.

'As it's your first visit,' Bosomworth grunted to Heneage, nodding in the direction of the corpse, 'perhaps you'd like t' be t'first t' examine 'im. I'd like your views.'

Heneage took one look, moaned 'Good God!' and collapsed gracefully to the floor.

'Nay,' Bosomworth shook his head. 'I don't think it's t'Almighty. Somethin' vaguely blasphemous about that. Does 'e always do this?' he asked Lestrade.

'Only in the presence of corpses and lizards,' the sergeant told him.

'Well, shovel 'im up, Smurthwaite. Makes t'place look untidy.'

The constable of that name helped the mortuary attendant to carry the fallen Heneage to another slab in the corner.

'Get a lump of ice from outside and put it on 'is 'ead,' Bosomworth bellowed. ' 'E'll be all right. Now then, Lestrade. What do you make on t' this? Or are you goin' to go swimmy too?'

Lestrade would not go swimmy. He had seen the Sights before.

No doubt he could stand one more. The dead man was about his own age, with light brown hair cropped short. His face had been pulverized with a heavy object, the nose flattened and the nostrils flared, caked in dark-brown blood. Where the eyes should have been were sightless holes, like the sockets in a skull. The teeth, as he peeled back the blue lips, were broken and jagged and the chest had been ripped by diagonal cuts that crossed each other. Neat. Precise. Almost in a geometric pattern.

'Bit of a facer, in't it?' Bosomworth observed, tilting back his bowler. 'I'll confess we don't get many o' these in Ilkley.'

Or anywhere else, mused Lestrade. 'Who washed the body?' he asked.

'I did,' a wizened little creature hobbled back from the unconscious Inspector.

'This is Ben Thirkettle,' Bosomworth said, 'T'stoker to t'Pump Room boilers. 'E also lays folk out.'

Lestrade doubted that. At least not for a long time. Still, old Thirkettle could conceivably have been a flyweight in his youth.

'Which way did the blood run?' Lestrade asked.

'Come again?' Thirkettle squinted at him.

'When you washed the body, the blood on the chest; which way did it run?'

'Well, 'e'd bin froze, y' see,' the toothless man told him, with much gratuitous smacking of the lips. 'T'blood were crusty, like. I 'ad to scrape it off wi' a trowel.'

'From here,' Lestrade's finger traced the line of the diagonal cut, 'Did it run down or up?'

'Er . . . down. Nay. Nay. Wait a minute,' Thirkettle closed his eyes and chewed his lip in concentration. 'Aye. Up. Nay. Down.'

'Bloody 'ell as like,' Bosomworth stamped his feet. 'Mind like a razor, this one.'

'Down.' Thirkettle flashed a defiant glance at him. 'I'm sure. It were down.'

'And here?' Lestrade said, following the line of the other cut.

'Down again. Towards 'is 'ip.'

Lestrade nodded. Suddenly, as Bosomworth and Thirkettle watched, he crouched over the torso, something gleaming in his right hand.

'What t'bloody hell . . . ?'

Lestrade held up a set of brass knuckles with a four inch blade that shone in the lamplight, 'A little cosmetic surgery,' he said. 'I'm sure our friend won't mind.' He dipped the point of the knife into one cut, high on the chest. Then into the other. Then he tickled the point between the nipples where the cuts crossed. 'Right,' he stood up and clicked home the blade before consigning the weapon to the pocket of his Donegal.

'Is that t'Metropolitan issue?' Bosomworth asked, frowning.

'Not exactly,' Lestrade said. By now he was peering at what was left of the face.

'The eyes . . .' he said.

'Rooks,' said Thirkettle.

Lestrade looked at him. 'It was merely a civil question,' he told him.

'Nay, lad,' Bosomworth explained. 'Rooks. Y' know. Big black bloody birds.'

'Oh, rooks,' Lestrade gave it the southern pronunciation.

'Aye,' said Thirkettle, 'that's what I said. T'rooks would 'ave 'ad 'em out. Anythin' layin' on t'moors for a day or two is fair game.'

'I'll tell yer somewhat,' Bosomworth grinned, ''E's not goin' to see us through t'week, that's for certain.'

Thirkettle broke into a donkey's bray of a laugh, his jaw chewing round and round.

'These wounds', Lestrade ignored them both, 'to the head. Which way was the blood running here?'

'Down,' Thirkettle was sure this time. 'Both sides of 'is face.'

'Not off the chin?'

'Nay. Out to t'sides.'

'Well,' said Bosomworth, lighting his pipe, 'I'd be impressed if I knew what t'bloody 'ell you were talking about.'

Lestrade stepped back from the body, 'I *think* I know what happened,' he said.

'Go on then, lad,' Bosomworth urged him, 'I'm all friggin' ears.'

'The chest wounds came first,' the sergeant told him. 'This one', he drew his finger from the left shoulder to the right ribs, 'delivered first, the other second.'

'Which means?'

'Our man is right-handed.'

'Well,' Bosomworth's lucifer had found its mark at the end of his pipe and his stolid features flashed eerily in the dim light, 'that reduces it t' nine in every ten. What made the cuts?'

'The murderer,' Lestrade said, somewhat surprised. Surely, the Yorkshire Constabulary wasn't *that* deficient?

'What weapon, man?' Bosomworth snapped.

'Butcher's knife,' Lestrade guessed, 'meat cleaver. Something of that sort. Long and sharp. He was still standing when the blows struck. Which means that our man is both strong and fast. What was he wearing when he was found?'

'Er . . . combinations, waistcoat, shirt, trousers and jacket.'

'Right,' nodded Lestrade, 'the cuts are quarter of an inch deep. Allowing for a thickness of clothing, the blows must have been delivered with a great burst of energy. Demonic, almost.'

'De what?' Bosomworth asked.

'As though by t'devil,' Thirkettle piped up.

The Inspector rounded on him, 'May I remind you you're t'bloody boilerman at t'Pump Rooms. There's a certain perspective t' be kept around 'ere. What about t'head?' he asked Lestrade.

'I think he'd have died from the chest wounds,' the sergeant told him. 'The blows to the head were delivered later, with a heavy object. By this time he was lying on the ground. The direction of the blood tells us that.'

'Does it?' Bosomworth asked.

'If he'd been standing, the blood would have trickled *down* his face, not across it.'

'Why bash 'im as well as slash 'im?' the Inspector wanted to know.

Lestrade shrugged. 'Perhaps he wasn't sure he was dead.'

'The meat cleaver,' Bosomworth sucked hard on the briar, 'would it 'ave 'ad a sharp point?'

'Probably,' Lestrade said. 'It's more a butcher's knife, but single edged, I'd say.'

'So why didn't 'e finish 'im off wi' t'point?' Bosomworth's logic was inescapable.

'I don't know,' Lestrade confessed. 'Can I see his belongings?'

Thirkettle shuffled over to a drawer and jerked it open. ''Ere,' he said, 'a 'anky. A' Albert watch. A letter.'

'What are they?' Lestrade pointed into the drawer.

'Oh, bloody 'ell,' Thirkettle said, 'I knew I'd put 'em somewhere,' and he fitted his dentures back in with much lip-smacking ceremony.

The handkerchief was of finest Irish lawn and in the corner, the embroidered initial 'N'. Nigel? mused Lestrade. Norris? Norman? Nellie? The computations were endless. The watch was a beauty. Silver gilt and worn. Something of an heirloom, he imagined. The glass was cracked and the thing had stopped at ten to two.

'I reckon that's t'time 'e died, y' know,' Bosomworth said. 'That butcher's knife 'it 'im an' 'it at that precise moment in time.'

'Does that help us, sir?' Lestrade asked.

'Wi'out knowin' which bloody day this were, nay,' Bosomworth said. ''Cept it gives me a perfect alibi. I've been on t'midday shift every bloody day this month. At least *my* whereabouts are accounted fer. Nice watch though, in't it?'

The inscription on the back was in a foreign language. Lestrade spelt it out. 'N-o-u-b-l-i-e-z-p-a-s-e-y-l-a-u. What's that?'

'I dunno,' Bosomworth said. 'It's in a foreign bloody language.'

It wasn't Latin. Lestrade knew that. All those years on the first declension at Mr Poulson's Academy had given him a taste for the tongue. Unless of course it was the *second* declension.

'This is foreign too,' Bosomworth held up the letter. It had no date. It had no address. It began '*Mon cher Louis*' and it was signed '*Maman*'. The rest was gibberish. Lestrade held it over the lamp. No discernible watermark.

'What about his clothes?' Lestrade asked.

Thirkettle shuffled across to a coat-stand on which a solitary jacket hung. ''Ere,' he said.

Lestrade examined it. A coarse northern tweed, he guessed. No label. No name. The pockets empty. Both elbows were gaping and someone had inexpertly resewn the ragged edges across the lapels made by the lightning butcher's knife. 'Where's the rest?' he asked.

Reluctantly, the newly-toothed Thirkettle took off his waistcoat, the one with the bad, new stitching, and began to unbutton his recently-slashed shirt. 'All right,' Lestrade held up his hand, 'I don't think we need go further. Can I assume that there is nothing to help us identify the man in the clothes you're wearing?'

'Layer-out's perks,' Thirkettle explained at what he took to be

Lestrade's righteous indignation. 'Unfortunately, Mrs Thirket-tle's somethin' of a slouch when it comes t' needlework.'

Lestrade was less horrified by that than the fact that there *was* a Mrs Thirkettle at all. 'Come t' think of it,' the boilerman/mortuary assistant chewed on, 'I don't think I'll bother,' and he proceeded to strip to what appeared to be his own combinations.

'Is this a local cloth?' Lestrade asked Bosomworth.

'Yorkshire, as like,' the Inspector examined the weave, 'but us is a bloody big county, y' know. I wouldn't like t' be specific about t'Ridin'.'

'Have the Gentlemen of the Press got hold of this yet?' the sergeant asked.

'Press?' Bosomworth spat vaguely at the floor. 'Gentlemen?' he spat again. 'Neither o' them words 'ave any meanin' for a police-man,' he said. ''Sides, t'Mayor 'as threatened to 'ave my balls on a breadboard if one single word gets out. Remember t'tourist trade. They'll be swarmin' up 'ere from York an' Doncaster an' Leeds by t'week after next. Only if t'buggers get wind o' this, they'll bugger off t' 'Arrogate.'

'Or they might bugger off here in droves, sir,' Lestrade said. 'They still do guided tours of the Ratcliffe Highway where I come from – and those killings were in 1811.'

'Aye, well, that's as may be,' the Inspector clamped anew on his briar stem, 'but that's Lunnon for yer. Wouldn't do up 'ere, I assure you. There's nowt s' queer as folk. 'Appen.'

Lestrade was quickly losing the thread of this conversation, but he held on. 'I just thought that an article in the local paper might help identify the man. We're not going to get very far with a face like that.'

'Agreed,' said Bosomworth. 'But you'll 'ave t' find another way.'

'All right,' Lestrade sighed. 'Do you mind if I keep this letter? And this watch? Maybe my guv'nor can shed some light.'

Bosomworth turned to the prostrate policeman who lay like the death of Chatterton. ''Im? Couldn't shed skin, 'e couldn't.' The clock in the corner caught his eye. 'Bugger me. 'Alf past. My Rest Day started twenty minutes ago. If you need me, I'm not abloo-dyvailable until Monday.'

'Good God, Lestrade,' Inspector Heneage was muttering as Lisbon flew hither and thither with the smelling salts, 'are you telling me that you *regularly* have to view . . . things like that?'

'Bodies, sir? Oh, yes,' Lestrade applied his frozen hands to the radiator. 'They tend to crop up now and then in the course of a murder inquiry.'

'Good God. Oh, Lisbon, do stop fussing, there's a good chap. I'm perfectly all right.'

'I promised Lady Heneage, sir,' the man's man reminded him.

'I know you did, Lisbon,' the Inspector said, taking the ice pack off his head, 'but Mama of sainted memory has been in Kensal Green now these eight years. Having spent a term on Humanism at Oxford, I'm not convinced she's actually aware of what's going on nowadays.'

Lisbon managed to look outraged and crestfallen at the same time, but busied himself in preparing the mid-evening eggnog with his portable Silber and Fleming eggnog maker.

'So, Lestrade,' Heneage did his best to concentrate, 'what did you learn from that revolting spectacle?'

'Very little, sir, I'm afraid,' the sergeant said, 'unless you want an infantry of the dead man's wounds.'

'No,' Heneage said, a little too quickly to be casual. 'No, I don't think that will help. Do we have an inkling of who he may once have been?'

'Ah, well,' Lestrade unlaced his boots and wrung his socks out over the carpet. 'Er . . . you don't mind, sir? Only, I've been tramping the moors again while you've been . . . um . . . resting and I can't actually feel my feet.'

'Quick, Lisbon,' Heneage called, 'hot water. And plenty of it. Towels. Jump to it, man.'

A pompous face appeared around the adjoining door. 'Is Mr Lestrade about to give birth, sir?' he enquired.

'Oh God,' Heneage's colour drained, 'if that's the approach of gangrene on your left big toe, Lestrade, I feel I might "go" again . . .'

'No, sir,' Lestrade was quick to reassure him, 'that's just the combination of a hole in my boot and wet grass. It's difficult on a sergeant's pay to make ends meet.'

'Particularly the ends of one's boots, apparently,' a disapproving Lisbon said, sweeping in with a bowl of steaming water.

'Immerse your nether limbs in that lot, sir. And would you mind not screaming? The walls in this establishment are paper thin.'

'I'll try,' promised Lestrade and had to bite his lip to keep his promise. 'Hot pains,' he winced, 'hot pains.'

'Bravely borne, dear fellow,' said Heneage. 'Now, about that poor chap's identity.'

'Ah, yes,' Lestrade wiped the tears from his eyes as the feeling returned to his feet, 'that's the thirteen bob question. This might help.'

'Aha,' Heneage took the first item. 'It's a handkerchief, Lestrade.'

'Very good, sir. What do you make of the initial?'

'Now that's an "N", Lestrade. Forgive me for being blunt, but do you have the basic skills?'

'Sir?'

'Can you actually read?'

'Quite well, thank you sir,' the sergeant felt his hackles rising along with the agony in his calves. 'I was hoping you might know who "N" was.'

'Oh, I see,' a frown darkened Heneage's handsome features. 'Hmm. That's a bit of a facer, isn't it? Could be almost anybody.'

'Thank you, sir. What about this?'

'Ah, now that's easy. That's a watch, Lestrade,' the Inspector caught the look on his sergeant's face, 'but I suspect you'd already deduced that. Let me see, it's an Albert. Belcher chain. Ah, Lisbon, the nog. Many thanks,' and he sipped it from the silver mug. Lestrade wasn't offered any. 'Oh, it's broken. What a shame.'

'Inspector Bosomworth believes it was broken in the attack, sir.'

'Tsk, tsk, how dreadful,' muttered Heneage. 'Wait a minute. What's this?' He had found the back of the watch.

'It's an inscription, sir. In a foreign language.'

'Foreign be damned, Lestrade,' the Inspector sat up, 'it's French.'

'It is?' Could there be some usefulness in this idiot after all, Lestrade wondered.

'N'oubliez pas Eylau,' Heneage mused with a perfect accent. 'Don't forget Eylau.'

'Eyelow? Who's he, sir?'

29

'Damned if I know, Lestrade,' the Inspector shrugged. 'Could it be the dead man? Could he be Eylau?'

'Why would he carry a watch reminding him not to forget himself, sir?'

'Ah. Yes.'

'Unless . . .'

'Yes?' Heneage put down the eggnog.

'Well, it's an old watch, sir, I'd say. Older certainly than the corpse under the Cow Rock. If it's a family heirloom, say, then it might refer to an earlier Eylau altogether.'

'Brilliant, Lestrade. How does that help us?'

'I'm not sure it does, sir,' Lestrade rescued his feet from Lisbon's caustic bowl and applied the soothing balm of the towel, 'but this might.'

'Ah,' Heneage took the letter, *'une lettre d'amour*, if I'm any judge.'

'If you say so, sir,' Lestrade said.

'Oh no,' Heneage turned the thing over, 'it's signed *"Maman"*. Unless of course we've stumbled upon an example of the Oedipal strain.'

Strain was the very word surfacing in Lestrade's mind at that moment, for all sorts of reasons. 'Is that French too, sir?'

'Yes. It says, "My dear Louis. Thank you for yours of the 4th ult. I hope you are wearing your long combs in this inclement weather. I am glad that things continue to go well for you at The Shop, but please, no more of the Alpine Club. All is well with us. I remain, your devoted *Maman*." Well, well. Deductions, Lestrade?'

'We may assume then that the man is a Frenchman . . .' the sergeant postulated. After an hour on the moors, it was hardly surprising.

'Further,' Heneage was in full cry now, 'we may assume that his name is Louis Eylau. And that he is a shopkeeper and member of the Alpine Club.'

'You know the Alpine Club, sir?' Lestrade asked.

'Never heard of it,' Heneage said, 'but if this Eylau was a Frenchman, he may have climbed those noble peaks often. He may even be, not French at all, but Swiss. Although . . .'

'Although?'

'Well, there are certain peculiarities of Swiss French, as

30

opposed to French French, I mean. I don't detect them in this letter.'

'It's an old letter,' Lestrade told him.

'Is it? How do you know? There's no date.'

'Look at the creases, sir,' the sergeant said. 'Brown edges along the folds. That letter's been in a drawer for a while, perhaps years. Can you show me the word for "shop", sir?'

'Shop? Yes . . . er . . . here it is. "*Épicerie*". What about it?'

'What kind of shop is that? Greengrocer's? Baker's?'

'General store, I suppose.'

'Does that word usually have a capital letter?'

'Er . . . no, not usually. Not in the middle of a sentence anyway. Perhaps Mrs Eylau is not as literate as she ought to be. Lestrade,' Heneage leaned forward, 'you have a strange expression on your face. What is it?'

The sergeant leaned back against the radiator until the heat on his neck made him sit bolt upright again. 'I can't help wondering why a Frenchman is found hacked to death on a Yorkshire moor, wearing the clothes of a Yorkshire labourer.'

'Hmm,' Heneage mused. 'It is a bit of a teaser, isn't it?'

'And there's something else.'

'Oh?'

'His face was unrecognizable.'

Heneage quivered.

'Why should someone go to the trouble of attempting to destroy a face and then leave so many clues about pointing to the man's identity?'

'No,' said Heneage. 'You've got me there.'

It took three days for Lestrade to interrogate all eighteen of Bosomworth's suspects. It would have taken him one, were it not for the presence of Inspector Heneage, who persisted in checking the antecedents of all of them and sending them back to their cells with a well-delivered diatribe on the morality of the Saucy 'Seventies. At first sight, the last of them, old Samuel Clinch, was the least prepossessing of all.

'Good God!' Heneage read the documents on the table before him. A solitary candle lit the gaunt, yellow face of the man across the room from him, hardening the features into a mask of evil. So much for Lestrade. Old Samuel Clinch looked the soul of integrity. Indeed he was wearing his collar backwards. 'It says here, Clinch, that you exposed your person to three little maids from school.'

'Parson, sir,' Clinch said. 'That's a misprint, is that. T' should say, 'e exposed 'is parson, *id est*, I revealed to t'lasses as I were a lay-preacher.'

'Skilled at the laying on of hands, we gather,' Lestrade said from the relative darkness behind the man.

'I do God's work, wherever and whatever,' Clinch told the policemen.

'No, no,' Heneage said, 'that can't be right, Clinch. I have the sworn deposition here from a Miss Daisy Applegate who says that you dropped your trousers and called to her from the Calf Rock on 12 February last.'

'Aye. I 'ad a wasp in my kicksies, sir,' Clinch explained. 'Nearly stung my unmentionables, did it.'

'In February?' Lestrade growled. 'How often do you see a wasp in February?'

'Well, that's just t'point, sir,' Clinch turned to him, 'I didn't see this one until it were inside my clouts.'

'You called to the young lady,' Heneage quoted, '"have you ever seen one as big as this?"'

'T'wasp, sir,' Clinch insisted, 'I were referrin' t' t'wasp. Proper 'uge, it were.'

'According to Miss Applegate, you proceeded to . . . in February? Good God, man, you could have died of exposure.'

'Nay, nay,' said Clinch, 'It were all a misunderstandin'. I fully intended t' pull my kicksies up as I approached the young lady, but I stumbled and was unable to do so.'

'How far away were you when you stumbled?' Lestrade asked.

'Er . . . ooh, about thirty yards or so.'

'The ground,' Lestrade asked, 'was it level?'

'Aye. 'Appen,' nodded Clinch.

'So you "stumbled" for thirty yards across completely flat ground and landed with your hand on this young lady's breast?' Lestrade had read the deposition too.

'I felt a right tit, I can tell yer. Well, I *did* apologize.'

'Later that day, you did the same thing to a Miss Emily Tripp, on her way home from the Corn Exchange. This time you were in an alleyway and merely unbuttoned your flies,' Heneage read.

'Still looking for the wasp?' Lestrade yawned.

'I'ad cross-threaded my kicksies from t'wasp incident earlier in t'day,' Clinch assured the interrogators. 'My combinations were in something of t'bunch. *Most* uncomfortable, I can tell yer.'

'Sadly for you,' Heneage said, 'Miss Tripp is a Latin scholar from the Ilkley Grammar School. She says she quite clearly saw your *membrum virile* and it was erect.'

'I don't know what she's talkin' about,' Clinch said blandly.

'And on Thursday, Miss Evadne Grimaldi reported that you offered her sixpence to hold the very same *membrum virile* while you answered a call of nature, as both your hands had been burned in a fire and you were unable to pass water unaided. Is that true?'

'Empathetically, no,' Clinch contended. 'Anyway, you can't trust a word any of the circus people tell yer.'

'Circus people?' Lestrade echoed.

'Aye. Lord George Sanger's circus. Wintered 'ere, they did. In Ilkley. Left town three days ago. Gipsies, tramps and thieves. That's all they are.'

'What have you to do with the body of a man found at the foot of the Cow Rock?' Heneage asked.

'Bugger all,' Clinch held his arms out, 'I told that Inspector Bosomworth, it's all a case of mistaken identity. That's what it is.'

The answer to Lestrade's telegram came two days later. From Inspector Bacharach of Criminal Records. No Louis Eylau. Stop. Fourteen hundred and eighty-three possibles with initial 'N'. Stop. Was Lestrade aware there was no 'N' in 'Louis Eylau'. Question Mark. There *were* a number of suspicious Frenchmen known to be in the country, but Mr Vincent refuses to sanction any contact with the *Sûreté* in case they realize he'd pinched their system of the CID and get funny about copyright. Stop. So there. Stop. By the way, you still owe me for the Christmas Dinner. Stop. Bacharach.

'What a scandal,' mused Lestrade. But he hadn't time to reflect on the shortcomings of the back-up from Headquarters. As if to underline Inspector Bosomworth's edict that the murder of Louis

Eylau should be kept as discreet as possible, His Worship the Mayor of Ilkley had called in person on Inspector Heneage and insisted that no house to house inquiries should be made. Since His Worship's uncle had gone to Balliol, a nod was clearly as good as a wink to a green Inspector and Heneage assured him that on no account would such a thing happen. Odd then, that the *Ilkley Advertiser* should plaster, all over its front page, 'Frenchman Slaughtered On T'Moor' and 'Did You Know This Tyke?' with a rather amateur attempt to sketch the mangled features. Readers were invited, on page two, to visit the remains in the basement of the Hydropathic Pump Rooms where Mr Benjamin Thirkettle, Assistant Boilerman, would be delighted, for a small fee, to pull back the shroud several times a day between the hours of ten and three. Perhaps not surprisingly, by midday on the seventh, not only was the said Mr Thirkettle looking for a new job and the basement of the Pump Rooms securely locked, but the *Ilkley Advertiser* had a new editor. The old one was to be found in various Ilkley hostelries sobbing into his ale that the story was given to him by a ferret-faced man in bowler and Donegal with a hole in his boot. The new editor, in the edition of the eighth, as well as lamenting Sir Bartle Frere's lack of judgement in Zululand, also offered a reward for apprehension of the shabby miscreant described above.

By the time that edition appeared however, the shabby miscreant, his boot resoled, his toes nearly working again, was rattling east by courtesy of the Great Northern Railway, his Inspector and his Inspector's man in tow.

There'd been another one in Harrogate.

3

She sat alone in the Sun Pavilion, the light of the leaden Yorkshire sky streaming in through the yellow and green of the glass dome, flecking her golden hair with spring. A desultory quartet in the corner had gone off to lunch, it not yet being the season to keep them there full time and the only sound was the rattle of tea cups and the distant clatter of tureens.

Two men, one in fashionable astrakhan, the other in a rather nasty tweed Donegal, stood awkwardly in the doorway. She noticed the Maitre d'Hotel approach them, all three glance in her direction and then cross the carpeted floor between the empty tables to reach her.

'Miss Clare,' said the Maitre d', with a French accent by way of Knaresborough, 'zese gentlemen are from ze police.'

She looked up at them, her face pale, her eyes dark.

'Inspector Heneage, Miss Clare, from Scotland Yard,' the senior man said. 'This is Sergeant Lestrade.'

'Gentlemen,' she nodded.

Heneage took her hand and kissed it. 'May we?' he asked.

'Please,' she waved them to their chairs.

'Will Madame be taking ze luncheon?' the Maitre d' asked.

'No, thank you, Pierre.'

'Gentlemen?' he turned to them, notepad at the ready, pencil stub poised in an expectant white-gloved hand. 'The Brown Windsor is particularly legendary zis morning.'

'Thank you, no,' Heneage said, 'just a coffee. Arabica.'

'Wiz or wizout sulphur water, sir?'

'Without,' Heneage said quickly.

'Very good, sir,' and the Maitre d' bobbed away.

'Please accept our condolences, Miss Clare,' the Inspector said. 'This must be a perfectly beastly time for you.'

'Thank you, Mr Heneage. The truth is I'm feeling rather guilty.'

'Guilty?' Lestrade's notepad was to the fore as the Maitre d's had been.

'Why, yes. As a token of respect, the Manager has closed the dining-room today, but he neglected to tell the kitchens. There are, I believe, *poissons* to the ceiling and one could drown in the Brown Windsor. Personally, I couldn't eat a thing.'

'Understandably so,' Heneage nodded. 'Painful as it must be, Miss Clare, we have to ask you a few questions.'

'I know,' she sighed, 'Inspector Bottomley intimated that you might.'

'Bottomley?'

'He of the Harrogate Constabulary.'

'Ah, yes,' Heneage remembered, 'we have exchanged telegrams. Tell us, Miss Clare, um . . . about the deceased . . . ?'

'Yes?'

35

'No,' Heneage shifted a little uneasily, 'I'll rephrase that, shall I? Um . . . tell us about the deceased.'

She drew herself up, her bosom heaving against the frothy bodice of her day dress.

'Finest Arabica,' the Maitre d' arrived at that moment with a silver tray. There was a delay as he fiddled and fussed, arranging doilies and whipping the folds out of napkins.

'Thank you, my man,' said Heneage, 'Now be a good fellow and toddle off, would you? Miss Clare and we are not to be disturbed.'

'Very good, sir,' the Maitre d' said, his nose at the horizontal with umbrage.

'Shall I be mother, sir?' Lestrade asked.

It didn't seem at all likely to Inspector Heneage.

'No, no, sergeant,' Miss Clare took the pot, 'this is woman's work. I wouldn't expect to drive a coach and four.'

Neither would Lestrade. Not without killing someone, anyway.

'You were asking me about William,' she said, her eyes full but her hand steady. 'We were to be married, you know.'

'Congratulations,' said Heneage solemnly, though it seemed less than appropriate and he could have kicked himself.

'We were staying at Harrogate for the waters, Miss Rudding and I. William was on leave.'

'Miss Rudding?' Lestrade asked.

'My companion, sergeant. Jane Rudding. My parents went of the diphtheria some years ago – although it is something of a family joke that my father went rather than see Mr Disraeli at Number Ten.'

'Understandable, Miss Clare,' Heneage nodded.

'Since then Jane and I have been inseparable.'

'Where is she now?' Lestrade asked, seeing no one at Miss Clare's elbow.

'Lying down.'

'The shock?' Heneage asked.

'The water,' Miss Clare said. 'You were wise to decline it.'

'Kill or cure,' smiled Heneage. 'Oh, I do apologize. Rather tasteless.'

'Rather like the water,' said the lady, 'but I suspect that Monsieur Pasteur would be horrified at what he found in it. Jane was

36

here, ironically, for the nervous tension. The water seems to have cured that, but has given her chalybeate tummy.'

'You said that your intended was on leave, Miss?' Lestrade asked, anxious to make *some* headway before the quartet returned.

'Yes. My fiancé was a Lieutenant in the Artillery, Mr Lestrade. He was staying in room 31, here at the Gascoine.'

'And you and Miss Rudding?'

'Have adjacent rooms on the floor below, 25 and 26.'

'How long had you been here when disaster struck like a bolt from the blue?' Heneage asked.

'Four days.'

'Um. Right. Well, I think that will be all, Miss Clare. Once again, please accept . . .'

'Er . . . just a couple more things, sir,' Lestrade chipped in. 'Do you know who found the body?'

'No, sergeant.'

'Was anything taken, from the body, I mean?'

'I don't believe so.'

'Where was the body found?'

She stood up suddenly, Heneage rising with her, 'I believe it was on the edge of a park called the Stray. I'm sorry, gentlemen. I thought I could . . . perhaps another day?' And she swept from the room, the Maitre d' holding the door open, before rushing to hang the 'Dining-Room Open' signs on the front of the building.

'Well, really, Lestrade,' Heneage sat down heavily, 'that was appalling.'

'A little odd, certainly,' the sergeant agreed.

'What was?'

'Miss Clare not wearing mourning like that. A coffee-coloured day dress two days after the man she is to marry is found butchered . . .'

'I was referring to your badgering,' Heneage snapped. 'That sort of thing may be suitable for some East End rough, but to a lady of some refinement, such as Miss Clare . . . Do you realize you used the word "body" three times in as many sentences?'

'Did I?' Lestrade asked.

'Such a word has connotations, Lestrade. Apart from the grisly aspects to which it apports here, there is a gravely sexual innuendo.'

'There is?' Lestrade had lost all contact with this conversation, but he looked around on the carpet wondering who could have dropped it.

'In future, sergeant, *I* will ask the questions. It's luncheon-time. Lisbon has booked us into the Royal.' He slammed down his cup. 'At least there, I expect they serve a decent cup of coffee, Arabica or no. You will do what you seem to enjoy – view the deceased, the scene of the crime and whatever else detectives do and report back to me. *When* Miss Clare is feeling better, *I* will question her again. And I will do it alone. Understand?'

'Perfectly, sir,' said Lestrade.

Harrogate was larger than Ilkley. And more opulent. As such, it boasted its own mortuary. And its mortuary attendant was full-time, not sharing his dubious skills with those of boiler-stoking. He even had his own teeth. Only his leg was someone else's – of excellently carved mahogany. His own hapless limb had fallen victim to a Sikh tulwar in the second war against those beastly but determined fellows.

He dragged the timber around the slabs of the floor. 'Now, where did I put 'im?' He hauled up a tarpaulin, 'Nay, that's old granny Westerby. Bit of a to-do at t'moment as t' who's goin' t' bury 'er – t'Westerbys or t'parish. T'workhouse were 'er second 'ome.' He tried another. 'Nay, that's Dan McLivett. Look at that,' Lestrade would rather not, ''Ung like a bloody dray'orse. There's many a 'arrogate lass 'ad sight o' that over t'years. Nasty thing, syphilis. It must be 'im over 'ere, then.'

It was. What was left of William Lyle, Lieutenant, Royal Artillery, lay pale and dead on the last slab in the green, windowless room. A handsome face, with neat military moustache, stared sightlessly up at Lestrade in the yellow green of the gas-jets. At least the eyes were still there, once a cornflower blue, and the face was unmarked. Across the muscular chest however, the same tell-tale cross that had carved the marker of Louis Eylau below the Cow Rock at Ilkley. Lestrade used his switchblade again. The same angle. The same cause of death. Whoever it was who had killed these men, he was a craftsman.

'Inspector Heneage?' a voice made him turn.

'Lestrade,' he said, 'sergeant.'

'Ah,' a middle-aged man with a still boyish face and falling blond hair shuffled into the gloom. 'Inspector Bottomley, Harrogate Constabulary. I was expecting a Mr Heneage.'

'He's been detained, sir,' Lestrade lied. 'I'm afraid you'll have to make do with me.'

'Now, don't do yourself down, my dear fellow. I was a sergeant myself once. My, you've got a few in today, Potter,' he said to the attendant.

'Nay, lad, 'tis nothin' t' Chillianwallah. T'usual, Mr Bottomley?'

'Why not?' the Inspector asked rhetorically. 'Hot toddie, sergeant? The sun's over the yardarm.'

Considering that Lestrade had not seen the sun since they arrived in the county, he had to take Bottomley's word for that.

'Well, I'm glad you fellows could get over, actually. I don't think we've had a murder in Harrogate since 1832. And that was the Reform Bill Riots, so it's understandable. What do you make of it?'

'Where was the body found, sir?'

'Sir? Oh, no, sergeant. One professional to another, eh? You can call me Nobby.'

'Thank you, sir,' Lestrade said, sensing a need to feel his back against something solid, 'but it's Metropolitan policy.'

'Oh, quite. Quite,' Bottomley nodded, 'Very ... sound, I'm sure. Nice-looking man, though, wasn't he?' He peered through his pince-nez at the corpse. 'Very nice.'

'I've seen this before,' Lestrade said.

Bottomley looked at him, 'Well, you would,' he said, 'man of the world as no doubt you are. When I was last in Villiers Street . . .'

'No, sir. I mean the wounds. These cuts.'

'Really?' Bottomley perched himself on a stool nearby, 'ooh, I just can't get comfy. Where?'

'On the corpse of a Frenchman at Ilkley.'

'Ooh, I read about that in the *Harrogate Organ*. A piece they'd clearly pinched from the *Ilkley Advertiser*, if I'm any judge of local hackery. Not best pleased, the Mayor of Ilkley, I shouldn't think. We're bigger here, of course, more established as a Watering Place.' He licked his finger and slicked down an eyebrow. 'My back is broad,' he said. 'We can take a little salacious press-

39

mongering. And don't they monger, those chappies from the Press?'

Potter clacked over the flagstones with two steaming mugs.

'Here's looking at you, tyke,' the Inspector raised the cup that cheers.

Lestrade sampled the brew. Cocoa with more than a hint of brandy. It laced his moustache until Bottomley flicked it off for him. 'So, what's your theory?' the Yorkshireman asked.

The sergeant shrugged. 'Damned if I've got one,' Lestrade found a stool and angled it safely in the corner. 'Two men. One known. The other not. Both in their twenties, one with a pulverized face. Both died by slashes to the body caused by . . . what? A large knife?'

'Hm. That's what I thought.'

'Sword,' said Potter, mopping the floor around their feet.

'What, chuck?' Bottomley asked.

'T'were a sword what killed him.'

'How do you know?' Lestrade asked.

'I've used a few in my time,' Potter stood upright. 'T'weren't no picnic at Chillianwallah, I can tell yer.'

'What kind of sword?' Lestrade asked.

'Three-bar hilt,' Potter dragged his leg behind the mop again. 'Isn't that a cavalry sword?'

'Aye. 'Appen,' agreed Potter. 'I served near eight year wi' 14th Light Dragoons. 'Ad one of them bastards on my 'ip every bloody day.'

Presuming the man referred to a sword rather than a 14th Light Dragoon, Lestrade asked, 'How can you be sure it's specifically a three-bar hilt?'

'Look 'ere,' Potter staggered back to the cadaver, 'just the width. Too wide for t'tulwar. Too narrow for t''oneysuckle 'ilt the 'Eavies carry. And I'll tell yer somewhat else.'

'What?'

''T were a foreigner what done it.'

'Now, Potter . . .' Bottomley wagged a finger.

'What makes you say that?' Lestrade persisted.

'Any cavalryman in our army uses t'cuts, in t'Manual, like. Them cuts aren't in t'Manual. Not in any Manual I've ever read, any road up.'

'What sort of foreigner?' Lestrade said and was rather surprised to see Bottomley cover his face with his hand.

'Nigger,' growled Potter, his wooden leg rattling on the flagstones. 'Sikh, I shouldn't wonder. They 'ad my leg, y'know, Mr Bottomley,' he screamed.

'Aye, chuck, I know,' the Inspector patted the attendant. 'Look, why don't you get a bit of fresh air? They're open by now.'

He pressed a warm coin into Potter's clammy hand.

'What's a bloke goin' t' do wi'out 'is leg?' Potter wondered, clumping away to the steps.

'I'm sorry about that, sergeant,' the Inspector said, patting the man's knee. 'I didn't have time to interrupt your train of thought. Every death in Harrogate over the last thirty years Potter has laid at the door of Duleep Singh or some other dusky heathen. He hasn't realized they've been utterly loyal to us now since 1856. And how any of them could have sent the influenza or the flash flooding of the Tewit Well back in '71, I have no idea. I'm afraid he's sold you a bit of a pup, there, cluely speaking.'

'You think he's wrong about the sword?'

'I think he's wrong about the foreigner. Do you want to see his clothes?'

'Snappy dresser, is he, Potter?'

'No, no,' chuckled Bottomley, 'not the mortuary attendant. The deceased.'

He led the way – and Lestrade was glad he did – to a broom cupboard at the back. Several brooms fell out on him as he opened the door, but beyond them, hanging against the back wall, was a ripped tunic.

'Undress frock,' said Bottomley, 'Serge. Top quality, mind you. No rubbish. But not that lovely Melton of full dress. Give me no nap for preference every time.'

Lestrade examined the garment. Diagonally below the scarlet collar, the dark blue was stiff with blood. 'Odd,' he muttered.

'What, chuck?' Bottomley was replacing the brooms.

'I understand that Lieutenant Lyle was on leave.'

'So he was.'

'Wearing his regimentals?'

'Oh, yes, I see what you mean. Still, he p'raps didn't want to get his civvies dirty, what with the elephants and everything.'

41

'Elephants?' Lestrade wondered if the conversation had returned to the Sikhs again.

'Why, yes. That's why we think he was there that morning. On the Stray. That's where Sanger's circus was camped. He'd told Miss Clare that he hadn't seen a circus since he was a boy.'

'Were they performing here?' Lestrade asked.

'No. It's not the season yet. But they're limbering up, taking on hands and so on. It's funny, one of Harrogate's most respected citizens up and joined one last year. Chartered accountant he was.'

'Ah, it's the razzle-dazzle, I expect,' Lestrade said.

'Oh, I don't know. There's precious little razzle-dazzle in an accountant's office. It's not like being an actuary. Now that really *is* a walk on the wild side.'

'Who found the body, sir?' Lestrade asked.

'Jem Buttersnaite, old Mr Wedderburn's head gardener.'

'Mr Wedderburn?'

'Aye. Local squire, you might say. Wedderburn House is just off the Stray. The rhododendrons are an absolute picture in the summer. Do you like flowers, Sergeant? I'm a petunia man myself.'

Lestrade didn't doubt it. 'Well, sir,' he grinned, 'in a busy life...'

Bottomley raised both hands, 'Oh, I know, chuck. I know. Not enough hours in the day. We found this in his pocket.' He passed Lestrade a locket, edged in gold. Around the rim, the legend ran, 'To my darling, on our engagement, November 1878. Emily.' And on the glass face beyond it a sweep of deep chestnut hair.

'Emily?' Lestrade said.

'Emily Clare,' Bottomley explained, 'the dead man's fiancée. Have you talked to her yet?'

Lestrade looked again at the dark hair. 'Apparently not,' he said.

The management, it was true, weren't totally in approval of Detective-Sergeant Lestrade rummaging through the room of a deceased guest. In fact, so much so that they told him he couldn't. Inspector Heneage would have to get permission from Inspector Bottomley, who in turn would have to approach the

Chief Constable, who, being of an Evangelistic nature, would have to ask God. Far easier for Lestrade to shrug, then wander down the relevant corridor at the Gascoine before daylight left the room and loiter outside number 31. While loitering, his brass-knuckled switchblade just happened to click into the lock and he slipped inside.

As he had hoped, Miss Clare had not taken possession of her fiancé's things, so the wardrobe still contained his tunic and japan-boxed helmet. Lestrade ran his finger over the bullion cuff and the velvet-blue of the sleeve. Bottomley was right – there was a certain something about handling Melton. But it was what lay against the back of the wardrobe that held his gaze. It was a three-bar hilt cavalry sword. He slid the weapon from its scabbard and noted the etching on the blade – 'W.L.' on one side and 'Royal Artillery' with lightning flashes and the Queen's – God Bless Her – cypher. So, the artillery also carried the three-bar hilt. Of course, had he attended the Sharp Objects That Cause Death lecture back at the Yard last month, Lestrade might have known that all along. He checked the blade's edge for signs of caked blood. Nothing. Either this was not the murder weapon or it had been wiped meticulously clean.

Still, he had an hypothesis to test. He placed the scabbard on the table in the gathering gloom and turned to face the ottoman. Remembering (however vaguely) his Cutlass Drill For Riots learned as a uniformed constable, he bent both knees, offered point and scythed downwards to his left. A diagonal gash sent clouds of horsehair into the air. Bringing the blade up to head protect, he hacked backwards, slicing diagonally from left to right. The thud and rip sent more stuffing skywards and he was left with the same cross that had ripped the life out of the two men. The same, but not quite. Now, police cutlass drill, he knew, was based on the same military manual to which old Potter had referred. Lestrade had executed the cuts of the British Army, more or less – and they were not quite the same as the wounds on the chests of the deceased. Was Potter right, then? Was some foreigner using a different manual? Or was it merely Lestrade's lack of expertise and the relatively unyielding qualities of the ottoman?

Perhaps if he tried again . . .

'Stop!' an outraged voice screamed behind him. Lestrade's

blade hurtled downwards, causing him to stumble as it fell and it brought a rush of crimson to his left thigh. 'What is the meaning of this?'

Lestrade had seen irate hotel managers before, most recently in the Case of the Irate Hotel Manager in Rickmansworth, but never one whose face had gone quite so purple.

'It's all right,' Lestrade dropped the sword on the bed and began surreptitiously tying his handkerchief above his knee to act as a tourniquet to staunch the blood, 'I'm a policeman.'

'I know that perfectly well,' snapped the manager, 'and I told you not ten minutes ago to keep clear of this room. Now I find you destroying the furniture. Your superior shall hear of this.'

'I have no doubt of it,' Lestrade winced, tying the knot as tightly as he could. 'In the meantime, I would like a few minutes with these ladies.'

Behind the sturdy frame of the manager, as appalled as he was, stood two demure young ladies, one blonde in a coffee-coloured day dress, the other dark in full mourning.

'Out of the question!' the manager stood his ground.

'It's all right,' said the blonde, 'Sergeant Lestrade has some questions, I believe, that he did not have a chance to put to me earlier.'

'That is correct, Miss Clare. Or should I say, Miss Rudding?'

The women looked alarmed. The manager looked askance.

'Thank you,' the blonde pushed him gently out of the door and locked it.

'Jane,' the brunette said, 'some water from the wash-stand. Mr Lestrade may bleed to death.'

'A mere technicality,' Lestrade said, but he was grateful all the same to collapse into the rattan chair.

'I'm sorry about our little subterfuge,' said the dark lady, untying Lestrade's improvised bandage, 'I couldn't face any more questions today. Jane suggested that she take my place, especially since you Yard men would not know us apart. The Maitre d' was kind enough to help.'

'It could be described as hindering the police in the course of their inquiries,' Lestrade said.

She looked deep into his eyes and something leapt within him. Searing pain tore through his leg as he jerked violently.

'I'm sorry,' she said, wiping the blood with the handkerchief. 'You really should let us cut those off.'

'Miss Clare,' Lestrade's eyes widened, 'apart from the propriety of the situation, those trousers cost me three and tuppence. The tear can be mended,' his eyes widened still further, 'that is, if it's the trousers you're talking about.'

She smiled, the first time he had seen her smile. It was, he was sure, the most beautiful of the sights in Harrogate. 'How did you find out?' she asked.

'First,' he told her as Miss Rudding brought the water, 'Miss Rudding was wearing coffee, days after her fiancé was murdered. I know this is 1879, but there are limits.'

'Very shrewd,' Jane Rudding said, handing her companion a flannel.

'Second, Inspector Bottomley showed me the locket found on Lieutenant Lyle. It bore Miss Clare's name and what I took to be a lock of her hair. It was dark.'

'Well,' she shook her long tresses free of her shoulders, 'it was a silly, schoolgirl prank that we played and we're sorry for it. I'm ready now, sergeant.' She wiped his sweating face and stood up, while Jane took away the bloody water. 'How can I help?'

'I understand that Lieutenant Lyle went out on the day of his death to see the circus leave?'

'He told me he was going to at dinner the previous night, yes.'

'You dined here at the hotel?'

'In the Sun Room, yes.'

'Was the Lieutenant his usual self?'

'I think so. In fact, he was very excited.'

'Excited?'

'Yes. He said he'd seen an old chum with the circus. Or thought he had. He couldn't actually believe it.'

'Why?'

'He didn't say. I remember . . .' her face twisted in concentration, 'I remember he said it couldn't really be he.'

'Who?'

'I don't know. At that stage the fish arrived and we changed the subject. Do you remember, Jane?'

'He didn't give me a name, darling. But I remember he said "It can't actually be he" and I asked why not. And he said "They'd never allow it".'

' "Never allow it"?' Lestrade repeated, 'what did he mean by that?'

Miss Rudding shrugged, 'Perhaps that's why he went back to the camping ground that morning. It was early, before breakfast, I believe. Perhaps he went back for another look at his old chum.'

There was a thunderous knock at the door.

'Oh,' said Miss Rudding, 'that'll be that perfectly foul idiot of a manager – and your superior, I shouldn't wonder, Mr Lestrade. Mr Lestrade?'

But the sergeant wasn't receiving any more visitors. Was it the heady perfume of Miss Clare? The effect of swinging a sabre? Or the excruciating pain from the sword slash to his left leg? Whatever it was, he toppled backwards on to the bed and all the lights went out.

'Outrageous!' was the first word that Lestrade heard. It was also the second. It might have been the third, but it was masked by the slamming of a fist on a desk. The sergeant sat bolt upright, wincing anew as he remembered his left leg. He dispensed with the 'where am I?' question, for he recognized his rather dingy little room at the Royal, the one they reserved for gentlemen's gentlemen, the one he shared with the disapproving Lisbon. The next question was also superfluous – 'who are you?' It was perfectly obvious. Across the table from him stood Inspector Heneage, the muscles of his jaw flexing, blinking in fury. And 'what happened?' was totally redundant. Lestrade remembered all too well.

'Breaking and entering,' Heneage snapped. 'Destroying an ottoman worth eight pounds, fourteen shillings and ninepence ha'penny. Bleeding over a carpet and rattan chair, the cost of cleaning which will be a week's wages for you. Those are the indictable offences. Then there is the wilful disobedience occasioned by you interviewing Miss Clare, expressly contrary to my instructions.'

'I . . .'

'That is precisely the point, Lestrade,' Heneage interrupted. 'I. This monstrous ego of yours. May I remind you that you are a sergeant in the Detective Department of the Metropolitan Police? At the moment, that is. I am an Inspector. As such, I outrank you a hundred to one. To say nothing of the obvious disparity in our intellects. I have a degree, Lestrade – something to which you could never aspire.'

'But . . .'

'What stage have your inquiries reached?'

'The inquiries you ordered me not to make, you mean?'

'Causticity will not endear you to me, Lestrade. Have a care. You are within a whisker of losing your metaphorical stripes.'

'You mean, apart from the fact that Miss Clare and Miss Rudding changed places?'

'An understandable subterfuge,' Heneage dismissed it. 'What else?'

Lestrade steadied himself on his elbow. 'Both men died by the same method, sir,' he said. 'The cuts to the body.'

'Yes, yes. We know all that. Did you disobey orders and offend two charmingly genteel young ladies to ascertain something we already knew?'

'The other common feature, sir, is the circus.'

'Circus?'

'Lord George Sanger's circus. It wintered in Yorkshire, near Ilkley. It moved to Harrogate to recruit and now has moved on.'

'Where?'

'I don't know. But Lieutenant Lyle went twice to see it limbering up on the Stray. According to Misses Clare and Rudding, he recognized an old friend there.'

'There? You mean, on the Stray?'

'With the circus itself, I understand.'

'You really believe that there is a connection?'

Lestrade shrugged. 'It's a good place to start,' he said.

'Very well,' Heneage crossed to the door, 'that's what I shall do.'

'If you'll give me a minute, sir, I'll just get my leg into action,' he flexed it painfully.

'I have no need of you or your leg, Lestrade. Were it not for Miss Clare's intervention, I would have suspended you without . . . what do you call that stuff . . . wages? I would have suspended you without that indefinitely. As it is, Miss Clare interceded.'

'That was very kind of her,' Lestrade said.

'Uncommonly,' Heneage agreed. 'And as it is, I am sending you home. This room is paid for until tomorrow. Thereafter you will vacate it and travel back to London by whatever means at your disposal. You will report to Mr Vincent himself and prepare to receive whatever the Director deems it fitting to throw at you. Understood?'

'Sir . . .'

'Oh, no, Lestrade. You've conflagrated your maritime conveyances. It is all far too late.'

'Don't go to the circus alone, sir,' Lestrade warned.

'I went often as a child,' Heneage told him, 'I believe I can manage now.'

'As a child, you weren't chasing a murderer, sir,' the sergeant said.

'And I don't believe I am now,' Heneage told him, 'but I know that the ethos of the department implies that no stone shall be unturned, so I am prepared to follow this unlikely lead.'

'But how will you find it?'

'A two-mile convoy on the road?' Heneage swung open the door. 'Come, come, Lestrade; as I may have told you earlier, I have a degree.'

Emily Clare thought she recognized the limping man with the rain driving through his Donegal and bouncing off his bowler. He seemed to be making his inquiries in the usual way, in the ticket office at Harrogate station, side entrance. What she hadn't seen was that he had tried the main entrance in order to have a roof over his head, but the revolving door had got him and beaten him back. Had she been a trained detective, she would have noticed that he was limping on his *right* leg, not the result of a sabre-slash but a dastardly and unprovoked assault by a door-jamb.

'Mr Lestrade?'

'Good morning, Miss Clare,' he tipped the sodden rim of his hat.

'Are you leaving Harrogate?'

'By the next train,' he told her.

'Can your inquiries be complete?' she asked.

'No, madam, I have been ordered south by the Inspector.'

'But why?'

'Let's just say I am rather persona non regatta at the moment.'

'If it's that business in poor William's rooms, I shall speak to Inspector Heneage at once.'

'I fear he too has gone,' Lestrade told her, 'in search of the circus.'

'Ah,' she said, 'You poor man, you can't possibly manage that heavy Gladstone. I will fetch a porter. But first you must let me buy you a cup of tea. Just the thing on foul mornings such as these.'

'Look,' the wizened little operative behind the grimy glass rapped on the counter, 'do you want a bleedin' ticket or don't yer?'

'My good man,' Miss Clare pressed her nose to his window, 'you are addressing a Detective-Sergeant of the Metropolitan Police.'

The operative was unmoved. 'Well, fan my fly-buttons,' he growled.

Lestrade was contemplating adding to his list of misdemeanours by putting one on the operative when Miss Clare led him away to the warmth and snuggery of the station tea rooms.

'I am making the arrangements,' she told him over a steaming brew. 'Poor William will be taken the day after tomorrow. The funeral will be at his home on Thursday.'

'Where is Miss Rudding?' he asked.

'Sending telegrams,' she said. 'William's commanding officer has expressed a wish to attend with a contingent from his company. Riderless horse, reversed boots in the stirrups, all the paraphernalia of death. I suppose you see it every day, Mr Lestrade?'

He nodded, gazing into the patient, dark eyes. Eyes a man could drown in. 'Some days,' he told her.

She closed to him, her hand for a moment on his. 'Will you find him, Mr Lestrade?' she whispered. 'The man who did this?'

He pulled his hand back, suddenly afraid of the emotions within himself. 'Yes,' he vowed, 'I will find him.'

She smiled, then whipped out a pretty lace handkerchief. He thought she would cry, but she held it at arm's length. 'For you,' she said.

'What is it?'

'It's a handkerchief,' she told him.

'Yes. No. I mean . . .'

49

'Do you read the Romances, Mr Lestrade? Sir Walter Scott?'

'As a child I always had my nose in a book,' he told her, 'but that was because I rather liked the pressure of the pages on my nostrils. I got over it. You're not referring to the Walter Scott who wrote "Ear Lobes and Their Place in Modern Detection"?'

'Er . . . I don't think so,' she smiled, '*Castle Dangerous, Ivanhoe*. Stirring tales of derring-do. In most of them, a knight errant vows to carry out some fine tasks for a lady, to do her some inestimable service. She in turn gives him her colours, to wear on his sleeve as he champions her in the lists.'

Lestrade was listing quite badly that morning, what with sabres and revolving doors.

'Of course . . .' she began.

'Yes?'

'Of course, in Scott, the lady's colour is a love token,' she said, 'but my love has gone. Taken from me.'

Instinctively, he gripped her hand, 'I *will* find him,' he said, looking into her eyes as he tucked the handkerchief into his cuff.

'I know,' she said, closing her eyes briefly at his touch and the earnestness of his promise, 'I know.'

'Now,' he broke himself free of the spell that bound them both. 'One good handkerchief deserves another. Does the initial "N" mean anything to you?'

'Napoleon,' she said.

'Napoleon?' he sat up, frowning.

'Napoleon Buonaparte, Emperor of the French. Monsieur l'Escargot, my tutor, allowed himself to become quite boring on the subject.'

'He did?'

'Yes,' she poured a second cup for them both. 'You see, Buonaparte, like poor William, was an officer of the artillery – though not, you understand, ours. But he was a self-made man in unstable times. He rose from the squirearchy of Corsica to become the greatest general the world has known. The letter "N" was his trademark, so to speak. He had it embroidered on his slippers, engraved on his glass goblets, branded on to the withers of his army's horses.'

'And sewn on to his handkerchiefs,' Lestrade nodded, suddenly understanding.

'Certainly.'

'Tell me,' he forgot his painful legs in the excitement of the moment, 'does the name "Louis Eylau" mean anything to you?'

She shook her head, 'I don't think so,' she said. 'Louis of course is a popular French name. Eylau is a place.'

'Is it?'

'The site of a battle I believe. I don't remember exactly which campaign; Monsieur l'Escargot had me reciting lists of them.'

'So,' Lestrade snapped his fingers, '"Remember Eylau" doesn't mean a person; it means remember the battle.'

'Er . . . what is the significance of this?'

'I'm not sure,' he told her. 'This Lescargo, did he teach you French?'

'*Mais oui*.'

'No,' Lestrade smiled, 'French, did he teach you French?'

'Yes,' she laughed, 'he did.'

'Marvellous. What does the word "*épicerie*" mean?'

'"*Épicerie*"? It's a shop. A sort of grocer's, I suppose. Why?'

He looked at her. For six years he'd been a policeman; a detective for four. All his training had been 'give nothing away. Reveal nothing'. He could see the fierce old Scots face of Dolly Williamson now, his sidewhiskers glowing in the eerie firelight of his grate at the Yard. He could hear the creaking leather of his voice – 'A detective, laddie, should be like one of the three wise monkeys. An average detective sees all; a good detective hears all; but a great detective does all that and keeps his bloody mouth shut.' In a single second of madness, Lestrade broke every rule in the book, 'I have reason to believe', he whispered, checking that no one in the station tea room was too close, 'that your intended died by the same hand as another, whose body we found at Ilkley, not three days since.'

She blinked at him. 'Who was this man?'

'I don't know,' he shrugged. 'We christened him Louis Eylau because he carried a pocket watch with the inscription in French "Remember Eylau" and a letter, also in French, which was addressed to Louis and appeared to be from his mother. That letter mentioned the shop.'

'The shop,' she repeated.

'Yes. "*Épicerie*". You said it meant shop. So did Inspector Heneage.'

'Yes, but was it shop or The Shop?'

It was Lestrade's turn to blink. 'There's a difference?'

'Yes. Did the word *épicerie* appear in the middle of a sentence?'

Lestrade racked what passed for a brain. 'At the end. Why?'

'Did it have a capital "e"?'

He shut his eyes and chewed his moustache. If only he hadn't let that idiot Heneage take the damned letter with him, 'Yes,' he blurted, 'yes. It did.'

'Well, that's it,' she said, 'It's not any old shop, Mr Lestrade. It's *The* Shop. William was always talking about it. It's the cadets' nickname for the Military College at Woolwich, where they train officers of artillery and engineers.'

'Is it?' Lestrade still chewed his moustache, 'is it indeed?'

'So this Louis Eylau was an officer of artillery too, like William?'

'It would seem so,' Lestrade nodded. 'Miss Clare, when was your intended a cadet at Woolwich?'

'Er, let me see. He obtained his commission in February 1877. That means he joined in the spring of '75. Does that help?'

Lestrade struggled to his feet and took her hand, 'I don't know,' he said, 'but it can certainly do no harm. Please excuse me, Miss Clare – I have to send a telegram. But rest assured,' he patted the handkerchief at his wrist, 'I *will* find the man responsible.'

His Royal Highness the Duke of Cambridge was wearing his other hat that afternoon, that of the Colonel of His Own 17th Lancers, the rather natty one with the silver battle honours and drooping white swan's feathers. He was less than his cheery self. That confounded idiot, Drury Lowe of his regiment, had sent him another ridiculous despatch from the Seat of War in Natal. Just because Cambridge was Colonel of the Regiment, that didn't mean he wanted to be kept informed every time a horse of the 17th farted in the lines.

He fidgeted with his pouch belt and got his thumb jammed into his pricker chains – always a trial for a cavalry officer. Mr Snowdon, the Photographer Royal, peered at him from behind the black hood. 'Do we have a problem, Your Royal Highness?' he ingratiated.

'You may,' His Royal Highness blew through crimson cheeks, 'I however do not.'

'Could we move our mameluke a teensy weensy threat to the left?'

Cambridge slid the sword sideways.

'Oh, dear. No, the light is flashing on our fly buttons. Better move it back again. Now, chins up. Just a feather. That's it. Watch the birdie . . .'

'My Lord,' an aide burst in, 'urgent telegram, sir.'

'Oh bugger and damnation, Blithering. Can't you see I'm having my photograph taken?'

'I'm very sorry sir,' Blithering turned beaming to the camera, quickly slicking down his hair. 'It's from the Prime Minister's Private Secretary.'

Cambridge's whiskers positively drooped, along with his swan's feathers. He threw the lance cap at Blithering who caught it expertly in exchange for the telegram. Unfortunately, in his haste, His Royal Highness had forgotten that he was still attached to the thing by his caplines and he collided with the aide, almost bowling him over.

'Well, don't just stand there, man. Unhook me from this bloody thing, you idiot, Blithering.'

While the aide fumbled with his chief's accoutrements, a quaking Cambridge read Disraeli's words with watery eyes. No doubt you've heard. Stop. Inquiries being made by one Lestrade, comma, from Scotland Yard. Stop. Questions asked at Woolwich. Stop. He wants to know if they had a cadet called Louis Somebody. Stop. Get over to The Shop. Stop. Stop any answer. Stop. I know this Lestrade. Stop. An idiot, comma, but a persistent one. Stop. I'll lean on Howard Vincent. Stop. And get Lestrade recalled. Stop.

'Good God,' the aide and the photographer heard Cambridge's prickers rattle. 'Blithering, get me a cab. Where's my bloody cape? If I don't get over to Woolwich before they shut the post office, you'll be looking for another job – and so will I.'

Snowdon sighed, folding up his apparatus. 'We must do this again some time,' he said, and then, when His Royal Highness had clumped off in a gust of plumes, 'bastard!'

Lestrade had extended his welcome as long as he dare. He was receiving some funny looks from the clerk at the Royal, who knew a member of the relatively unwaged when he saw one. If Heneage did not get back soon, Lestrade would be unable to pay for his room. As it was, he had taken to eating at Mrs Mordecai's, where the shepherd's pie was cheerful, but above all cheap. On the other hand, when Heneage returned, he'd find Lestrade still there rather than walking the beat on a chilly London night with a pointed blue hat on. And where *was* Heneage . . . so long at the fair?

The sergeant received a speedy reply to his telegram; come to think of it, for the army, an extraordinarily speedy reply. There was no mention of 'triplicate' or 'receiving every consideration' or 'in the fulness of time'. Instead, a simple telegram which said Sergeant Lestrade. Stop. Only Louis we had was Louis la Point Virgule. Stop. Cadet 1791–93. Stop. Killed at Salamanca. Stop. 1812. Stop. Glad to have been of inestimable help. Stop.

Not only the speed and uselessness of the reply struck Lestrade but the fact that the telegram appeared to have come, not from the Military College at Woolwich, but from the office of the Commander-in-Chief. Was the Duke of Cambridge himself minding The Shop these days?

It was the second telegram that troubled Lestrade more however. It was from Howard Vincent, Director of Criminal Intelligence at the Yard and it demanded Lestrade's immediate return to London. There was nothing for it; the sergeant began to pack his bag and wonder how he could scrape together enough to pay his bill. In the event, his problem was solved in a rather unexpected way.

A little before eight, as whatever there was of daylight in that desultory spring faded in the west, a frantic knock shattered the stillness of the converted lavatory that was Lestrade's room.

'Lisbon?' the sergeant had never seen a man so pale, at least not one with his cranium still intact and not lying on a marble slab, 'what's the matter?'

'Sergeant,' the man had to steady himself on the door frame, 'oh, sergeant.'

Lestrade caught him as he stumbled forward and together they staggered into the nearest chairs.

'Man and boy, man and boy,' the valet mumbled. 'That it should have come to this . . .'

Lestrade was confused. 'That what should have come to what?' he asked.

Lisbon looked at him through mad, red-rimmed eyes, madder and redder in the firelight. 'It's Mr Heneage,' he muttered, 'the Inspector. He's dead.'

4

Howard Vincent, Director of Criminal Intelligence, sat the next morning in his office at the Yard, sharing an apple with his iguana. He had a few moments before the divisional chaplain arrived, so he was thumbing idly through the Thunderer when a smallish headline struck him rather forcefully.

He sat bolt upright, spitting fruit in all directions. 'My God, Ignatius!' he screamed, 'have you read this?'

Either the beast had not or he had no comment, for he simply rolled an eye and chewed on, urinating quietly on Vincent's blotting paper. It was not many Directors of Criminal Intelligence who had an iguana that was office trained.

' "Scotland Yard man found dead",' he read aloud. 'Blah, blah. "Stabbed to death by the roadside near Knaresborough yesterday morning. Blah. Blah. Local police baffled." Well, what's new? Ah. "Inspector Hastings Heneage was investigating the recent murder of Lieutenant Lyle RA. His Number Two, a Sergeant Lespade, appears to have disappeared." Disappeared!' He thumped the table and the iguana visibly leapt, feeling one of its headaches coming on.

The Director's own head was buried again in the Thunderer so that he barely acknowledged the knock on the door. It was followed by the click of a stick and the clearing of a throat.

'With you in a moment, Chaplain,' he said.

'I've been called many things in my life already,' the visitor said, 'but never that. Never chaplain.'

Vincent looked up and stood up in quick succession. 'Mr Prime Minister,' he gulped.

'Mr Director,' Disraeli hobbled to the chair where he hoped the iguana might never sit. 'I've come for a word.'

'Of course, of course. Er . . . did I know you were coming?'

The old Jew looked over his proboscis at him, 'I really can't answer that,' he smiled. 'Lovely reptile.'

'Oh, thank you, Prime Minister. Er . . . tea? Coffee?'

'Thank you, no.'

'I am extremely flattered that you took the time to call. Mr Cross didn't say . . .'

'That's because Mr Cross doesn't know. It doesn't do to tell one's Home Secretary everything. They tell me *you* have certain political leanings, Mr Vincent.'

Vincent straightened up immediately, 'Oh, no, sir. Nothing of your eminence, I assure you.'

'Don't do yourself down, Director,' the Prime Minister said. 'It wasn't all opening railway stations and royal audiences, you know. I've been a hack writer, lawyer, dabbler in shares, traveller, novelist. It took me five years to get into the Commons. And as for my maiden speech . . . yucchh, what a disaster.'

'Ah, but now, sir, you have reached the top of the greasy pole.'

'True,' smiled Disraeli, his lower lip jutting more than usual, 'but you got to kiss an awful lot of babies. Nice place you got here, Mr Vincent.'

'Thank you, sir.'

'Er . . . could you sit down, do you think?'

'Oh, of course, Prime Minister,' and he did.

'No, it's not all Berlin Conferences and being called "Benny" by Bismarck. You have to talk to people like W.H. Smith.'

'Tsk, tsk,' Vincent felt for the man.

'I've come myself today, Director, on a matter of the utmost gravity – too personal for my personal secretary; too private for my private secretary.'

'Really?' Vincent craned forward.

'Does the title Prince Imperial mean anything to you?'

'It's not one to which I personally aspire, Prime Minister, reserved as I believe it currently is for a member of the Buonaparte family.'

'Quite. But do you know where he is?'

'Er . . . well, if *The Times* is to be believed, en route for South Africa, isn't he? Should be virtually there by now.'

'No, Mr Vincent,' Disraeli licked his curl back into position on his forehead.

The lizard turned his head in something akin to interest.

'Not?' Vincent frowned.

'No, *The Times* is not to be believed. The newspaper for which I once wrote, *The Representative*, could have knocked it into a cocked hat. But that is ancient history and we are concerned with current affairs. The plain fact is . . .' and he checked the walls for ears, '. . . the Prince Imperial has absconded.'

'Abs . . .?'

'Gone walkies,' Disraeli explained.

Instinctively, Vincent clapped his hands over the iguana's ears. 'Sorry,' he grinned, 'but they're very intelligent, you know. Like dogs, there are some words to which they become accustomed. We never use the "w" word here. You've no idea how long Whitehall is until you've traversed it with an iguana on a lead.'

Disraeli could believe it.

'Er . . . I feel bound to ask, Prime Minister, where the Prince Imperial has gone and indeed why.'

'Why?' Disraeli smiled his most oily smile. 'Is it so hard to imagine?' He raised his hands in supplication, 'You and I are creatures of duty, Mr Vincent. You have your Detective Force and I half the civilized world to look after – not to mention five-sixteenths of the uncivilized. Have you never, even for a moment, wanted to throw open your casement window and gambol in the grass?'

'Well,' Vincent cleared his throat, 'I am forty feet up.'

'It's spring,' Disraeli beamed, 'or it would be if the weather got better. In spring an old man's fancy . . . the primroses are out at Osborne now. And, ah, to see the branches stir across the moon at Portchester . . .'

'So the Prince Imperial . . .?' Vincent thought he ought to prevent the old man from wandering *too* much. After all, half the civilized world relied on him, apparently.

'. . . was facing a dull, routine campaign, *watching*. Oh, you see, we couldn't actually let him *fight*. Imagine the furore were he to be killed! He knew he was bound for weeks, perhaps months, of inactivity, so he simply didn't go.'

'I see,' said Vincent, 'But I don't quite see . . . I mean, why am I involved?'

'Well,' Disraeli gushed, 'you see, your second question is a little harder to answer than your first, Mr Vincent. I can understand entirely *why* he went. *Where* he went is another matter. That's where you come in.'

'Yes, of course. You want him found. Well, I see entirely. How many men would you like? Fifteen? Twenty? We are a *little* stretched just at the moment, what with the corruption charges, dismal pay and so on.'

Disraeli shuddered. 'Discretion, Mr Vincent, *please*,' he said, 'I fear that if the great British public got hold of the Prince's absconding, they would level at him charges of cowardice. That would of course mortify his mama, the Empress, who would bend the ear of the Queen, God Bless Her, and where would that leave any of us?'

'Yes, of course,' Vincent nodded gravely, 'Consider your drift caught, Prime Minister. Perhaps one intrepid man . . .'

'Lestrade,' Disraeli said quickly.

'I beg your pardon?'

'Lestrade,' he repeated. 'I understand that he is a Detective-Sergeant now.'

'Indeed,' Vincent was astonished. 'Do you know him, sir?'

'We met when he was too young to grow fuzz on his upper lip. A rooky greener than grass. I suggested he grow a moustache to add gravitas to his appearance.'

'Well, he certainly took your advice. He has quite a luxuriant growth now, for a sergeant, I mean,' and he patted his own monstrous lip-camouflager with pride. 'But I fear he is working on a case.'

'Oh dear,' Disraeli frowned, pursing his lips, 'anything vital?'

'Well . . . er . . .'

Disraeli arched an eyebrow, then loosened his cape to reveal the dazzling bullion frock-coat he had worn at the Berlin Congress and almost every day since, just to overawe people. It worked again.

'Ah, but of course, I can tell you. He is assistant to Inspector Heneage of the Headquarters, here. A new man, Harrow and Balliol.'

'Some of us', Disraeli smiled, 'graduated from the University of Life.'

'Oh, quite, quite,' Vincent agreed, frowning solemnly.

'I was particularly hoping that Lestrade could be released. It's a silly thing, I know, but you see, he and I went to the same school.'

'Indeed?' Vincent swallowed in disbelief. Even the iguana looked dubious. But then, to most people, all iguanas do.

'Then of course it was the Reverend Potticary's. More recently, I understand, a Mr Poulson's. But the same school nonetheless. Er . . . this case he's on?'

'Oh, yes. Rather curious, really. The Yard has been called in by the Yorkshire Constabulary. Two rather ghastly murders, I'm afraid. One of an unknown man at Ilkley, the other of a Lieutenant Lyle of the Artillery.'

'The Artillery?'

'Yes.'

'Tell me about the unknown man.'

'Well,' Vincent ferreted through his filing cabinet. 'Ah, here we are. Cause of death, deep slashing cuts to the thorax. Face badly disfigured . . .'

'This is Lestrade's report?'

'Heneage's, yes sir. The senior man always submits the report. This arrived five days ago.'

'Does it say how old the victim was?'

'Mid-twenties, they assume.'

'Anything else?'

'A number of clues.'

'Oh?'

'A handkerchief, a watch and a letter.'

'What did the letter say?'

'Well, here it is, sir. Please read it for yourself.'

Disraeli did. The colour drained slowly from his face. 'My God,' he whispered.

'What is it, Mr Disraeli?' Vincent asked. 'What's wrong?'

'Er . . . nothing,' the Prime Minister said, 'I . . . er . . . am just a little surprised at the dreadful handwriting of a Balliol man, that's all.'

'I'll have a word with him about it,' Vincent promised prematurely. 'Oh, no . . .'

Disraeli caught the stumble. 'No?'

'Er . . . have you . . . er . . . read *The Times* this morning, sir?'

'I told you, you can't believe a word that's printed there. Why?'

'Well, you may be right, sir, for I have received no report from Lestrade. But then . . .'

'You are talking in riddles, Mr Vincent,' Disraeli snapped.

'I'm sorry, Prime Minister. *The Times* of this morning reveals that Inspector Heneage is dead; found murdered by a roadside in Knaresborough.'

'Recall Lestrade.'

'That's just it, sir. I already have. I wanted him to report in person, just to see how Heneage was shaping up – Mr Cross's scheme for a bit of élitism in the Force, you know. And yet I can't. He's disappeared.'

'Disappeared?' Disraeli clawed for his stick and hauled himself upright. 'How can a sergeant of detectives disappear?'

'I'll go to Yorkshire myself, sir, and find out.'

'Do that,' the Prime Minister snarled, staggering for the door. 'Do that,' and calmer now, 'and do keep me informed, there's a good fellow. I would very much like to talk to Mr Lestrade as a matter of some urgency.'

'Leave it with me, sir,' Vincent said. 'The moment I find him, I'll send him back to you, even if I have to conduct the case myself.'

'Excellent, Director. Excellent. Mr Vincent's in his Heaven and all's right with the world.'

'Tickety-boo,' beamed Vincent in agreement.

In the hallway, Disraeli met his Private Secretary, buckling under the weight of a recently-arrived despatch. 'Get a telegram off to that old bugger Cambridge,' he snapped. 'Tell him the Peelers have found the Prince Imperial. Then get me that private detective, what's his name?'

'Steele, sir. Oliver Steele.'

'That's right. My study at Number Ten, five sharp. Whether he wants to know the time or not, I want him to find a policeman.'

'Very good, sir.'

Howard Vincent had relaxed from the total rigidity he had assumed during Disraeli's visit. After all, he was an ambitious man. Politics was indeed his next step. But when it came to toadying, Vincent was as green and cold as his reptile.

'Even so, Ignatius,' Vincent lounged with his lizard, stroking its hideous head, 'there's something Mr Disraeli isn't telling us, isn't there? Something about the death of that man at Ilkley. My God,' he leapt upright again, riffling frantically through the files. He slapped his forehead, infuriated by his own stupidity. 'Of course,' he said, 'That's *it*. A handkerchief with an embroidered

"N". A pocket watch saying "Don't forget Eylau" and a letter to Louis and referring to The Shop. It's him. The dead man at Ilkley *is* the Prince Imperial. My God! My God!'

He sat down heavily. 'Well, why not?' he said to the iguana. 'Heneage is dead and Lestrade must be hopelessly out of his depth by now. Time I did some field work. Sorry, old thing,' he packed the creature into a soggy cardboard box, 'I don't think the Yorkshire air would agree with you. Now, don't look at me like that. It was the same when I had that invitation to Ireland last year. You didn't like the Londonderry air, either, did you?'

'How frightful, Emily,' Jane Rudding said, 'it is simply too ghastly. I couldn't bear to hear it again. Oh, well, then, just once. *Where* did you say they found him, that poor Inspector of Scotland Yard?'

'By the side of the road,' her companion told her, sipping her umpteenth cup of tea that morning. 'Near the Dropping Well.'

'The Dropping Well?'

'Reputedly the birthplace of Old Mother Shipton, the prophetess of Knaresborough.'

'Oh yes – "And the world to an end shall come in eighteen hundred and eighty-one." Two years to go. How depressing.'

'Fiddlesticks, Jane. I happen to know that the original verse referred to *seventeen* hundred and eighty-one. Or was it sixteen hundred? Either way, it hasn't happened yet.'

'Lisbon was pretty shaken, I suppose.'

Emily Clare nodded. 'As though by an earthquake. He was distraught, poor man. You know these manservants, Jane. All his life he'd been taught to fetch and carry, in sunshine and in rain, never complaining.'

'Yes,' Jane nodded, 'well, they don't have feelings, do they, people of his class? Not like you and me, I mean?'

'No,' Emily agreed, 'I suppose not. And yet the murder of his master utterly destroyed him. It was as though he had come unglued.'

'And he was stabbed, you say?'

'Through the heart.'

Both ladies shuddered.

'Emily,' Jane was loath to raise it, but the idea sat irritating in her mind and she simply had to, 'what has Inspector Heneage's death to do with poor William?'

'That's what I'd like to know,' she said, staring wistfully at the violets that intertwined their way through the glaze of her cup, 'and so would Sergeant Lestrade.'

'Ah, yes,' Jane said, looking up, 'Where *is* Sergeant Lestrade?'

The great circus rolled and rattled its way east from the Forest of Knaresborough. First the hunched camels of the night and the giant pachyderms, the darting herd of skewbald Shetlands and the huge, lumbering wagons with the rest of the menagerie. Dogs yelped and snapped at the straining beasts and the groaning wheels. Dawn saw them at Kirkby Overblow. They took their elevenses at Clap Gate. Everywhere, children ran with them, whistling, shouting, marvelling at the caged beasts, mesmerized by the jingle of bits and the snorting horses. By evening, they'd crossed the River Cock and tethered their wagons on that same field where, eternity before in the winter of the Roses, Yorkist had killed Lancastrian and the snow of Towton was stained red.

He sat in the flickering lamplight on his great gilded wagon, a man the wrong side of fifty-three, an elegant beaver top hat at a rakish angle above a face sculpted by the weather, worn smooth by the driving rain on the road. His eyes twinkled like fireflies in their dark-ringed sockets and he patted the belcher chain and huge fob that dangled from it across his silver-thread waistcoat.

'Well now,' he said, pausing to remove a vast cigar, 'what can you do?'

'Oh, a bit of this,' the man before him said, 'a bit of that.'

'Yes,' the top-hatted man said, 'there's a lot of this 'n' that in the circus. But you see, son, Sanger's circus is the biggest on the road this season. We open tomorrow at Tadcaster and I'm a wireman down.'

'Are you?' the young man asked.

The top-hatted man leaned forward, 'Mr . . . er . . . Lister, is it?'

'Yessir,' he answered.

'No, no, lad. No "sirs" here. To the great fee-paying public, I am Lord George Sanger. But round here, it's George or Boss. My ol' dad was a travelling showman; carried a peepshow on his back for twenty years, man and man. He was on the deck of the *Victory* when Nelson went down, you know.'

'Good Lord!'

'Yes. Exactly. We Sangers are no strangers to fame. Who were you with last?'

'Er . . . ?'

'You said you'd got circus in your blood,' Sanger reminded him, 'so who were you with last? Bostock's?'

'Yes, for a while,' Lister said, 'Bostock's.'

Sanger leaned out of a side window, 'Nell, my love, can you spare a minute?'

There was a muffled reply.

'Well, put a poultice on it,' Sanger suggested and catching sight of a practice act beyond the campfire snarled, 'you'll never get a triple that way, Curtis.'

There was a clatter on the wooden steps behind him and a pock-marked lady stood there.

'Nell, my darling. I believe you two know each other.'

The lady peered in the lamplight at the young man before her. He looked useful enough, a little spare, a little rangy. 'No,' she said. 'Do we?'

'Well, I . . . er . . .' Lister hedged.

Sanger stood up. 'Here,' he said and suddenly threw a cudgel at Lister, who missed it and it dropped heavily on his toe. 'Tsk, tsk,' Sanger shook his head, 'wireman, eh? Well, perhaps, but you're no juggler, I'll tell you that. Nell, my princess, have you got Ziggy?'

'George, it's past his bedtime.'

'Oh, I think Mr Lister would like to meet him.'

She smiled and clattered back down the steps.

'You see,' Sanger retrieved the cudgel and twirled it expertly in his hand, 'I'm surprised that my good lady wife didn't recognize you, nor you her, you being from Bostock's an' all. She is of course, Lady Pauline de Vere, to use her show name, the Lion Queen of Bostock's. In fact, old Bostock didn't like it at all that I pinched his star attraction, but that's show business, isn't it?'

'Oh, Pauline de Vere,' Lister clicked his fingers, 'it's this bad light. I didn't recognize her.'

There was a sound behind Lister that he'd never actually heard before. It was like someone with appalling adenoids trying to clear his throat. When he turned, he leapt upwards, landing neatly on Sanger's desk. A half-grown lion was looking up at him, his pale-pink tongue licking his stubby whiskers and his paws huge, spread out on the floor.

Sanger laughed, 'That's not bad,' he said. 'Maybe you'll make a decent wireman after all. Hmm,' he glanced at the mess at Lister's feet, 'only two ink bottles broken. Not bad.'

Lady Pauline popped her battered old head around the corner, giggling. 'That's only Ziggy, Mr Lister,' she said, 'he's only a cub. He only wants to play.'

'Yes,' squeaked Lister, 'well, I haven't been well.'

'And you haven't been near a circus, either,' Sanger said slowly, 'not Bostock's nor anyone else's. Thank you, my love, I think Ziggy has made our point for us.'

'Come on, poppet,' and she took the hairy beast by the ear and led him away, muttering soothing things to him, 'no, that nasty man didn't mean to frighten you, darling. Mummy will beat him severely with her whip. Yes.'

'Do you intend to stay up there all night?' Sanger asked.

'Do you have any more surprises for me?' Lister asked.

'That depends on the answer to my next question.'

'Which is?'

'Which is,' Sanger closed his wagon door and slid the bolt, 'who are you really and what's your bloody game?'

Lister had not moved by the time Lord George's ash had tumbled from his cigar. He clamped the thing between his thin entrepreneur's lips and said, 'Judging by your position up there, anyone'd think you'd seen a mouse, not a lion. And if you're circus,' he pulled the cheroot out and pointed to it, 'this is a monkey's tadger.'

'All right,' said Lister, lowering himself carefully, 'it's not Lister, it's Lestrade. Detective-Sergeant Lestrade, Scotland Yard.'

'I'd gathered that much,' Sanger whipped a small, gilt-headed thing from his hip pocket.

Lestrade slapped his own, but it was too late. 'My tipstaff,' he said.

'Something of a give-away,' Sanger chortled, 'You might as well have worn your blue hat. Snort?' he threw the tipstaff on to the table and held up a flat-bottomed decanter, half full of amber nectar.

'Not when I'm on duty, sir,' Lestrade said, 'so please don't embarrass me by offering tomorrow. But for tonight, yes, I'd love one.'

Sanger chuckled and poured a glass for them both.

'There are a few gentlemen I know east of Temple Bar who'd give their eye-teeth for your sleight of hand, Mr Sanger,' Lestrade said of the tipstaff.

'Out of sleight, out of mind,' the showman shrugged, throwing his hat to the nearest peg. 'Rummaging through other people's pockets can be an invaluable pastime. How long have you been a Miltonian?'

'A detective? Nearly four years.'

'Hmm,' Sanger sipped his brandy, 'green as a rag in the weather. Two things, if you're a-going under cover in the course of your detecting. Don't carry your tipstaff and don't stand too close to the likes of me. Now what d'you want? I'm a busy man. We open in Tadcaster. We next play Pontefract. It's ...' he checked his watch, 'nearly midnight now. We must be away by five, all packed and trim.'

Lestrade perched himself on the edge of a travelling trunk, 'I have reason to believe that an Inspector Heneage visited your show the other day.'

'No, we haven't officially opened yet. Tadcaster is the first night.'

'Not as a member of the audience,' Lestrade explained, 'but in the course of his inquiries.'

Sanger frowned and screwed up his leathery face. 'He didn't get to me,' he said and stuck his head out of the window again. 'Johnnie? Got a minute?'

A muffled voice called back.

'I'm going to do you a favour,' Sanger told Lestrade. 'Whatever I say in the next few minutes, you play along. Savvy?' and he slid back the bolt.

An outsize head appeared above the wagon's floor, followed by a pair of pallid hands with stubby fingers and a dwarf tumbled in a tight cartwheel into Lord George's presence.

'Evenin', Boss,' he chirruped.

'Can I do the business?' said Sanger. 'Major John, this is Mr Lister. He's with the *Weekly Graphic*. ... Come to spend a few days with the greatest show on earth.'

65

'Charmed,' the dwarf bowed.

Catapulted into the Fourth Estate, Lestrade reacted quickly. 'Major,' he said, shaking the little man's hand, 'you do a midget act, I presume?'

Lord George turned away with an inrush of breath.

The dwarf stiffened and squared up to Lestrade's navel, 'No,' he said coldly, 'I am the show's accountant. I just happen to be on the short side.'

'Ah, I see,' Lestrade cleared his throat, 'sorry.'

'You know how it is, Johnnie,' Sanger said, pouring the dwarf a brandy, 'in the Press as it is on the road. Always somebody else, somebody trying to muscle in, pinch your pitch, hit the town first.'

'Do I!' echoed John, gulping the glass's contents. 'Here's shit in your shoes, gentlemen.'

The others raised their glasses.

'Well, Mr Lister thinks there's another newshound sniffing around, a Mr . . . er . . .'

'Heneage,' Lestrade had caught the showman's drift.

'The crafty old bugger,' John said.

'You met him?' Lestrade asked, accepting Sanger's refill.

'Oh, yes.'

'Why wasn't I informed?' Sanger said. He could be as pompous as the Prime Minister if the mood took him.

'Keep your titfer on, Boss,' the accountant said, 'I didn't tell you because Mr Heneage claimed he was a copper. From Scotland Yard.'

'Well, well,' Lestrade giggled, 'the crafty old bugger.'

'My words exactly,' John reminded him.

'What did he want?' Sanger asked.

'He was talking a load of bollocks, Boss,' the accountant held out his glass for more, but Sanger ignored it. 'Some camel shit about a murder back in Harrogate. Mind you, when you played Harrogate last season, it *was* murder, do you remember? Stuck-up load of bollocks, they are, in Harrogate, Mr Lister – and you can quote me on that.'

'Who else did Heneage speak to?' Lestrade asked him.

'Nobody. Oh, only Stromboli.'

'Stromboli.'

'The august,' Sanger explained.

'August?' Lestrade felt everybody was suddenly speaking a different language.

'Clown, Mr Lister,' John told him. 'Bloody 'ellfire, son, you've got a lot to learn.'

'So this Stromboli . . .' Lestrade ignored the jibe.

'. . . brought him to me, rather than bother the Boss. I sent him packin', I can tell you.'

'Stromboli?'

'No, the copper. Only now you tell me he ain't a copper.'

'Ah, life's full of illusions, Johnnie,' Sanger blew smoke-rings to the gilded ceiling where baroque angels smiled down at him. 'Well, I'm sure you want to get back to your books. You balance them so beautifully.'

Realizing that a second drink was unlikely tonight, the dwarf bowed and took his leave. 'I estimate three hundred bums on seats tomorrow night, Boss,' he called.

'Excellent, Johnnie. Merry counting,' and Sanger slid the bolt again.

'Why did you do that?' Lestrade asked.

'Because I don't want us to be disturbed.'

'No, I don't mean the bolt. I mean why did you invent the journalist story?'

Sanger poured them both another brandy and sat back in his chair, 'I don't know. Sixth sense, I suppose. If two Scotland Yard men come a-sniffing around a circus, I'd say there's trouble in the wind. I get the impression, Mr Lestrade, that you're going to need all the friends you can get in the days ahead. And you won't get them playing your cards straight. But then, you know that already. That's why you came to me to sign on, wasn't it?'

'Let's just say I thought I'd learn more as Joe Lister than as Sholto Lestrade.'

'Maybe,' Sanger nodded through clenched teeth around his cigar, 'but the name has possibilities – "The Great Sholto",' he imagined it blazing in naphtha flares across the sky. 'So where's this Inspector of yours? Sent you undercover, did he?'

'No,' Lestrade said, 'he's lying on a marble slab in Harrogate. About now, an Inspector Bottomley of the Yorkshire Constabulary is admiring his face while sipping a hot toddy.'

'Bugger me,' muttered Sanger darkly. 'I think you'd better tell me all about it.'

Perhaps it was the warmth of Sanger's gilded caravan. Perhaps it was the effect of four brandies in a quarter of an hour. Perhaps he hadn't quite recovered from his close encounter with the king – well, prince – of the beasts. Whatever the reason, Lestrade decided to come clean. Something about Lord George Sanger inspired that in a young policeman.

'Inspector Heneage was investigating a murder . . . well, two, to be exact. His makes the third.'

'Fancy,' muttered Sanger, the eyes bright in the sallow face. He outsallowed Lestrade easily.

'You travelled out of Harrogate by way of Knaresborough?'

'Yes,' said Sanger.

'Why?'

'Eh?'

'Knaresborough lies to the north-east of Harrogate. Yet now you're travelling south-east to Tadcaster and Pontefract.'

'That's simple,' Sanger said, 'Howes and Cushing.'

'Who?'

'It's a cut-throat business on the road, Mr Lestrade,' the show-man rested his boots on his table-top. 'Now I've got Astley's in London, Lord George Sanger is the biggest show in the country. This season, the biggest threat comes from the Americans – Howes and Cushing arrived at the Port of London two weeks ago.'

'I don't follow.'

'Neither do I,' Sanger said, 'I lead. I've got blokes all over the place. Come here,' he led the pie-eyed policeman to the window, 'look there. What do you see?'

Lestrade took in the camp-fires, now being kicked out for the night; the great black wagons silhouetted against the Yorkshire sky. From the lines, the Liberty horses snorted and whinnied softly in their sleep and the occasional elephant trumpeted. Only Sanger had elephants that could play the trumpet.

'A circus,' he said.

'No,' Sanger shook his head, 'an army, Mr Lestrade. This is the van. I am the General. Major John is my Adjutant. Everybody out there knows his place in the ranks. And ahead are my light cavalry. Blokes posted in all the major ports, the major cities.' He consulted his watch. 'It's nearly one. I've got three riders spurring south as we speak, fanning out in an arc to watch the roads.

68

Any sign of Howes and Cushing – or anybody else for that matter – and they ride hell for leather to tell me. Then we switch towns, double back, even, if we have to, commandeer the railway. The move to Knaresborough was a feint, designed to confuse Howes and Cushing's riders, 'cos they got 'em too, make no mistake. It seems to have worked so far. Last I heard, their show was making for Manchester.'

'A regular Buonaparte, aren't you?' Lestrade slurred.

Sanger chuckled. 'Now he *was* a showman.'

Lestrade subsided gratefully into his chair again. 'Well,' he said, 'when you left Knaresborough, you left in your wake a dead man – my Inspector.'

'Where was this?'

'Not far from the road, near a place called the Dropping Well. Do you know it?'

Sanger ferreted in a gilded cupboard, heavily chased with cherubs, and spread a map across the table, careful to avoid Lestrade's spilt ink. 'Show me,' he said.

Lestrade focused with difficulty. Sanger nodded as the detective's finger eventually found its mark. 'Yes,' he said, 'we passed within half a mile of there. How did your man die?'

'Stabbed', Lestrade told him, 'with a sharp-pointed weapon.'

'Sword?'

'No,' Lestrade shook his head. 'I have two other corpses on my hands,' he said, 'and I have reason to believe that all three men met their untimely ends by the same hand. Except the first two died by being hacked to death with the very weapon you just mentioned. This one is different.'

'Why?'

Lestrade shrugged. 'I don't know. Perhaps our man was short of time. Perhaps he'd left his sword at home. I've never quite seen a wound like it.'

'Quite?'

'Well,' Lestrade found his glass being refilled as he struggled to remember, 'the hole was through the heart, implying expert swordsmanship, but it was round. No sword-blade I've ever come across could make a hole like that. And there was something else.'

'What?'

The sergeant swayed around the caravan, lurching a little with each step. 'A bruise. To the right of the wound.'

'Don't all stabbings cause bruising?'

'Not like this. Depending on the force of the thrust, there's bruising all the way around the wound. This was just to one side.'

'Was it now?'

'Mr Sanger,' Lestrade straightened, 'I have a job to do. You've been very kind, covering for me with Major John and so on. But a policeman is dead. Killed in the line of duty. Oh, he was an idiot and not very expr . . . ex . . . good at his job, but nobody kills a policeman and just walks away with it. Nobody. Besides . . . I promised a lady.'

Sanger smiled. 'All right, Mr Lestrade. You travel with us. Keep up your pose as Mr Lister of the *Graphic*. Ask what questions you like. *But* I must be kept informed. Savvy? Circus folk don't take kindly to gojos – strangers – whether they're newshounds or coppers or whatever they are. You'll take some knocks – and you'll be on your own. And I'll tell you this. None of my people killed your Inspector. Circus folk don't do that. Oh, they kill themselves occasionally in the pursuit of excellence, but they don't go round killing passers-by, not even copper passers-by. Not *real* circus. You've got a good face,' Sanger held him by the shoulders, 'and you're young and you need a break, so for now, I'll string along with you. Who you really are will be our little secret, for the time being.'

'Thank you. Thank you, Mr Sanger.'

'Boss,' the showman said, 'Boss.'

'Boss,' Lestrade repeated. 'Any ideas about the Inspector's wound? The weapon that caused it, I mean?'

Sanger chewed the last of his cigar. 'Try the elephant man,' he said and stepped backwards as Lestrade slid, unconscious at his feet.

It took Lestrade a while to come to terms with the pounding in his head. There seemed to be a dry rattle reverberating through his ears and a tickling sensation above his lip. Pervading all was a rather strange smell he'd never encountered before. He pawed the air, idly trying to remove the irritation. Expecting a fly or

70

perhaps a cobweb, he sat bolt upright, screaming, when he felt fur.

In front of him a hideous face with gleaming teeth stared back. But it was not Lady Pauline de Vere, glancing back from driving the wagon, that had terrified him, but the little colobus monkey sitting on its perch, chattering.

'He was only grooming you, Mr Lister,' the showman's wife said. 'Say hello to Minkey, Mr Lister. He'll shake your hand if you ask him nicely.'

'I'm sure he will,' Lestrade said, but he had no such intention. 'Where are we?'

'Just coming into Appleton Roebuck. We'll be on the ground by noon. Then you'll see some action for your readers,' she winked.

'My readers? Oh, yes, of course, my readers.' Lestrade thought he'd better nip into Tadcaster when they arrived and buy himself a newshound's notepad.

'Yes, it'll be "All hands to the tilt".'

That was precisely how Lestrade's head felt as he tried to make the view beyond Lady de Vere and the plodding horses' heads focus.

'Ah, he's a one with the brandy is my George,' she laughed, 'but you'll get over it. Would you like Minkey to stroke your forehead? He's a Temple monkey. He's used to it.'

'No, thanks,' Lestrade almost screamed. 'Perhaps I'll stretch my legs. Have a little walk with the elephants.'

Lestrade hit the ground at a run, especially when he realized that the monkey was making another determined bid for his nuts. The sprain wasn't too bad, though, and he hobbled out of the way of the herd of speckled Appaloosas that trotted behind Lady de Vere's wagon. Standing to one side, he watched the great cavalcade roll past, stretching as far as the eye could see in both directions.

A horseman cantered along the roadside, leaning in the saddle and glancing behind him every so often. He drew rein beside Lestrade. 'Hello,' he said, 'another new face.'

'Er ... Joseph Lister,' Lestrade extended a hand, *'Weekly Graphic.'*

'Harry Masters,' the rider shook his hand, 'I'm the vet. Seen a camel with the colic?'

71

'No,' Lestrade couldn't see a camel at all, what with the dust on the road. Spring had suddenly arrived with the circus.

'Damn, I hoped somebody would have. Damned if I know what to do. I knew I should have joined the Camel Corps, not the 47th Foot.'

'Not many camels in the infantry?' Lestrade commiserated.

'Well, none, actually,' Masters admitted. 'They only took me on to service the regimental goat. Well, the Boss doesn't pay me to sit here talking all day. We'll have a chat later.'

'Where are the elephants?'

'At the back,' the vet called. 'They always start at the front, but the stupid buggers are so slow. Can't stand 'em personally. Good luck,' and the intrepid outrider was gone. 'The Sultan of Ramnuggar's your man.'

Lestrade sat on a milestone, the first he'd reached in his career, and waited as the rest of the menagerie came past. One black panther had a nasty turn in his eye and Lestrade was heartily glad that there were iron bars between it and him. He knew the elephants by their long, swinging trunks and great flapping ears. There were a dozen of them, a huge monster at their head. Above his grey, domed skull sat a lithe young man with blond hair and freckles.

'I was looking for the Sultan of Ramnuggar,' Lestrade bellowed above the snorting and thump of the beasts. The smell was indescribable.

'You've found him,' the sandy man called down. 'Just a minute.' He patted the animal behind the ear and the monster curled up its trunk and coiled it around his master's waist before putting him down, so gently, at Lestrade's side. 'Walk on,' the Sultan called and the great beast obeyed.

'That's extraordinary,' Lestrade said, gaping.

'Oh, that's nothing. You should see 'em waltz. I'm working on the Lancers, but it's a bit fast for 'em.'

'No, I mean that you are the Sultan of Ramnuggar.'

The Sultan grinned. 'Yeah, well, actually, that's Ramnuggar Road, Stepney.'

'Oh, I see.'

'Well, you know 'ow it is. Nobody's goin' to pay good money to see a Cockney ride an elephant. So it's the ol' cork and turban. Wait 'til tonight. Who are you, by the by?'

72

'Er . . . Joseph Lister. I write for the *Graphic*. The Boss has given me permission to ride with the circus for a few days.'

'Well, well. You'll want to know about my girls.'

'Ah. How many do you have?'

'Twelve.'

Lestrade looked askance as he walked alongside the Sultan. The man was, what, twenty-two? Twenty-three? To have sired twelve daughters already was a prodigious feat. But then, presumably, he didn't use his feet.

'Edna's the eldest. She's sixty-one.'

'Sixty . . . ?' Lestrade stopped.

'I wouldn't do that, Mr Lister,' the Sultan said in alarm, but it was too late. Lestrade felt as though a house had hit him in the back and he sprawled forward, grazing his cheek as he hit the loose chippings on the road. He rolled instinctively and found himself staring up at something he'd only ever seen from an entirely different angle – and then it had been stuffed with umbrellas. Now, the elephant's foot was inches from his face and joined to a ton and a half of elephant.

'Esmerelda,' the Sultan scolded and jabbed something into the creature's flank. It lowered its foot carefully beside the prone policeman and walked on.

'That was close,' the Sultan helped him up.

'I'll say it was,' Lestrade's heart only now descended from his throat.

'Yeah, she normally piddles on anythin' under her feet. You got off lightly. First lesson, then, Mr Lister. Never stand still in front of a movin' elephant.'

Lestrade mentally added that to his list of moving things he must never stand in front of. It was a comfort.

'Now,' the Sultan went on, 'I've told you about Edna. And you've just met Esmerelda,' he closed to his man. 'I've got to whisper this, 'cos if they hear, there'll be hell to pay. My favourite is Erica. That's her over there, third from the right. Look at them eyelashes, eh? Is she a little darlin' or what?'

'That's a nifty thing, Mr Sultan,' Lestrade said. 'Is it a goad?'

'Ankus,' the Sultan said, holding up the prod he had jabbed Esmerelda with, 'that's what they call 'em in Inja. Want a 'old of it?'

Lestrade took the weapon in his hand. It was eighteen inches

73

long, damascened with silver and had a spike at one end. What interested him most, however, was the iron projection that curled away next to the spike. He twisted it in his grip so that the curl was on the right. Through the clouds of dust behind the elephants, Lestrade shouted, 'A nasty weapon.'

'Not to a elephant,' the Sultan shouted back, ''cos they're so thick-skinned, y' see. Literally, I mean, not metaphysicsly. There's nothin' what takes umbrage quicker than yer average elephant. In fact,' he hung back from the beasts still further, 'I'm takin' a chance just usin' that dread phrase "yer average elephant". 'Cos they're all special, y' see. But no, the ankus doesn't hurt 'em. Whatever those bastards from the RSPCA tell yer.'

'It would hurt a man though,' Lestrade observed.

'Oh yeah,' the Sultan took the thing back, 'it would kill a man, I should think. In the wrong hands. 'Specially if it got him in the heart. Now, about my girls . . .' and he proceeded to bore Lestrade to death all the way to Tadcaster.

Tadcaster stood on both sides of the river Wharfe, dominated, in the dusk of a spring evening, by the great granite tower of St Mary's church. The Romans had come here, many years ago and called it, wrongly, Calcaria. It was most famous however for its beer and Lord George had called the entire show together to warn them that if he smelt liquor on any man, woman or child, there'd be no pay that Friday.

Lestrade could only watch in astonishment as Sanger's people went through their paces. Arriving when he did with the elephants, his boots somewhat browner and stickier than before, much of the ground work had been done. On the field Sanger's agent had selected, carefully tearing down Powell and Clarke's posters first and replacing them with Sanger's, a little man with powerful shoulders was barking orders to a crowd of navvies in bright shirts and moleskin trousers. Around him lay enough canvas to fit out the fleet in the olden days, all quarters laced together with ropes. As Lestrade watched, he heard the shout 'All hands to the tilt' and from everywhere people came running, taking their places at the canvas edge, with the speed of trained performers.

'Come on,' Major John belted the detective in the kneecap as he ran past, 'nobody gets out of this. It's tradition. I'm an accountant and I have to do it.'

And so it was that Detective-Sergeant Lestrade became part of the circus. He watched the tiny accountant grab the canvas and did likewise.

'Tilt!' bellowed the tentmaster and with a great cry, everybody took the strain. The ropes, coiled and slack, suddenly tautened as muscle and sinew bore the brunt. Across the field, four of the Sultan's girls were meandering, it seemed idly, to the points of the compass, but as they did so, the great canvas lifted. Higher. Higher. Until, little by little, it slid along the frame ropes to the poles and darkness closed over the field.

'Mind your feet,' Major John called to Lestrade as the navvies came loping at a trot around the great tent, driving in the guy hooks with their mallets. Inside the vast arena, other men were shovelling tan and sawdust from a slowly moving cart. No time was wasted, for time, as George Sanger constantly told people, was money. One by one, the naphtha flares were lit in their iron cages and the entrance flaps were pinned back. Rows of chattering women bustled together under the auspices of Lady Pauline, setting out terraces of canvas chairs.

'Ah,' Lord George positively sprinted across the ring, 'the smell of the crowd.'

'No Parade today, Boss?' a man twelve feet in the air on stilts called.

'Not worth it at Tadcaster, Shorty,' the showman shouted back. 'Let's warm up tonight and we'll parade at Castleford, eh?'

'Right you are,' and he tottered off to fasten some fittings.

High above them all, half a dozen young men and women, the core of the famous Flying Buttresses, swung to and fro from poles and perches, some with rods, some without.

'Nets!' thundered Sanger from the ground.

'Oh, Boss, come on!' a Buttress shouted, ''ave a 'eart.'

'Nets!' Sanger repeated. 'Or you don't go on.' He winked at Lestrade. 'Always the same the first night, Mr Lister. Daredevilry run riot. Like little kids, they are.'

The little kids arrived first, scampering with their parents across the darkening grass to the magical naphtha glow of the Big Top. The man on stilts welcomed them; 'This way, ladies and gentlemen and children. Walk up! Walk up! Step this way for the main attraction. Step right up! It's a sight to see. Come on, kiddies, that's it, bring your Mamas and Papas.' And each sentence was punctuated with a thunderous crash on the bass drum.

They took their places inside, as the tentmen hauled down the canvas of the entrance way and rolled and roped it away on a wagon, ready for the off. Then all was colour and spangles and stardust.

The Sultan had undergone a metamorphosis. His golden hair was pinned under a lilac turban and his freckles buried under the burnt umber of the Central Indian Plain. His girls cavorted and swayed in the ring, screaming through their noses and tossing their great plumed heads. They lovingly linked, trunk to tail and twirled first this way, then that.

The Lipizzaners, in feathers and sequins, cantered nobly around the circle, spangled sylphs on their backs, pirouetting as they rode. In the centre, Lord George, resplendent in a scarlet coat, barked the acts by way of introduction, and the applause was deafening. It took Lestrade back to his childhood, when he had seen the mighty Van Amburgh, the Brute Trainer from Pompeii, pop his head inside a lion's mouth to tickle the animal's tonsils with a feather. He had not known that Van Amburgh was actually from Fishkill, New Jersey and a martyr to incontinence. It wouldn't really have surprised the little boy from Pimlico – his first inclination on putting his head inside a lion's mouth would probably have been to wet himself too. As it was, the young Lestrade had watched his mother's face shining in the showlight, her eyes bright, her hands, red from years of wrestling in the suds with other people's laundry, hovering in anticipation. He had watched his old dad, whose watch he still carried, the naphtha flaring on his tunic numbers. Somebody in the row behind had asked him to remove his helmet. He had – it made a change from somebody knocking it off.

The trumpets blared to announce the highlight of the evening – 'And now, ladies and gentlemen, the ever-popular story of Dick Turpin and his ride to York!' Sanger bellowed. He cracked his whip and a magnificent coach and pair slid into the arena, the lights dancing on its frame, the coachman hauling at the coloured reins and snaking his whip over the heads of the prancing greys. From across the sawdust ring, a lone horseman, mounted on a glossy black stallion, thudded into the centre.

76

'Good old Bess!' the audience shouted and the animal reared up, pawing the air and loving the roars of the crowd. Then Turpin brought him down again and caracoling sideways, drew two horse pistols and yelled 'Stand and deliver!' behind the mask. The coachman tugged at his leathers, bracing his feet on the board and the vehicle skidded to a halt.

'Your money or your life!' Turpin demanded in time-honoured tradition and fired his blank into the air.

'You'll not take this coach, you blaggard!' the guard shouted and stood up to draw his blunderbuss. Turpin was faster and steadying the frisky horse, fired again with his second weapon. The guard jerked, looked down at the dark stain spreading across his spangles and buckled at the knees. Before the coachman could catch him, he toppled forward, bouncing on the rump of the left-hand horse before pitching into the sawdust. Turpin dropped his pistol as the smoke cleared. The crowd roared its approval, but the coachman lashed his horses and careered round the arena, making straight for the exit. Before he got clear, a clown tumbled on to the tan, his huge shoes flapping, his orange hair jerking up and down. He produced a huge bouquet of flowers from his trousers and lovingly planted them near the fallen guard. Turpin wheeled Bess away and cantered off.

'August! August!' the audience roared, 'Stromboli! Stromboli!' The clown bowed to them all, then snapped his gloved fingers and four others came running, expressionless in their white faces, the glycerine tears sparkling on their cheeks. They took up the fallen guard, one at each corner and carried him shoulder high.

'Turpin! Turpin!' the crowd chanted, but Stromboli wasn't having any. He scuttled across the ring and grabbed two buckets, screaming at the audience in his Italian-English. 'Eh? Wassa matta? Never min' that Turpin. 'E's a Dick. You! You're too adry, thatsa your problem!' and he hurled the contents of the first bucket at the front row. They screamed and recoiled, showered in confetti. But Stromboli had gone, threatening and bullying the audience on the other side.

In the tack room near the Big Top, Lestrade had got there late. A crowd of clowns stood disconsolately around, together with an anxious-looking Sanger, his whip dangling from his wrist. Dick Turpin, the highwayman, stood to one side, looking slimmer and younger than she had on Black Bess a moment ago. Her face was deathly pale. But not as pale as the man on the floor. His greatcoat had fallen back and his tricorn hat still lay in the ring. The crowd laughed and clapped hysterically at the antics of Stromboli beyond the canvas. But the ring was a charnel-house and a man lay dead, an ounce of lead where his belt buckle had been.

5

He led her by the hand up the steps into the gilded caravan. The crowds had gone home, the wires come down. The Sultan's girls were demolishing a well-earned few tons of hay, as were the horses and the camels. Several sheep had been provided by Messrs Langton, Butchers and Meat Purveyors of Tadcaster, to keep the lions and tigers from the door. The great canvas tent had come down at the cry again of 'All hands to the tilt' and some of the wagons were already on the road to Pontefract.

He held out a glass. She shook her head.

'Take it,' he insisted. So she did. 'There,' he said.

'Thanks, Boss.' Her voice was barely a whisper. And she began to cry.

'Now, now, lassie,' the showman put an avuncular arm around her, 'that's no way to go on. It was an accident.'

'No, it wasn't,' Lestrade spoke for the first time, leaning against the bolted door.

'Now, you keep out of this,' Sanger snarled. 'This is circus business.'

'It's my business too,' Lestrade insisted. 'A man is dead.'

The girl looked up at him with tear-filled eyes and a crimson nose. 'Who's he?' she asked.

'This is . . . Mr Lister,' Sanger told her. 'He's a reporter on the *Graphic*.'

'A reporter?' she jumped. 'Shouldn't we call the police?'

'No police,' Sanger said levelly, looking hard at Lestrade. 'The show must go on.'

'I have *some* experience in these matters,' Lestrade said. 'I'd like to ask you a few questions, Miss . . . ?'

She looked at him. Then at Sanger. 'It's all right, lass,' the showman said, 'Mr Lister isn't going to write about this in his paper. Are you, Mr Lister?'

'Not a word,' Lestrade promised. 'I'm just trying to help.'

'All right,' she sniffed, 'What do you want to know?'

'Your name,' he sat down beside her.

'Miss Muffett,' she said, 'Angelina Muffett.'

'A circus orphan, Mr Lister,' Sanger said. 'Little Angie's Ma and Pa died of the smallpox in '65. We brought her up.'

'You and Lady Pauline?'

'Me and the whole show,' he said, lighting a cigar. 'There's lots of orphans in a show this size – take little Evadne Grimaldi, for instance.' Lestrade would rather not. For a start he was far too busy and for afters, Samuel Clinch had already tried that.

'This act you do, Miss Muffett,' he said, ' "Dick Turpin's Ride To York" – have you done it before?'

'Oh, yes,' she blew her nose and an elephant answered, yards away, 'many times.'

'It's one we inherited from Astley's,' Sanger told him. 'Always went down well there in old Batty's time. The star of course – and I know Little Angie won't mind me saying this – is Black Bess. That's what the crowd come to see.'

'Is he all right, Boss? Blackie? He wasn't frightened by the firing?'

'No, he's fine, Angie,' he reached down and patted her long dark hair, 'getting his oats by now in the lines. Don't you worry.'

'How old are you, Miss Muffett?' Lestrade asked.

'Nineteen, sir,' she told him.

'How long have you been riding?'

'Since I could walk, sir.'

'Born in the saddle, Mr Lister,' Sanger said proudly. 'Balloons and banners, toe to pommel, baguette – you name it, Angie's the girl. Why, she can do things on a horse that'd make your eyes water.'

Looking at Miss Muffett's sturdy thighs under her riding breeches, Lestrade didn't doubt it.

'Tell me about the act,' he said. 'What usually happens?'

'Well, the coach circles the ring three times, then I appear on Blackie. I shout "Stand and deliver" and the guard delivers a speech.'

'I didn't hear that tonight,' Lestrade frowned.

'He didn't deliver it', Angelina sniffed, ''cos it was Joey Atkins, not George Tullett.'

'Tullett? Atkins?'

'George Tullett is the usual guard, but he's laid up.'

'Fell off a wagon day before yesterday,' Sanger said. 'Sprained his ankle, so Joey filled in. Best cudgel man I've seen since Stepney Fair.'

'Cudgel man?'

'Juggler. Ever kept twelve balls off the ground at once, Mr Lister?'

Lestrade shook his head. He had to admit two was his limit.

'He'll be a hard act to follow.'

'Was he supposed to draw his blunderbuss?' Lestrade asked the girl.

'Yes. And then I fire . . .' her voice faded away and she shuddered, suddenly taking another gulp from the glass.

'What normally happens?'

'The . . . the coach is robbed. I take the ladies' trinkets, the gentlemen's watches and then gallop to York, chased by the Charlies.'

'After much racing round the ring, "Black Bess" collapses and dies,' Sanger went on. 'Slowly of course. You can't kill a good horse like that all at once. By the time Blackie finally rolls over in the dust, there isn't a dry eye in the house, I can tell you.'

'Tell me about your guns,' Lestrade took the murder weapon from Sanger's table. 'Flintlock?'

The girl shrugged. 'I don't know,' she whispered, 'I can't tell one from another. Dakota-Bred does all that.'

'Who?' Lestrade asked.

'Jack Carver,' explained Sanger, 'known as The Medicine Man or Dakota-Bred. Remember those twelve balls I was talking about? Well, Dakota-Bred can shoot 'em out of the sky before they drop. Not a man to fall out with.'

'And he loads the guns?'

'That's right,' Angelina said.

Lestrade stood up, cradling the horse pistol in his hands. 'Where will I find him?' he asked Sanger.

'End caravan,' the showman said, 'next to "The Shoal of Trained Fish" exhibition. You can't miss it.'

But Lestrade could. And did. He found the wagons in a circle, dark against the night sky of March. The wind moaned through the horse-lines, promising early rain. Only the smoke of the fires wafted silently through the darkness. From the beast cages he heard the throaty snore of a lion, dreaming no doubt of the broad yellow grasses of the Serengeti and smacking its lips on the off-chance of running into Doctor Livingstone. The door of the end caravan was slightly ajar and a pale glow shone from inside. Lestrade pushed and the thing creaked back on its hinges.

He let his eyes get used to the blackness to his left. To his right a single tallow candle burned, its flame steady again now that he had closed the door. Before him stood a huge glass tank, full of water and on its surface bobbed little wooden ships of the line, bedecked with sails and flags. In the murky waters beneath, gold-finned shubunkins flashed this way and that. A lofty angel-fish paused to look at him and slid away to the weedier corners.

'Hello.'

The voice made Lestrade shriek but he did his best to turn the scream into an answer. 'Hello,' he managed, as if those two balls he'd been talking about had not yet descended.

'Fin rot.'

'I beg your pardon.'

A head had emerged from behind the tallow candle. 'Fin rot. Only one or two, not the whole shoal. Still, it's a bugger when it gets a grip. I'm just wondering if there's a connection with the fowl pest that's going the rounds at the moment. Farmers are having rather a hard time of it just now, what with the foot-and-mouth and this appalling weather. We're in for the worst harvest of the century, I shouldn't wonder. Oh, my dear chap. You've turned a little pale. Did I startle you?'

From the conversation and the thrust of the head, Lestrade had at last made out who his companion was. 'Mr Masters,' he said, 'you're the vet.'

'That's right. You're the chappie from the *Graphic*. Sorry if I startled you, but you need quiet to diagnose fin rot. Quiet and subdued light.'

'You must be kept busy,' Lestrade said, 'with so many animals.'

'Oh, it's a living,' Masters looked for somewhere to dry his hands, having plopped a goggle-eyed Moor back into the water.

He settled for his waistcoat. 'Of course, this is my first season on the road.'

Mine too, thought Lestrade, but he wanted to keep his private life as private as possible.

'It's the oyster I'm worried about.'

'The oyster?' Lestrade echoed.

'Sanger's Smoking Oyster. Do you smoke, Lister?'

'Cigars,' Lestrade said.

'Not attached to a yard and a half of rubber tubing, though?'

'Er . . . not usually,' the detective-turned-journalist confessed, 'I'm sorry, I thought you said "Sanger's Smoking Oyster". It must be earwax,' and he rammed home a finger to alleviate the problem.

'No, no,' Masters assured him, 'It's definitely an oyster. A genuine specimen of *Oyster Edulis*, the common European bivalve. Admittedly, I cannot yet be sure of its sex. It may well be hermaphrodite which puts it, I suspect, on a par with Dorinda the Bearded Lady – have you met her?'

'No.'

'Lucky man. Take my advice. Stay away. No, the oyster *appears* totally healthy, but then, nothing is quite what it seems in the circus, is it? There is a theory . . .' and he closed to Lestrade, extinguishing the lone candle as he did so, 'there is a theory that smoking can seriously damage your health.'

'Really?' Lestrade had not heard that, 'how?'

'Gives you violent headaches,' Masters almost mouthed the words.

'Do oysters have heads?' Lestrade had rarely pondered the question before. He knew of a place called Oystermouth in the West of Wales, so presumably it was feasible.

'Not in so many words,' Masters explained, then stopped abruptly. 'Wait a minute. Is any of this going in the *Graphic*?'

'Well, I . . .'

'Oh, no,' the vet shook his head, 'no, no, Mr Lister. I'm preparing a paper on the effects of smoking – not just in bivalves, you realize, but generally. It could have earth-shattering implications. You'll forgive me if I don't share the products of my researches with you just yet?'

'Oh, of course. Of course. I was actually looking for the wagon of "Dakota-Bred" Carver.'

'Really? Oh, it's behind this one. Over to the left. Well, good-night, Lister. See you on the road.'

'Good-night,' Lestrade called and wandered off in search of his quarry.

He crossed the yard behind the fish exhibition, feeling his boots squelch in mud. He thought he heard a faint whirring sound behind him, but before he had time to turn, he felt a searing pain across his throat. Not since the time he was garotted (unsuccessfully) in Flower and Dean Street had he felt pain like this. Then he had jabbed backwards with his elbow and brought his assailant down. This time, he only jabbed thin air and lost his balance. A second whiplash slashed around his ankles and as his hands came up to release pressure on his throat, a third roped his wrists together.

'Well, I'll be hog-tied,' a lazy voice sounded above him and he saw himself being stared at by what appeared to be a huge Stetson hat. Then there was much unwrapping and loosening and he felt his adam's apple sink to its proper place before a strong pair of hands hauled him upright. 'Say, ain't you that there newspaper fellah?' the voice drawled again.

'Indeed,' rasped Lestrade. 'Are you Dakota-Bred?'

'Thru an' thru,' the American shook his hand, 'Jack Carver. Gee, I'm sure sorry 'bout them rope burns. An' that mess on your suit an' all.'

Lestrade let the cowboy help him up into a wagon. In the lamplight, he saw a spare-looking man, a year or two his senior, with clear blue eyes and a healthy tan. He wore a loud check shirt and the widest leather trousers Lestrade had ever seen.

'Never min',' said Carver, 'you'd be surprised how quick the skin grows back. This is likely to hurt a tad.' Lestrade screamed for the second time that night and left the chair he had only just collapsed into. 'There, I told yer it would. But there ain't no substitute for horse liniment on a rope burn. You'll thank me in the mornin'. I'm awful sorry, mister, but when I see a fella a-comin' out o' the darkness with a gun in his hand, why, I just do what comes natural.'

'Yes,' grimaced Lestrade, eyeing with malice the lariat that had just brought him down.

'Jest be lucky you ain't a dogie.'

Whatever that was, Lestrade certainly was.

'Else, havin' roped yer, I'd be burnin' your butt about now with a red-hot brandin' iron. Ceegar?'

Lestrade was past caring what it did to oysters and since Dakota-Bred didn't seem to be offering any rubber tubing, he took the cheroot as it was.

'Actually,' the cowboy lit up for them both, having struck the lucifer on his fancy boot, 'I gotta confession to make.'

Lestrade was all ears, especially the left one, which had got caught up in Carver's rope and was throbbing madly. He craned forward.

'Ah ain't from Dakota at all. Ah'm from the sovereign state of Alabama. Trouble is there ain't many cowpushers in Alabama. Oh, I was raised in the West, sure enough, so I guess it ain't too much of a lie. What paper you work fer, Mister?'

'The *Graphic*,' Lestrade said, hoping that wasn't too much of a lie either. 'I wanted to talk to you about your guns.'

'Why, sure,' the cowboy, creaking as he walked, crossed to a large wooden chest at the far end of the wagon. 'This here', he pulled a nickel-plated revolver from a blanket, 'is a Thumb-Breaker – have a heft o' that an' you'll know why.'

He threw it at Lestrade who missed it expertly and it clattered at his feet, 'Careful, boy,' Carver said, 'that thar's reel ivory handles. This'n,' he hauled out a second pistol, larger than the first, 'is ma pride 'n' joy. It's a Navy Colt, made for General Bedford Forrest hisself.'

Lestrade had always assumed that Bedford Forrest was a football team, but perhaps this wasn't the place or the time to say so.

'Now, this'n,' Carver yanked out a heavy Dragoon pistol, bigger than anything he'd produced so far. He'd thrown nothing else Lestrade's way and noting the size of the latest weapon, the detective was very glad of that. 'This'n's got a kick like a Tennessee mule. Now, if it's rifles you gotta hankerin' fer . . .'

'I was rather referring to this one,' Lestrade held up the horse pistol which he had recovered from the mud on his way into the wagon.

'Aw, that ain't mine,' Carver frowned.

'But you load it for Miss Muffett's act – Turpin's Ride to York?'

'Sure. She's jest a li'l ol' slip of a girl. Don't know tiddly squat 'bout shootin' irons. Not like Annie Oakley. Now there's a missie who can fan ma hammer any time.'

'Is it a flintlock?'

'That?' Carver took the butt of the proffered gun. 'No, sir. Oh, it's dressed up to *look* like a flintlock, but flintlocks is jest too goldarned unreliable fer show work. See here,' he flicked off the fancy serpentine, 'that's jest fer show. What you've got here, Mister, is a good ol'-fashioned percussion cap.'

'It fires one bullet?'

'Ball, fellah, ball,' Carver corrected him, but it was rather late and Lestrade felt he'd disturb people if he complied, so he stayed silent.

'Did you load the gun tonight?'

'Yup.'

'As every night?'

'Yup.'

'Were you in the ring when Joey Atkins died?'

'No sir. Ah was puttin' on ma duds ready for ma act.'

'Which is . . . ?'

'Well, in the ring, ah do some bronc-bustin'.'

' "Bronc-bustin' " ?'

'Yeah. Okay,' Carver chuckled, consigning each gun to the chest again, having twirled them like lightning around his fingers before Lestrade's very eyes, 'not much of a bronc, I'll admit. But you put a burr under the saddle of a sofa, an' ah'll guarantee you *some* kind o' reaction. Old Paint – that's ma horse – Old Paint bucks around a little, then settles down when ah pat him in the right place. Know'd a woman like that once. Struggle like a hell-cat she did, 'til ah put ma hand on her . . .'

'Yes, Mr Carver, thank you. Er . . . the act?'

'Oh, yeah. Well, then ah rope the odd geeraffe or llama. Darn things spit like an ol' Tennessee Spittin' Contest. Ah tell yer, most nights ah come off soaked in spit. Occupational hazard, ah guess.'

'Do you do any shooting in the ring?'

'No sir. Too plum dangerous in a Top this size. Oh, it's okay at Olympia, with a real roof an' all. But even in yer goddamned English weather, there's a chance of a spark hittin' the canvas. Anyhow, Lord George, he say "no" to live ammunition.'

'But you use blanks?'

'Sure. In ma other act, I recreate the battle of Adobe Walls.'

'What happens there?'

85

'Ah get to kill me some injuns. 'Course, they ain't reel injuns, on account o' the last injun to live in Britain was ol' Pocahontas, but she took sick.'

'And as far as you know, you loaded Miss Muffett's pistol with a blank charge tonight.'

'Sure. Here,' he tossed a box of cartridges to Lestrade. 'Blanks, all of 'em. Want me to prove it?'

'All right,' said Lestrade.

Carver caught the box Lestrade threw back to him and one by one loaded them into the gun. Each time, he placed the muzzle to his head and squeezed the trigger. Each time, the explosion shook the caravan and wreathed the smiling cowboy in smoke.

There was a thump on his door and a top-hatted gent appeared above the steps. 'Everything all right, Dakota-Bred?'

'Jest hunky-dory, Boss,' the cowboy waved. 'Ah was jest provin' to Mr Lister here how ah didn't fix the killin' of poor ol' Joey.'

'Of course you didn't,' Sanger frowned. 'Come, come, Mr Lister, you can't go around accusing my people like this, you know.'

'I made no accusation, Mr Sanger,' Lestrade said.

'Good,' the showman straightened his lapels, 'I'm very glad to hear it. No more firing, then, Dakota, there's a good bloke. Cicero's got one of his heads.'

'Cicero?' Lestrade repeated.

'My oldest lion,' Sanger said, 'I've given him a mustard poultice, but he's off his food something chronic. 'Night all,' and the door clicked shut.

'Where are these guns kept?' Lestrade asked.

'Right here, in ma wagon,' the cowboy told him.

'When did you load them tonight?'

'Six o'clock. Give or take . . .'

'And you're sure you put blanks in both?'

Carver leaned forward, his hat tilted on the back of his head. 'Look, Mister, ah've been handlin' guns since you was wearing diapers. If ah couldn't tell a blank from the reel thing, ah'd hang up ma spurs. Now, if you don't mind, ah've got to get to bed. Castleford tomorrow.'

He tugged off his boots, his bandana, his shirt; then climbed out of his leather trousers and peeled down his red combinations. When he was standing in only his hat, he hauled back the untidy covers on his equally untidy bed. A dark-skinned woman suddenly sat up, her long black hair framing a pair of large breasts whose nipples protruded over the sheets.

'This is Rain-In-The-Butt,' Carver explained, 'half-Oglala, half-cut. She's never gotten used to the white man's fire water.'

Lestrade leapt to his feet in astonishment, transfixed by the woman's naked body and impassive features.

'Ah know, ah know,' the cowboy said, waving his hat at the sergeant, 'ah said the last injun livin' here was Pocahontas, but ah wasn't includin' ma good lady squaw. Won her in a poker game down in the ol' Panhandle. Her English ain't so good, but her ass is somethin' else. Say, you wouldn't care to . . . ?'

But Lestrade was an Englishman, through and through. He'd already tipped his hat and left.

It rained all the next day, but the show went on regardless, as Sanger had insisted it should. Mr Oliver, the Boss's agent, had done his advance bookings work well. Castleford was packed, the razzle-dazzle of the show in marked contrast to the misery of the South Yorkshire spring.

Though it went against every rule in the book, they buried Joey Atkins quickly, on a grassy knoll outside the town, as the light of another dawn saw the circus-folk bare-headed and weeping and the wagons rolling again. Lestrade had found time, when the show was at its height, to steal into the wagon that doubled as a hearse, to see what story Joey Atkins had to tell.

They'd stripped him of his coachman's livery and dressed him in his best suit, his hands clasped over his chest. A little bunch of primroses lay in his cold fingers, with a card that said 'From Angie. Sorry, Joey'. He opened the jacket and prised up the waistcoat and shirt. A black hole, wiped clean of blood by the Women Who Do These Things, gave Joey Atkins the appearance of having a second navel. With difficulty, Lestrade turned the corpse over. There was no hole in his back. The bullet must be lodged there, inside him. No point in trying to dig it out, especially by candlelight. The sergeant knew which gun had fired the fatal charge. And he knew whose finger had been on the trigger. Neither of those were the questions at issue.

'I hope I look as peaceful,' a voice made Lestrade turn. A clown stood silhouetted against the distant naphtha flares, his hair protruding in manic tufts from a bald pate, his nose a little red ball. His eyebrows were painted halfway up his head and under the ever-smiling red lips, his own were drawn and tight. 'Poor Joey,' he said and placed a bouquet on the dead man's chest.

'You did that last night,' Lestrade said, 'in the ring.'

The clown nodded, 'I was supposed to give the flowers to the Lion Queen later,' he said, looking at the body below him, on the black-draped table. 'It came to me in a flash. You see, the show must go on, Mr Lister. Joey would have wanted that.'

'Did they realize, do you think? The audience?'

'No,' the clown sighed, perching himself in his huge trousers on the corner of a stool, 'The circus is not all it seems. It is illusion and patter – a veneer. Like a bubble – bright and magic – but one blow and it's gone. If the audience had known that Joey was dead, the bubble would have burst. The magic would have gone.'

'You're Stromboli, aren't you?' Lestrade asked.

The clown bowed, his tie whizzing round and his hair standing on end.

'They say you're the greatest clown in the world.'

Stromboli chuckled. 'They say you're a newspaper man.'

'What?' Lestrade felt a surge of colour to his cheeks which he hoped didn't show in the candlelight.

'I'm sorry,' Stromboli said, 'it's just that I've never seen a newspaper man who did not make notes before. Where is your little black book?'

'In the caravan,' Lestrade said, neglecting to mention that it had the words 'Metropolitan Police' stamped on the front. 'I'm not here to write about tragedy.'

Stromboli lifted his head at the roar of the crowd above the band. 'Comedy, then,' he said. 'Tragedy tomorrow. Comedy tonight. That's my cue.'

'You aren't Italian?' Lestrade had not caught a trace of the accent he had heard in the ring.

'No, I'm Swiss,' Stromboli said, though that accent wasn't apparent either. 'Do you know what happened?'

'An accident,' Lestrade said.

The clown looked at him. 'And I'm Queen Victoria,' he said. 'This may be my first season with the Sanger circus, Mr Lister, but I know a murder when I see one. They're playing my tune,' he

88

half turned in the doorway, his bow-tie still whizzing, 'I just called to pay my last respects to Joey. He was the best.'

They had moved without him. Lord George Sanger, in his full ringmaster's outfit, had stood over the grave in the rain as they lowered him to the flowers. 'Good roads, Joey,' he had said, throwing the earth. 'Good times and merry tenting.'

And Sholto Lestrade began to piece together, as he had already countless times before, the shattered fragments of a stranger's life.

'The man you are looking for, Mr Steele,' said the Prime Minister, 'is to be found in the pages of this book. Page eighty-three if my tired old eyes don't deceive me.'

He looked out across the lawns at Hughenden, to still – and always – rural Buckinghamshire, showing, as yet, few signs of spring and no signs at all of any fizz.

The private detective was a handsome young man, about three hundred years Disraeli's junior. He had a shock of black hair and glittering brown eyes and a jaw like the prow of a ship. 'Lestrade,' he read, 'Constable Sholto Joseph.'

'He's aged a little, I suspect,' the old Jew warned him. 'That was taken on his admission to the Metropolitan Police; H Division, I believe. He's grown a moustache, I have it on reasonable authority, and is of course now plain-clothes. He won't be wearing that rather silly pointed hat.'

'May I ask, sir, why you want this man?'

Disraeli fidgeted irritably with his rings. 'Is the remuneration insufficient, Mr Steele?'

'No, sir,' the young man answered, 'more than fair.'

'And are your daily expenses being met?'

'Most handsomely.'

'Then what can be the need to ask questions, Mr Steele?'

The detective smiled. 'Forgive me for saying this, Lord Beaconsfield, but I have been in the business of amateur sleuthery now for eight years. Before that, I aided my dear old dad, Truaz, in many a covert operation. I am totally familiar with all his cases. No doubt you've read his memoirs, covering many years – *Steele Eye Span*?'

'No,' sneered Disraeli, who read no books but his own.

'Well, in all my time; and in all my dad's time, neither one of us has been called upon to look for a policeman. We've both been called in to find people when the police can't find them. But an actual policeman? Never.'

'Get to the point, Steele,' Disraeli drummed his fingers on the chiffonier.

'I've already made it, sir,' the man told him, 'I'd like to know why you want him.'

Disraeli turned, exasperated, to the French window and back again. He looked the dissolute young man in the eye and recognized something lurking there. True, there was no gardenia in the buttonhole; no deafening of the check in the suit; no chains dangling from lapel to lapel, but good taste aside, there was *something* of the young Disraeli peering out behind the charming smile.

'Very well,' he said, 'I'm going to take a chance on you, Mr Steele. Because I see in you a man much like myself . . .'

'You flatter me, sir,' Steele bowed.

'Yes, I do, don't I?' the Prime Minister flashed a glance at the ceremonial trowel in the corner. 'But never make the mistake, Mr Steele, of flattering yourself. We are men of the world, you and I. Unlike the poor Prince of Denmark, we know a hawk from a handsaw. And I suspect that we have one especial trait in common.'

'Oh?'

Disraeli smiled broadly, his foetid breath snaking out in the chill of his study. Somewhere, a clock stopped. 'We are both, at heart, dishonest,' he said.

'Oh.'

'Tell me, Mr Steele,' the Prime Minister sat back on the sofa to take the weight off his gout, 'where is the Prince Imperial at this moment?'

'Er . . .' Steele frowned, finally shrugging in defeat. It was rather like being asked to name the survivors of the *Birkenhead*. 'Somewhere in Africa?' he guessed valiantly.

'Yes, that is what the papers keep telling us, isn't it? Actually, he's somewhere in England. Not terribly far, I wouldn't imagine, from the base of the Old Cow Rock in Ilkley, Derbyshire.'

'I'm afraid you've lost me, sir.'

'Yes, just as he has lost Lestrade. I avoided telling Mr Howard Vincent, Director of Criminal Intelligence at Scotland Yard, that the man found dead at the foot of said Rock was the Prince Imperial. He, idiot though he is, and somewhat overfond of a particularly repulsive reptile for my liking, has by now no doubt drawn the inference I intended he should and reasoned it out.'

'That the dead man is the Prince Imperial?'

'Quite so. Only he isn't.'

'Not?' Steele frowned. 'Look, sir, do you mind if I sit down?'

'Be my guest,' the old Jew proffered a cadaverous hand. 'But before you do, Mr Steele, be so good as to empty your pockets.'

'My . . . ? Very well,' and the detective did.

'Place the contents on this priceless Louis Quatorze table, would you?'

Steele scattered his belongings. Disraeli perused them. 'Would you say', the Prime Minister asked, 'that these items constitute your daily pocket contents?'

'I should think so,' Steele said.

'Right. A bus ticket. Three pounds and elevenpence . . . three farthings. A piece of knotted string. And a watch. Inscribed?'

'Plain,' Steele shook his head.

'No letters?'

'No,' Steele shrugged.

'No handkerchief?'

'No, sir,' Steele admitted, a little shamefacedly, 'I use my sleeve, I'm afraid – an old Bermondsey custom.'

'Yes,' Disraeli nodded, 'I daresay sleeves were invented before handkerchiefs. Well, there you have it!' And he sat back, as triumphant as he had been the year before, when he'd thrashed Prince Bismarck at Snakes and Ladders in Berlin.

'I do?'

Disraeli sat upright again. 'The dead man at Ilkley was carrying a handkerchief monogrammed with the initial "N" – "Napoleon" – the cypher of the Buonapartes. He was carrying a watch which was a memento of one of Napoleon's battles. The First's, that is. The Prince Imperial's dad was Napoleon III – he can't possibly want to remember any of *his* battles. And he was carrying a letter addressed to him by name – Louis – and making mention of "The Shop" – in other words, the Artillery School at Woolwich where he trained for the British Army. If you were found at the foot of

91

the Old Cow Rock, Mr Steele, from the contents of your pockets, no one would know you from Adam. Any more than they would me – except that, like the Queen – God Bless Her – I never carry any money. He might as well have had blazoned in firework letters five feet tall "I am the Prince Imperial".'

'But the face,' said Steele, 'your face, for instance . . .' and he lost his nerve.

'Ah, quite. It's not everyone with such a rare profile – the aquiline nose, the Apollonic lips, the fairy hair. No, most people are like you and the Prince Imperial, Mr Steele – very ordinary indeed. Unless they carry papers that pertain to their identity, no one would know them. But you see, the man at the foot of the Old Cow Rock had no face left. It had been smashed to a pulp.'

'My God.'

'Indeed. But a better reaction would have been to ask why.'

'Why?' Steele complied.

'To make us believe that the Prince Imperial is dead. Some innocent passer-by of approximately the right age and height was done to death and the handkerchief, the watch and the letter were planted on the body, so to speak, to send the police off on a wild goose chase.'

'I see,' said Steele, 'so where is the Prince Imperial?'

Disraeli stumbled with his stick and his gout to the rain-streaked window again. 'When I first met the little abortion,' he said quietly, 'he was no more than ten years old. He was wearing a little uniform and carrying a little sword and he was swinging it backwards and forwards, much after the fashion of German students in what they call the Schlägerei, the duel. When he saw me, he said, "Mr Disraeli, Mr Disraeli" – always an excitable child – "Mr Disraeli," he said, "Mama and Papa have taken me on the most wonderful outing of my life. We've been to the circus. When I grow up, I'm going to join the circus."' Disraeli turned to the seated detective, 'I don't know where Lestrade is,' he lisped, 'but I know where the Prince Imperial is. He's with the circus.'

One half of the Monteverdi family was padding down the road that leads to Pontefract under a sullen, Yorkshire sky.

'Can you imagine,' he was saying in a somewhat muffled way,

to the man from the *Graphic*, 'what it's like to keep putting your hands in puddles?'

Lestrade couldn't, but then he wasn't tottering upside down, his feet nodding level with the sergeant's head. 'You couldn't . . . sort of . . . walk the right way up?' he suggested. 'That way, only your boots would get wet, wouldn't they?'

'Probably,' Monteverdi said, 'but I need the practice. I'm forty-seven next month. The old biceps are going a bit. Got to toughen 'em up.'

'What part of Italy are you from, Mr Monteverdi?' Lestrade asked.

'Ramsgate,' Monteverdi said, 'and my cousin Giacomo's from Wigan. Nothing in the circus . . .'

'. . . is quite what it seems,' Lestrade chimed in. 'Yes, I'm just beginning to understand that. Tell me about Joey Atkins.'

'Ah, poor Joey,' Monteverdi paused to wipe his nose, not an easy task in his present predicament. 'You will let me know, won't you, if those bloody llamas are getting too close, only they'll pee on anything, you know. No respect at all, they haven't got.'

'I will,' Lestrade promised. 'Er . . . Atkins?'

'Ah, poor Joey. He was the best, you know.'

Yes, Lestrade knew.

'Been with the Boss now, nigh on fifteen year. Did a spell with Powell's and Clarke's before that. All rounder was Joey – slack wire man, clown, even did a bit of fire-eating for a while.'

'He gave that up?'

Monteverdi nodded, though it may have been to avoid camel-droppings steaming on the road. 'Gave him heartburn,' he said. 'But as a cudgel man he had no peer.'

'Was he married?'

'Nah,' he spat something out of the corner of his mouth, ''cept to his job, of course. Mind you, there was a bit of bother a couple of years back.'

'Oh?' Lestrade kept glancing across for the man's facial expression. He was to be disappointed however – his hobnailed boots gave precious little away. 'What was that?'

'Dorinda, the Bearded Lady, set her cap at him.'

'That caused bother?'

'Yes, because Tinkerbelle did, too.'

'Tinkerbelle?' This all began to sound like a fairy story.

'The Strong Woman. It all got a bit nasty. Fur flying in all directions.'

'Are they both still with the circus?' Lestrade had been warned already about Dorinda, but Tinkerbelle was new to him.

'Larger than life,' Monteverdi said, 'but I doubt they'll tell you much. You may as well ask the Pig-Faced Woman.'

They camped that night on the low hills that ringed the broken bridge for which Pontefract was named, under the black outcrop of the castle in whose dungeons Richard II was said to have come to a sticky end, and not by eating Pontefract cakes. Tomorrow they would parade for the first time in the tenting season; all the glitter of the greatest show on earth. But first, Lestrade had three ladies to talk to.

He crossed the park where they held race meetings every third Thursday and reached Tinkerbelle's modest, two-horse wagon. Blazoned across its side, Michelangelo Philbrick, the circus painter, had captured a vast woman with pectorals the size of tall-boys. And he wasn't exaggerating, for a giantess opened the door to Lestrade's knock. He had indeed come to the mountain.

'Yes?' her voice was surprisingly shrill for a woman with the build of a drayhorse.

'Lister – of the *Graphic*,' Lestrade lied, tilting his bowler backwards much after the manner of Fleet Street. 'Could I ask you a few questions, Miss Tinkerbelle?'

'Come in,' she stepped back to reveal a pretty chintzy interior in Cartland pink. A wizened old crone sat knitting in the corner. 'Mummy, this is Mr Lister. He's from the newspapers. Mr Lister, this is Mummy.'

'Charmed,' smirked Lestrade, but there was something about the old girl's pipe he didn't care for.

'Take the weight off your bollocks, sonny,' she trilled, 'Tinker was just about to do 'er exercises, wasn't you, Tink?'

'Not now, Mummy,' the large girl blushed, 'Mr Lister doesn't want to see . . . all that.'

Lestrade could see at a glance there was an awful lot of that to see. 'No, no,' he said, 'I'd be delighted. But at the moment I'm writing a piece about the late Joey Atkins.'

The blue eyes of the Strong Lady suddenly brimmed with tears and she ripped a spangled costume dangling on a hook in her bare hands and began to sob uncontrollably.

'Oh, I'm terribly sorry,' Lestrade said, fumbling for a handkerchief. Then he remembered he'd lent it briefly to half of the Monteverdi family after their little chat; and he quickly put it away. He was about to offer her Miss Clare's, the token she had given him long days before in Harrogate; the sign that said he was her champion. He put that away too.

'Ooh, you've done it now,' the old girl whipped out her briar, 'she'll be blubbin' all night. All right, Tinker, my sweet. You just go through your paces, my pet. I'll talk to the gen'l'man.'

Tinkerbelle, her massive chest heaving in anguish, adopted a theatrical pose and proceeded to tear in half a copy of Mr Gladstone's book on church and state. It was for such purposes that the great Liberal had written it. She then twisted sideways, snatched up a brass poker and began to curl it into a horseshoe. Her shoulders bunched and rippled under her bodice to an alarming degree.

'Well, then, sonny,' the old crone went on, admiring the expertise of her little daughter, 'folks'll tell yer that ol' Atkins was the best. Am I right?'

'You are,' Lestrade could not take his eyes off the performance in front of him.

'Well, that's a load of bollocks, is that.'

'Is it?'

'Oh, 'e was a tolerable juggler. Tolerable, mind jer. Nothin' more. But the way he treated my little Tinkerbelle; I'll never forgive 'im for that.'

'He treated her badly?' Lestrade called over the wailing. Tinkerbelle picked up a hockey stick, having discarded the poker, and snapped it across her thigh. It broke like matchwood.

'Despicable,' tutted the old girl. 'Tell 'im what 'e did to yer.'

A heart-rending sob was the only reply.

'Oh, never mind, I'll tell 'im. Tailed 'er,' the old girl clamped her toothless gums on the pipe. 'Tailed 'er in this very wagon. I was out or I'd never 'ave allowed it. Well, you get pretty broadminded in the circus, what with donkeys and llamas all over the place. Took my little Tinker's virginity, 'e did. Here, darlin',' and she threw the wailing girl a clean handkerchief which Tinkerbelle tore to shreds. 'No, my little Tinker never stood a chance.'

Little Tinker, still crying as though her heart had burst, was placing walnuts in the crook of her knee and cracking them, first singly, then two at a time. Lestrade had seen the naked body of the late Joey Atkins and the floor show he was watching now gave him a pretty fair idea of the broad outline of Tinkerbelle's never standing a chance. She could have flattened the juggler with one swipe.

'Dirty bugger,' the crone was going on. Lestrade was about to protest his innocence, that the mighty thighs of Tinkerbelle had aroused him but little, when it became clear that she was still talking about Atkins. 'And as fer that bloke in a frock.'

A shriek from Tinkerbelle announced that she could take no more and she collapsed, sobbing, into the old crone's lap, narrowly missing death by knitting needle.

'Er . . . bloke in a frock?' Lestrade was confused.

The old girl held a cadaverous finger to her shrivelled lips. 'Nuff said,' she whispered. 'I wouldn't be surprised if there's your murderer, Mr Newspaperman. No, darlin'. Tish, tosh, Mummy's here, Mummy's here,' and she cradled the muscle-bound thing in her arms, crooning softly an ancient lullaby.

While Lestrade hesitated in his chair, she opened her red-rimmed eyes and glared at him. 'That's our way of saying "bugger off",' she spat.

Lestrade did and as he left the caravan's – and Tinkerbelle's – glow, he heard the old girl say, 'You'll never be in a fit state to carry that camel tomorrow, now.'

One down, Lestrade thought, two to go. So, Joey Atkins wasn't the paragon people made him out to be. He'd seduced the Strong Lady, however, so he must have had something about him. But perhaps the old lady's vitriol had been tinged with jealousy. Perhaps she was secretly miffed that the juggler had not warmed to her charms. But with charms as wrinkly as that . . . Lestrade shook off the thought in the clear night air, before the stench of the elephants got to him again. He was still a young man, just starting out. Time enough for wrinkly thoughts later.

He knocked lightly at the door of the second wagon and a bearded head popped out of a side window.

'Dorinda, the Bearded Lady?' Lestrade asked.

'No,' answered the hirsute head, 'try next door.'

Lestrade was confused. Not even Sanger's circus boasted *two* bearded ladies, surely? He tried again. This time he'd guessed right and she led him into the comfortable recesses of her gilded caravan. Velvet drapes framed the double bed which filled one end of it and she pushed him gently back on to it.

'Can I get you a drink?' she purred.

'Well, I . . . it's a little late,' Lestrade tugged at his collar.

'Nonsense, I don't have to be in my booth till ten. Dorinda,' she insinuated her hand into his, 'it's Mr Lister, isn't it?'

Lestrade was wishing about now that he was the Incredible Disappearing Man, but there was little chance of that, given his lack of prestidigitation. 'Yes,' he gulped.

She wandered away in her frothy négligé, lifted from Sanger's Parisian tour of the previous year, and poured them both a stiff something or other. She didn't take her eyes off him the whole time. 'We'll start with two fingers, shall we?'

'Er . . . pardon?'

'The Scotch,' she held up the frosted glass, 'two fingers' worth. You can always come back for more,' and she wormed her way close to him, her bustle rustling on the eiderdown. 'My, but they're breeding them handsome in Fleet Street these days.'

'Well,' Lestrade coughed, 'Thank you, Miss . . . er . . .'

'You can call me Dorrie,' she moaned, looking at him under her luscious, drooping lids. 'What can I call you?' and she ran a beringed hand over his thigh, 'big boy?'

'No,' Lestrade squeaked, 'that wouldn't be . . . very honest, really, would it?'

'Oh, I don't know,' she raised an eyebrow and twirled her moustache, 'I'm sure we can do something about that.'

He cleared his throat and his head in one fluid movement and gripping the glass tightly with one hand and the bed with the other, tackled the problem head on. 'I've come to ask about Joey Atkins,' he said.

'Poor Joey,' she sighed, 'yesterday's man.'

'Precisely,' he said, 'I want to know how he became that.'

'Because', she flicked his tie out of his waistcoat, 'today is another man. You.'

'Yes,' his grin had frozen. 'But I'm alive.'

'I can tell,' her hand had crept up his leg.

'Please, Miss Dorinda. A man is dead.'

'Dreadful,' she shook her head. 'But this is the circus, Mr Lister, dearest. These things happen.'

'When they're planned, they do.'

She sat upright. 'What do you mean?'

'I mean that Joey Atkins was murdered.'

'Surely not?' she frowned.

'Take my word on it.'

'Good Lord,' she swept away to her window, where the lights of Pontefract still twinkled in the early hours. 'Who?'

'I was hoping you could tell me,' he told her.

'I?' she turned wide-eyed, 'why I?'

'Because you and Mr Atkins were . . . lovers.'

'Lovers,' she shuddered at the word. 'Sorry,' she said, 'if I shuddered at that word. But it's so delicious, don't you think? So redolent of soft sheets, firm flesh, huge . . .'

'And because Mr Atkins also made love to Miss Tinkerbelle?'

'Nonsense,' she snorted, sweeping her dress out of her way and pouring herself another Scotch, 'how can any man make love to a cart-horse?'

Lestrade thought it best not to tell her. 'Jealousy, Miss Dorinda,' he said, 'is a terrible thing. It eats hearts, twists fate . . .' he closed to her, 'provides a damn good motive for murder.'

She turned to face him. Suddenly she put down her glass, and tore open her bodice. Instinctively he stared open-mouthed at her firm, pert breasts, the large pink nipples pointing skywards. 'Magnificent, aren't they?' she purred and let the dress descend from her shoulders. She parted her legs and stood there, hands on hips. 'Superb, I think you'll agree.'

The sergeant blinked, several times in succession.

'Do you think', she asked him, 'I have problems taking – and holding – a lover? Do you think I'd have lost Joey Atkins – or any man – to another man like Tinkerbelle Watson? Oh,' she suddenly laughed, 'it's the beard, isn't it? I'm sorry, you didn't think this was real, did you?' she stroked the luxuriant growth. 'In the circus, Mr Lister, nothing is quite what it seems, you know. There!' and she snatched off the black facial fuzz to reveal the merest hint of stubble underneath. 'That's better, isn't it?' she twirled her own moustache while the fake one lay on the bed. 'Mr Lister? Mr Lister?'

But the sergeant had gone.

She popped her head and breasts out of the window and howled into the night, 'Maryanne!'

Lestrade was not ashamed, in later years, to admit that he ran, positively ran, to the safety of the lion pens. The beasts sniffed him on the wind and sank back to sleep. He was in search of the Pig-Faced Woman and for all her tragic title, she could hardly be more of a freak than the two he'd just met.

He knocked on the relevant door. No answer. He tapped again. Nothing. So he pushed the door. In the murk, at the back of the wagon, he saw the nodding frame of an old lady in her rocking-chair. She smiled at him under her old-fashioned poke bonnet. Lestrade had vague memories of his granny wearing one. Her arms were swathed in long evening gloves and her shapeless fingers, probably bent with arthritis, lay useless in her lap.

'Miss Stevens,' said Lestrade, 'I know the hour is late . . .'

The old lady grunted, living up to her sobriquet.

'But may I come in?'

Another grunt.

He tried to see her face in the gloom, the pale skin on which the sun never shone, the little vicious eyes.

'My name is Lister,' he told her, 'I am a journalist on the *Graphic*, and I would like to ask you about the late Joey Atkins.'

The old lady cocked her head, as though listening intently.

Lestrade reacted accordingly, 'Joey Atkins,' he shouted, 'I've come to ask you about him.'

Miss Stevens frowned.

'The juggler,' Lestrade roared. 'He was killed in the ring two days ago.'

The enigmatic Miss Stevens chuckled. *Another* one who had nothing good to say about the late lamented? Lestrade appeared to have opened a can of worms. He sat down quietly beside the old lady. Years of playing the booths and the penny gaffs had not been kind. Her profile was even more repulsive than her full-face; her nose was a snout and her jaw-bone, with its peculiar structure, obviously made it difficult for her to talk. What must it be like, Lestrade wondered, to show your hideous face day after day for children to point and adults to snigger? To appear in the broad glare of naphtha or sunlight, when all you really want to do is to hide in the darkest corner on God's earth. On an impulse, he took Miss Stevens' hand in his. His scalp crawled. She had no fingers, just a bloated, swollen hand. But she recognized his humanity and dropped her great, misshapen head on his shoulder. And ran a long, pink tongue over his face.

He leapt across the wagon, thumping into the wall before he heard it – a stifled, mocking laugh.

'Who's there?' he yelled.

At first there was no movement but for the gently rocking Miss Stevens, her head still lolling to one side, the bright eyes looking at him. Then a hand emerged from the recesses of her dress, then another. They were followed by the head of a dwarf. One who wasn't Major John. The little man rolled out from under the runners of the rocker and stumbled about, pointing at Lestrade and holding his stomach with the pain of the laughter.

'Very funny,' the sergeant said, hands on hips. 'I came to talk to the Pig-Faced Woman.'

'Many do,' the dwarf managed between hysterics. 'She don't say much back, mind. Not unless I prod her with this.' He held up a stick. 'Ain't that right, Miss Stevens, darlin'?' He jabbed the bustle and the old girl grunted in reply.

'But . . . she's . . . she's a . . .'

The dwarf nodded, 'Brown bear are the words you're gropin' for, Mr Lister.'

'Brown bear?' Lestrade repeated.

'Of the family *Ursidae*,' the dwarf said, untying the ribbons of the bonnet. The beast looked down at him, even in its sitting position, and licked the top of his head. 'Geroff, you daft bugger. Soft as shit, she is,' the dwarf slipped a sugar lump into the animal's gaping mouth. 'One tooth,' he waggled it, 'and that's hangin' by a thread.' He pulled off the gloves and the paws boxed the air. 'There,' he kissed the bear on the nose, 'that's better, ain't it, Missy? Nobody'll pay to see a bear sittin' in a rockin' chair, Mr Lister. But to see Miss Stevens, the Pig-Faced Woman, well, that's different . . . Folks'll trudge miles for that. 'Course, we 'ave to keep her face shaved, so's it looks like human flesh. But you don't mind, do you, Missy?' and he hugged the beast. 'When this gentleman's gone, I'll help you off with your dress. I'm sorry, Mr Lister, I was just puttin' Missy to bed when I heard you a-coming. I couldn't resist it. Hit me with a slapstick if you like, but I couldn't help meself. Look, don't take it wrong. You can throw me about tomorrow if you like.'

'Throw you about?'

'Yeah,' the dwarf untied the apron strings that bound them, chair and bear. 'When I'm not workin' the bear and the ether, I'm star of the Dwarf-Throwing Contest. Forty-three feet's my best. Mind you, that were a throw by Tinkerbelle. I doubt there's many men can better that.'

So did Lestrade. 'No, thanks,' he said. 'I'll decline, if it's all the same to you.'

'It's all the same to me,' the dwarf said. 'Somebody'll throw me. It's all part of the show.'

Lestrade shook his head and clattered down the wagon steps. 'About Joey Atkins,' the dwarf said quietly, 'I'm real sorry Miss Stevens couldn't help.'

6

'Bendy' Hendey, the India Rubber Man, shaved that morning as he always did, with his left arm wrapped round his neck, scraping the cut-throat down his right cheek. The little man he shared a caravan with sat upright in his bed and saw the sun gilding the textile mills and the pit derricks. He breathed the air from the open window. 'Good day for a Parade, Bendy.'

A grunt had to suffice as Hendey was working on his moustache-place, the trickiest operation of the lot. One slip now and he'd lose a lip, perhaps two.

'What do you make of that newspaper bloke?' the dwarf asked.

'Mm-mm-m,' Hendey observed.

'Well, that's easy for you to say,' the little man gambolled over the edge of the bed. 'Know what I think?'

'Mmm?' said Hendey, still scraping.

'Now I know you'll say this is silly,' he elbowed the taller man aside and splashed his face with cold water. 'Towel?!' he shrieked, eyes closed, little stubby arms flailing.

Hendey threw it to him, with his left foot of course. 'This is silly,' he said, complying as he always did with the little man's every wish.

'There you are,' the dwarf caught him a deft kick on his ankle. 'But I think,' he beckoned the acrobat down to his level, 'I think the bloke's a copper.'

'Get away!' Hendey snatched the towel and proceeded to poke his ears out.

'Consider,' the dwarf bounced back on to the bed and began to haul on a tiny pair of scarlet tights. 'Ooh,' he squeezed himself in, 'each time I put these on, I realize anew why they call me Huge Hughie. Consider. He's a bloke, what, twenty-five? Twenty-six? See the way he wears his bowler?'

'No,' Hendey didn't notice these things.

'Straight. Every newshound I've ever seen wears it tilted, on the back of his head.'

'So?' Hendey shrugged, lacing his mauve kicksies above his taut abdomen.

'All right, all right,' Hughie conceded, 'not conclusive, I'll grant you. But cop a load of this – he come looking for advice from the Pig-Faced Woman.'

Hendey guffawed, 'Well, he fell for that one, all right.'

'Exactly. How many newspapermen do you know would go to a freak for advice? Begging your pardon, Bendy, of course.'

'And yours, Huge,' the acrobat slipped on his sequinned jacket.

'Now, a copper – that's a horse of a very different collar. Your average copper is architecturally that stupid.'

'I think you're imagining things, Huge,' the India Rubber Man said, tucking his ears under his little cap. 'Seen my plume?'

'Last time I did it was in the mouth of that 'orrible little monkey of Dame Pauline's.'

'Oh, thanks. Is that it, then?'

'What?'

'The extent of your theories about Lister of the *Graphic*.'

'No,' the dwarf tugged on his doeskin boots, the ones with the gold tassels. 'No, it isn't, as a matter of fact, Mr Clever Clogs, it's what he's asking about clinched it for me.'

'Oh? In what way?'

'Has he been anywhere near you? Asked about your flexes? Has he buggery! Did he quiz me on my throwing? The trick with Missy? The ether thing? Not on your twisted torso, he didn't. All he wanted to know about was Joey Atkins and how he died.'

'Get on! Well, I'm ready. Whose turn is it for breakfast?'

'Yours. You know I never eat a thing on throwing days. Better to be safe than sorry. The punters want to see a dwarf chucked; they don't want to see a dwarf chucking up. I'll tell you what I think. Just a tea for me, Bendy. I think he's a Miltonian brought in by the Boss.'

'What for?' Hendey checked his appearance in the full-length cheval in the corner.

'Tsk,' the dwarf nudged him aside and tilted the glass so that it fitted him. 'You know,' he said, 'I could be a tall bloke in a funny mirror, couldn't I? He's brought him in to find out who done for poor old Joey.'

'I thought Angie done for him, Huge.'

'Yeah,' the dwarf pushed him out of the door, 'but you thought a camel was a cigarette until I told you different. Mind you, I reckon I'll have to tell him about what I saw.'

'What?' Hendey flexed his legs and wrapped his arms under his backside, testing the grass with his fingers.

'The other night, the night Joey died. What I saw coming out of Dakota-Bred's caravan. Or should I say "Who"?'

'I dunno, Huge,' the acrobat uncoiled himself. 'Should you?'

'I dunno,' the dwarf screwed up his face. 'Give me a chuck, will you, Bendy? I'm stiff as an elephant's tadger this morning.'

The acrobat shielded his eyes from the sun, scanning the fires on which this morning's bacon sizzled. 'Madame Za-Za's?' he asked.

'Yeah, that's about right for the first throw of the morning.' Hendey stooped, grabbing his little friend by wrist and ankle and twirled with the natural grace of the superb athlete he was.

'Mosholatubbee!' the dwarf yelled as he sailed majestically through the air before hitting the side of Madame Za-Za's caravan with a sickening thud. He rolled in the dust, groaning.

'How's that, Huge?' Hendey called.

The dwarf, winded, waved back at him as a grizzled head appeared out of the window, complete with black eyeshade and cigar. 'Stop bouncing off my caravan, you annoyin' little bugger!' she shrieked.

'Ah, Za-Za, my love,' the dwarf gasped, 'fragrant as ever, my petal.'

'You'll come to a sticky end, you will, Huge Hughie. See if you don't.'

The dwarf staggered upright and made his way back to the breakfast fire. 'Evil eye,' he chuckled to the India Rubber Man, jabbing the air over his shoulder with his thumb, 'old Za has put a curse on me, Bendy.'

'That's without a glass ball,' the acrobat waved at the old girl, still spitting blood at her window.

'That's what I've got,' the dwarf eased his leather trousers, 'a glass ball. And I don't even want to think about the other one. Still, I'm ready for anything now.'

'Walk up! Walk up!' Lord George Sanger was banging his own drum in Pontefract that morning. Not for him the comfortable life of a permanent office in London. He could have stayed at home at Astley's and counted his money. But it was the road, the crowd, the bright faces and dancing eyes in the naphtha light – that's what kept his blood racing. He still liked the old tricks best, the ones he'd done as a shaver at his old dad's side, in the penny gaff and the horse fairs. The Ether Trick always brought them in.

And today was no exception. They'd paid their money – happily collected by Major John, sitting on a blue-draped pedestal, and they stood in the sunlight of the park, eight deep around the little stage. The multi-talented Huge Hughie had landed badly on his eighth throw that morning, his thrower being a little the worse for drink, and he was glad of the respite. While Bendy Hendey was dangling from a tree branch with his legs behind his ears and a copy of the *Circus Gazette* over his unmentionables, Sanger went into his patter.

Lestrade had finished his breakfast near the Big Top and had spent the morning in the rather dangerous company of Dakota-Bred, watching in astonishment as the cowboy shot straws out of the hand of his good lady squaw, who proceeded to stand in her sacking with the same degree of animation as half a hundred-weight of murphies. Had she come from Eastern Europe, she'd have passed for a totem pole. But above the crash of gunfire, there was suddenly a scream, then several, and Lestrade turned to see women and children hurrying away from the ether booth, while a bald-headed George Sanger was appealing to them for calm. As

Lestrade's stride turned to a run, he saw the India Rubber Man unsnake himself and drop silently from his tree before racing across to the little stage, elbowing people aside and twisting through them like quicksilver.

By the time Lestrade got there, it was all over. Huge Hughie lay writhing on the boards, his mouth a livid white. Dark, bloody vomit had splashed over his scarlet jacket and he was doubled up, his knees under his chin.

'Huge! Huge!' Hendey broke through the cordon of horrified onlookers.

'That's bloody realistic,' one of them muttered.

'Help me get him behind the curtains, Bendy,' Sanger hissed.

'Got him, Boss,' the acrobat had snatched up the little twisted bundle and whisked him out of the public gaze. In the cramped darkness behind the drapes, Lestrade crouched with the others.

'It's the throwing,' said Hendey, trying to straighten the little man out, 'it's hurt him inside. Twisted something.'

'Throwing, be buggered,' muttered Lestrade, 'this man's been poisoned.'

There were mutterings that night. And dark forebodings. Two deaths in four days. They all took chances, every one of them. If an elephant went berserk; if a tiger got spiteful; if a rope snapped . . . circus folk walked hand in hand with death and they did not fear it. But this – this was different.

The Parade of course had gone on – the flags and the prancing horses and the plumes and the brave tones of the marching band. The show had gone on too – to a packed Top of Pontefract punters. And the canvas had come down and the wagons rolled again. All except one wagon. The one shared by the India Rubber Man and the dwarf. That still rested, the Clydesdales cropping the flattened grass nearby at their tether ends, the rain bouncing off their steaming flanks. The India Rubber Man had said his tearful goodbye. 'Well, old friend,' he'd squatted beside the little body, 'you've had your last throw.'

George Sanger had taken the little cold hand in his. 'Your tiny hand,' he murmured, 'it's frozen. Good roads, Hughie, good times,' he placed the hand across the breast, 'merry tenting.' And they watched a tear roll down his cheek.

Now, it was just the three of them – Lestrade, the policeman, Masters, the vet and Hughie, the dead man. Three men in a wagon. By the oil lamp's glare, Masters worked quickly, his sleeves rolled up, a grubby apron tied across his waistcoat. Lestrade held the lamp closer.

'Are you sure we should be doing this, Lister?' he asked.

'You've done it before, haven't you?'

'On a giraffe or a horse, yes. But a man . . .'

'We must know what killed him, Mr Masters,' Lestrade said.

The vet sighed and ripped open the abdomen. He looked up at Lestrade.

'The viscera,' the detective said, 'note the position of the viscera.'

Masters shook his head. 'It all looks so different in an Aberdeen Angus. Pass me that jar.' He lifted out the stomach with his forceps and went to work on the gullet with his ivory-handled knife. 'Are you all right?'

Lestrade's green pallor had nothing to do with the matter in hand – it was the shade of the lamp that was to blame.

'Check the mucous membrane,' he said.

'You know a devil of a lot about post mortems,' Masters said, 'for a journalist.'

'My dad was an undertaker,' Lestrade lied. 'This sort of thing stays with you.'

'Too right it does. Look, I don't know what you hope to learn by all this. I've no microscope, you know. Not even a retort.'

The last thing Lestrade wanted was repartee, so Masters' remark seemed irrelevant.

'Well, that's the best I can do,' Masters dumped his bloody instrument on a sideboard. 'Where did I put my cocoa?'

Lestrade peered under the lamp. The dwarf's lips were still pale, his tongue swollen and bloated. The stomach lining and the oesophagus glowed a worm-eaten white. 'Pass me that bottle, Mr Masters, the one George Sanger used.'

The vet did so and Lestrade sniffed it. There was little smell. He placed a finger in the glass neck. 'Lister!' Masters cried, but it was too late. Lestrade's face contorted and his cheek muscles twitched. He spat viciously, then snatched Masters' cup of cocoa and downed it in one.

'Are you mad?' the vet demanded to know.

106

'Quite possibly,' Lestrade said, 'there's no sugar at all in that cocoa. Tell me, Mr Masters,' he kept his tongue moving so that it didn't swell, 'can one horse pull this wagon?'

'Yes, of course. A full-grown Clydesdale could pull three of these in tandem – not for long, of course, or at very great speed. Why?'

'Because I have to go back into Pontefract and I'll need to take a horse to catch up with you again. You'll find Sanger's burial party down the road. Somewhere near pines. Old Hughie was partial to pines apparently.'

'Look, Lister, you're a man of the world. Is all this burying at crossroads and so on strictly legal? I mean, oughtn't we to be calling in the police and the appropriate authorities?'

'Yes and no,' Lestrade hedged, lifting up the stomach and placing it into a knapsack, careful to ensure it was secured in the glass jar first of course. He stuffed Sanger's bottle into his pocket. 'I believe the Boss sees himself as authority enough in these matters,' he said, still feeling the burning sensation in his mouth so that his teeth ached, 'at once magistrate, vicar and captain of his ship. As for legal, what's going on in this circus has nothing whatever to do with the law, if you see what I mean.'

'Where are you going, exactly?' Masters called as his man all but disappeared in the driving rain.

'Just popping out for some matches,' Lestrade said.

Now Lestrade had never quite taken to the equestrian side of life. It was for people like him that the young Gottlieb Daimler and the even younger Carl Benz were working, that very night, on various internal combustion engines, somewhere in Europe. True, Lestrade had done his stint in the Mounted Division, but he and his horse, Killer, had not represented a marriage of minds and the vicious animal had, on more than one occasion, thrown him into the Thames mud with unerring accuracy and then proceeded to attempt to demolish his head. Indeed, the helmet so pulverized by the beast's flying hindhoofs was destined to be on display for many years in the Police Museum at Scotland Yard.

This animal filled him with even greater trepidation. Certainly, it lacked Killer's fiery spirit. Its very name – Sloth – spoke volumes for its persona, but the thing stood nearly eighteen hands high and even when Lestrade had managed to rope it and mount it, by climbing up the side of the wagon, the span of his legs as he straddled its great bare back brought tears to his eyes. Early morning risers, tramping to work in mill and mine on their clattering hobnails, stared under their flat caps at the apparition – a bowler-hatted man, bedraggled to within an inch of his life, the sodden Donegal dripping from every fold. His feet were at right angles to his body and he seemed to be riding a sofa with legs. It was as well they couldn't see, in the dawn's early light, the contents of the glass jar in the knapsack under his arm. And as well for the drunken Irishman who had caught the Clydesdale's bridle on the road and demanded a swig from said jar, that Lestrade had been less than convivial.

He slid wetly off the horse's back and staggered like a man with tin legs to the doorway. Here he hammered, too wet and cold to care how many neighbours he woke. Eventually, lights glimmered in the upper windows and a sash slid upwards.

'Yes?' a peeved voice croaked.

'Are you the chemist?' Lestrade shouted.

'Do you dough what time it is?' the head demanded.

Lestrade fumbled under the folds of his coat for his half-hunter. 'It's nearly four o'clock,' he said, 'I'm sorry, but my business is urgent.'

The͏re were growled mutterings from above. 'They told be,' he said, 'they told be "Do't live over t'shop", but did I pay ady heed? Did I hell as like.' And he vanished, only to emerge later in nightgown and dangling cap, carrying an oil lamp.

'Thank you, Mr ... er ... ?'

'Dudstad,' said the chemist.

'Dudstad?' Lestrade repeated.

'Dudstad!' the chemist pointed at the brass plate off which the rain bounced.

'Oh, Dunstan,' Lestrade read aloud.

'Dat's what I said,' the chemist explained, 'I'm a bartyr to by siduses. Always the sabe. Every April ad Bay like clockwork. Dow, who are you ad what do you want?'

'My name is Detective-Sergeant Lestrade, Scotland Yard, and I want you to have a look at this.'

He held up the glass jar and the chemist recoiled, horrified.

'What the bloody hell is that?' he wheezed, clutching his throat.

'I was hoping *you'd* tell *me*,' Lestrade said. 'Can I come in? Only I'm quietly catching pneumonia on your doorstep.'

Dunstan led the way through a murky passageway into a back room, filled from floor to ceiling with an astonishing array of phials and jereboams full of garishly-coloured liquids.

'Who is it, Digel?' a voice called from another room.

'It's dobody, Daddete. Go back t' sleep, will yer? By wife,' he explained.

'She has sinus trouble too?' Lestrade sympathized.

'Dough,' said the chemist, 'whatever bakes you think that? Hag on, let be get sobe bore light in here.'

He applied his taper to various wicks and the laboratory lay bathed in light. 'Dow,' he said, 'show be that . . . thig again.'

Lestrade placed the jar on a table. The chemist squatted beside it, peering through a misty pair of pince-nez. 'If I didd't dough bedder, I'd say that that was sobebody's stobach. Though it looks as though a traid chibpadzee has taken it out.'

'And you'd be right,' Lestrade said, 'about the stomach, I mean. I can't speak for the removals man.'

The chemist looked at him in horror. For the first time he took in the yellow-faced young man in the dripping Donegal. He could have escaped from somewhere. 'Do you have ady proof that you're a detective?' he asked warily.

'About as much as you have of being a chemist,' Lestrade said, wondering where his tipstaff had landed after he'd flung it to the verges on the advice of Lord George Sanger.

'Ay, well, you bust adbit, it's a little . . . peculiar, shall we say? You turd up here at four id t'bordig ad say "Here's sobebody's stobach".'

'Please, Mr Dunstan,' Lestrade urged, 'a man is dead.'

'I should hope he is,' the chemist crouched by the jar again. 'Well, what do you want be to do about it?'

'Examine that stomach,' Lestrade said. 'Confirm what I already believe. How did the owner of that die?'

Dunstan tutted and muttered, but began his preparations nonetheless. Holding the jar at arm's length, he placed it on a table. Then he stood there. 'Do you bind?' he said, 'oddly, I'b dot usually called upod to haddle people's stobachs. Sort of goes against the graid, if you dough what I bean.'

Lestrade pulled back his sodden cuffs, screwed his courage to the sticking place and lifted the mucous substance out on to the slab.

'Could you wring it out?' Dunstan asked.

'Ring . . . ?'

'Like you were a washerwobad. Like you were a bangle.'

Lestrade's old mum had been a washerwoman. And one of the first household implements he'd caught his fingers in had been a mangle, so he was on home ground. Even so, he could think of more pleasant ways to spend an early Sunday morning. He squeezed and twisted and a considerable amount of liquid dripped into Dunstan's dish. This the chemist whisked quickly away. 'This is a job for the borgue, you know,' he said.

'Has Pontefract got one?' Lestrade asked.

'A borgue? We haven't eved got a public uridal. Here, hold this.'

Lestrade took a test tube with slimy fingers. Dunstan put a match to his Bunsen burner and proceeded to tilt the tube this way and that. As the men watched, the colourless liquid disappeared, leaving only a red sticky residue at the bottom.

'Well?' Lestrade asked.

'Defiditely dead,' the chemist said, 'that's blood left id the bottom there, that's all.'

'So where's the other stuff gone?' Lestrade asked, 'the liquid?'

'Disappeared,' said the chemist.

'Why?' Lestrade kicked himself for not having attended that Bunsen Burning For Pleasure And Profit lecture at the Yard.

'Because it's oxalic acid ad that's what happeds whed you heat it up. Bore thad that I caddot tell you, seeig as how it's half past four id the bordid and it took be eighteen years to grasp eved the basics of chebistry.'

'Would I be right in assuming that this oxalic acid is the same as acid of sugar?'

'You would,' the chemist told him.

'The same stuff that's used to clean metal?'

'The sabe. Dyers use it too – ad leather ad brass bakers. It dissolves iddigo ad bakes laudry blue – that is, blue used id laudry, dot all your clothes blue, if you divide the differedce.'

'Yes,' Lestrade said. 'My old mum was a washerwoman. As soon as I smelt the bottle, I knew I recognized it.'

'Well, there you are, thed,' Dunstan growled, 'didd't deed to get be up at this Godforsaked hour, did you? What bottle?'

'This one,' Lestrade produced it from his pocket, 'can you test this too?'

'Why? What's it supposed to codtaid?'

'It's supposed to contain ether. But that would be too slow. It actually contains more of the same – oxalic acid.'

'Aye, well,' Dunstan said, 'it's what I've always said – you shouldd't buck about with aitch-two-see-two-oh-four-two-aitch-two-oh, should you?'

'I try not to,' Lestrade told him.

'That'll be three ad tedpedce.'

Back he spurred like a madman, but he stopped short of shrieking a curse to the sky. Actually, of course, he had no spurs and leap about on the Clydesdale's back though he might, the contented beast merely ambled along at his walking pace anyway. So it was nearly dawn when Lestrade arrived, shivering and saddle-sore, at the great gilded caravan of Lord George Sanger.

The impresario had not yet dressed and what little hair he still had hung in curling tongs around his ears.

'Ah,' the showman smiled, taking in the sight, the trembling knees, the widely-separated thighs, 'bit of a cockchafer, old Champion, isn't he?'

'Champion?'

'Bendy Hendey's Clydesdale. I was thinking of billing him a year or two back as "Champion the Wonder Horse", but I don't think the world's ready. Masters told me you'd ridden off to get some matches,' he hung the detective's Donegal and bowler over the little grate. 'Are you all right, Lestrade?' he asked. 'You look terrible.'

'So do you,' the sergeant said, 'and it was Sloth I rode, not Champion.'

'Well, can you wonder at it? Two deaths in a week. It's not natural. What's going on, Lestrade?'

'It's as I told you, Mr Sanger. There's a maniac here in your circus and I don't know where he'll strike next.'

111

'Are you sure it's a man?' Lady Pauline appeared from behind a bead curtain with two steaming mugs of tea. 'Fire that down your clack, Mr Lestrade. You look like you need it.'

The sergeant eased himself down beside the fire and let the warmth of the mug seep through to his blue fingers. Obviously, the Boss had confided to his good lady lion tamer Lestrade's true identity. It was only a matter of time of course.

'Tell me about the Ether Trick,' he said.

Sanger sat opposite him. 'That's a secret,' he said.

'It's because somebody's keeping secrets that people are dying,' Lestrade shouted; then calmer, 'look, Mr and Mrs Sanger, I could stop this circus now. In my capacity as a Detective-Sergeant of the Metropolitan Police, I could close you down.'

'But . . . the season . . .' Sanger protested.

'Exactly,' Lestrade nodded. 'You'd lose a fortune, I know. And for that reason, I'm prepared to let you go on – for now. But you've got to be totally honest with me. How is the Ether Trick done?'

Sanger thought for a moment, glancing from Lestrade to his wife and back again. 'Very well,' he said, 'but you must promise me, Lestrade, that this will never leave these four walls. I'd be drummed out of the Showman's Guild.'

'You have my word,' Lestrade promised.

'All right, then. I've been doing this one way or another for over thirty years. It all started in the '40s when anaesthetics were a new thing and Doctor Simpson was making a fortune out of giving them to the Queen – God Bless Her.'

Lestrade raised his mug in a loyal toast while Lady Pauline saw to the more comestible sort for breakfast.

'I hit upon the idea of putting a boy to sleep on stage, using ether. But the trick was, he was in mid-air. More recently, I took to using dwarfs – more of a crowd puller and you don't get the cruelty people on your back. As yesterday's events prove, there's no complaints authority about misusing a dwarf. Anyway, Hughie, same as always, stood on stage. He appeared to be free-standing, but in fact he was resting on a steel frame hidden by a curtain. I came on with the little bottle of ether – which was actually pump water, by the way – and went through the patter. You know, bit of mummery about the miracle ether, etc. and then I poured some on to a pad. That pad then went over Hughie's nose. Now, usually, he'd pretend to fall asleep, go rigid and there he'd be, apparently sleeping soundly, resting on his elbow only, his body and legs stretched out. Actually, of course, his feet were supported too. It was all the rage at the Egyptian Hall for years.'

'And yesterday?'

'Well,' Sanger's face darkened as he took his wife's toast and dunked it into his tea, 'yesterday followed the same routine. But as soon as Hughie touched the pad, he fell off the pedestal and started writhing around. I thought he'd got cramp, or something . . . until I saw the blood. He was sicking up blood, Lestrade. I've seen some sights in my time, but that . . . By the time I'd got up on stage, the poor little bastard was dead. What was it? Did I kill him?'

'Let's say you fired the shot,' Lestrade said, 'but you didn't load the gun.'

'You mean, like Little Angie?'

'Exactly. Who puts the pump water into the bottle?'

'I do,' Sanger said.

'And you did yesterday?'

'Yes.'

'From that time until you used the bottle, was it ever out of your sight?'

'Er . . . yes. Yes, it was. It was just there.' He pointed to a sideboard's surface.

'For how long, would you say?'

'Oh, I don't know. An hour, perhaps more.'

'Ample time,' said Lestrade, 'ample time for anyone to have entered this wagon and tampered with it. I take it the wagon was not locked.'

'No,' said Sanger, 'it's always open house. Wait a minute . . . you were here, Nell. Did you see anybody come in?'

'I wasn't here much longer than you, George,' she dropped the bacon into the sizzling fat. 'No one came in while I was here.'

'What did you mean, Lady Pauline?' Lestrade asked, 'a minute ago, when you said "Are you sure it's a man"?'

'Well,' the Lion Queen fanned the smoke away from her face, 'I don't know, really. I don't know much about murder, but I do know the killer avoids doing it himself. That's rather cowardly, don't you think? Rather like a woman?'

George Sanger chuckled. 'That's richer than you know, Mr

Lestrade, coming from the bravest woman in the world – the first woman ever to put her head in a lion's mouth. Go easy on the bacon, pet. I'm not ever so hungry this morning.'

She teased his ringlets around the curlers. 'Poor Georgie,' she cooed, 'Mr Lestrade?'

'I could eat a horse,' he said and nobody had any doubt which one he meant.

In the caravan of the clowns, the Walker brothers were putting on their make-up.

'I tell you, it's him,' Whimsical Walker insisted, 'it's that bloke from the *Graphic*. He's doing the murders.'

'He says "It's that bloke from the *Graphic*",' Mrs Whamsical was brushing a bright blue wig that looked like an old one of Disraeli's.

'Tell him', Whamsical was painting the white line around his lips, 'that that, as usual, is cobblers.'

'He says "That's cobblers", Whim,' his sister-in-law relayed the message.

'Yeah,' muttered the elder brother, 'that's what he always says. But I'm right. You see if I'm not. We had no trouble at all 'til he come here. Now folks are droppin' like flies. Tell him.'

'"Folks are droppin' like flies" he says, Wham.'

'I know they are,' Whamsical hauled on his outsize red and green check trousers and hooked the braces over his shoulders.

'He knows that, apparently, Whim,' his brother's wife told him.

'Well,' Whimsical stood up to have the blue wig put on, 'I'm not answering any of his bloody questions. Calls himself a newspaperman. I'm not talking to him at all.' And he clattered out of the wagon.

'He's not going to talk to him, Wham,' Mrs Whamsical précised.

Whamsical Walker pressed the catch that made his hair stand on end. 'That'll make a change,' he muttered.

Mrs Whamsical stuck her head out after her retreating brother-in-law. 'He says "That'll make a change", Whim,' she called.

The wagons rolled south-west towards Wakefield, Lord George

Sanger as always at their head. They had not heard from Mr Oliver, the agent, for over twenty-four hours. Even so, the assumption was that Wakefield was booked and ready and the world was Sanger's oyster – the smoking one, of course.

It was just as they rattled into Purston Jaglin under a leaden sky that the balloon went up. There was a ripping sound and a roar and a giant elm crashed across the road, causing Sanger's skewbalds to rear and buck. Old waggoner that he was, he held them fast and spoke soothingly to them, while Lestrade, on the board beside him, wedged between the Sangers, as it were, allowed his heart to descend again to its usual place. As they watched, a sturdy frame with a shock of wild, white hair clambered through the still-quivering branches of the fallen tree and stood on top of the trunk.

'Repent ye, Sanger,' the apparition screamed, 'and turn ye again.'

'Oh, God,' the showman moaned.

'Who's that?' Lestrade asked him.

'I am the Reverend Zephaniah Hale, Priest-in-Charge of the parish of Purston Jaglin. And you are trespassing.'

'That's brilliant,' said Lestrade in admiration, 'I didn't know voice-throwing was one of your many accomplishments, Mr Sanger.'

'I thought he was away,' the showman muttered, lighting a cigar, his fingers still threaded through the reins.

'You know him?'

'Oh, yes. We met four years ago. Since then – and before that, I gather – he's been in and out of madhouses. To say he's as insane as a snake is an insult to my reptiles.'

'Reptile!' roared the clergyman, his collar-end flapping in the morning, 'you are ambassadors of the Evil One. You will not set your cloven hoof in *my* parish. Tell him, Overmantle.'

A tall, rather gormless young man with thick spectacles and a silly way of carrying his head clambered through the undergrowth. Like the vicar, he wore a billowing cassock and he was carrying a piece of paper. He read from it, intoning as though from a psalm. 'The Ether Trick,' he whined, 'an abomination in the eyes of the Lord.'

'Who's this?'

'Herbert Overmantle, his curate. You'd think the odds against

115

having *two* loonies in one church were fairly long, wouldn't you? I'd like five minutes with their bloody bishop.'

'The Intelligent Pigs,' the curate moaned on. 'Bestiality at its very worst.'

'Women!' Hale roared, pointing at the Lion Queen, 'cavorting in states of nakedness that would put Gomorrah to shame.'

'Shall I hit him with my whip, Georgie?' Lady Pauline asked out of the corner of her mouth.

'Let's see how it goes, Nell, my dove.'

It was as well Sanger waited, for as they watched, smocked labourers, with varying degrees of hatred written on their faces, began to muster on each side of the road, flanking the fallen elm. They carried scythes and pitchforks that glinted in the sharpening light.

'Do you get a lot of this?' Lestrade asked.

'Now and again,' Sanger told him. 'Used to be a lot more in the old days, of course. Some of these bumpkins see a trained animal and they imagine it's witchcraft. God knows what they'd say if I showed them Madame Za-Za.'

'The Pig-Faced Woman,' Overmantle intoned, 'scoffing at the Lord's handiwork.'

'And women!' Hale bellowed. 'Don't forget that.'

'We just want to pass through,' Sanger called to him. 'We won't be putting on a show in Purston Jaglin.'

'No,' Hale thundered, 'you certainly won't. Neither will you go on to that Sodom of the South Riding.'

'Wakefield,' Sanger explained to Lestrade.

'Really?' the sergeant said, 'I had no idea.'

Sanger rolled his eyes skyward.

'You can't just roll in 'ere,' a labourer growled.

'Thank you, Thwaite,' the vicar stared him down. 'Leave the verbal assassination to me, will you? You haven't the wit for it.'

'Sorry, your 'oliness,' the labourer acknowledged his place.

'Snakes,' intoned Overmantle, still reading from his list.

'Now the serpent', the vicar boomed, 'was more subtil than any beast of the field.'

'Ah, but the chimpanzees are smarter,' Sanger smiled, between puffs. Behind him, wagons were rolling to a stop. The lanky Dakotan, in wide-brimmed hat and chaps, reined in his quarter-horse alongside Sanger.

'Well, I'll be,' he tilted back his head, 'a welcomin' committee. Would you like fer me to shoot his eyes out, Boss?' he asked.

'I think Lady Pauline asked first, Dakota-Bred,' the showman said. 'Ride back a bit and tell everyone it's elevenses, will you? Oh, and get the elephants up.'

'You are spies,' Hale roared. 'To see the nakedness of the land ye are come.'

'Ah, yes,' Sanger said, 'talking of spies, have you seen a Mr Oliver, my agent?'

'Aye, an 'e won't be botherin' anybody for a bit,' the loquacious labourer shouted.

'Shut up, Thwaite!' Hale rounded on him. 'Sanger, you are a boil breaking forth, with blains. Unstable as water, thou shalt not excel!'

'What if we go round?' Sanger asked the priest. 'Skirt the parish?'

'A trespass upon the Lord's holy ground,' Hale countered. He jumped down from his tree-pulpit, 'I know thy pride, Sanger, and the naughtiness of thine heart. Turn your wagons around.'

Sanger handed his reins to Lestrade. 'All right,' he said, 'this has gone far enough. I haven't used my fists on a man since I was a lad, but buggered if I can think of what else to do.'

Before Lestrade could stop him, as the circus folk formed a semicircle at his back, Sanger had leapt down from the wagon, stroking his skewbalds as he passed them and stood before Hale, a good head shorter than the deranged vicar of Purston Jaglin.

'I warn you, Sanger,' Hale snarled at him, 'I boxed for Toynbee Hall. Put on the whole armour of God, lads,' he roared to his parishioners, then pulled back. 'Herbert, hit him.'

Sanger stepped back too, pirouetting out of the way. He needn't have bothered, because the yard of pump water that was Herbert Overmantle didn't move. The parishioners closed ranks a little.

'Prepare to receive cavalry!' bellowed Hale, ever a student of General Jacob Astley whose armies had clashed through his parish three hundred and fifty years earlier. It was cavalry of a rather different kind that the men of Purston Jaglin had to face however; and the Reverend Hale would have done better to have studied Hannibal. Sanger twirled round, pawing the air with his fists rather as Lestrade had seen the tic-tac men do at racecourses.

From nowhere, the ground shook and the teacups in Sanger's wagon rattled. There was an involuntary trumpet and the elephants came forward at the gallop, ears flapping, trunks swaying, eyes flashing.

'Mother of God!' gulped Overmantle and turned to hack his way through the branches of the elm.

'Let your loins be girded about!' Hale roared and rushed after him. For a second, perhaps two, the parishioners stood their ground, gripping their assorted weapons; then they broke and ran, clutching their smocks and hats as they disappeared across country.

The Sultan of Ramnuggar, bouncing with ease on the back of the lead elephant, whistled and shouted something incomprehensible and the great beasts wheeled and halted, splashed with the mud of South Yorkshire.

'*There's* a story for your paper, Mr Lister,' the elephant man called, and he leaned down, clapping his hands over his animal's ears. 'Be sure to spell Elvira's name right, won't you? She's very sensitive.'

And so they got to Wakefield. And the cry went up 'All hands to the tilt' and the great canvas giant spread, red and white, brightening the dull spring day. Then the Parade and the dazzle. But there were no dwarfs to throw. And no cudgel man balancing his balls in the air. Like the true professionals they were, Sanger's people went through their paces. The Walker brothers and Stromboli were never funnier, sliding about in gallons of custard, hurling buckets of confetti, roaring with umbrage as their shetland-drawn carriage fell to bits. The crowd roared with them in pure delight and gasped in horror as the Flying Buttresses went through their death-defying routine of leaps and whirls on the high wire. And the whole presided over by Lord George Sanger, resplendent in his hunting pink, cracking his jokes along with his whip.

Night came to the circus and in the damp stillness, while a camel farted on the wind, the clown Stromboli came to visit a little kipsey-sack tucked out of the wind under a props wagon.

'Were you asleep, Mr Lestrade?' he asked.

118

The sergeant jerked upright, clouting his head on the axle shaft. 'Lister,' he said. 'Lister.'

'Look,' Stromboli lit a pipe from the embers of the fire, 'we're two men light as it is. Don't you think you need a little help?'

Lestrade looked at the face under the make-up, 'Don't you ever take that off?'

'Of course,' he said, 'but only on Sundays. A true august never appears in public without make-up. He lives for his art. As, I suspect, do you.'

'Ah, the newspaper business,' Lestrade beamed, nodding sagely. 'Yes, yes.'

'How is old Winkworth these days?'

'Who?'

'Winkworth,' the clown repeated, 'the editor of the *Graphic* – Archie Winkworth.'

'Oh, Archie,' Lestrade bluffed, 'oh, he's fine. Fine.'

'Got over his old trouble, then?'

'Well,' the detective was in uncharted waters, 'you know how it is.'

'Oh, yes,' said Stromboli, his own face grim under the grin of the greasepaint. 'I know exactly how it is. Archie Winkworth is editor of the *Sketch*. The editor of the *Graphic* is Rufus Murdoch.'

'Ah.'

'So, Mr Lestrade, couldn't we learn to trust each other, you and I?'

The sergeant knew when the game was up, when the writing sparkled in fireworks on the wall. 'How do you know me?' he whispered.

'The ears of a clown,' Stromboli waggled them backwards and forwards.

'Do you always snoop outside the Boss's caravan?'

'Except on Sundays,' chuckled Stromboli. 'I'm a deeply re-ligious person.'

'Who else knows?'

'Your guess is as good as mine. Circus people aren't stupid. They'll jump to it sooner or later.' The august offered his briar to Lestrade.

'No thanks, I'm trying to give them up.'

'You'll get nowhere with them,' Stromboli said, jerking his thumb over his shoulder.

'Who?'

'Circus folk. They're a clannish lot. They won't tell you anything.'

'But you're circus folk,' Lestrade said.

'Not *this* circus,' Stromboli told him. 'Until this season, I was with the great Circus Rentz in Germany.'

'What brought you over here?'

'Let's just say Mr Sanger made me an offer I couldn't refuse. But there's something you should know, about circus folk, I mean.'

'What's that?'

'They'll pull together for the public. Today on the road, for example. If Sanger hadn't sent in his elephants, they'd have died to a man fighting the yokels. But that's the exterior – the front.'

'Don't tell me,' Lestrade said, 'nothing is quite as it seems in the circus.'

'Exactly. Underneath that one big happy family, there are passions and jealousies and hatreds.'

'I've already found that out,' Lestrade nodded.

'Take the Walker brothers, for example – Whimsical and Whamsical. You've met them?'

'No.'

'My fellow clowns. They hate each other. Haven't spoken for years, though they share the same caravan.'

'Why not?'

Stromboli shrugged. 'That's circus for you. Was it a mistimed trick? A piece of slapstick that went wrong? I don't know. But this I do know – both of them hate me more than they hate each other.'

'Why?'

'You said it yourself,' Stromboli leaned back against the wheel arch, 'and I'm blushing under my make-up to admit it – I'm the greatest clown in the world. Bringing me in has brought additional tension to the clowns. I shouldn't think either of them is particularly fond of Lord George Sanger at the moment, either. It was, after all, his idea that I joined.'

'All right,' Lestrade sat up again, careful this time to mind his head. 'Who else?' he said, 'who else should I know about?'

'Ha, ha,' said the clown. 'You've got to put a few more cards on the table than that, Lestrade. I've got a stake in this too, you know. I could be next.'

The detective chewed thoughtfully on a wisp of straw, then realized it had come from the llama enclosure and threw it away. The great clown was right. He needed a friend. Somebody on the inside. As a sergeant of detectives, he usually had an Inspector above him, directing, controlling, organizing. Below him were always constables; dim perhaps, rookies invariably, but people at least off whom to bounce ideas. But there was no one, no one in this whole mad menagerie he could trust. Unless . . . .

'This is how we do it at the Yard,' he said. 'We have a board. On the wall. Green, it is. And on it are pieces of paper. Names. Places. Coincidences. My guv'nor – that's the Inspector in charge of the case – ties up all the ends he can, oh, with my help of course.'

'Which I'm sure is invaluable,' Stromboli patronized.

'So . . .' Lestrade shifted in the kipsey-sack so that he was as comfortable as possible.

'We've got two men dead,' Stromboli scarcely had to remind him.

'All right. Tell me about the first one.'

'Joey Atkins. I hardly knew him. First-rate cudgel man, though.'

'Cause of death?'

'Er . . . bullet.'

'Ball, to be precise. The gun that killed him was an old-fashioned percussion-cap pistol. The ball must have penetrated his stomach and lodged in his spine. Judging by how fast he died, it probably hit the spinal cord.'

'Who fired it?' Stromboli was very good at this.

'Angelina Muffett, bare-back rider. I've seen some murderers in my time, Mr Stromboli. I pride myself in knowing one when I see one. There's something about them. An indefeatable something. She's innocent.'

'Not if you listen to the Reverend Hale,' the clown chuckled.

Lestrade remembered the girl's magnificent thighs again. 'Of the murder, I mean,' he smiled. 'Then there's the man who loaded the gun.'

'Ah, that would be Dakota-Bred Carver. The Medicine Man.

Best shot I've seen. We had nothing quite like him at Rentz. Could he be your man?'

'He *could* be,' Lestrade shrugged. 'He certainly has the technical expertise.'

'There is one thing,' the thought had just occurred to Stromboli.

'What?'

'Well, am I right in thinking that Joey Atkins was filling in that night in the ring? That he wasn't the usual guard on the York coach?'

'That's right. Why?'

'Well, what if . . . oh, no, that's not likely.'

'I'll be the judge of that,' Lestrade told him. 'What?'

'What if Atkins wasn't the target at all? What if the *real* guard was? What's his name?'

'Tullett.'

'Yes. What if it was *he* who was the intended victim? You've talked to him of course?'

'Er . . .' Lestrade hedged, 'I was just about to when Huge Hughie died. I've been rather busy since then.'

'Right,' Stromboli was in his stride now, 'the second murder. Huge Hughie, the dwarf.'

'Cause of death?' Lestrade asked the imaginary green noticeboard.

'Er . . . poisoning?'

'Yes, but not by ether as you might expect.'

'No?'

'No. The dwarf's stomach and the bottle applied to his nose and mouth contained a reasonable amount of oxalic acid.'

'What's that?'

'A chemical found in cleaning fluid. Laundresses use it. It's also used to clean brass, remove rust and so on. As such, it's available to anybody. You can buy it over the counter in any hardware shop or grocer's. You don't need to sign for it.'

'Who administered it?'

'Lord George Sanger.'

'Who filled the bottle?'

'Lord George Sanger.'

Stromboli blew rings to the sky before he spoke again. 'I'm new to all this of course,' he said, 'but wouldn't you say that sort of points to Lord George Sanger?'

'Too obvious,' Lestrade shook his head. 'He wouldn't be fool enough to administer poison to a victim in full view of a crowd of people.'

'Why not?' Stromboli asked.

'Hm? Oh,' it had dawned on Lestrade, 'I see what you're getting at. Yes. Yes. What better way of carrying it out? People would say what I just said – "Too obvious" – and they'd illuminate him from their inquiries. You should have been a detective, Mr Stromboli.'

Stromboli refrained from returning the compliment for fear of hurting the man's feelings. 'Isn't this a bit odd, though?'

'What?'

'Well, I don't know very much about murder, Mr Lestrade. Give me a custard pie and a mop and I'm in my element. Murder is not my business, but I did read somewhere that if a man kills more than once, he will use the same method.'

'That's usually so,' Lestrade told him, 'Unless...'

'Unless?'

'Unless our man is an exceptional murderer. One of those you come across once in a lifetime. A man so clever, so far above the commonplace, that he can turn his hand to anything. Any weapon, any method. Such men are very dangerous – and they're hell to catch.'

Stromboli nodded.

'You see,' Lestrade said, 'I haven't been totally honest with you.'

'Oh?' the clown raised a painted eyebrow.

'Joey Atkins wasn't the first of our friend's victims.'

'No?'

'No. He was the fourth. And Huge Hughie was the fifth.'

'Who were the others?'

'The first I don't know. An anonymous man at Ilkley.'

'The circus wintered there,' Stromboli said. 'That's where I joined them. Why is the man anonymous?'

'Because the murderer wanted him to be. He demolished his face so that he'd be unrecognizable.'

'I see. And the second?'

123

'Lieutenant Lyle of the Royal Artillery. An officer on leave at Harrogate.'

'That's where we moved to from Ilkley.'

'Quite,' Lestrade nodded. 'It was that link with Sanger's circus which led me here in the first place. I wasn't sure I was right – until Joey Atkins died.'

'You said Atkins was the fourth victim. Who was the third?'

'My own Inspector, Hastings Heneage. He visited the circus. You spoke to him.'

'Not me,' Stromboli said. 'The first two men were ... what? Battered to death?'

'The first one, yes. The second, no. But the actual cause of death was sword-cuts.'

'*Sword*-cuts?'

Lestrade nodded. 'So you see, Mr Stromboli, our friend is more versatile than you thought. He has used a sword twice, an elephant goad, gunshot and poison. And I haven't the faintest idea what he'll use next time.'

'You're sure there will be a next time?' the clown asked.

'Oh, yes,' nodded Lestrade grimly, 'I'm sure.'

7

Dawn had barely slashed crimson-mauve in the eastern sky when Lestrade felt a toe nuzzling his ribs. Once again his cranium collided with the wagon-workings. He peered out from his blankets. Thank God. Whatever had nudged him awake, it was too tall for a colobus monkey, and it wore its top hat at too rakish an angle.

'Mr Lestrade,' the silhouette above him crouched to reveal the leathery features of Lord George Sanger, 'fancy a little ride?'

'Er...?' the sergeant was rather non-committal. After all, it was not yet daylight and he wondered what beast Sanger had in mind for him to straddle.

'Don't worry,' Sanger sensed the man's unease, 'we'll take my gig.'

Lestrade hauled on his shirt and trousers, fumbling with his waistcoat buttons as he ran in the showman's wake. They crossed the dead fires, not yet rekindled for the morning's breakfast, squelched through the straw-strewn mud where the elephants swayed and rattled their chains. Misty figures in the dawn light joined them. An ox of a man Lestrade had not seen before took the reins of a wagon, his red beard still damp with dew. Beside him, in rather more conventional attire now, Tinkerbelle Watson arranged the folds of her pelisse over her biceps. A rangy man with the spine of a snake hopped up behind them and last, a cowboy in a long duster-coat, then fashionable in Wyoming, leapt aboard.

Sanger halted beside them, then patted Dakota-Bred's arm. 'Don't take your guns to town, Jack,' he smiled, 'leave your guns at home, son. Don't take your guns to town.'

The Dakotan sighed and hauled a sawn-off shotgun out of his coat, then a Henry repeating rifle, two revolvers and a Derringer. 'Aw, shucks,' he said.

'I think you know everybody,' Sanger introduced Lestrade as 'from the *Graphic*'. 'Oh, have you met Jim? Jim Crockett, lion tamer.'

The huge man with the auburn beard nodded and grunted. Too long with his lions had made him monosyllabic, terse. At least he showed no inclination to roll over and lick Lestrade, so the sergeant was grateful for small mercies. Sanger stepped up on to the running-board of his gig and urged on his horse as Lestrade gripped iron beside him.

'Where are we going?' the sergeant asked, as the circus camp faded in the mists behind them.

'Wakefield jail,' Sanger told him. He checked back that Crockett's heavier wagon was keeping up, the spotted horses getting into their stride.

'Wakefield jail?'

'As far as they know, you're covering a story on the extra-curricular activities of the circus. In reality, I may want you to use your metaphorical tipstaff and get us inside.'

'Why?'

'Because they've got my agent and I want him out.'

'You can't just break people out of jail,' Lestrade said, suddenly aware of the situation.

'Why not?' he turned in his seat and shouted, 'Dakota-Bred!'

The cowboy leapt from the lurching wagon and sprinted alongside the gig, hauling himself up on to the boards. 'Yo!' he announced himself.

'Tell Mr Lister about the time you sprung your friend in Apache Wells.'

'Why, sure. This pardner o' mine was put in jail fer killin' a fellah.'

'Murder?' Lestrade frowned.

'Nah. Some guy called him an injun-lover. That ain't murder. That's self defence. Anyhow, the guy drew first.'

'Drew?' Lestrade had no idea that artists were involved.

'His gun. He slapped leather, but my pardner was quicker. Drilled him good. Gut shot. Anyhow, the dead fellah had some purty powerful friends in town so they took him to the jail and was fixin' tuh lynch him come mornin'.'

'Tsk, tsk,' Lestrade shook his head. That didn't sound like Wakefield at all.

'So ah sprung him. Blowed away the front of the jail with dynamite. Boy, did that jailhouse rock!'

'You're not ... you're not intending to ...?' Lestrade was horrified.

Sanger held out his hand, palm uppermost. 'Thanks, Dakota-Bred,' he said.

'Aw, gee, Boss,' the cowboy hauled a bundle of dynamite sticks from his duster-coat.

'Now, toddle back,' Sanger smiled.

'Say, Boss, how high is this jailhouse?'

'Don't know,' Sanger shrugged. 'Never seen it. Why?'

'Well, me and Bendy got an idea if we can git to the roof.'

'I'll do the ideas,' Sanger insisted. 'Tell Jim to keep up. Last one in Wakefield gets 'em in.'

They rattled across the nine-arched bridge that spanned the Calder, past the little medieval chantry, cold and Gothic in the morning.

'Six hundred years old, this bridge, y' know,' Sanger said, pausing in mid-crack with his whip to light a cigar. That fact gave Lestrade no comfort at all. Past Doctor Crowther's almshouses they sped as the city crawled into life. A solemn bell tolled the hour of six from the great spire of All Saints, its gilded weather-vane two hundred and forty-seven feet above the Kirkgate.

Sanger hauled on the reins and the gig stopped. 'That's bad,' he muttered.

'What?' asked Lestrade.

'Have you seen a single bill for the circus? I haven't. Looks like Ollie didn't have a chance.'

'You didn't tell me why your agent is inside,' Lestrade said.

'Trumped-up charge by the mad old vicar of Purston Jaglin,' Sanger said. 'It's happened before. All part of the show's rich tapestry.'

'How do you know?' Lestrade asked.

The showman tapped the side of his nose, 'I told you. I have riders everywhere.'

Crockett's wagon creaked to a halt alongside them.

'Right, Jim,' Sanger leaned across while Dakota-Bred tethered the horses. 'Plan A.'

The circus folk alighted and stood around in various degrees of nonchalance, trying to blend in with the Wakefield stone. Admittedly, a red-headed giant in a scarlet-braided tunic, a woman as tall and broad as he, a man in a Stetson and spurs and another man who casually scratched his left ear with his right hand *behind* his head, didn't do a very convincing job. All in all, they made Lestrade look quite ordinary. Sanger had vanished and the sergeant kept his place on the gig's seat until he could work out what was happening.

A moment later, a furious showman emerged from the corner of King Street, his hat in his hand, his bald head gleaming in the first rays of the sun.

'Plan B, Boss?' Crockett grunted.

'What happened to Plan A?' Lestrade asked Sanger.

The showman briefly flashed the lining of his titfer. It was crammed full of pound notes. 'Plan A is always the simplest, most direct,' Sanger said, 'plain, old-fashioned bribery. It never failed in the good old days. But people today ...' he spat copiously. 'When turnkeys aren't on the take, you know there's something wrong with society.'

'So what's Plan B?'

'Well,' Sanger chewed his cigar, 'I hesitate to use it. Tink?'

The big girl blushed, nodded and she and Crockett took up

positions on the little green below the courthouse, grey and grim and foreboding.

'Plan B is blank-moulding,' said Sanger in answer to Lestrade's look of utter bewilderment, 'perhaps with a bit of nobbing if all goes well.'

Lestrade had hoped that nobbing had gone out with the Contagious Diseases Act, but it wasn't his place to say so. 'Blank-moulding?' he asked.

'Putting on a show in the street, from cold. Always hard work, but at six in the morning, diabolical. The tog-tables take too long and anyway we'd probably be arrested.' He crossed to the giants among his people. 'I counted eight blokes in there,' he said to Crockett. 'When you see eight faces at the window, you give me the sign.'

The lion tamer nodded, then roared deafeningly, 'Walk up! Walk up! See the greatest sensation of the age. Tinkerbelle, the strongest woman in the world.'

He unsnaked his whip and it cracked like a gunshot over the girl's head. As Lestrade watched open-mouthed, Tinkerbelle oozed out of her pelisse and began to flex her thorax. One by one the buttons pinged off her bodice until she rippled on the grass in her blouse. An astonished group of locals began to gather, nudging each other, muttering in approval, drooling. From nowhere, Crockett had produced a side drum and he began to beat this with his fists, roaring a welcome to the crowd. They rose as a man when Tinkerbelle dropped her skirts and stood in a steel-framed corset, her huge thighs flexing and straining, her back rippling with the effort. Slowly, the steel of her stays began to buckle. Crockett casually glanced around him and began to count. 'One face,' he roared, 'two faces, three faces.'

The blank-moulding seemed to be working.

'What for is he a-doing that, our Egbert?' a young shoe-black whispered.

'It's circus, in't it?' Egbert told him, with his two or three years' extra wisdom. 'That's 'ow they do it in t' circus, you know. Circus folk do it standin' up.'

'Six faces, seven faces,' Crockett roared. Tinkerbelle's eyes were closed tight, the laces snapping at her back. But it wasn't her eyes or the laces the crowd on the green were looking at. Neither for that matter were the crowd at the courthouse windows.

'Keep an eye open, Lestrade,' Sanger whispered, 'if you possibly can. We'll be back.'

'Eight faces,' thundered Crockett as Tinkerbelle rolled to the floor, writhing and flexing. The crowd surged forward, eager for a better view. Soon the only sound was Crockett's insistent drum-beat and the puffing and grunting of Tinkerbelle. Lestrade hadn't noticed Sanger, Dakota-Bred and Hendey slip around to the front of the building.

Suddenly, a roar went up as the corset burst.

'Bloody 'ellfire!' shouted Egbert, for whom life down on the farm would never be the same again. He stared at the phenomenal frontage of Tinkerbelle Watson, still muttering 'bloody 'ellfire. Bloody 'ellfire'. More importantly, the eight jailers were rapt too, their faces pressed to the bars at the windows.

Even so, it was a routed trio of showmen who came back a few minutes later.

'All right,' snapped Sanger, 'so they've got *nine* blokes in there. How was I to know? And how was I to know the ninth bloke was a bloody Maryanne, with no interest in naked women whatsoever. Put your clothes on, Tink,' he shouted, 'you'll catch your death. Jim, nob.'

And the lion tamer nobbed, while the time was ripe. He snatched the Stetson from the head of Dakota-Bred and went among the sizeable crowd, hoping for pennies.

'Come along now, gentlemen,' he said genially, 'you've had a sight for sore eyes this morning. It must have brightened your way to work. Come along now. We need to buy this lady a new corset. And you, sir,' he slapped a hand on young Egbert's shoulder, 'for a mere twopence, you can have her old one.'

It wasn't working. Clearly miffed that Bendy Hendey had thrown a blanket over Tinkerbelle, the crowd began to move away.

'All right,' sighed Sanger. 'Plan C.'

Without warning, the lion tamer lashed out with his fist at the nearest labourer, sending teeth flying into the morning. Dakota-Bred brought his head up under another's jaw and Hendey twisted aside from a retaliatory blow before pirouetting forward to land a well-timed kick on his man's head. Suddenly, there was a battle going on on the little green outside the courthouse. Most of the locals made a beeline for Tinkerbelle, to see if she needed rescue. It turned out that she didn't and she cracked together the skulls of her first two saviours.

'Plan C involves you,' Sanger shouted to Lestrade. The sergeant jumped down from the gig, ready to mix it with the roughs. He didn't like the look of their hob-nailed clogs at all and he'd left his brass knuckles in his Donegal.

'No, no,' Sanger dragged him to the lee of the building, 'you get in there and get my man out. We'll be all right out here. How you do it is up to you, but I'd keep my back to the wall, if I was twenty-five and single.'

Lestrade ducked a flying fist and dashed into the building.

'Who are you?' a rather dapper young constable asked him, a natty little cerise cravat slung nonchalantly over his collar-numbers.

'Detective-Sergeant Lestrade,' Lestrade said, 'Scotland Yard. You are holding a man I need to take with me.'

As they spoke, the counter swung up and eight burly constables rapidly arming themselves with cutlasses, clattered past them. 'Can you 'old t'fort, Annie?' one of them asked.

'Oh, aye, lover,' the young man minced, 'I'll be all right.'

'Annie?' Lestrade cocked an eyebrow.

'Oh, don't worry,' the young man twinkled, 'it's just a nickname. My real name's Peregrine. What do the lads call you, on your Force, I mean?'

'Sergeant,' said Lestrade, vaguely horrified.

'Look, er . . . I hope you don't mind my saying this, only it is a *little* unusual for a Metropolitan detective to turn up unannounced in his shirt-sleeves. Especially when we've just 'ad a bribe offered us to take that particular prisoner, rapidly followed by a full frontal attack on this very desk.'

'Can you wonder you've been offered a bribe?' Lestrade spread his arms, while thinking on his feet. 'My coat, hat and jacket were ripped from my person on the street outside. What kind of police station are you running here? I'd been led to believe that Wakefield was top-hole.'

'Oh, it is, sergeant, it is, I assure you,' the constable patted the detective's hand in a flourish of civic pride. 'Look, I'm sorry. It's a very strange morning, this morning. As soon as I got up, I said to Fat Tom, I said . . .'

'Fat Tom?'

'He's my ... friend. "Fat," I said, "I feel one of my heads coming on. It's goin' t' be one of those days."'

'About the prisoner?'

'Oh, Oliver,' the constable shuddered, 'not my type at all.'

'On what charges is he being held?'

Both men glanced out of the high barred window as the din of battle redoubled outside.

'Distributing filthy pictures,' the constable said. 'Charges brought by the Reverend Hale of Purston Jaglin. Mind you, he's as mad as a snake. Look, I hate to ask you, sweetie, but do you have a teensie-weensie bit of identification? I wouldn't ask, only...'

'In my coat,' Lestrade shrugged, 'the one ripped off my back under your very nose.'

'Oh, quite, quite,' the constable sympathized. 'Well, we'll say no more about it, shall we? Do you want t'other bloke as well?'

'T'other bloke?' Lestrade found himself lapsing.

'Aye. T'Reverend Hale brought in both blokes. Both of 'em passing out these filthy pictures. Is that why you want Oliver?'

'Er ... yes, that's right. You ... er ... you haven't got an example of these filthy pictures, have you?'

The constable shuddered. 'In t'safe, lover,' he said, 'I tell you, I went quite cold when I saw 'em. I certainly wouldn't let Fat Tom see 'em. Well, we *are* the guardians o' t'nation's morals, aren't we?'

Lestrade had never looked on his rôle in quite that way, but he hadn't time to argue semetics. He peered out of the window while the constable wrestled with the safe's combination. Crockett, Dakota-Bred, Hendey and the girl were hemmed in by an increasing mob of yokels and boys in blue. At the back, skirmishing around the line like a terrier at the ankles of a bull, Sanger gave more than he got and waded in again.

'Look at that,' the constable threw the pictures down in disgust, having held them at arm's length. They were posters for Sanger's circus.

'These are posters for Sanger's circus,' Lestrade said. Such perspicacity had earned him the metaphorical stripes of a sergeant of detectives in only four years.

'Ah,' smiled the constable, 'that's where they've been so diabolically clever, lover,' he lisped. 'And what t'Reverend spotted straight away. Look at that!' his trembling finger pointed to a rather bad painting of Angelina Muffett, baguetting on the saddle of a Lipizzaner. 'A painted, naked woman,' the constable shuddered. He closed to Lestrade, 'performing with an animal.'

'Er . . . oh, quite, quite,' Lestrade said, 'but this is nothing in comparison with the stuff he's been peddling in London.'

'Ooh, no,' the constable shook his head in disgust. 'Don't tell me they do it on bicycles as well. By t'way,' he closed to his man, 'do you know anything about this circus?'

'No,' Lestrade lied. 'Why?'

'Oh, nothing,' the young man said. 'I just wondered if they had any daring young men on flying trapezes, wearing very tight clothing . . .' and his voice trailed away.

'Ah, well,' Lestrade smiled, 'in the circus, nothing is quite what it seems.'

He always felt guilty, in the years ahead, that he had left Sanger and his people to fight it out. The showman didn't mind. He'd clashed with the authorities before. He even introduced it into the show later as 'The Second Battle of Wakefield'. True, three constables ended up in hospital and there was a bit of damage to the cathedral windows, but, unlike the upright constables who guarded Wakefield jail, the magistrate before whom Sanger appeared the next day was understanding itself. Especially when Lord George emptied the contents of his hat on the man's desk and threw in Tinkerbelle's discarded corset for good measure. All the showman got was a caution – and he was that already.

Four men sat in Lord George's caravan the next night and smoked cigars. The rain drummed on the roof and Lady Pauline had put her teeth in the glass and gone to bed.

'I can't get over that old bastard Hale,' Sanger said, pouring everybody their second glass of brandy. 'Fancy trying that old one about the filthy pictures.'

'You could have knocked me over with huge ticket sales when he made a citizen's arrest,' Oliver said. 'Especially as I thought he was chained to a wall in Wakefield Asylum for Incurable Curates. How did you get us out, Mr Lister? You never said.'

Lestrade looked at Sanger's agent – a neat little man in a screaming check, his thumb and index finger worn smooth by years of pinning up circus posters and greasing the palms of local authorities.

'Oh, years of experience,' he said. 'You'd be amazed what working for the *Graphic* does in the corridors of power.'

'Mr Samson,' Sanger said, 'it was good of you to come to Ollie's rescue.'

'Well,' the fourth man said, blowing smoke up to the cherubs, 'it's not every day you see two clergymen belabouring a chap around the head. I mean, fair play and all that.'

He was a good-looking man, with black hair, dark, sparkling eyes and a jaw like the prow of a ship.

'And what do you do?'

'Me? I'm a rigger looking for work.'

'A what?' Lestrade asked.

'I rig wires for the trapeze,' Samson explained. 'I was about to introduce myself to Mr Oliver here when the thunderbolt of Purston Jaglin struck.'

'The ways of the Lord are strange,' pondered Sanger. 'Who were you with?'

'A couple of years with Clarke's,' said Samson, 'but I *am* rusty, I'll admit. Did a turn before the mast last year. Round the Horn.'

Sanger shook his head. 'It's beyond my ken how people can do that,' he said. 'Not much of a sailor myself, despite my old dad and Trafalgar.' He suddenly stooped and hurled a silver-painted cudgel at Samson who caught it deftly and slipped it quickly to Oliver, who did likewise. The agent hooked it under his arm to Lestrade and it dropped loudly on his feet.

Sanger smiled broadly. 'Looking for work, then, Mr Samson?' he asked.

'I was down to my last tanner,' the rigger-sailor told him. 'It could have been downright embarrassing if the Yorkshire Constabulary hadn't offered to find me a bed for a couple of nights,'

'Good,' the showman said, 'we'll try you out in the morning. You'd better ride south when you're rested, Ollie. Something tells me we've outstayed our welcome in Wakefield.'

'What's going on, Boss?' the agent leaned forward.

'How d'you mean?' Sanger lit a new cigar.

'I heard about Joey and Huge. What's the score, Boss?'

'You know circus, Ollie,' Sanger said. 'Accidents will happen.'

The agent gave him an old-fashioned look, 'I've been on the road with you for eight years, George Sanger. Before that, I did ten with Wombwell's. If it weren't for this leg of mine, I'd still be up there on the silver wire, you know that. People don't die of accidents like being shot dead with blanks and drinking pump water that shrivels their insides to seaweed.'

'You're very well informed,' Lestrade observed.

'It's my job,' Oliver told him, limping across to the window. 'There's wiremen out there, trick riders, lion men, cudgel men, elephant men, riggers, acrobats, freaks and labourers. Nearly three hundred people on your payroll, Boss, and they're being picked off one by one. How long before you do something about it?'

Sanger looked at the three faces in front of him. Yes, he'd known 'Ollie' Oliver for years. Outside his Nell, Major John, his brother in Birmingham, Jim Crockett, Maccomo, the Walker brothers and a few dozen others, there was no one he trusted more. He looked beyond the agent to the dark camp through the window. Nearly three hundred people – a caravan nearly two miles long on the road. Family. *His* family.

'I am doing something about it,' Sanger said. 'Mr Samson, you're new to Sanger's circus, so I'll take a chance you're pure as the driven snow. I know I can trust you, Ollie. Gentlemen, I'd like you to meet Sergeant Lestrade of Scotland Yard.'

There was an expectant hush in the Big Top. The naphtha lit a handsome young man in sequinned tights, one of those, no doubt, about whom the young constable in Wakefield had been enquiring – he who was unlike other constables. He wore a white shirt with lawn sleeves and while one arm was extended to his left and the drum roll thundered from the orchestra pit, the other held the blade of a swept-hilt rapier, its pommel wobbling in the air, its tip against his lips.

'Hoop-la,' called his luscious, leggy assistant and the drum stopped with a clash of cymbals and the blade came down. There was a gasp of horror from the crowd. People were on their feet, shouting, crying. Children screamed.

The young man in the centre of the sawdust ring staggered, the rapier somersaulting out of his mouth, blood spraying in an arc from his throat. His knees buckled. His hand went out for a moment to his luscious, leggy assistant and he died.

'Unbelievable,' Lord George Sanger shook his head. He suddenly looked older than his fifty-three years and tired and ill. 'Nell, my love, how's luscious, leggy Lucinda taking it?'

'Lying down, as always,' the Lion Queen scowled.

'Not tonight, surely?' That, to Sanger was unbelievable too.

'I'd better go and bed down the lions. Jim's in no fit state.'

Lestrade tipped his bowler as the old girl made her exit. What was left of Alistair Brodie lay in the Props Wagon, his spangled tights brown with dried blood, his shirt ripped back where Sanger had rushed to try to revive him.

'Not in all my born days have I seen anything like it,' the showman muttered, his eyes bright with tears. 'Two, two of my people to die in my arms.'

'Couldn't be suicide, could it?' Masters the vet asked, almost apologetically.

'Shut up, Harry,' Sanger growled.

'Well, could it, Lister?' the vet persisted. 'You seem to have experience of these things. I remember a captain in the 47th fell on his sword after a particularly vicious game of bridge one night. I blamed his partner, of course.'

'In my experience,' Lestrade said, 'suicides do the deed in dark corners. They die in their beds in that loneliest of hours between two and three. Those who advertise it don't want to die at all.'

'Ah, yes,' Masters nodded, 'a sort of cri de coeur.'

'Well, Harry,' Sanger reminded him, 'early start in the morning. We'll need to put out in Sheffield.'

'Yes,' the vet sighed, 'I think we're all put out enough at the moment,' and he clattered away to check the horse-lines.

'Put out?' Lestrade asked.

'We'll be staying in Sheffield for three nights,' the showman told him. 'In that situation, the artistes find what lodgings they can in the town. That's called putting out. If you take my advice you'll make for Mrs Minogue of Effingham Street. Does the meanest Barnsley Chop in the world, I shouldn't wonder, though how I can even mention food at a time like this, I don't know.'

Lestrade mechanically checked the wound again by the flickering oil lamp. Outside a rising spring wind was rattling the caravans and making the great beasts restless. Circus folk sat in their wagons or huddled in their kipsey-sacks and watched each other. The big cats could smell the fear on the wind. Alistair Brodie's throat was sliced perfectly in half – his windpipe by the sword divided. Apart from the look of agony on his pale, handsome face, it appeared for all the world as though he was a subject for the surgeon, an example for eager, fresh-faced young medical students to profit by.

'Why is Jim in no fit state?' the detective asked, ever the picker-up of unconsidered conversations, especially other people's.

'Jim virtually brought the boy up,' Sanger said. 'His own mother died in the same epidemic that took Little Angie's parents.'

'His father?'

Sanger shrugged, 'Second Battalion, Grenadier Guards, if my memory serves me aright. Always very accommodating was Liza Brodie.'

'Scottish?'

'That persuasion, certainly. I never enquired too deeply. Well, when you've got a wife that wrestles lions for a living, Lestrade, you don't really feel inclined to look at other women.'

'So Brodie had been with you all his life?'

'Yes,' Sanger perched himself on a bed of flats across which painted elephants scampered, trunk to tail, 'Circus-bred, through and through.'

'How long had he had the sword act?'

'About three years. Before that he was a rigger – fixed the wire for the trapeze artistes. Billed himself more recently as the Great Bolus. Lucinda provided the glamour.'

'Ah, yes,' Lestrade remembered, 'luscious and leggy.'

'Most people found her so.'

'What did Harry Masters mean – suicide?'

'Man's an idiot,' Sanger's face glowed orange and sinister as he lit a cigar. 'Oh, I'd offer you one, but there's no smoking in this wagon. What he knows about animals' workings I could write on a pin-head. By the way, Ollie tells me Howes and Cushing have got the Pin-Headed Man. I'm bloody furious about that, I can tell you. I suppose Masters is talking about Henrico.'

'Henrico?'

'El Magnifico – the Magnificent.'

'What does he do?'

'A bit of this, a bit of that,' Sanger winked at him, 'but mostly he throws knives at the luscious Lucinda – and that's not all.'

'What else does he throw at her?'

'No, I mean, he is familiar with the sleeping quarters of her caravan.'

'Oh,' Lestrade's ears pricked up, 'how long has this been the case?'

'Nearly a year.'

'Did Brodie know?'

'Unquestionably.'

'And what was his attitude?'

'He was furious. They had a fight.'

'When was this?'

'Nearly a year ago.'

'And since then?'

Sanger shrugged. 'Since then, they've all rubbed along, so to speak. But there was no love lost. Rumour was that Lucinda was going to leave Alistair and run away to the circus – another circus, that is.'

'Did you notice Brodie recently? Did he have any . . . I don't know . . . changes of mood?'

'I don't think so. He seemed his usual self. He was always a bit on the surly side, was Alistair. Well, I suppose when you slide three feet of steel down your gullet on a daily basis, your disposition isn't likely to be sunny, is it?'

He rapped on the wagon door.

'*Quien es?*' a rather foreign voice called.

He knocked again.

The upper section of the door swung wide, catching Lestrade's nose in its sweep. He staggered back.

'*Si?*' a magnificent head of jet-black hair was framed in the lamplight.

'I was looking for Lucinda,' Lestrade mumbled, blinking the tears from his eyes.

The black-headed man turned and muttered something incomprehensible, then opened the lower half of the door as well. He grabbed Lestrade's hand and pulled him quickly up the steps. 'They will talk,' he muttered cryptically.

'Will they?' Lestrade asked. The lady in the bed was luscious indeed, though how leggy she was was moot in that a vast eiderdown covered her lower portions. 'Please accept my condolences, Mrs Brodie.'

'You're the newspaperman,' she said, reaching for a mirror to check that she was presentable.

'Joseph Lister,' he held out a hand. She took it with a warmth that shook him and her fingers lingered a trifle longer than was strictly necessary, given the situation surrounding Lestrade's visit. 'I'm doing a story on sword-swallowing in the '70s,' he lied. 'Although I have no wish to impose on your . . . grief, I hoped you might tell me about your late husband's technique.'

'Clearly, it wasn't very good,' she said, patting the bed beside her.

Lestrade took the chair, but stood up again suddenly, a second crease having been created quite painfully by a sword that lay there.

'Sangria?' the dark-haired man suggested.

Lestrade took in the bed, the lady, the man and didn't see how they'd all fit. 'It's rather late,' he smiled, hoping to avoid the Spanish peccadillo. The dark-haired man shrugged and poured himself one anyway. 'You must be Henrico El Magnifico?'

'*Si.*'

'Don't tell me,' Lestrade could judge the myth that was circus now, 'you're from Sydenham.'

'*Que?*'

'Oh, no . . . no, wait,' he studied the darkly handsome features, 'Penge,' he slapped his knee, 'I see it in your eyes.'

Henrico looked confused. Lucinda gabbled something to him in Spanish and he understood. Drawing himself up to his full height, he said, 'I am Henrico Jesus Santiago de Compostella Ortega. I am from Burgos in the province of Castile. I have never heard of this Penge. It sounds like a disease of elderly peoples.'

Lestrade had never thought of it like that, but he saw the

Spaniard's point. And he knew that this man threw pointed knives for a living. He wasn't about to upset him. 'Er ... Mrs Brodie ... about your husband's technique ...'

'Oh, yes,' she yawned, 'the Extendable Epiglottis, the Open Oesophagus, the Gaping Gullet – he used them all.'

'Er ... you wouldn't care to divulge ...?'

'How it's done?' She took the glass of red wine offered by the Spaniard and teased her nightdress open another lace hole. She had a cleavage that threatened her navel. 'Look for yourself. You sat on it.'

Lestrade gingerly removed the sword and sat carefully on the arm of the chair, where he hoped there'd be no more hidden blades.

'It's a swept-hilt rapier apparently,' Lucinda told him. 'What would you say, Henrico? Late 1620s, Toledo?'

'Early 1630s,' the Spaniard gabbled.

'Except it isn't,' Lucinda said. She suddenly ripped her bodice open to reveal a magnificent frontage. Lestrade tried not to gasp, but it was not a sight a young detective was treated to *all* that often in his career. Several times on this case, it was true, and he thought he ought to indulge himself a little while he could. 'Thrust,' she commanded.

'I beg your pardon?'

'Lucinda,' the Spaniard frowned, '*por favor!*'

'It's all right, silly,' she scolded him, 'Mr Lister is from the newspapers. He's seen a woman's all before.'

'All' was an understatement in this particular instance. 'No,' said Henrico. 'The risk.'

'Give point, Mr Lister,' she ordered. Something, some fire in her eyes, an urgency in her throat, made him obey. He lunged, as he'd been taught to in cutlass drill and caught her high in her left breast.

'Ah,' she shuddered, 'close to my heart, Mr Lister.'

Lestrade recovered his footing and stared. The blade had slid up into the hilt on impact, leaving nothing but a small red mark on the girl's breast.

'I'm sorry,' he said, 'did I hurt you?'

'No,' she smiled, '*that's* how it's done, Mr Lister. Trick swords. They *look* real enough. Now, take that one in the corner.'

He hadn't seen it before. A weapon identical to the one in his hand, its blade-tip dark brown. 'Is this . . . ?'

'. . . the weapon that killed him,' she said. 'And please, Mr Lister, don't try that trick again or you'll kill *me*.'

'So, how . . . ?'

She lay back, neglecting to relace her nightdress. 'Each sword swallower does it his own way. It's all to do with the angle of the oesophagus, the muscular contractions of the throat and the neck. Indigestion of course is always a risk. Alistair could manage the odd knife – he liked stilettos the best because they're slim-bladed. Bowies were beyond him – too bulky.'

'Spanish clasp knives of the kind they make in Zaragossa, he found equally problematical,' Henrico added.

'But swords,' Lucinda went on, sipping her wine, biding her time, 'they were out of the question. I don't need to paint you a picture of where the tip of a three-foot blade would end up if you sank it to the hilt down your throat, Mr Lister.'

Indeed she didn't. Lestrade's eyes misted at the very thought of it.

'Hence the trick swords. He had three of them – the swept-hilt, the small sword and the three-bar hilt.'

'A three-bar hilt?'

'Yes, the type the cavalry uses.'

'And the artillery,' Lestrade mused.

'If you say so,' Lucinda said. 'He had three duplicates made, each one with trick blades, designed to collapse on themselves. He would fence with the real ones in the ring, bending the blade, clashing the tiger bars with it, drive it point down into the tan of the floor and balance on it with one arm – all to prove to the punters that the weapon was real. Then he'd switch blades at the last minute from a cabinet we had on stage and shove the trick one down his throat. The blade only went in as far as an average dentist or blacksmith would. And, hey presto, the Great Bolus does it again.'

Lestrade metaphorically kicked himself. His own dear companion of a mile, the switchblade in his pocket, acted on a similar principle. Release the catch and the blade slid harmlessly back into the brass knuckles. Leave the catch alone and it was a weapon every bit as lethal as the swept-hilt rapier.

'Forgive me for saying this, Mrs Brodie,' Lestrade said, talking

140

to her nipples as much as to the woman herself, 'but you don't seem very upset at what's happened.'

She put her glass down, 'I know this is 1879,' she said, 'and that full mourning is still just about fashionable in some circles. The Queen, they say, wears black still. But she's an old trout, Mr Lister, and not circus. She's also an old hypocrite, I dare say. I didn't love Alistair Brodie. Ours was a marriage made in the Big Top – which is every bit a marriage of convenience as if we had been titled heir and heiress. I rest my body where it pleases me, Mr Lister. Alistair Brodie pleased me for a while, but he was a boring, inadequate old fart. At the moment,' she looked seductively under her lids at the Spaniard, 'Henrico is my all.' Then she turned the full pout on Lestrade, licking her lips as she did so, 'at the moment.'

The Spaniard stood impassive. Only a flickering muscle in the side of his jaw betrayed his fury. He had fought one duel over this fatal femme already – would Lestrade be his next protagonist? The detective rose to go, lifting the bloody sword as he went. 'Can I take this with me?' he asked.

'Anybody'd think you were a copper,' she smiled, 'all this interest in death. It's morbid, Mr Lister. Not natural.'

'Neither is murder, Mrs Brodie,' he said. 'Tell me, did anybody have access to these swords, real and trick?'

'In the wagon, no. Alistair was meticulous about them. But in the ring . . .'

'In the ring?' he paused at the door.

'In the ring, there are acrobats, dancers, animal acts, the ringmaster, clowns. The world and his wife could have switched the swords back.'

'Thank you, Mrs Brodie,' Lestrade nodded briefly to the Spaniard, 'and good-night.'

He wandered the night. The prospect of a damp kipsey-sack did not appeal. His sword-blade caught the light of the flitting moon as he trudged the campfires. The elephants swayed at their chains and looked at him from tiny, twinkling eyes. He reached out a tentative hand and patted the rough, hairy skin, wrinkled under his fingers.

'You never forget, do you?' he whispered. 'You must be alone in this circus. Nobody else remembers a damned thing.'

'Careful, Lestrade!' he spun at the whisper of his name. Damn!

He had to get better at this. Aliases were only preserved as long as they were adhered to.

'Who's that?' he whispered, hand on the sword-hilt.

'You'll be talking to the animals next.'

He recognized the white lips and crazy hair of Stromboli padding out of the darkness on his enormous shoes. 'And he wrote in the letter, saying, "Set ye Uriah in the forefront of the hottest battle and retire ye from him and that he may be smitten, and die." '

'What?'

'Two Samuel, Chapter 11 – Uriah the Hittite.'

Now, it had to be confessed that Lestrade had never really followed the scriptures at Mr Poulson's Academy for the Sons of Nearly Respectable Gentlefolk. He didn't know an Ephesian from his elbow.

'You'll have to explain that one,' he said.

The august slipped Edna a sugar lump under the clouds, patting the great beast and stroking her trunk.

'I couldn't help noticing you came from Lucinda's wagon. You're not familiar with the story of Uriah?'

'That wouldn't be Uriah Heap, would it? Only I always thought Thackeray rather overrated personally.'

'No,' Stromboli smiled, 'Uriah the Hittite.'

'Hittite?'

'An ancient Middle-Eastern tribe,' the clown was patience itself. 'The story goes that the great King David saw Bathsheba, Uriah's wife, at her ablutions. He liked what he saw, and slept with her. But there was a problem.'

'Hebrew's Droop?'

'Marriage. Bathsheba was married to Uriah, a captain in David's army.'

'I see.'

'So David arranged that Uriah should lead his vanguard in the central part of the battle, where the risks were greatest. He calculated right. Uriah was killed.'

'Really?'

'So the Good Book tells us.'

'And Bathsheba?'

'Married David and "bare him a son".'

'Happy ending, then?'

'Unless you're Uriah,' Stromboli said. 'Or the Lord.'

'The Lord?'

'"But the thing that David hath done displeased the Lord."'

'Ah,' Lestrade smiled. 'Divine retribution.'

The clown nodded. 'In the form of one Nathan, who said "Thou hast killed Uriah the Hittite with the sword . . . . Now, therefore the sword"', and he tapped Lestrade's hilt, '"shall never depart from thine house."'

'Fancy,' said Lestrade. 'I don't quite . . .'

'The Spaniard,' Stromboli explained as though to an idiot. 'He is King David.'

'Ah, I see. Lucinda is Bathsheba . . .'

'Alistair Brodie is Uriah. That ring, Lestrade,' the clown gazed to the dark outline of the Big Top, 'that's the battlefield. The hottest of battles. That's where Uriah died.'

'So Henrico switched the blades?'

The clown shrugged. 'Stands to reason.'

'Too easy,' Lestrade wrestled with it for a while. 'Too obvious.'

'Of course,' Stromboli chuckled, 'whoever the murderer is, Lestrade, you're looking for a showman. Someone who kills in public and takes delight in it. Not for him the murk of a darkened room or the silence of an alleyway. He kills in the sawdust ring with the full glare of the crowd on him. That's what makes him so dangerous.'

Lestrade looked at his man. 'So you suspect the Spaniard?'

It was the clown's turn to look at him, 'I'm a clown,' he said, rather sadly, 'an august. I don't suspect anybody. Except . . .'

'Except the Spaniard. Yes, I know.'

'No. Not him only. We were talking of the Scriptures a moment ago. Do you know Revelations?'

'Er . . . in a busy life . . .' Lestrade blustered, by way of explanation.

'The Revelation of St John the Divine,' said the clown. '"And I looked, and behold a pale horse: and his name that sat on him was Death and Hell followed him."'

'Er . . . one of the Liberty horses?' Lestrade guessed. The Lipizzaners were all the right colour.

But the clown shook his head. 'A grey I've seen trailing the show on the road for the past two days,' he said. 'A tall man, muffled, indistinct.' He leaned to the detective, swinging round

143

Edna's rocking trunk. 'If you're Nathan,' he said, 'sent by the Lord to avenge Uriah's death, then who's he on the pale horse?'

Lestrade followed the clown's gaze to the stand of elms beyond the camp and the great, grey, steel-making city beyond that.

'Who indeed?' he muttered in the darkness.

8

Sheffield, the City of Plate, lies in the lee of several hills, interlaced with wooded valleys. The south Pennine slopes provided the raw material for the city's lifeblood and in those days, the Georgian elegance of Paradise Square, where Wesley had preached, was swamped by the Victorian slums of Philadelphia and Jericho. The Master Cutler was second only to the Lord Mayor in terms of importance and anybody who was anybody was in iron. As opposed to the riff-raff, who were in irons in the local jail.

The Parade clattered and clashed its way across the river Don, where the Sultan's elephants took a certain umbrage at the passing rolling stock of the Manchester, Sheffield and Lincolnshire Railway. No harm done and the crowds lined Spittal Hill and Wicker Street before the great beasts and cavorting artistes swung north-west up Snig Hill and West Bar to throw an arc of magic around the city. Both the Mayor and Master Cutler were there, chains clashing in civic competition, making presentations and speeches to Lord George Sanger, who noted with relief that Ollie Oliver's posters were everywhere and the circus had indeed come to town.

They camped on Crooke's Moor, a little to the west of Mushroom Lane and the cry went up 'All hands to the tilt' as the Big Top rose white and scarlet in the morning. The man on stilts invited the good people of Sheffield to walk up and walk up they did. No one noticed the solitary horseman on the grey. No one had time to check the lonely Miss Stevens and to pat her on the chin. In a packed tent, under the flare of naphtha, the Lipizzaners pranced their tan circuit, little Angelina bouncing from one back to another with an agility which amazed the crowd. As the Buttresses flew on their high wire and the riggers ran this way and that, tautening slack, tying knots, a pin dropped in the audience. Lestrade cursed himself with embarrassment and picked it up, hooking his lapel together again with it.

Stromboli rolled and slipped his way around the ring, bumping into Sanger, skidding under the lumbering feet of the elephants, presenting bouquets of fake flowers to ladies in the front row, who shrank back from the limelight, grinning stupidly. No one knew that the sword-swallowing act had gone, that the jugglers were short of a cudgel man, that dwarf-throwing had been quietly removed from the programme. The Ether Trick booth stood silent and empty.

The show had gone on and it was a tired troupe who shambled into Mrs Minogue's at 86 Effingham Street late that night, its sign over the door – 'Duntentin'. The lady in question was a large patroness of circus folk. When she opened her portals to Lestrade, she seemed to have a bust akin to a sofa and a mob-cap over her riot of grey, barbed-wire hair.

'You'd be Mr Lister,' she said, raising a glass at him, 'come in.'

'Thank you, Mrs Minogue,' he wiped his feet.

'You can call me Kindly,' she said, 'everybody does.'

'Thank you, Kindly.'

She held out a hand, 'That'll be eightpence for the bed.'

'Ah,' he fumbled in his waistcoat pocket, 'here you are.'

She caught it expertly, flipped it and bit it, then slipped it into her cleavage. She could have carried a coffer in there for all Lestrade knew. She stopped him in the entrance hall, her hand out again. 'And tenpence for the breakfast.'

'Right.' He found the coppers again.

'Ta, duckie,' she pinched his cheek, 'a glass of sherry-wine?'

'Well,' Lestrade smiled, 'it's a little late for me.'

'Suit yourself,' she said. 'You don't mind if I do?'

'Of course not.'

'Sign the book, duckie.'

She bustled behind a counter and pointed to a ledger. Lestrade took the quill and almost signed his real name in his tiredness, but he checked himself in time.

'Joseph,' she said, spinning the register to her side. 'That's a nice handle. Coat's a little drab for your namesake, but never mind. Married?'

'Er . . . no.'

'I was, you know,' and she led him with an oil lamp up a rickety staircase. 'This', she lifted her glass to a portrait on the wall, 'is Mr Minogue, manufacturer of Britannia metal. I shouldn't speak ill of the dead, of course, but he *did* have a drink problem.'

'Really?'

'What's your tipple, Joe? You look like a brandy man to me.'

'Well, I . . .'

'Mine's sherry-wine,' she smiled at him. 'Oh, purely for medicinal purposes of course. My lungs,' she wheezed, gripping the bannister, '. . . old Doctor Proctor said I should really be in Switzerland with my lungs. Still, what did he know? They struck him off in the end.'

'They did?' Lestrade had never known stairs go on for so long.

She paused and closed to him. 'Little girls,' she whispered.

'Ah.' That said it all.

'This', she held the lamp to another portrait on the second landing, 'is Mr Ledbetter, my third husband. German silver.'

'That's what he made?'

'No, that's what killed him. He was an extremely careless man and would drink cocoa at his work place. I warned him. I said "Charles, stick to alcoholic beverages" I said. "It's a lot safer in the end."' She checked herself expertly as her carpet-slippered foot stumbled on a loose stair-rod.

'And here we are.' She stood at last on the third landing.

'My room?' Lestrade hoped.

'No,' she held up the lamp to yet another portrait, 'Mr Carpenter, my second husband. Optical instrument maker.'

'Deceased?'

'As a dodecahedron. The diphtheria carried him off. Had no resistance, you see,' she tapped the glass. 'He didn't imbibe. Of the temperance persuasion.'

'Tsk, tsk,' Lestrade shook his head.

'This is your room,' she flung open the door. 'No visitors, please, Joe,' she warned, 'I run a respectable establishment. I know some of these showgirls.'

So did Lestrade.

'Mr Slingsby wouldn't approve.'

'Mr Slingsby?'

She led the way into the tiny garret room, the one with the

appalling, peeling wallpaper, and put down the lamp before a portrait above the bed. 'My first husband.'

'Diphtheria?'

'Wallasea.'

'I beg your pardon?'

'He's living in Wallasea – and in sin – with a Mrs van Houten. She is of Dutch extraction. We have a lot of Dutchies in Sheffield on account of the excesses of the Duke of Alva back in the olden days. You might say Mr Slingsby is living with his dear old Dutch.'

'And Mr Slingsby wouldn't approve . . . ?'

'Under his own roof, no. Under Mrs van Houten's roof – well, that's another matter.' She tapped him viciously on his lapel, so that the pin fell out again. 'But that's men for you. Breakfast's at seven sharp. The Girl Who Does will knock you up with hot water at six. Sure I can't tempt you?' she wobbled the glass under his nose.

'Thank you, no,' and he closed the door.

'Good-night, Joe,' she called.

God, apparently, was love. Or so it said under the ghastly portrait of Mr Slingsby. Lestrade hauled off his jacket and climbed out of his trousers. There was no wardrobe, so he folded them as well as he could over the chair. The bed left much to be desired – for example, a pillow – and his head crashed back so that he found himself staring up Mr Slingsby's fiercely flaring nostrils. Even so, the mattress was marginally preferable to the hard ground under a kipsey-sack and he sank gratefully on to it. The rain stung the little window that looked out on to the sleeping city. From where Lestrade lay he could see the scaffold-shrouded cathedral of St Peter and St Paul where they had just started work on a new nave. Beyond that, the city slept. And so, after a while, did the sergeant of detectives.

Was it a dream, he wondered for a moment? That soft hand stroking his chest, the heady perfume filling the room. He felt the soft ripeness of her breasts, the flat expanse of her stomach, the gentle pressure of her thighs. His hand roamed upwards over the smooth flesh to the stubble of her upper lip.

He sat bolt upright, banging his head on the sloping ceiling.

'Good God!' he shouted, then disappeared below the covers. In the dark tent of the blankets, he heard her say, 'At last. At last.'

Then he was out on the threadbare carpet, shivering in disbelief. 'Madam,' he whispered.

'Dorrie,' she reminded him. 'I'm so glad you decided to stay at Mrs Minogue's.'

'What are you doing here?' he leaped for his trousers.

'Do you know what it's like to be a freak?' she asked, sitting up, her breasts draped over her knees.

'Well, the chaps at the Yard . . . er . . . in Fleet Street, used to say . . .'

She dashed across the room to him, 'I don't care what they said. To me you'll always be normal.'

'Oh, thank you.'

'Kiss me, Joseph.'

'No . . . I . . . It's late.'

She pinioned his arms and he was just grateful that she was not Tinkerbelle Watson. 'It's never *that* late,' she said. 'Hold me!'

'I . . . can't actually move,' he realized.

'Sorry,' and she let him breathe again. 'We have passions too,' she assured him breathlessly. 'It's not all just taking our clothes off for money and letting people stare at us. I'm sorry I called you a Maryanne. It obviously wasn't true.' She glanced feverishly down at his manhood.

'But Mr Slingsby,' Lestrade hissed in desperation.

'Who?'

He took her hand, as much to keep it out of his fol-de-rols as anything else, and led her to the bed – a dangerous move, but he was up to it. 'Mrs Minogue's first husband.' He found his lucifers and lit the lamp. The glow lit Dorinda's naked body, her gorgeous shoulders, her ripe, pert breasts, her carefully macassared beard.

'He looks a miserable old sod,' she muttered.

'Quite. And I have been assured by Mrs Minogue that I am allowed no visitors.'

'It's only a portrait,' she said.

'Ah, but is it?' he lifted the lamp to illuminate the old skinflint's features. 'Look at the eyes.'

She did.

'They sort of . . . follow you round the room, don't they?'

'Do they?' she squinted at it.

148

'Take my word for it. Tell me, Dorinda,' he took her hand again, 'aren't you cold?'

'No,' she shuddered, 'I'm hot.' She wrapped her leg round his.

'Stand here,' he said, dragging her sideways and placing her carefully in a draught. 'Now?'

'Well, it is a *bit* chilly here,' she conceded, standing alone again.

'That's Mr Slingsby.'

'What is?'

'That cold sensation. Cold to chill you to the marrow. Cold from the grave.'

He saw Dorinda's eyes flicker in the flame.

'What do you mean?'

'Have you stayed here before?' he asked.

'No,' she told him.

'I have,' he became serious, watching the leaping shadows in the corner, 'and I begged not to be given this room.'

'Why?' she frowned, the hairs on her upper lip bristling uncomfortably.

'Him,' Lestrade barely mouthed the word, 'Mr Slingsby.' He closed to her, watching her nipples stiffen in the draught from the window. 'He went of the diphtheria, these twenty years ago.' He put his lips against her ear lobe, 'But he's still here. He's here now. Watching us. Watching you. Listen . . .'

In the corner, the pin dropped from his lapel.

'. . . You can almost hear him . . . breathing.'

But Dorinda wasn't listening. She'd snatched up the frothy nightdress she came in and leapt from the room, leaving her heady perfume and a small beard-trimming razor in her wake.

Lestrade heaved a sigh of relief, locked the door and went back to bed.

He heard the clock strike the hour. Two. That loneliest of times. The dark before the dawn when men's hearts beat empty at doorways and the knives come out. He heard a rustling sound. It came from the corner of the room. His eyes were open. He was awake. By the dim light from the window he could make out a female form, undulating out of a tight-fitting costume. He didn't move. Not even to pinch himself.

'Why don't you put the lamp on,' a soft voice purred, 'if you want a better look? And you *do* want a better look, don't you?'

She swayed towards him, peeling a spangled vest over her bare shoulders, shaking her long, blonde hair across her breasts. He fumbled for his matches, rattling the chimney of the lamp in his panic. He'd locked that door. He knew he had. The glow fell on the undeniable charms of the luscious Lucinda and she was indeed as leggy as they said. Her nether limbs went up in fact to her . . . .

'What are you doing here?' Lestrade felt it best to interrupt his own train of thought.

'What they pay me for,' she said, running her elegant fingers over her body. 'Showing myself.'

'But . . .'

'Oh, I know. Dear old Lord George would have you believe that people come to marvel at the dancing, the grace, the speed, the skill. I suppose some of them do – the women, the little kids, the old men. But the young men, the able-bodied – anything between fifteen and sixty, shall we say – they come to look at what you see before your eyes. Only they never manage it, do they? Never quite see what you're seeing now. In the circus, nothing is quite as it seems.' She kicked off her high-heeled boots and stood naked before him. It was turning into one of those cases.

'How . . . how did you get in?' he had to clear his throat several times.

'Through the door, silly,' she pulled back the coverlet. 'Oh, dear, do you always wear trousers in bed?'

'Only on Mondays,' he said.

'Well, then,' she said, tugging at his belt, 'it's Tuesday now.'

'But I locked the door.'

'Prestidigitation,' she murmured. 'Any circus person worth their salt can pick a lock. How do you want me?'

'Back in your own bed,' he said firmly, shaking his head to clear the spell of her. 'What would Mrs Minogue say?'

'Sanctimonious old hypocrite,' she sat on the bed beside him, running her hands over his chest. 'She's just miffed 'cos she didn't get here first. Lift your bum.'

'What?'

'So that I can get your kicksies off.'

Lestrade was desperate. 'What would the Spaniard say?'

'You couldn't pronounce it,' she giggled. 'But I am not any man's plaything. At the moment he shares my act and my bed. Nothing is for ever. Make love to me.'

'Er . . . I . . .'

'You know you want to,' she was as expert with someone else's buttons as she was with her own, patting his manhood approvingly.

'There's something you should know,' he said.

'That you're a copper from Scotland Yard? I know.'

He gulped.

'That you're investigating the murders in the show? I know.'

He gulped again.

'That you've a body like a whip,' she fell on him, 'I know.'

'No,' he pulled her hair until she sat up, 'no, I mean, I am not as other detectives.' Further denial seemed useless. His hand fell on Dorinda's razor on the bedside table, 'This,' he waved it at her, 'this is just for show. As a matter of fact . . . I was rather admiring that fetching little chemise you were wearing. You haven't got one in powder blue, I suppose?'

She sat upright, straddling him so that her breasts stared down at him. 'What are you saying?'

He looked up at her, pursing his lips and arching his eyebrows. 'Nature played a cruel trick on me, Mrs Brodie. Here you are, in your prime, no doubt. And I', he sighed languidly, 'simply could not rise to the occasion.'

'That's a pity,' she said coldly, 'because there are things I could tell you. Things you need to know.' And she cocked a supple right leg over his head and cartwheeled across the floor to her pile of clothes.

'What things?'

'Oh, no,' she tugged on her chemise. 'And I *don't* have a powder blue one.'

He clawed his way out of bed, fumbling with his fly buttons. 'What things?' he repeated.

'Things!' she shouted.

He caught her firmly by the shoulders and shook her. 'Three men from the circus are dead,' he growled, 'and I don't know who's going to be next. Now if you know anything, tell me.'

She wrenched herself away from him angrily, spinning back as she reached the door, 'I know who I saw by Alistair's swords; by the cabinet he used in the ring.'

'Who?' Lestrade shouted.

She looked at him, the woman spurned. She drove her powerful arms into the sleeves of the bolero jacket. 'A better man than you could ever be,' she hissed. 'A real gentleman.'

He closed to her. 'You *do* realize that this real gentleman could have killed your husband, don't you?'

'Life's too short, Lestrade,' she scowled, 'and by morning this feeble imposture of yours will be over. I shall take great delight in telling everybody who you *really* are. See how many murderers you can catch then, Mr Scotland Yard!'

And she slammed the door and was gone.

Was it the thud that woke him? Or the scream? Either way, as the cathedral clock struck the hour of six, he was sitting bolt upright again with yet another lump on his cranium from that damned ceiling. Instinctively he checked the bed beside him. No one, with or without a beard. No naked girl in the corner either. He rolled sideways, narrowly missing the guzunda and poked his head around the door. A slip of a thing in an apron was rushing along the landing below and heads were appearing at doors and up the stairwells.

There was a loud slap as the screaming girl collided with the less-than-sobering influence of Mrs Minogue's right hand. 'Stop that, gel,' Lestrade heard her hiccough. 'Come and have a sherry-wine. It'll soothe your nerves.'

He dressed in seconds and with shirt-tails flapping, dashed along the landing.

'Mr Lister,' it was Dakota-Bred, buckling on his guns, who found him first, 'what the Sam Houston is going on?'

'I hoped you'd know,' Lestrade said, 'I heard a scream.'

'It's the Girl Who Does,' Lord George hurried past them both, still in dressing-gown and smoking cap, his curlers dangling over his shoulders. 'Coming from Lucinda's room.'

'What's the trouble, Georgie?' Lady Pauline's grizzled old head popped out of the necessary office. Without her veil she could have turned the morning milk.

'Probably just a mouse, Nell, my dove. Go back to . . . er . . . sleep.'

Dakota-Bred let out a long, low whistle. With the instinct of a man used to danger, his pearl-handled .45 was already in his hand, nudging Lestrade's elbow.

'Do you mind?' the sergeant gingerly moved aside the dark steel muzzle.

On the bed under the window lay the naked body of Lucinda Brodie, her blue eyes crossed and staring sightlessly up at an ugly knife that jutted grotesquely from the centre of her forehead.

'That's a beauty,' the cowboy had spun the revolver back to its holster and crossed the room in a single stride.

'Don't touch it!' Lestrade shouted and shut and locked the door. He crouched beside the bed. The girl's hands had clutched the sheet convulsively and her mouth was open, her teeth clenched. The blood was a dark mask over her once lovely face and flecks of it had splashed into her hair and over her breasts. Lestrade looked at the coverlet. It had been pulled back around the girl's ankles and there was no blood on it. He looked at her body, her arms rigid in rigor mortis, her legs splayed.

'Hey!' Dakota-Bred grabbed Lestrade's hair and pulled him up, 'what kinda pervert are you?'

'I am Detective-Sergeant Lestrade of Scotland Yard, cowboy. Let go of my hair or I'll break your arm.'

The cowboy did. 'Y . . . You're a copper?'

Lestrade smoothed down his parting, suddenly aware of the hammering at the door.

'Dakota-Bred? Lister? Let me in. This is *my* circus.'

And over Sanger's voice they heard another. 'And this is *my* house.'

Lestrade flicked the key. Mrs Minogue took one horrified look at the corpse on the bed, then at Lestrade, his shirt-tails dangling. She swung her hand up and brought it down on the sergeant's neck with a force surprising in a middle-aged dipsomaniac. He lolled back alongside the leggy, no-longer luscious Lucinda.

'When you spoke of Mrs Minogue's Barnsley Chop,' Lestrade winced, trying to get some sensation back into his left shoulder, 'I thought you were referring to her culinary expertise.'

153

'That too,' Sanger passed the man a brandy, marginally stiffer than Lestrade's neck. Or the corpse on the bed.

'How long have I been out?'

'About an hour,' the showman told him.

'Now keep still, Mr Lestrade,' Lady Pauline was applying a hot poultice to his ruptured tendons. 'This always works on my lions, but you've got to give it time.'

'What did she hit me with? A poker?'

'Just the side of her hand,' Sanger said, 'I wish I'd known about that, years ago. She'd have been great in a side-show, splitting bricks.'

'Yes,' Lestrade staggered to his feet, 'as opposed to shitting bricks, which is what I nearly did – begging your pardon, Lady Pauline.'

The old Lion Queen dropped her poultice back into the bowl. She patted his cheek. 'You look after yourself, sonny,' she said, 'there's a maniac loose, you know.' She looked at Lucinda, shook her head and wandered away.

As the door closed behind her, Sanger moved from his place lolling against the wall. 'She's taking this pretty bad, Lestrade,' he said. 'What's going on? Can you see a pattern in this madness?'

Lestrade grimaced as he hauled his shirt back on. His left hand dangled uselessly. 'She's trapped a nerve,' he winced.

'She's got one, certainly,' Sanger said. 'That's what I like about old Kindly – why we keep coming here whenever we're doing the northern circuit. Doesn't suffer fools gladly, doesn't Mrs Minogue.'

'Has anybody called the police?' Lestrade looked at the dead girl.

'I thought you were the police,' Sanger said.

'No, I mean the local police.'

The showman shook his head. 'Mrs Minogue won't hear of it. It would ruin her reputation. Number 86 – Home to the Stars. Sounds good, doesn't it? Number 86, Home Where You Might Get Stabbed To Death loses an edge, don't you think?'

Lestrade had to concede that it did. 'So we keep this one in the family again, do we?'

'Look Lestrade,' Sanger laid a hand on his bad shoulder and

watched his man turn a whiter shade of pale. 'Oh, sorry. My people are dying. Lucinda is the fourth. *And* she's a woman.'

'Yes,' Lestrade could not fail to notice, 'yes, she is. Who covered her up?'

'Lady Pauline and Mrs Minogue. They said it wasn't decent.'

Lestrade looked with annoyance at the corpse. 'And they put her arms like that, across her?'

Sanger nodded. 'It wasn't easy,' he said, 'she'd gone stiff as a wagon board.'

'And they took out the knife and cleaned her up, I suppose?'

'Yes. Did they do wrong?'

Lestrade sighed. 'No,' he said, 'no, they didn't do wrong. Where's the knife?'

He watched as Sanger pulled it from his pocket. The hilt was of ebony, ridged for a firm grip and the blade broad and single-edged.

'It's a Bowie knife,' the showman told him, 'and before you ask, both Dakota-Bred and Henrico el Magnifico carry them.'

Lestrade felt the weight of it in his hand. Suddenly, without warning, he threw it at the headboard. It hit it and plopped on to the bloody pillow beside the dead girl's head.

'Hmm. Not a throwing knife, then?' he said.

Sanger crossed to retrieve it. 'Ordinarily, no. It was invented by Colonel Jim Bowie. I expect Dakota-Bred can tell you all about him. Legend goes that Bowie's brother lost some fingers in a hunting accident, so he designed a knife with a crosspiece to prevent the hand from slipping. No, it wasn't designed to be thrown. But . . .' he crouched silently, his right arm snaking out to the horizontal. The weapon hissed through the air and its murderous tip bit deep into the headboard.

Lestrade blinked in disbelief. 'Don't move,' he said. He wrenched the knife free and placed the tip into the dark, puckered hole between the girl's eyebrows, bruised now and shiny. Her eyes had swollen and the colour had gone from her cheeks.

'That's it,' Lestrade said, 'that's where the murderer stood when he killed her. Just where you're standing, Mr Sanger.'

'From which you deduce?'

'That our murderer is strong – but we already knew that. He is an expert with a throwing knife. And . . .' he turned to the showman, 'the luscious, leggy Lucinda was offering herself to him when he killed her.'

The Girl Who Does sat in the little cane chair in the kitchen, not far from the black-lead stove which filled most of her waking hours. She was barely sixteen, Lestrade guessed, by her pale face and willowy form under the grubby apron. Her cap had slipped on the skew and she was rocking gently from side to side, looking at him as though from a long way away and she was giggling as she spoke.

'No, sir,' she said, 'I live in. My room is along under t'stairs.'

'And what time did you turn in last night?' the sergeant asked.

''Bout midnight,' she told him, 'I 'ave t' be up by five t' get t'breakfast things on and t'hot water.'

'Which order do you do the rooms?'

'I start at Mrs M's and go on up t' attic.'

'So mine would be the last room you'd get to?'

''Appen,' she hiccoughed.

'Except that this morning you didn't get beyond the third floor.'

'Nay,' her face darkened at the memory of it, but Mrs Minogue leaned over and poured her another sherry-wine so that she was all right.

'Tell me what happened,' he said quietly.

'Well, I got t' room, y' know, t'one with ... *her* ... in it. I knocked.'

'You always knock?'

'Of course,' Mrs Minogue interrupted, 'I told you, Mr Lister, I run a respectable establishment.'

'Quite,' he smiled icily at her. So respectable was Mrs Minogue's establishment that two women had inveigled their way into his room and one of them had been stabbed to death in the space of six hours. He himself had been temporarily incapacitated and the entire domestic staff were well on their way to becoming paralytic. So much for Victorian values. 'What happened then?'

'Well,' she gulped gratefully at the amber nectar, 'I remember t'door was open, like. Not on t'latch.'

'Ajar?'

'Nay, thank you, sir,' she raised her glass, 'I'm all right for t'moment.'

'You went in?'

'Aye. She were there . . .' her eyelids flickered, her knuckles whitened on the glass, '. . . On t'bed. Dead.'

'You knew she was dead?' Lestrade checked.

'Oh, aye,' the girl shuddered, 'she were starin', like, at t'ceilin'. Her eyes were crossed, like she 'ad a turn. An' that knife thing, stickin' in 'er 'ead. Fair gave me t'willies, I can tell yer.'

'You screamed?'

'Did I?' she frowned, looking to Mrs Minogue, 'I don't remember anythin' else until Mrs M were slappin' me round t'head, offerin' me a drink.'

'Which you took?'

'Nay,' the girl straightened, 'I'm of t'Methodist persuasion. I don't touch a drop.'

'Quite,' nodded Lestrade. 'On the stairs. In the kitchen. Did you see anyone else as you delivered the hot water?'

She thought hard. 'Nay,' she shook her head.

Lestrade leaned back. It didn't surprise him. It would have been too simple if she had.

'Only that big tyke.'

He leaned forward again. 'What big tyke?'

'That tyke wi' t'beard.'

Lestrade blinked. 'You mean Dorinda, the Bearded Lady?'

'Do I?' the girl frowned at her glass. 'Mrs M,' she said, 'this medicine for soothin' t'nerves. What's it called again?'

'Sherry-wine, dear,' the old girl told her.

'Aye. Does it make yer see things, like?'

Lestrade looked at the patroness, as intrigued to catch her answer as the girl was.

'Only after a prolonged dose of treatment, love,' she said. 'Things like mice and cockroaches.' She looked coldly at Lestrade. 'So they tell me, anyway.'

'But I see *them* anyway,' the girl said.

'Not in *this* house, though,' Mrs Minogue was quick to assure Lestrade.

'Oh aye . . .' the girl began.

'Why do you ask?' Lestrade cut in.

'What?'

157

'Why do you ask if sherry-wine makes you see things?'

'Well, this tyke I saw, t'one wi' beard. Didn't look like a woman.'

'Big?' Lestrade suggested.

'Like t'barn,' the girl explained.

'No one of that description is currently staying in my house,' Mrs Minogue assured them both. 'You can't have been properly awake, girl.'

'But I were, Mrs M,' the girl was quietly adamant before she slithered to the floor, 'I were.'

By mid-afternoon, when most of the circus folk had gone to the Big Top to practise and Lord George Sanger was already making arrangements with Ollie Oliver to move south to Chesterfield, Lestrade had pieced together the movements of the night. On the wall of his garret room, next to the reminder that 'As Ye Sow, So Shall Ye Reap', he had stuck a plan of the house, hastily sketched by Mrs Minogue, anxious as she was to keep the lid on the melting-pot that was 'Duntentin'.

Anyone had access to Lucinda Brodie's room, at any hour of the night, for she never locked it. All the gents at number 86 bore witness to the fact that her caravan door was always open too. Lord George Sanger had gone, perfect commanding-officer and father-figure that he was, to break the news to Henrico el Magnifico and the Spaniard had wept copiously all over him, then gone out on to the practice ground and thrown his deadly knives into the heart of a wooden, painted man. Time after time the razor points had bitten into the wood, until the whole area around the heart was chewed and ripped. Nearly two miles away, Detective-Sergeant Lestrade sat on his bed, chewing the end of a cigar. Whoever Henrico was throwing his knives at, Lestrade had the same target in mind. But who? Who was the flat, wooden man with the painted face? The face in the crowd?

He went through it again, for the umpteenth time that day. George and Pauline Sanger were in bed on the first floor. He said she was snoring; she said he was. They *had* heard movement, about midnight, but assumed it was Mrs Minogue, locking up. Why should either of them have crept from the double bed, risking the creak of a floorboard, the rattle of a doorknob, to hurl a

Bowie knife into the head of a girl who had never harmed either of them? And the Sangers had a point.

The great Stromboli had been asleep on the second floor. That put him nearer to Lucinda's room and since he was alone, he had no alibi. The man knew Lestrade's secret. He made no bones about the fact that he went down to the kitchen at nearly two in search of a drink of water. No, he had seen nothing. On the first floor he had heard communal snoring coming from the Sangers' room.

Dakota-Bred Carver had the room along from Lestrade's. He had been up oiling his guns until well past midnight; then he had thrown his blanket down on the floor, rested his head back on his saddle, lowered his Stetson over his eyes and gone to sleep. As was his custom, he was up at four and strapping himself into his chaps. He had not left the room, however, the whole time. Not until he heard the girl scream. And then he had come a-running, carrying iron.

Major John had been up most of the night – a combination of the accounts he had to work on and the probable effects of Mrs Minogue's dumplings. His was the room on the third floor back, but he had spent much time passing it. On his many comings and goings to Mrs Minogue's usual office on the second floor, he had seen quite a few people wandering about. One was the Girl Who Did. She seemed to be in a trance, floating in her nightdress along the first landing, carrying an empty bowl and muttering 'Hot water, hot water'. What time was this? Lestrade had asked. Around one, perhaps a little later. The dwarf had led her gently back to her own room, near the kitchen, kicking aside the mice and flicking the odd cockroach off her bed. Was it then, Lestrade wondered, that she had seen the bearded man? Major John had a face like a baby and anyway, not even in the wildest stretches of sherry-induced exaggeration could he be described as big. Indeed, unless the Girl Who Sleepwalked had glanced down, she wouldn't have seen him at all.

Another apparition the little accountant had seen was Dorrie, the Bearded Lady. She looked furtive, he said, and had a high colour. She seemed to be making for the attic and when she saw him, claimed that she had put her razor down somewhere and was looking for it.

Yet a third was the deceased herself, the wife of the Sword

Swallower, mistress of the Knife Thrower. She too had been moving in the general direction of the fourth floor, about an hour after Dorinda. She looked more luscious and leggy than ever. When she saw the dwarf, she winked, patted him on the head and said she was off for a tumble. The little accountant noticed that during his interrogation, Lestrade did not once ask him who with.

Dorinda herself wasn't speaking. Yet Lestrade knew full well where she had been at least at certain times during the night. Then of course she had an alibi. And anyway, the corpse had told its own tale. Given the late Lucinda's proclivities, it didn't seem likely that she would have lain on the bed, naked and ready, for another woman, albeit a rather follicularly-advantaged one. Her caller – her killer – had been a man. A man she knew. A man for whom she was prepared to lie naked and exposed. A man who had crept into her room, announced or otherwise, and who had enough expertise to throw the knife that killed her at about two o'clock. This he knew from the stiffness of the corpse. At that time, he was sure that one person and one person only was in the clear – and that was a Detective-Sergeant of the Metropolitan Police.

'You'll have a sherry-wine before you go?' she asked him, resting her carpet-slippered feet on a pouffe.

'Thank you, no.'

'Tsk, tsk,' she said, 'and I thought you Fleet Street men liked your liquor. I'm sorry about clouting you, by the way, Joe. It was shock, I suppose. No one's died under this roof since Mr Minogue – and never by a knife in the head. It's not a very nice way to go, is it, duckie?'

No, it wasn't. 'That's all right,' Lestrade said, 'the feeling's nearly come back to my arm, now. And the neck muscles are relaxing.'

'Ah, good,' she refilled her glass. 'That'll be Lady Pauline's poultice. What a wonderful woman.'

'Indeed. And talking of women, how long has your girl been with you?'

'The Girl Who Does? Ooh, she's been a-doing now for . . . ooh, must be three years.'

160

'And she lives in?'

'Oh, yes. Her father kicked her out, the drunken old sot. Beat her something cruel, he did. Well,' she shook her head, 'that's the drink for you.'

'Yes,' nodded Lestrade, 'shocking. Do you trust her?'

'With my life,' the landlady was solemn.

'With your secret?'

She straightened, 'I beg your pardon?'

'Did you know the girl walked in her sleep?'

'I believe she does, yes. What has this to do with a secret?'

'She said she saw a bearded man.'

'Dreaming,' Mrs Minogue dismissed it. 'If memory serves me right, of the men staying here last night, only you and Lord George have moustaches. The others are clean-shaven. She must have seen the Bearded Lady.'

'That's possible,' Lestrade agreed, 'but there is another possibility.'

'Oh?' the landlady reached for her decanter. Lestrade risked all by gripping her arm.

'What time did you say you locked up?'

'At midnight, Mr Lister,' she said. The 'Joe' had vanished from her conversation. 'I told you that. The girl saw me do it.'

'And someone else saw you unlocking again less than half an hour later.'

'What?' she wrenched her arm from his grip. 'Who saw me?' she was standing now, shouting. 'What are you talking about?'

'I'm talking about murder, Mrs Minogue,' he said flatly, 'And about a murderer you let in at approximately twelve thirty this morning.'

'That's nonsense,' she snapped, 'I let no one in.'

'You did,' Lestrade insisted. 'What he did between twelve thirty and two I have no idea, but perhaps I can guess that to a woman who has worked her way through four husbands, the wee wee hours of the morning must hang heavy on her hands...'

'How dare you!' the deadly hand was raised again. This time Lestrade was faster and he caught it on his forearm before swinging backwards and slapping the old girl across the head. The glass fell from her hand. Her teeth flew across the carpet and she lay, sprawled and beaten, in the recesses of her sofa.

Lestrade crouched beside the couch. 'I'm sorry,' he said, 'I don't normally hit women. But you, madam, are an accomplice to murder.'

She looked at him through terror-struck eyes. 'You're no newspaperman,' she hissed.

'No,' he told her, 'I am Detective-Sergeant Lestrade of Scotland Yard. Now you tell me about the bearded man.'

She relaxed and sighed and he let her sit up. He even poured her another glass to replace the one she'd dropped. He stopped short of retrieving her teeth. There were some things even policemen didn't do. Even in 1879.

'Who saw me?' she asked after a moment's composure.

'No one,' Lestrade said, returning to his chair, 'I made that up.'

The look on her face was a picture. For a moment he thought she'd go for him again, but she subsided. 'Very clever,' she said, 'but isn't that what they call entrapment?'

'Mrs Minogue,' Lestrade leaned forward, 'Lucinda Brodie is the seventh victim of a madman I have been chasing for over two months. I have to stop him before he claims an eighth. If you like, I'll hand you, your house and your fancy man over to the Sheffield Constabulary. By the time you get out of jail, "Duntentin" will have fallen into rack and ruin. And you won't find an admirer then.'

Secretly, although he was far too kind to say so, Lestrade was astonished that she had an admirer now. Still, perhaps the man was visually disadvantaged – that would explain it.

'Very well,' she'd thought it over, raising her glass for him to fill it. Lestrade had never met a chain-drinker before. 'Your wild guess was very accurate, Mr Lestrade. I let in my gentleman friend at just on twelve twenty. He's ever so punctual when he's in town.'

'He is a regular visitor?'

'Indeed.'

'Who is he?'

She looked quizzically at him, 'I regret I cannot tell you.'

'And I regret that you must.'

'He is not, I suspect, unknown to you.'

'That narrows the field only a little, madam,' he told her.

'Very well. He is James Crockett.'

'The lion tamer?'

162

'A lion tamer, certainly. I understand that Lord George has several – Maccomo, the blackamoor – and that's not particularly easy for me to say; then there's Fearless Fortescue and Lady Pauline, of course.'

'So Crockett . . . ?'

'Pays me a visit whenever the circus comes to town.'

'Why doesn't he stay here?'

Mrs Minogue looked horrified. 'Please, Mr Lestrade. What would people think?'

'But surely,' the sergeant said, 'one more guest among several. Dakota-Bred was an unattached man last night, as was Major John. As was I.'

'Yes,' she scowled, 'but one of them is a dwarf and the other an American. And the third – as I thought and was led to believe – a newspaperman. No one would imagine that a lady of my refinement would . . . with them. But a full-blooded male like my Jim, well . . .'

'So what did you do, you and your Jim?'

She stood up sharply. 'That's a very indelicate question, sergeant,' she said, 'and I positively refuse to answer it. Let's say it's all still possible even in the twilight of one's years.'

'I see,' Lestrade knew a brick wall when he met one. 'How long did he stay?'

'Until half past five. My wretched alarm didn't go off and we overslept. Jim had to hotfoot it before the girl woke up.'

'But he mistimed it?'

'Clearly,' she pursed her shrivelled lips. 'The girl saw him.'

'Tell me, Mrs Minogue,' Lestrade rose with her, 'can you vouch for Jim Crockett's whereabouts the whole time that he was in the house?'

She blinked. 'Of course,' she said, 'only . . .'

'Yes?'

'Nothing,' she said, 'except that you can't suspect my Jim. He's as gentle as a lamb. And I'm sure I locked the front door again when I let him in. Yes, I'm sure of it.'

Cabs weren't plentiful in Sheffield, not at that time on a Saturday afternoon anyway, so Lestrade was grateful to recognize on the driving board of a trap, Samson, Sanger's new rigger.

'Mr Lestrade,' he called, hauling on the reins, 'come aboard. Making for the circus? I've just been on an errand for the Boss.'

'Yes,' he said. 'Mr Samson, I hope you'll keep my identity a secret,' he straightened his bowler as the pony jolted forward. 'You appreciate the delicacy of the situation?'

'Oh, of course, of course,' the ex-sailor grinned, 'but I wonder if you do?'

'If I do?' Lestrade turned to him.

'Hey up, Jocasta!' the pony swung to the left at the touch of the whip and the rigger brought the trap round under a stand of elms. They were on the edge of the city, the clanging of steel like a distant peal of bells in some mad belfry. He hauled on the reins and wrenched on the brake.

'The other night, when Lord George Sanger blew the whistle on you, Ollie Oliver was talking about two men dead, that's Atkins and Hughie the dwarf.'

'That's right.'

'Since then, it's doubled. The Brodies down within twenty-four hours of each other.'

'That's right again.'

'How many more are we talking about?'

'I don't follow.'

Samson lit a cigar and put his feet up on the board. 'All right,' he sighed, 'if you're going to play it cagey. What about the man on the moor at Ilkley – wi'out a 'at and wi'out a face? The dead Lieutenant of Artillery and the deceased Inspector of the Metropolitan police?'

Lestrade felt his hackles rising. 'Who are you?' he turned to face his man.

The rigger chuckled, 'John Samson,' he said. 'My friends call me Delilah, but I'd rather you didn't noise that abroad.'

'Circus rigger?'

'Certainly,' Samson blew rings to the budding branches above his head.

'Ex-sailor?'

'Correct.'

'What ship?'

'The *Belinda Leigh*. Port o' London to Rotterdam. Her Captain is a Mr Meecham. Her First Mate Tom Jackson. She was built at Jarrow on the Tyne in 1865, displaces 40,000 tons . . .'

'All right,' Lestrade said, 'you've convinced me. But how do you know so much about my cases? Unless . . . ?' his heart froze. For a moment he panicked, clutched his pocket convulsively, sitting on the board of a pony-trap at the edge of Sheffield with a glib, cigar-smoking murderer.

Samson laughed. 'Unless I'm the man you're looking for? No, Lestrade, I'm sorry to disappoint you. I'm just a man with a message.'

Lestrade looked at the dark eyes, the lantern jaw. 'You mean you're Unitarian?'

'No,' he said, 'I'm a detective – like you. Well, not quite like you. For a start, I earn a day four times what you do in a week and for afters, I know what I'm doing.'

'I'm happy for you,' Lestrade said. 'Who are you working for?'

'The Highest in the Land.'

'The Queen?' Lestrade was impressed.

'Do listen, Lestrade,' Samson said. 'I said the Highest. The Jew at Number Ten.'

' "Old Clo"?'

'The same. He knows you, Lestrade. Speaks of you; not highly, I'll admit, but with a certain fondness. Actually, I owe George Sanger a favour. I'd only got a bad photograph of you to work from and Dizzy was right – you do look different with a moustache. I wasn't *quite* sure it was you at first, but when Lord George obligingly introduced you, well . . .'

'One handle deserves another,' Lestrade told him.

'Yes, I suppose it does. My name is Steele. Oliver Steele. Steele and Steele, Private Inquiry Agents. Tell me, have you heard of a chap called Sherlock Holmes?'

'I don't think so,' Lestrade said, 'why?'

'Oh, nothing. There's a rumour in London that this deranged amateur is trying to muscle in on us professionals.'

'I thought *we* were the professionals,' Lestrade said.

'After your performance?' Steele scowled. 'Good God, man, do me a favour.'

'Are you serious?' Lestrade asked, 'about Disraeli knowing me?'

'Oh, yes. Said, if I remember right – "He's an idiot, but a persistent one".'

Lestrade looked a little crestfallen.

'Cheer up, Lestrade,' Steele ordered, 'after all, bad publicity is better than none at all. I don't suppose the Prime Minister, responsible as he is for most of the civilized and an extraordinarily large bit of the uncivilized world, knows the name of many sergeants of police.'

'Yes,' the professional detective reconsidered, 'I suppose I should be flattered. But why are you here?'

'To take you home,' Steele said. 'After all, you have been a teeny bit naughty, you know. What my friends in the East End would call "doing a runner".'

'Hardly that,' Lestrade told him, 'I had merely gone underground in pursuit of my inquiries.'

'Aren't you supposed to be ordered to do that?' Steele asked, 'by a superior, I mean?'

'There wasn't time. Men were dying.'

'Well,' Steele clamped the cigar between his lips and took up the reins, 'shall we go?'

'Where?'

'Home,' he said, 'back to dear old Lunnon town. You've got some explaining to do.'

Lestrade held his rein arm, 'I can't do that,' he said, 'not yet.'

Steele let the reins fall loose, grinning. 'Good,' he said, 'I hoped you'd say that. I must admit I was intrigued when the old Jew asked me to find you and bring you back. But I was even more intrigued when I got here. How much headway have you made?'

'First, tell me why the Prime Minister wants me off this case. You have to conceive it's a little peculiar.'

'Ah, yes, but then it's a little peculiar you're looking for.'

'Er . . . no,' Lestrade frowned. 'You've lost me.'

'Any idea who your man is?'

'Yes. I'm on my way to arrest him now.'

Steele's prow-like jaw sagged a little. 'You are?'

'Of course. Ironic really, isn't it? When he killed in the full glare of the naphtha it was as though he was invisible. But in the cramped confines of a lodging house, somehow you can't miss him.'

'Who?' Steele shrieked. 'Who is it, for God's sake?'

'Jim Crockett,' Lestrade announced.

'The lion tamer?'

'That's him.'

'Balderdash!'

'What?'

'If Crockett's your man, I'm the Emperor of Japan.'

'We're bound to have our professional differences, Your Omnipotence,' Lestrade bowed.

'All right,' Steele was an indulgent man, up to a point, 'all right, you tell me why Crockett.'

'The oldest problem in the book,' Lestrade said, pulling out a cigar of his own. It was his last and his wages had all but gone, but the case was over and he could afford to be generous to himself. 'One of the many problems incoherent in murder cases – how to get in and out of a murder scene without being seen.'

'Somebody saw him?'

'As a matter of fact, no – not exactly. But I have it from the lips of Mrs Minogue herself – she's the landlady – that he arrived at twelve thirty and was seen leaving at five thirty.'

'When did the Brodie girl die?'

'About two, I estimate.'

'Who let Crockett in?'

'Mrs Minogue.'

'And do we know where he was between those times?'

'Apparently with Mrs Minogue, though she was rather cagey about it.'

'So we only have her word?'

'That's right.'

'Yes, well, it's plausible enough,' Steele stroked his powerful chin. 'What about motive?'

'Mad as a snake,' Lestrade shrugged, 'I don't know. All I know is that he had opportunity.'

'So did the others in the house. What about the weapon?'

'Bowie knife, thrown at her head.'

Steele winced. 'Knife thrower, is he, Crockett?'

'Well, no, but . . .'

'Come on, Lestrade,' Steele emptied his boot of llama droppings, 'you're clutching at straws, man. Take my word for it, Crockett's not your man.'

'Really?' Lestrade sighed, 'I suppose you're going to tell me why.'

'Certainly,' Steele obliged. 'How tall is Crockett, give or take?'

'Er . . . oh, I don't know, six foot two, three.'

'What does he weigh, would you say?'

'Er . . . seventeen, eighteen stone.'

'His beard – is it real?'

'His beard?' Lestrade had had several close shaves himself recently. 'I suppose it is – although in the circus . . .'

'Nothing is quite what it seems. Yes, I know,' Steele nodded. 'But I also know that James Crockett is not the Prince Imperial.'

Lestrade wondered for a moment where his companion had escaped from. 'Who?' he asked.

'Let me take you back', Steele said, resting his hands over his knees, 'to the first murder – the man without a face at Ilkley.'

'What of it?'

'The clues you found there . . .'

'A handkerchief. . . .' He remembered the other handkerchief, the one Emily Clare had given him, still tied around his wrist under the cuff.

'. . . with a letter "N". "N" for Napoleon.'

'Napoleon,' Lestrade repeated. So Emily had been right. 'What else?'

'An Albert watch. With an inscription.'

'An inscription that said "Remember Eylau".'

'You're remarkably well informed,' Lestrade said.

'It's my job,' Steele told him. 'Eylau was one of Napoleon's battles, 1807 if memory serves.'

Emily was right again.

'And the third clue?'

'Er . . . a letter, written in French.'

'Precisely. By a mother to her son – to a little boy called Louis. Only the little boy had grown up. He had become a soldier in the British Army. He had trained at Woolwich – The Shop – and she warned him to beware of the Alpine Club because it was too dangerous. The mother was the Empress Eugenie and the son was Napoleon Eugene Louis Buonaparte, the Prince Imperial.'

'You mean . . . the body below the Cow Rock was the heir to the throne of France?'

'No,' growled Steele, 'that's what you were supposed to think. Unfortunately, with you on the case, there wasn't much chance of that. Our friend made the basic mistake of assuming that the British Police are halfway intelligent.'

Lestrade ignored him, 'So who . . . ?'

'Who killed the Prince Imperial? No one has . . . yet. It's going to be a bit of a race, Lestrade, between you and me, to see who does it first.'

'What? Do you mean . . . ?' Realization was beginning to dawn.

'Exactly. The Prince Imperial has lost whatever slight hold on reason he might once have had. Not much of a head start, poor bugger, a grasping Spic of a mother, a father half-adventurer, half-daydreamer. And the poor little bastard given the Legion of Honour when he was two days old. It's a lot to live up to.'

'Then . . .'

'He's not in South Africa, before you ask,' Steele said.

Lestrade hadn't intended to.

'He jumped ship, as it were, even before he got on the train. Vanished for a while, but obviously had made his way north. We know he was at Ilkley because that's where he hacked a passing labourer to death with his Royal Artillery sword and took his identity. He knew people would come looking for him. He hoped to shake them off for ever by dying. But there was a problem there. He has one of the most ordinary faces I've ever seen, but somebody will recognize him – Jaheel Carey, for instance, his ADC. So he picked off a passing labourer who bore a passing resemblance to him and bashed his face to a pulp for good measure. Then he planted those obvious clues – the handker-chief, the watch, the letter. Then he joined the circus.'

'And that's where Lyle recognized him,' Lestrade kicked him-self metaphorically.

'What?'

'The day before he died, Lieutenant Lyle went to watch the circus. They were at Harrogate then, coming out of winter quar-ters, taking men on. Of course he recognized him. They'd been at Woolwich together. *That's* why he couldn't believe it. What was it he said – "They'd never allow it"? Well, of course they wouldn't. The very idea of the Prince Imperial working for a circus is impossible. What a superb hiding place.'

'All right,' Steele agreed, 'so Lyle had to die. He killed both men the way he'd been taught – the cuts of the German Schläge-rei, the student duel, as popular in France as it is in Germany. Of course, your Inspector was different.'

'You know about him too?'

'Of course, Lestrade,' Steele sighed, 'I am a detective. I tend to detect.'

'But Heneage was harmless,' Lestrade told him. 'Couldn't investigate a rice pudding.'

'Yes, but the Prince Imperial didn't know that. He probably panicked. Realized that here was an officer from Scotland Yard on to him.'

'So he killed him.'

'Yes, he'd already dropped the sword. Stashed it somewhere, I shouldn't wonder. And then his mind began to work. With that curious brilliance sometimes found in the insane, he hatched a wicked plan. Why not kill Heneage with a weapon that would point to somebody else being the murderer? He's been doing it ever since.'

'The ankus pointed to the elephant man, the Sultan of Ramnuggar.'

'Precisely.'

'The live ammunition in the pistol to Dakota-Bred Carver; the acid of sugar in the ether bottle to George Sanger; then of course there was the tangled web of the Brodies, what with her persuasions and so on.'

'He hoped you'd go for the Spaniard.'

'Which I nearly did. But why kill Lucinda?'

'Because she knew something would be my guess.'

Lestrade remembered it all too well. How she had lost her temper and stormed from his room, taunting him with what she knew. But he wasn't telling Steele that.

'So the Prince Imperial isn't Jim Crockett?'

'Of course not. The ginger beard's no fake. The height. The weight. It's all wrong. This man is elusive, but he's not a master of disguise. Crockett's been with Sanger for years. Our man has arrived recently. And all I've got to do is to see three more people.'

'Three?'

'You forget, Lestrade, I know what the Prince Imperial looks like.'

'What?'

Steele laughed. 'Oh, no,' he said, 'I'm not handing him to you on a plate. I've come too far and worked too hard for that. Just leave the crime solving to me, Sholto, m'boy. You're in over your head. By tonight, I'll have met everyone in this damned freak show. Take my word for it, there'll be no more murders in the sawdust ring.'

9

Oliver Steele sat in the chair, upright, rigid. His shirt and jacket hung in threads, draped around his body, and his boots were ripped and twisted. His face was as black as any nigger minstrel's, and his teeth bared in a permanent grin. His scalp was dark and devoid of hair and across his chest were deep lacerations, blacker than the surrounding skin that exposed a grey-looking rib on one side below his heart. His knuckles were a deathly white and across his arms and shoulders reddish-brown tree-leaf mottlings had left their mark.

'For Christ's sake, Lestrade,' Sanger whispered, his terrified voice barely audible, 'nothing human could have done that.'

Lestrade muttered, 'Here's another fine mess you've got yourself into, Oliver.'

Nathaniel Isinglass was a little the wrong side of forty. The fact that his spectacles slanted across his face betrayed the dismal truth that he had ears at different levels. He was also a martyr to asthma and years of getting his head down in wet kipsey-sacks and facing the lashing rain of the road had done nothing for him. He was the boffin of Sanger's Circus. Rumour had it that he had a degree in science from Leyden University, where they had lots of jars. He sat in Sanger's wagon that night, shaking his head and doing his best to breathe now and then.

'Nat,' Sanger was saying, 'Nat. What went wrong?'

The boffin shook his head again.

'Here,' the Boss shoved a large brandy under the man's nose.

'Thanks, Boss,' Isinglass gulped at it.

'I've never seen anything like it,' Sanger muttered.

'I have,' Harry Masters stretched out his booted legs. He had been on the road in search of camel fodder for two days and it had taken its toll on his nether limbs. Indeed, below the waist, he was quite dead.

'Where?' Lestrade asked.

'Saarland, on the German border. I saw a man killed by lightning. Damnedest thing I ever saw.'

'What happened?' Sanger asked.

'Actually, it's not all that uncommon,' the vet began to lever off his hunting boots. 'Between eighteen and twenty persons each year are killed in England from lightning bolts. Not to mention animals. It depends on all sorts of things of course – the intensity of the charge, what the unfortunate is wearing, where he is standing. And on the size of the individual. A sheep, for instance, is more likely to die than a man. Wham! Instant navarin of lamb.'

'Are you saying John Samson was killed by lightning?' Sanger asked.

'No, no,' the vet said, 'I don't think that's possible, is it? I mean, the wagon around him was untouched, except for the floor.'

'He would have died instantly?' Lestrade asked.

'Look, Lister, I haven't the faintest idea. I'm only a vet, for God's sake. An old soldier.'

'You're the nearest thing we've got to a doctor,' Lestrade told him, 'and to a forensic scientist.'

'A what?' Sanger asked.

'It's what they call a man who gives expert testimony in a court of law. Er . . . I've often reported on them in the Temple, for the *Graphic*, you understand.'

'What were you working on, Nat?' Sanger looked at the boffin. He sat hunched and silent. Slowly the frosted eyes came up. 'An electric chair,' he said.

They all looked at him.

'Perhaps you can explain that, Mr Isinglass,' Lestrade suggested.

The boffin swigged again at the brandy balloon. 'You remember Tom Norman, Boss? His Electric Lady?'

'Oh, yes,' Sanger clicked his fingers to focus his memory, 'Gladys Eck – "A Lady Born Full of Electricity".'

'That's right. Tom made a fortune by getting people to watch sparks fly out of her body and give her hand a shake.'

'Shocking,' chuckled Sanger. 'Man after my own heart, Tom Norman. How was that done, Nat?'

'Simple,' the boffin said. 'Gladys was wired up under her frock to an induction coil. Another lead was attached to a metal plate under a dampened carpet. The punters stood on the carpet and when she touched them, their hair stood on end and their fingers tingled. Two thirds of 'em kept coming back for more.'

'Brilliant,' nodded Sanger. 'She's dead by now, I suppose?'

'Anyone can do it, Boss,' Isinglass wheezed. 'It's the wiring, not the woman. I was trying to go one better than that. My wiring was the same, except that it was hooked up to a dynamo of differing frequency.'

'Er . . . ?' Lestrade dithered for them all.

'Has the rain stopped?' Sanger asked. 'You can show us, Nat.'

'No,' the boffin said quickly, 'no, Boss, I . . . couldn't go there. Not tonight. I couldn't look him in the face . . .'

Sanger patted the man's quivering shoulder. 'Right you are, Nat,' he said softly, 'just tell us,' and he poured the man another snort.

'The dynamo is a bicycle – a three-wheel Facile – I bought it in Harrogate. By fixing it to the ground outside the Sparks Wagon . . .'

'The Sparks Wagon?' interrupted Lestrade.

'My laboratory, Mr Lister. You must have seen it around. It's always parked a little away from the other caravans in case of fire or in case the static unnerves the animals. As I was saying, by fixing the dynamo to the ground outside, I can wire up the leads and pedal like blazes. Of course, because it's fixed, I'm not actually going anywhere, but the faster I pedal, the greater the power surge.'

'Isn't that . . . rather dangerous, Nat?' Sanger asked, looking at the others.

'Damnably!' growled Masters.

'No,' Isinglass insisted, 'not if you pedal sensibly. The only way the charge would be great enough to be dangerous is if somebody pedalled like mad. They'd have to be very fit. And . . .' he looked around the assembled company like a frightened hare, 'they'd have to do it deliberately.'

'What time did you close the Sparks Wagon last night?' Lestrade asked.

'Let's see,' the boffin clutched the glass with both hands, 'it must have been about ten. The show was just finishing. I had some last-minute adjustments to make.'

'Did you lock the wagon?' the sergeant checked.

'Oh, yes. You can't be too careful,' Isinglass told him, 'Howes and Cushing's people are about by now, I shouldn't wonder.'

'Yes,' Sanger nodded, 'it's about that time, isn't it? We've had a fortnight of shows ahead of them. Now would be about right. I'm doubling the watch at night.'

'When I checked the wagon a few minutes ago,' Lestrade said, 'the lock had been picked.'

'Expertly?' Sanger asked.

'Not particularly,' Lestrade told him, 'but it's a Beaver and Black. I know four year olds who can pick one of those.'

'What time was the big bang?' Masters asked.

'You weren't here?' Lestrade asked.

'No,' the vet said, 'I told you, didn't I? I've been on the road. I'd only just got to my wagon when I saw people running in all directions and the flames going up. Was that from the floor?'

'And the curtain to one side of him,' Lestrade nodded. 'The explosion must have been about two o'clock.'

'Two ten,' Sanger said. 'It knocked the clock off my shelf. Caught Lady Pauline a nasty one.'

Everyone knew that Lady Pauline could stop a clock, but they were all too nice to say so.

'Certainly flustered the animals,' Masters muttered, 'I thought Cicero had had a heart attack.'

Sanger nodded, 'Minkey went berserk,' he said. 'Lady Pauline's been in the wars one way or another. First the clock, then the monkey. Bit her something terrible.'

Lestrade nodded too, but there were worse places the monkey could have bitten her.

'Well, there it is,' sighed Sanger, after a while. 'You know, I'm almost relieved.'

'Oh?' said Lestrade.

'Well,' said the showman, unbuttoning his waistcoat, 'that this one was an accident. Samson must have been nosing around in there. Whoever his accomplice was must have pedalled too fast and accidentally killed him.'

'Howes and Cushing?' Masters asked.

'Stands to reason,' Sanger nodded, 'I must be getting old, Harry. I took Samson on trust. Didn't ask enough questions. Pity, he was a damned good rigger.'

'Who's the accomplice?' Lestrade asked.

They looked at each other.

Sanger shrugged. 'Could be anybody,' he said.

'Could be the pale horseman,' Masters volunteered.

'Who?' the others chorused.

'Stromboli told me about him,' Masters said. 'I must admit I hadn't noticed. Then about three days ago I saw him.'

'Who is he?' Lestrade asked.

Masters shrugged. 'Buggered if I know,' he said. 'Nondescript sort of bloke. Big 'tache. Rides a grey. When I saw him he was just sitting, watching.'

'Anything in particular?' Lestrade asked.

Masters looked at him oddly. 'Well,' he smiled and frowned at the same time, 'it's funny you should ask that. He seemed to be moving his horse into different positions and he had a telescope. I can't imagine why, but . . . he seemed to be watching you, Lister.'

'It's the Apocalypse,' Isinglass whispered.

They all looked at him.

'No, Nat,' Sanger patted the man, 'it was an accident. Samson and the pale rider got greedy, that was all. Snooping for Howes and Cushing. They shouldn't have broken into your wagon. It's that simple. Now, gentlemen,' he stood up straight, 'it's late and it's Lucinda Brodie's funeral tomorrow. I've yet to see to John Samson – the laying-out and so on. Let's call it a night shall we? Try and get some sleep? Nell, my love,' he called back into the curtained recesses, 'look after Nat, will you? He's not so good.'

The Lion Queen staggered out dutifully, her fingers wrapped in bandages, her forehead badly bruised, victim as she was of clock and monkey. The guilty creature was obviously feeling quite contrite and was draped like a stole around her wrinkly old neck, kissing her chin every now and again.

'Come on, Nat,' she forced the sleep from her eyes and put her arm round the narrow, hunched shoulders, 'you tell Old Nell all about it – your big bang theory.'

'I can't understand it, Pauline,' the boffin muttered as they clattered down the steps, 'it shouldn't have happened. I got this letter from Sing Sing prison in America the other day. God knows

175

how they'd found out about it, my invention. I don't suppose they'll want it, now.'

'Well,' Masters yawned, 'I've just about had it. Must get some liniment on these legs. Good-night, Boss. Good-night, Lister,' and he squelched away through the mud, re-booted.

'Well, Lestrade,' Sanger yawned, 'I'll bid you good-night, too.' He reached to extinguish the lamp.

Lestrade didn't move. 'It's not that simple,' he said.

'What?'

'You once told me – in fact almost everybody's told me – that in the circus nothing is quite what it seems.'

'So?'

'So, you're right. John Samson wasn't what he seemed.'

'Obviously.'

'No,' Lestrade persisted, 'no, Mr Sanger, not obviously. He didn't play the spy for Howes and Cushing. He played the spy for . . . well, it doesn't matter who. The point is that he was looking for me. His name was Oliver Steele and he was a private detective.'

'Good God!' Sanger sat down heavily. 'He was still a damn good rigger. I'd swear he was circus. How did you find this out?'

'He told me. He knew who I was, of course, and one thing led to another.'

'So his death . . .'

'Was about as accidental as the Custer Massacre. You see, he was on to the murderer. He told me he had three more people to interview out of your entire company. Three more and he'd have had him.'

'Really?' Sanger was astonished.

'We can assume, I think, that Nat Isinglass was one of them. He and his Sparks Wagon are about as noticeable as dandruff on a white muff. I hadn't seen him. Chances are Steele hadn't either. And unless Isinglass is the best faker since Maskelyne, he's innocent as the driven.'

'I agree,' Sanger said, 'been with me for years. I don't know who's more shocked, him or Samson.'

'That means that Steele had narrowed it down to two. Two out of three hundred. Only I don't know which two.'

'That's a bitch,' the showman observed. 'Didn't he give you any clue?'

176

'Oh, I'm awash with clues,' Lestrade said, 'I know who I'm looking for.'

'Eh?'

'His name but not what he looks like.'

Sanger frowned. 'Any Irish blood in you, Lestrade?' he asked.

'Any Frenchmen with the circus, Mr Sanger?'

'Frenchmen?' Sanger thought. 'Er . . . let me see. Well, yes, all the Buttresses are.'

'The Flying Buttresses?'

'The same. They're really the Elbeufs, from Nancy.'

'Six in the troupe, aren't there?'

'That's right. Three men. Three girls.'

'Er . . . rather a delicate question, really,' Lestrade hesitated to ask it, 'but, they *are* girls, the three?'

'Of course they are,' Sanger frowned. 'That bastard Phineas Barnum's got the Human Hermaphrodite – Half-Man, Half-Earthworm. I'd kill for him, er . . . her . . . um . . . it.'

'What about new people?' Lestrade asked. 'Who's new this season?'

'God, a lot of 'em,' Sanger said. 'Riggers and labourers by the score. A circus can't function on its stars alone. You need a lot of hands. Dakota-Bred's new, of course. It's his first season. Henry Masters – except that he was vet with Powell and Clarke for years. Stromboli – he was with Gentz until last year. Quite a coup, he is. Then there's Maccomo.'

'The lion tamer?'

'That's the chappie.'

'Black?'

'As your hat. From French West Africa, I understand.'

'Is he?' Lestrade felt the hairs on his neck crawl. 'Is he now?'

'Does that help?' Sanger shouted as the sergeant dashed into the night.

'It might,' Lestrade called back. 'It just might.'

He crossed the compound under the shadow of the Big Top, a black silhouette against a threatening sky. The rain had stopped, but water still dripped from awning and roof, splashing in puddles that carried the reflections of the coming dawn. It was the middle of May, but the blossom nodded tightly budded on the trees and the nights were raw and cold still. Where was spring? Where was summer? Miss Stevens turned in her straw-filled bed at the crunch of his boots on the gravel. No, it wasn't Huge Hughie. She went back to sleep. And to wait.

'Lestrade,' the hissed name made him turn. The white lips, the orange hair, the softly whizzing bow tie. He'd seen them somewhere before.

'Stromboli,' the sergeant stepped up to his ankle in water, 'I'm in a hurry.'

'I know,' the clown said, 'but there's something I think you should know.'

'Really,' he backed with the august into the shadows as the camels chewed the cud behind them, staring with patient eyes.

'Something Bendy Hendey said the other day.'

'I've talked to Hendey,' Lestrade told him.

'I know you have. So have I. But this was just general chat. We were waiting to go on last night. The Sultan's elephants were in the ring. I was arranging my buckets with Whamsical.'

'Please, Mr Stromboli,' Lestrade said, 'I don't have much time.'

'Probably not,' the clown said cryptically. 'Hendey hasn't stopped talking about Hughie the dwarf since the little fellow died.'

'So I believe.'

'Grief,' the great clown said, 'I've seen it before. Apparently, Hendey remembered something Hughie had said on the day he died.'

'Which was?'

'He'd seen something – on the day Joey Atkins died. He saw someone coming out of Dakota-Bred's caravan.'

Lestrade looked at his man. 'Did he now? When did Hendey tell you this?'

'Last night, during the show.'

'I don't suppose Hendey told you who it was?'

The clown shrugged. 'Hughie didn't tell him,' he said. 'Where are you going now?'

'To arrest a murderer, Mr Stromboli. Want to come along.'

'You . . . you know who it is?'

'Let's just say he shouldn't have put his faith in burnt cork. Good-night.'

Tiger, tiger, burning bright in the cat-pens of the night. Lestrade had watched them perform of course for the past two weeks. But always there had been iron bars between him and them. There were still and he was grateful for that, but this time they were so much nearer. He could smell them. And they of course could smell him and had been able to for some time. They watched him pass them now, all of them apparently dozing, but all of them actually awake. The most cunning killers of all, the Bengal tigers, brindled in their deadly beauty. One of them lashed an elegant tail. Another twitched its ears and yawned. Lestrade preferred not to look too closely at the massive canines, the lolling tongue. He had never really followed statistical matters in Mr Poulson's Academy all those years ago. Even so he knew that the odds against him dying at the claws of a tiger were many millions to one. Now those odds had shortened considerably.

One of them growled as he reached the tamers' wagon. It was a sound from hell. And Lestrade did not look back. He trusted to padlocks. And he trusted to steel. But Steele was dead and what if those padlocks were made by Beaver and Black? He hammered furiously on the door and didn't wait for Jim Crockett to open it before he was up the steps and inside.

'Are you all right, Mr Lister?' the red-bearded giant couldn't help but notice that Lestrade's forehead was turning a rather nasty shade of purple where he had collided with the half-opened door.

'Who is it, Jim?' a voice called from one of the curtained sections at the back.

'Mr Lister, Freddie,' Crockett said. 'The man from the *Graphic*. He's not looking too chipper.'

'I'm looking for Maccomo,' Lestrade told him.

'Fearless' Freddie Fortescue popped his head around the curtain. A dapper little man with a central parting and twirled moustaches, his party piece was to waltz with his tigers while the band played on.

'Next door,' he said.

Lestrade got up to go.

'No, no,' Fortescue checked him, 'here, I mean. The next cubicle. Mac. Mac? Bloke to see you.'

They waited. Fortescue slid his curtain aside and slipped, appropriately, into his slippers.

179

'What's this all about, Mr Lister?' Crockett asked. 'Trouble with the cats?'

'Mac? Come on, you black bugger, wake up!' Fortescue hauled back the African's curtain. His bed was empty.

'Bugger me,' Crockett muttered, 'that's peculiar.'

'Where is he?' Lestrade asked.

'Search me,' the auburn man shrugged, but Lestrade had seen him in action. Searching him wouldn't be high on the detective's list of priorities. 'He was here last night, after the Sparks Wagon went up, I mean.'

'Hasn't been with you long, I understand?'

'Maccomo?' Fortescue ferreted for a loaf of bread, hacking it with a sinewy limb (attached to a bread knife, of course), 'this is his first season. He's good, mind. Had old Cicero eating out of his hand in minutes. 'Course, it's 'cos he's a nigger. Well, they're brought up to it, ain't they? Lions. They eat 'em for breakfast. Toast, Mr Lister?'

'No thanks. You say Maccomo was in his bed earlier?'

'Yes,' Crockett said, 'but I think I heard him get up.'

'Weak bladder?' Lestrade asked.

'Checking on the cats. Yes, he's good with lions, but he doesn't care for the tigers, does he, Fred?'

'Nah,' Fortescue took the marmalade out of a cupboard. 'Well, stands to reason, dunnit? Ain't got no tigers in Africa, have they? I didn't hear him get up.'

'No, well,' Crockett sat at the tiny table and began to help himself to the morning goods, 'you sleep like the dead, Fred. I definitely heard him get up. He's around somewhere.'

'Mr Crockett,' Lestrade looked up at him from the seat he'd felt he'd had to collapse into, 'could I have a word in private?'

'Er ... Fred?' Crockett glanced at his fellow-tamer.

Fortescue was in mid-bite, but played the white man, scooped up a few comestibles and was gone. 'I'll look for Mac, then,' he said.

'This tea's fresh, Mr Lister,' Crockett raised the pot.

'Mrs Minogue,' Lestrade said.

'I beg your pardon?'

'Please don't be obtrude, Mr Crockett,' the sergeant warned, 'I know you were at "Duntentin" the night before last.'

'Who told you?' the tamer demanded to know.

'The good landlady herself,' Lestrade told him. 'Says you and she have a thing going.'

'Well, what of it?' Crockett said. 'No law against it, is there?'

'None at all,' said Lestrade, 'I assume you and she are both adult and consenting. It's just Mrs Crockett...'

Lestrade had rarely seen a florid man lose his colour so fast. His hand shook so that the preserve plummeted to the floor with a soft plop. 'Mrs Crockett is living in Skegness,' he said, with the look of a man facing the drop. 'I write to her when I can. Not that it's any of your business, but we have not shared a marital bed since 1863. On that last occasion, we were celebrating the fall of Vicksburg, Mrs Crockett being a keen devotee of current affairs – and having a soft spot for General Grant.' He shuddered, 'Not, all in all, a happy memory.'

Lestrade wasn't sure whether Crockett was referring to starvation on the Vicksburg Bluff or a roll under the eiderdown with Mrs Crockett. Or possibly even her soft spot. He'd leave that stone unturned. 'So you take your pleasures where you can?'

Crockett nodded. If he had to take his pleasures with the likes of Kindly Minogue, here was a desperate man indeed. 'What time did you arrive at number 86?' Lestrade asked.

'I don't know,' the giant said, 'perhaps half past twelve. I wasn't carrying a watch.'

'I want you to think carefully,' Lestrade said. 'What happened when Mrs Minogue opened the door?'

The lion tamer closed his eyes. 'Er . . . oh, God, I'm no good at Hanky-Panky.'

'Don't do yourself down,' Lestrade urged. He was a generous man at heart, 'Mrs Minogue seemed to have no complaints in that direction.'

'Mrs Minogue?' Crockett seemed confused. 'What's it got to do with Kindly? Oh, I see. You thought Hanky-Panky meant . . . .' and he chuckled his booming laugh so that the table shook. 'No, Mr Lister, Hanky-Panky is circus for memory act. Shocking memory, I've got. Absolutely shocking.'

'I see. Well, let me help you, then,' Lestrade offered. 'She let you in. What then? Did you kiss her?'

'Er . . . yes, I think so.'

'Where was this?'

'On the cheek,' Crockett frowned. Not for him the Saucy 'Seventies.

'No, I mean, which part of the house were you standing in at the time?'

'Oh, the hallway.'

'Right. Then what? You made for her room?'

Crockett's eyes were shut tight again. 'Yes,' he nodded.

'Which is on the first floor. Now, *think*, Mr Crockett. Think carefully. After you'd got in, after you'd said "Hello" to Mrs Minogue and given her a kiss, did she lock the door?'

'Hers, do you mean?'

'No, the front door. Did she lock the front door?'

The lion tamer's face twisted with the effort. 'No,' he finally said as if it had been wrung from him, 'no, she didn't.'

'Are you sure? Because she said she did.'

'No, I'm sure,' Crockett insisted, ''cos she had her lamp in one hand and my . . . person in the other. How could she have locked it?'

'Yes,' nodded Lestrade, 'I can see she had her hands full. Thank you, Mr Crockett.'

'Look,' the lion man leaned forward, 'why does the *Graphic* need to know all this? You ain't going to *print* any of it?'

'No, no,' Lestrade answered him, 'rest assured, Mrs Crockett won't hear a word. I'll see myself out.'

Fearless Fred Fortescue was sitting as dawn came up like thunder, on an upturned barrel, stitching away at a scarlet tunic.

'Waddya think of this, Mr Lister?' he held it out to the passing newspaperman. 'Got it orff an officer of the Second Punjab Cavalry. Nice, ain't it?'

'Lovely,' Lestrade nodded.

'Makes the tigers feel at home, you know. Well, it's rough for 'em. Your tiger is a solitary beast, Mr Lister. And nocturnal. We 'ave 'em up all day practisin' and performin' and we puts 'em all together in a little cage. I likes to give 'em what creature comforts I can. Seein' this tunic what they wear in the Punjab reminds 'em of Inja, see?'

Lestrade saw. 'Did you find Maccomo?' he asked.

'Nah,' Fortescue went back to his needlework. 'He must 'ave gorn for an early breakfast in the Mess wagon.'

'Tell me about him.'

'What? Old Mac? He's all right, he is – for a blackamoor, I mean.'

'From French West Africa, I understand?'

'Yeah, that's right. Of the Sudanic peoples according to the classification of Professor Lepsius of Berlin. Mandingo, to be exact.'

'Really?'

'Mind yer,' Fortescue clamped the cotton suddenly between his lips, 'I think there's more than a touch of your Bantu about 'im.'

'Right. Look ... er ... Mr Fortescue ...'

'Fred. Call me Fred,' the sewing lion tamer said. 'Everybody does.'

'Fred. You've shared a wagon with Maccomo now, for how long?'

'Ooh, must be nearly three weeks. 'Course, 'e doesn't say much. What with the bone through his nose and his natural Mandingo taciturnity.'

'Of course,' Lestrade understood. 'But you've probably noticed him ... well, how can I put this? Undressing?'

'Yeah,' Fortescue said slowly. Then he chuckled. 'No,' he said, 'before you ask. It's not true.'

'What isn't?'

'That black blokes are hung like donkeys. Same as you or me. Well, me anyway. Now your male Bengal tiger, well, puts us humans in the shade, I can tell yer. Got a dong like Big Ben.'

'No, I didn't mean that,' Lestrade assured him, 'I mean, is he ... er ... is he black all over?'

'All over?' Fortescue stopped sewing in order to think about it. 'Well, not really, no,' he said.

'No?' the hairs on Lestrade's neck began to prickle again.

'No, the palms of his hands are pink; so, come to think of it, are the soles of his feet. As for his tadger ...'

'But, what I mean is, as far as you're concerned, he really *is* an African?'

'Well of course he is,' Fortescue said, 'black as your hat.'

183

Though it was true of course that Lestrade's bowler had no pink bits at all.

''Ere, why are you askin' that? What's it got to do with anythin'?'

'Nothing, nothing,' Lestrade said, quickly. 'It's just that in the circus, nothing is quite what it seems, is it?'

They buried Lucinda Brodie in a quiet spot far from the Chesterfield Road. The rain dripped on to her casket, lovingly made by the Sanger Company's chief carpenter, as Lord George said what by now were his all too customary few words. As the wagons rolled again and a tearful Spaniard knelt by the graveside and they shovelled on the earth, Sanger put back his top hat. 'Good roads, Lucinda,' he said, 'good times and merry tenting.' And they rumbled south, a stranger on a grey horse in their wake.

Chesterfield was a town of considerable antiquity on the banks of the river Rother. It was a cotton town, famous for its worsted stockings and for the twisted spire of its church, which bent, like a few men Lestrade had met in his career thus far, to the west. Most of the ten thousand souls who made up its population cheered the circus in. The weather was a bitch, but under the flares of the Big Top, all was colour and sound and magic.

It was when the Sangers had put up at the Angel that the note arrived. It was in beautiful copperplate, but the beauty ended there. It was a wet sergeant of police who met the circus owners in the hotel lounge.

'Eggnog, Mr Lestrade?' Lady Pauline was halfway through hers.

'Thank you, no,' he declined.

'I'll have yours, then,' she said and descended on another.

'Take off your Donegal, Lestrade,' Sanger was warming his backside by a crackling fire. 'I can't take the roads like I used to. In thirty years or so, I'll have had enough. Brandy?'

'Thank you,' that sounded infinitely preferable. 'Major John said there was some bother.'

He handed his hat and coat to the hotel flunkey and wrung out his trouser bottoms.

'Filthy night, Mr Lestrade,' Lady Pauline observed, absorbed between her game of patience and her nog. It was a game Lestrade himself could not afford to play much longer.

'It is,' he agreed. 'What's the bother?'

Sanger motioned him into an armchair near his own. The showman was taking an unusual night off and had replaced his hunting pink for a more sober black evening dress. 'I hear you've been asking after Maccomo?'

'That's right,' Lestrade said.

'May I ask why?'

The detective was grateful, now that his own supply had run out, to accept Sanger's cheroot. He'd have been even more grateful for a new one, but it seemed churlish to carp. 'Because it's possible he may be our man,' he said.

'I got the impression the other night that you were looking for a Frenchman.'

'Maccomo is from French West Africa,' Lestrade explained.

'Even so,' Sanger said, 'hardly an everyday sight sauntering along the Bois de Boulogne I shouldn't have thought.'

'Indeed not, but I'd like to get a closer look at his skin pigment.'

'So would I,' nodded the showman. 'That's why I sent for you.' He passed Lestrade the letter. The detective read it once. Then again. He looked up at Sanger, yellow, gaunt in the Angel's gas-lamps. Lady Pauline was searching in vain for a black king.

'Is this a joke?' Lestrade asked.

'If it is, I've yet to get the point,' Sanger said. 'What do you make of it?'

'These people,' Lestrade tapped the copperplate, 'the Fellowship of Animals' Friends . . . ever heard of them?'

Sanger nodded, 'They were featured in the *Travelling Times* two months ago,' he said. 'A new organization, a breakaway group from the curiously respectable Society for the Prevention of Cruelty to Animals. They have as their patron the Earl of Shaftesbury, no less. Nice old boy. Loves children and animals.'

'You don't think he'd be a party to kidnapping, then?' Lestrade asked.

'Well, I put a show on for him once,' Sanger remembered. 'He congratulated me at the end and said "I feel, Mr Sanger, that my business lies in the gutter and I have not the least intention to get out of it". Mind you, he's knocking on by now. Makes Disraeli look like a whippersnapper.'

'Ah, you're too trusting, Georgie,' Lady Pauline quietly cheated with the eight of spades. 'He's a self-righteous, vain, suspicious old bastard, that one. If he ever publishes his diaries, it'll all come out, you'll see.'

'Disraeli or Shaftesbury?' Lestrade asked.

The Lion Queen looked dully at him. 'Either or,' she shrugged.

'So you think he *could* be a party to kidnapping, then?' Lestrade pursued it.

'You're the policeman, Lestrade,' Sanger reminded him.

'I'm curious, Mr Sanger,' the sergeant warmed his cockles with the brandy. 'When Ollie Oliver vanished, you knew just where to go and what to do, albeit with a little help from me.'

'I took you along, didn't I?'

'Indeed. But now, you seem . . . what? To be asking for my help?'

'This is unfamiliar territory for me, Lestrade. I don't know Chesterfield. Ollie's been through – the posters are up, the tickets are sold and we parade at ten sharp tomorrow. But I don't know these maniacs who call themselves Animals' Friends. I don't know what they're going to do. We've had mad parsons have a go at us before – and we've been arrested on trumped-up charges. But kidnapping . . . well, that's a new business for us. Red three on black four, Nell.'

She blew a respberry at him, much to the horror of the passing flunkey who had never been happy letting gypsies book a room at the Angel. This one was even fortune-telling with cards.

'What do we do?' Sanger was serious, 'in cases of ransom, I mean?'

'Well, let's see,' Lestrade read the letter a third time, 'the instructions tell us to go to the cricket ground in Queen's Park. There we will find instructions as to what to do next. On no account are we to contact the police and we are to be carrying a suitcase stuffed full with one thousand pounds.'

'When you say "we" . . .' Sanger raised an eyebrow.

'All right, you,' Lestrade was more precise. 'Do you have a thousand pounds?'

Sanger looked desperate. He glanced at Lady Pauline, who was staring resolutely at the cards. 'I'll have to go to a bank tomorrow,' he said. 'It won't be easy.'

'How much credit *can* you get at the bank – that's easy, I mean?'

Sanger blew smoke from his thin lips. 'Say, two hundred,' he said.

'Right. Do it. Tomorrow morning, before the parade, go to the bank. Wear your top hat and carry a gardenia in your buttonhole. When you're there, make a fuss. Pretend the amount you're drawing out is the last penny you've got.'

'Why?'

'Because whoever wrote this letter may be watching you. They may know you're here now, talking to me, but we'll have to chance that. I think we can assume there's more than one of them, so who knows how well they've got the town sewn up. They'll be hoping you'll draw out a thousand, so make it sound as if it is. When you leave the bank, clutch the case as though your life depended on it – because perhaps Maccomo's does. Come straight back here and lock it in the hotel safe.'

'What then?'

'Go about your show business as usual. Not a word to anyone. How many tickets have you sold for tomorrow night?'

'Three hundred. The Top is full.'

'Right. Any one of those three hundred may be Animals' Friends. They'll be watching your every move. While the show's in full swing, I'll get over here. You will already have given me your key.'

'Why?'

'I'll ask the questions, Mr Sanger,' a plan was hatching nicely in Lestrade's addled brain. 'Before you leave the show, bring me some sticks of make-up – the sort clowns use.'

'All right,' Sanger said, 'but what . . . ?'

'They want to see that you get to the cricket ground at Queen's Park at midnight.'

'Yes,' Sanger remembered the letter's instructions. 'Where will you be?'

'The cricket ground at Queen's Park at midnight.'

'No, no,' Sanger hissed, shaking his head, 'that won't do, Lestrade. The letter says I must come alone.'

Lestrade smiled, 'So you will, Boss,' he said. 'So you will.'

It actually stopped raining the next day and the good people of Chesterfield strung flags across Knifesmith Gate, as much to

welcome the sun as the circus. Sanger made himself as ostenta-
tious as possible on the instructions of Lestrade. He raised his hat
to all and sundry, helped an old lady across the road (the old bag
had only just crossed the other way and was less than pleased)
and threw pennies to little boys and girls. In the Chesterfield
branch of Glyn, Mills and Currie, a pallid George Sanger spoke in
hushed tones to the teller – tones that carried to the entrance-hall
– that he had to see the manager on a matter of greatest urgency.
Lives were at stake, blah, blah, blah. No time to lose, blah. Large
sums of money, blah. For a man whose life revolved around
patter, this was bread and butter and tellers and clerks were soon
jumping in all directions and whispering in corners behind the
showman's back.

He waited in the vaults while the two hundred pounds were
solemnly counted out. Then he stuffed them into his battered
suitcase, buckled the straps and left, clutching the portmanteau
as though he were carrying the Crown Jewels or the head of
Pauline de Vere. Glancing nervously left and right, he made
straight for the Angel and insisted loudly that the case be placed
in the safe. Then, he went to work. The rest was up to Lestrade
and he sincerely hoped the lad was up to it.

The lad sat in the Sanger wagon while Stromboli slipped and
rolled his way around the tan, to the roar and delight of the
crowd. He sat in front of the mirror with the oil lamps around it,
painting his face as best he could to look like George Sanger's.
First, he clipped the moustache, then he thickened the eyebrows.
Finally he smeared the clown's greasepaint over himself to give
him the deathly pallor of the showman's parchment skin. He
could kick himself now that he hadn't more experience of this. He
should have accepted Howard Vincent's offer to play Ellen Terry
in the Police Revue after all. But no, there *were* limits. He was a
Detective-Sergeant of the Metropolitan Police. He would never
play a woman in the Police Revue. What if the woman won? He
took his eyes out a bit with a threat of magenta and just a little bit
of white to accentuate the nose. Then he pulled on the frock coat
with the gardenia buttonhole, tilted the beaver hat at just the
right angle and made for the Chesterfield night.

There was too much moon for his liking and it was nearly full. The clouds that had darkened the sky, it seemed since Christmas, had vanished and Orion and the Bear smiled down on him. In her cage a mile and a half away, old Miss Stevens sat in her evening gloves and mob-cap, licking the chintz, waiting for her little master to come back. Then she turned and went back to sleep and cried for Huge Hughie.

Lestrade crossed Low Pavement as the revellers made their way home. The show was over but he had given Sanger time to reach the wagon before he had darted out, suitcase gripped in his left hand, brass knuckles in the other. In the shadows, Lady Pauline and her husband watched him go.

'Slower, slower, sonny,' Lady Pauline whispered. 'Remember you're a man of fifty-five.'

'Fifty-three, my petal,' Sanger reminded her.

He took the corner at Beetwell Street, past the silent Market Hall with its porticoes and columns and crossed the broad concourse of Markham Road. The park lay dark ahead, its bushes shadowed under the moon. Once there, however, the ground was clear and he was bathed in light. The cricket square stood flat before him, a solitary stump in its centre. And something was flapping from it. He looked around. No one in sight. He reached the wicket and snatched up the paper he found tied there.

Even with the bright moon, he couldn't read it. He struck a lucifer, as near his face as he dared. Who knew who watched him from the bushes? Who knew how soon his greasepaint would smudge and melt? Rose Hill, he read silently, hoping his lips weren't moving with nerves. Where the hell was that? He turned back, for beyond him lay open country and the rest of Derbyshire. He retraced his steps, then found a passer-by and asked directions. He'd guessed right. Through New Square he paced, no sound in the town now but his own footsteps and a distant, barking dog. Ramnuggar's elephants must be asleep. At Rose Hill he stopped to read the nameplates. Damn! There was a Rose Hill East and a Rose Hill West. Not to mention Rose Hill itself. Which one was it? Then he caught sight of a paper flapping in the stiffening breeze, jammed behind a drainpipe. He ran to it.

Old Whittington, it said. The Cock and Pynot. Where the hell.... He saw the answer to a policeman's prayer. At the bottom of the hill, dozing at the head of a cab rank, sat a cabman on his growler. Lestrade grabbed his hat and thundered down the hill.

'Bloody 'ellfire!' the cabman woke with a start, steadying his horse in its traces. 'You're in a bloody 'urry.'

'Old Whittington!' Lestrade roared.

'There's no need to be bloody offensive, young man,' the cabman reminded him. 'Oh, I see. Old Whittington. Oh aye. All right then. Aye up, it's after midnight now – double fare, mind yer.'

'Just get there,' Lestrade ordered, 'I'll qua . . . qua . . . give you four times the fare if you're there in ten minutes,' and he fell backwards as the hack jerked forward to the driver's whip.

North across Newbold Moors they raced, the moon flying with them, until they clattered into the old inn yard of the Cock and Pynot. He poked his head out of the window, glancing up at the creaking sign. Like Lestrade himself, the sign painter had obviously drawn a blank trying to work out what a Pynot was and had contented himself with a painting of a Rhode Island Red heralding the morn. Lestrade alighted, slipped his man some silver and stood alone on the cobbles.

Dark in the dark old inn yard, a stable-wicket creaked. Lestrade stepped silently aside until his shoulder brushed the brickwork. There were no lights at the windows; only the breathing of the wind sighed with him. Then he heard it. The rattle of a chain. And the snick of a bolt. A chain he could probably handle. But if that was the bolt of a Martini-Henry, he probably wouldn't strike so lucky.

'Don't turn round, Mr Sanger,' a female voice called. 'Just put the case down where you are.'

'Where is my lion tamer?' Lestrade barked in an approximation of the showman's voice.

'Where he can't whip another lion,' came the reply. 'Put the case down.'

'Not until I see Maccomo.'

There was a muttering at his back. Lestrade guessed by the sound that whoever it was was at the casement, above and to his left. There was no telling how many of them there were, however, or where the lion man was.

'You really have no choice,' the woman said.

'Oh, but I do,' Lestrade still had not turned. 'If I choose to walk away now, you're one thousand pounds worse off.'

'And you'll have one dead persecutor of innocent beasts on your hands.'

He took his chance and turned, careful to keep the rim of his hat over his eyes. 'I've got other lion tamers,' he said.

'You'd allow your own man to die?' the woman's voice shook with disbelief. Under the overhang of the thatch, Lestrade could see she was not a bad looking piece, but with outsize teeth and a riding habit.

'Good-night, madam,' Lestrade called, 'it's been very pleasant having our little chat, but it *is* rather late and I've another show tomorrow. Got some elephants to beat to death.'

'No,' she screamed, 'wait.' She turned back into the room and there was more hurried conversation. 'All right,' she called to him. 'Wait there.'

So wait he did.

It was Maccomo who came out first, from the door below. Either that or he was a particularly careless coal miner who had not availed himself of a zinc bath in front of the fire. The man had manacles on his wrists but his legs were free.

'Put the suitcase down on the ground in front of you,' the woman ordered.

Lestrade did. 'Are you all right, Mac m'boy?' he shouted.

The negro grunted so that Lestrade was unsure of the answer. He couldn't *see* any damage to the man, but he was still in shadow. And he *was* black.

'Now you will come over here,' the woman said. Three men had clustered around her now, all of them young and well dressed. Not one of them appeared very good at this.

'Oh no,' said Lestrade. 'You send Maccomo to me. I'll stay here.'

She turned and whispered agitatedly to her co-conspirators.

'Here,' he threw the suitcase across the yard so that it landed halfway between him and them, 'one thousand pounds – oh and you can keep the case. But once Maccomo reaches it, you let him walk on to me and our business is done.'

The young men hissed angrily at her, pulling at her mutton-chop sleeves. She spread her hands, calming herself as much as them, then slipped the negro's chain and motioned him to walk forward. He walked steadily, the moonlight shining on the slope of his forehead and the tight curls of his hair. At the suitcase he stopped. In the silence, had Lestrade been wearing his own clothes, a pin would no doubt have dropped. As it was, only the sign creaked and the wind sighed.

'Now!' Lestrade shouted and the negro's shoulders bunched. His chained fists came up and his feet left the ground. In two strides he was at Lestrade's side, then running past him for the gate. Lestrade turned after him, saw the danger and ran backwards. Behind him, to block the runaway's path stood three more men, as young and well dressed as the others. Maccomo skidded to a halt on the gravel and stood there, tense and ready.

Lestrade had dashed the other way, leaping over the suitcase, and careered into the knot of Animals' Friends standing dithering in the doorway. He snatched the mutton-chop of the lady as he hurtled past and swung her with him, her arm tight behind her back, his switchblade at her throat.

'Let him go,' he bellowed.

The seven men in the yard all turned to look at him.

'When I was at the Sierra Leone Military Academy', the negro suddenly said, 'I was taught that the best method of defence is attack.' His left foot came up like lightning, jabbing into the stomach of his first captor. As the man jack-knifed, the right foot crunched against the second man's temple. The third was still standing there when the negro's two feet thumped him into the gate behind him – what is colloquially known as the middle of next week.

'And when I was at Mr Poulson's Academy in Blackheath,' Lestrade bellowed, not wishing to be outdone, 'I was taught to pick on people your own size, which is why I am holding a knife at your throat, Mrs ... er ... ?'

'Miss,' she gasped, 'Janet Spennymoor-Spalding.'

'Not the Dorsetshire Spennymoor-Spaldings?' Maccomo jumped on one of the three who still appeared to have some fight in him.

'Yes,' the woman gulped, 'do you know my family?'

'Rather,' smiled Maccomo, his teeth flashing in the moonlight. 'My great-great-grandfather was one of your great-great-grandfather's slaves.' He rattled his chains at her. 'Isn't it extraordinary how history repeats itself?'

'Now, then, gentlemen,' Lestrade said, 'I wonder if we could stop all this rather unpleasant head-stomping and lie on the ground? I'd hate to slip through sheer nerves,' he let the knife flash in the moonlight.

'You're not George Sanger,' the nearest young man said.

'Correct,' Lestrade told him, 'I am Joseph Lister of the *Graphic*. This will make a first-rate story in next week's edition. Is Spennymoor spelt with an m-o-r-e or an m-o-o-r?'

'I think you'll find that's m-o-o-r, Mr Lister,' Maccomo said, joining the group, 'as in blackamoor.'

'Right. And let's see, Miss Spennymoor-Spalding, your organization is the Society of Animals' Friends?'

'Fellowship,' she rasped, 'Fellowship of Animals' Friends. We are its militant branch.'

'And you disapprove of circuses?'

'Of course,' she winced. 'Will you let me go, you brute? You're hurting my arm.'

'What was the idea?' Lestrade ignored her, 'to bankrupt George Sanger?'

'We didn't want his money,' one of the men blurted, 'we wanted you . . . er . . . him.'

'Shut up, Charles, you poltroon!' she tried to lash him with her riding boot but Lestrade held her fast.

'I see,' he nodded. 'So that was your game. You weren't interested in cash, just the Boss.'

'Of course.' She struggled. 'He's one of the worst abusers of animals in the country. The time will come when they'll ban circuses, and zoological gardens. When vicars and people together will kneel down in common prayer for tamed and shabby tigers and dancing dogs and bears.'

'Not to mention the wretched, blind pit ponies, Janet,' Charles reminded her.

'Yes, and the little hunted hares,' another threw in.

'Well, I must confess to being rather hurt,' Maccomo assisted the men, as they lay down in accordance with Lestrade's wishes, by kicking their feet out from under them. 'First you didn't believe me when I told you that our animals are really quite well looked after. And now it transpires that you didn't want me at all, but Lord George.' He rolled his eyes and rattled his chains. 'Well, lordie, lordie.'

Lestrade dragged the woman backwards to the gate. 'Pick up that case, Maccomo, would you? It contains neat bundles of circus posters. I'd hate to lose those.'

'You swine!' Janet Spennymoor-Spalding hissed, 'you devious swine.'

'Steady, madam,' Lestrade said, 'that's very unkind to a very well-meaning body of pig. Maccomo, did they teach you to run at the Sierra Leone Military Academy?'

'Certainly,' said the negro, 'backwards of course, when discretion becomes the better part of valour. What about you at Mr Poulson's Academy?'

'In any direction, really. That's what educational freedom does for you.'

'From the gate, then?' Maccomo asked.

'Last one in his kipsey-sack's a cissy!' Lestrade clicked back the blade, pushed the struggling animal liberator forward so that she fell among her co-conspirators, and joined Maccomo on the long road back.

10

The Mandingo stretched himself under the elm tree that spread its arms across the road through Newbold Moor.

'You've done this before,' Lestrade wheezed, the greasepaint trickling with the sweat down his cheeks and behind his ears.

'In the blood, old boy,' Maccomo told him. 'The American branch of my family were always doing it, splashing through the mangrove swamps and wading through the Mississippi with an army of bloodhounds behind them. My second cousin Rastus was a stationmaster with Harriet Tubman's underground railroad.' He looked at the sunken eyes, the heaving chest of his fellow sprinter. 'If you think this is tough, you should try it with a ball and chain. By the way, I never thanked you for your timely rescue. It was deuced good of you to impersonate the Boss like that.'

'That's all right,' Lestrade said. 'Do you think they're following?' The road was a ribbon of moonlight over the purple moor. It looked empty enough.

'Well, they all ride velocipedes and such,' Maccomo said. 'Don't want to damage the flanks of any warm-blooded quadrupeds by riding *them*. Personally, I think we knocked the fight out of them.'

'I'm very glad to hear it,' Lestrade threw his hat on to the grass and rolled over in an attempt to catch his breath. 'Perhaps you'd like to tell me what happened?'

'Well, it was rather silly, really. I had this note from what I took to be an admirer.'

'Miss Spennymoor-Spalding?'

'Yes, but she didn't use her correct name. She simply signed it "Janet". Well, it was rather prurient, really.'

'It was?' Damn. Lestrade wasn't carrying his dictionary.

'I thought so. Let's put it this way, it wasn't the sort of letter I'd expect to receive anywhere along the Niger, I can tell you. It said that she was a new woman, whatever that meant. And that she had stirrings in her blood and longed to "go" with a black man. Well, Lister, as a journalist you'll appreciate the nuance of the inverted commas. It was an offer I couldn't refuse. Knowing, as I did, that all six of my wives back home have the adulthood to cope with this situation; that my marriages were sufficiently "open", I thought I'd give it a whirl, so to speak. Well, call it lust, call it vanity, call it damned foolishness, but out I went into the night at the hour suggested in the letter. I hadn't told a soul of course, because I guessed that my fellow tamers would try to talk me out of it. I'd just reached the Sparks Wagon . . .'

'The Sparks Wagon?'

'Yes. You know – on the edge of the camp – I'd just got there when, bop. Everything went black.'

'It would,' Lestrade observed.

'When I woke up, it was as though I'd had several pink gins. I had a bump on my head the size of Mount Loma and these chains on my wrists. I couldn't work out where I was at first. Then I realized by the constant clink of glasses, it had to be a pub.'

'The Cock and Pynot.'

'Precisely. My captors were perfectly pleasant, but the food . . . my dear chap, it was so *ordinary*. Not a mung bean in sight.'

'Were you able to learn anything about them?'

'Their first names. Apart from Janet, there were Charles, Algernon, Sidney and Maudsley. I didn't catch the others. They were all Merton men. Except for Janet of course, who doesn't qualify on either score. I suppose I should feel sorry for her, but then girls of my tribe are circumcised at eight and mothers by twelve. Alongside that, the terrors of a home tutor don't seem quite so awful, do they?'

'Amateurs, then?'

'Oh, grossly, yes,' the African began to flex his muscles to get some feeling back into his arms. 'They had me chained kneeling to a four-poster which wasn't pleasant, but I've known worse. Quite an *awful* eiderdown pattern. They were constantly arguing tactics. How to get Lord George and so on. Quite what they intended to do with him when they got him I don't think they knew.'

Lestrade loosened his tie. The gardenia had wilted spectacularly in his buttonhole, but at least his head was clearing now. 'I hope you won't take offence, Mr Maccomo, but your fellow lion tamers said that you didn't say much. But ... well ... you do speak excellent English for a ...'

'Nigger?' the man's teeth flashed white in the darkness of his face. 'Yes, I suppose so. I realized as soon as I arrived that my intelligence quotient was likely to prove something of an embarrassment. Circus folk are brave and talented, Mr Lister, but they're all a few elephants short of a herd. I thought it best to clam up. My superior education was all due to the High Commissioner in Sierra Leone really.'

'But I thought you came from French West Africa?'

'Oh, I do. At least I was born there, but they're an internecine lot, the Africans. Constant tribal warfare. As the son of a king I was a prized captive when the Wukari dragged me off.'

'You were a prisoner before this?'

'Oh, good Lord, yes. Well, there was the usual bartering and ransom and so on, but in the event I escaped. Blasted current in the Benue was so fierce it carried me the wrong way and I ended up in Lagos. Somebody found me washed up and took me to the British High Commissioner, Sir "Sandy" McPherson, OBE.'

'A good man?'

'The best,' Maccomo remembered with affection, 'Sandy the strong, Sandy the wise. He was always righting wrongs and he hated lies. I can see him now, laughing as he fought, working when he seemed to be playing. What a rôle model!'

'He taught you English?'

'Like a native,' Maccomo said. 'Took me into his own house-hold and treated me like one of the family. Put me down for Eton, but apparently they're full until the 1990s. When I was sixteen, I went back to papa – that's King Kaunda. Oh I was welcomed back with open arms, given the usual lion-skin shirt, the jackal neck-lace, run of the royal concubines and so on. But it just wasn't the same, Mr Lister. I'd tasted the Pax Britannica and I rather liked it. Not for me a mud hut on the Niger. There's a world out there and I decided to find it.'

'So you joined the circus?'

Maccomo laughed. 'Not exactly,' he said, 'I tried for a com-mission in the Guards but never received a reply. The Lords Taverners were equally reticent. I made for the Black Country, assuming I'd do better there, but it was just full of white men who worked in the potteries. In the end I had to face it. There are very few men like Sandy McPherson, who look beyond the colour of a man's skin to his soul. I was wandering through Stafford one day – well, you can't do much else but wander in Stafford – getting some very black looks, when I saw this circus poster. It showed a man in a leotard wrestling a lion. I thought to myself – I can do that. So I looked up the Boss a month or so ago and he took me on. In fact, and here's the coincidence, Lord George knew my father and, transversely, my father knew Lord George. The old king was on a goodwill tour of Paris when Sanger was touring there. Small world, isn't it?'

'It is,' Lestrade agreed, but his mind was racing on. A monosyl-labic moron with the courage of a lion he'd been ready for, but an intellectual with a cut-glass public-school accent had thrown him a little. 'Tell me, did you know John Samson, the rigger?'

The negro looked at him. 'No,' he said, 'why the past tense?'

'Oh, of course,' Lestrade said, watching the man's bloodshot eyes closely, 'you were . . . away. John Samson is dead.'

'Dead? Good Heavens. Fall?'

'Electrocution. He died of shock. His face was as black as . . . er . . .'

'. . . your hat, yes,' Maccomo smiled. 'How did it happen?'

'I thought you might know.'

'Did you?' Maccomo looked at him oddly, 'how strange. I have no knowledge whatever of electricity – that sort of thing is all part of the White Man's Burden, isn't it? Not for the likes of me – an everyday story of tribal folk.'

'He died strapped to Nat Isinglass' chair in the Sparks Wagon,' Lestrade said.

'Good Lord,' Maccomo tutted, 'what was he doing there?'

'That's what I want to find out.'

'I say, Mr Lister,' the negro leaned across to him, 'you aren't a policeman on the q.t., are you?'

'A policeman?' Lestrade hoped he wasn't blushing under the five and nine. 'Why do you say that?'

'Oh, I don't know. There was a chappie who used to hang around Sandy McPherson's residence back home. Forlorn-looking party with an air of mistrust. He was always asking people where they were going to or coming from. Always got the same reply too – your average Mandingo never knows whether he's coming or going. I believe he shot himself in the end. He was Chief of Police and there was something in his manner which resembles yours.'

'Oh, no,' Lestrade lied, 'give me an upright Remington and a pencil stub any day. I wouldn't know what to do with a truncheon and bracelets.'

They went on, walking this time now that the fanatical Fellowship seemed to have lost their spoor, and Lestrade asked as many questions as he dared, bearing in mind that this bearer seemed to be on to him.

'Of course, it's not easy,' Maccomo told him, 'being of the coloured persuasion at the moment. What with Cetewayo on the warpath. And our – sorry, your – fine chaps out there going down like ninepins. Bit of a blow, Isandlwhana, wasn't it? I do hope the Prince Imperial will be all right.'

Lestrade missed his footing on the outskirts of the town. 'The . . . er . . . Prince who?' he asked as innocently as he could.

'You know, Napoleon Eugene Louis Buonaparte. Something of a national hero in French West Africa – great white hope and all that. Well, we're all ardent royalists over there; it goes with the territory. Apparently, the Boss has a new finale in mind for the next port of call. It's called "The Prince Imperial Wins Through". I'm playing, with a certain predictability you might think, King Cetewayo and everybody else is blacked up.'

Lestrade looked at him under the green of the gaslight. 'No need for you to, though?' he asked, 'er . . . black up, I mean?'

'Are you attempting levity, Mr Lister?' the Mandingo asked, 'that is a *little* like taking coals to Newcastle, don't you think?'

What was left of Fearless Fortescue lay in the Props Wagon, by now the regular unofficial morgue of Lord George Sanger's circus. His right arm was dangling from his shoulder by a twisted thread of muscle and his face had all but gone. His throat had been torn out and his sequinned chest was dark brown with blood across the place where the great heart used to beat. The Indian cavalry jacket had been ripped off his back and all that remained of it was dumped over a chair.

The loquacious Maccomo took one look and sat outside by the blazing fire, his legs hooked beneath him, his arms outstretched. He spoke to no one and no one spoke to him. For all he had tasted the Pax Britannica, he was Mandingo at heart and the death of Fred Fortescue had cut to his roots. In groups and singly, Sanger's people came to pay their last respects to the greatest lion tamer on earth.

'When?' Lestrade asked.

'After the show,' Sanger said, the tears trickling down his cheeks. 'It didn't happen in the ring. No, no one saw it. No one saw it, Freddie,' he patted the man's good hand that someone had laid across the ghastly blood. He looked up at the sergeant of detectives. 'His tigers loved him, Lestrade,' he said softly, 'all of them. Why? Why would they do this?' He stood up suddenly. 'I'm going to get him, Freddie,' he said, 'whoever did this. Whoever caused it. He's going to pay. Tomorrow, Lestrade, I'm closing the show. It's over.'

'No,' Lestrade took the man's shoulder; identically dressed as they were, it made an odd sight.

'Don't tell me what to do with my own bloody show,' Sanger hissed, 'I want no more blood in the ring, do you understand? It's finished.'

'It will be if you close down,' Lestrade said. 'Whoever our man is, he'll just walk away – and start again somewhere else. And then,' he gripped both Sanger's shoulders, 'then, Boss, you'll never get him, will you? Now. Trust me. Can I have a word with your good lady wife?'

Lady Pauline de Vere, the Lion Queen of Bostock's, sat with her head in her hands and on her head sat the colobus monkey, similarly morose. Her veil was lifted to show the ghastly scarring that mottled her right cheek. Six of her 'family' were dead and like a mother too dumb with grief to cry, she just looked at Lestrade.

'What do you think happened?' he laid his bowler on the traces in front of the wagon, looking up at her.

She shook her head and the tears started. 'Who knows?' she sniffed. 'Perhaps he was too slow on the turn. Perhaps he slipped. They don't like it if a man goes down. It panics them. And they lash out.'

'How is it done? Taming tigers, I mean?'

She hooked the monkey down and let it run through her fingers, curling itself around in her lap. 'You never tame them, not really. Tigers are different from lions, lions from panthers and so on. And they're like us, Mr Lestrade, they're greedy and sullen and small-minded and vain. And they're irritable – and some of them are murderers, just like you and me. But they're also good and kind and fair. Give me a straight choice between a cat and a man and I know which I'd take, every time. The best cat tamers feed them themselves, first with a pole from outside the bars, then inside without one. You walk quiet, you look into their eyes, you never show fear. No fast moves, no harsh words, for it rouses the dormant devil in 'em. You stroke them down the back,' her hands were moving now, over and beyond the monkey, 'moving up to the head. If you've never heard a tiger purr, Mr Lestrade, you've never lived. And you've got him, for ever. Trust. It's all based on trust. Take, for instance, putting your head in a cat's mouth. You take his nostrils in your right hand, and you lower his jaw and lip. Keep this pressure up and he can't close his mouth. You're in more danger putting your head in a linen cupboard, what with the bugs and all.'

'How long had Fortescue been with tigers?'

'All his life,' Lady Pauline told him, 'I knew him at Bostock's and he did a stint with Wombwell's before that. Nobody finer.'

'*Could* this have been an accident?'

200

She mopped her eyes, red and liquid. 'I don't know,' she said. 'I just don't know. Perhaps he sneezed.'

'Sneezed?'

'A sharp noise like that would do it. A cough you can control, unless you know you're ill – in which case you stay out of the cage. But a sneeze – it comes up on you with the speed of a cobra and there's nothing you can do.'

'Was he feeding the cats?'

'Yes, it was their supper. We'd had the usual goats sent over this morning.'

'So there was nothing unusual about the routine?'

She shook her head. 'Nothing,' she said. 'The first I knew, there was a snarling and a screaming. Everybody ran outside. Jim Crockett was there before everybody else and he drove the beasts back with red-hot pincers Tom the smith had on his forge. They shook him around, poor Freddie, as if he was a rag doll. A broken, dirty rag doll.'

'You've no way of knowing which one attacked first?'

She thought for a moment. 'They all had their claws on him. But it was Bahadur with his jaws on Freddie's throat. He'd have started it. George will shoot him in the morning.'

'He will?'

'Of course,' she struggled bravely with her tears. 'He's tasted blood, Mr Lestrade. Not a three-day-old goat carcass, but fresh, warm, human blood. Nobody'd face him now.'

A silence between them.

'Mr Lestrade,' the old sinewy hand stretched out to him. 'Do you know?' she asked with a voice that dragged through his soul, 'do you know who's doing this? Can you stop him?'

'Madame,' he said softly, 'yes and no. Yes, I can stop him. But not until I know who he is. And no, I don't know who he is.'

He searched the canvas bags and rough kipsey-sack of Oliver Steele, the dead detective, one more time. In case he had missed anything before; in case a miracle should be lying there. Perhaps the list of those he had interviewed – the list of two hundred and ninety-seven names with only three missing. The three Steele hadn't seen. The three who weren't there on the days before he died. One of whom was the Prince Imperial, heir to the throne of

201

France, blue-eyed boy of his mother, Great White Hope of the Mandingo – and murderer.

Nothing. Just an expenses claim with a Downing Street stamp and a battered map and a book called *How To Rig Trapeze*, translated from the French by M Jules Leotard. He'd just finished when the camp began to stir itself and the rays of the May morning gilded the watch-fires of the night. But the spark had gone. The show would go on, because that's what the Boss had ordered. But the heart had stopped. Men tossed cudgels to each other through the air or somersaulted over the dewy grass. The Sultan of Ramnuggar polished the toes of his elephants, Dakota-Bred stripped and reassembled his guns. But the eyes were watchful, frightened, sharp. The smiles hollow and afraid. The band played solemn music, all of which sounded like the Dead March from Saul. George Sanger walked bareheaded through his people, his good lady lion tamer on his arm, the monkey round her neck like a stole. Everywhere, the whispered word, the hand on the shoulder, the fatherly hug. The Sangers held their children to them in the morning.

'The Nondescript, Lestrade,' George Sanger looked up from the furry beast whose glass eyes stared into him. 'Extinct, of course. This is the last specimen, shot off Zanzibar in the reign of his late Majesty King George IV. Sorry,' he shrugged, 'can't resist the old showman's patter. Actually, it's the skin and fur of a howler monkey stretched over a frame. Could be anything, though, couldn't it? Defies description.'

Lestrade found himself knee deep in pigs, that sniffed and snorted against his legs.

'I don't believe you've met my Intelligent Pigs,' the showman said, 'Gloucester Old Spots, brighter than Tamworths, friendlier than Cumberlands. Like to see 'em count to ten?'

'I'd like them to tell me who my murderer is,' Lestrade said, shaking his trouser leg where a porker had widdled on it.

'Hmm,' Sanger nodded, 'do you know, I had a pony once – an intelligent one. He'd trot round the ring until he found the wickedest man in the tent. Well, of course, he was trained to halt behind me, the ringmaster and the crowd would applaud. One night, though, he stopped by this bobby – no offence – and he

202

wouldn't move on. The bobby was in his uniform of course – they never took 'em off, did they, in the old days? He was getting his rag out I can tell you, but the crowd loved it. Funny thing was, of course, the pony was blindfolded.'

'Yes,' said Lestrade, 'there *is* a funny thing. Show as usual tonight?'

'Yes,' Sanger said determinedly, 'you were right. If I close now, we'll never nail the bastard. God, is that the time?' he checked his hunter. 'We're rehearsing the Zulu War for tomorrow night – "The Adventures of the Prince Imperial and How He Won Through".'

Lestrade smiled grimly. 'Change that,' he said.

'What?'

'The title – and the ending. Call it . . . "The Death of the Prince Imperial".'

'The death? But the man's alive. Isn't he?'

'At the moment,' Lestrade nodded.

'I'm not sure I want to tempt fate like that, Lestrade,' the showman said. 'I performed before him, you know, when he was a boy. He insisted on meeting me afterwards and said – I'll never forget it – he said "When I grow up, Mr Sanger, I want to join your circus".'

Lestrade looked the showman in the face. 'That's just it, Boss,' he whispered, 'he has.'

The lights burned dim in the caravans. The elephants stood like giant boulders against the pearl of the May sky. He tapped on the shuttered window and a gnarled old head in a tea towel appeared.

'Yes?'

'Madame Za-Za? It's Joseph Lister, of the *Graphic*.'

'So it is, sonny,' she said, peering at him under her lunatic fringe, 'I've been expecting you.'

He was not quite ready for the owl that stared back at him, its tufted ears upright, its talons and wings spread. Thank God it was, like the Nondescript, stuffed. The skull didn't move around much either, but the empty eye sockets seemed to watch him as he sat down in the candle-lit wagon, the sockets that reminded him of the dead man on Ilkley Moor where the Cow Rock meets the sky. Black wax dribbled over the eyebrow ridges and into the snaggle of the teeth from the candle stub fluttering on the cranium.

'Mr Za-Za,' the old girl chuckled softly, by way of introduction, catching Lestrade's fascinated stare. 'He's a bloody sight more useful to me now than ever he was when he was alive. Smoke?'

She waved a hookah at him. He shook his head.

'Well, perhaps later,' she smiled through teeth every bit as snaggled and brown as those of her late husband. 'You're looking for a murderer.'

He put the bowler down on the maroon table-cloth as calmly as he could. 'Am I?' he asked.

'No,' she cackled, 'it's not the crystal ball. It's common knowledge. Now, tell me, sonny,' she sat down, the light of the candle eerie on her wrinkled features, the bags under her eyes like great grey sacks, 'you're no more from the *Graphic* than Nell Sanger is a raving beauty. So what are you? Copper?'

'Is that what you think?'

'Oh, not me, sunshine,' she leaned back, her hands gnarled on the table-cloth, her talons outstretched, 'I am a receptacle, that's all I am, a tube, a conductor of the vital force between the world of man and the world of spirit. I am the seventh daughter of a seventh daughter – that makes me special, you know.'

'It does?'

She leaned forward. 'You ask a bloody lot of questions, don't you?' she rasped. 'See that?' She held up a withered arm, criss-crossed with ancient scars and purple weals, 'that's the mark of a survivor, that is. The blokes what done that to me also did for my father and mother. Killed 'em both back in the winter of '31. Drove us out, they did. Called us witches and worse,' her eyes flickered and for a while she was away, over some windswept moor, through the mists of time, only a short step from hell. 'They hanged him, you know, my old man. From a wild rowan tree. I can still hear the sound – the creaking of the taut rope. And her, my old mum. I can still hear the swish of her dress in the wild weather.' She was back with him suddenly, fiercely, 'and you want me to help you catch a killer.'

'I don't believe in tea-leaves,' he told her.

'Don't you, now? Well, then, give me your hand on it,' her own snaked out. He hesitated, then she caught his palm and twisted it into the light. 'There are seven types of hand,' she crooned, stroking his.

'Don't!' he withdrew it suddenly.

'Afraid?' she snapped.

'Ticklish,' he rubbed it on his trousers.

She snatched it back. 'Hmph!' she snorted, throwing it away, 'as I thought. The Elementary, clumsy and coarse, indicating the lowest type of mentality.'

'Thank you,' he'd never looked at his hand quite in that way before. It would be quite depressing if he weren't suicidal already.

'I, of course,' she twirled her jewelled fingers by the candle-light, 'have the Psychic hand, unworldly, supernatural. Still,' she sniffed and took his again, 'we must do what we can. Ah,' she bent his thumb painfully at right angles, 'you've a powerful phalange, sonny,' she said.

'I thought we were talking about hands,' Lestrade said, but she ignored him.

'Strong will,' she diagnosed. 'Ah, yes. Yes,' she tapped the base of his thumb, 'this is your problem, sonny. This is why you haven't caught the bastard yet. A feeble second phalange – no logic. Quite plump, though,' she wagged her own finger at him, grinning through her gritted teeth. 'The Mount of Venus, you naughty man. We'll draw a veil over your powerful, thrusting sexual urges, shall we?'

'I wish you would,' Lestrade said, hoping that the dim light spared his blushes.

'Then, of course,' she peered closer at his wrist, 'the Line of Lascivia is marked.'

'Is this helping?'

She sighed patiently, 'I am the seventh daughter of a seventh daughter,' she said. 'Trust me, sonny. I've got to know what *you* are before I can divine whether you're a match for the monster that stalks Sanger's circus.'

'Do you know who it is?' Lestrade asked.

'One thing at a time,' she lisped. 'Yes,' she shook her head, 'your Line of Head is irregular, broken.'

'What does that mean?'

'That you have the intellectual bite of a cucumber,' she said without taking her eyes off his hand. 'Mind you, there's an offshoot line up to your Mount of Jupiter – ambitious little bugger, on the quiet, aren't you?'

'Madame Za-Za . . .'

'Yes, yes, I know,' she tutted, 'that's enough about you. What about your Nemesis?'

'I've let you see – and hold – my hand, madam,' he said, 'let that be enough.' There was no way he intended the old lady to see and hold his nemesis as well.

'Very well,' she said, 'the leaves,' and ferreted for a cup.

'I told you . . .'

'What you told me in the balance of things against the dark forces is quite irrelevant,' she interrupted. 'Take heed of the gyppo's warning and shut up.' He was pleasantly surprised to find the old clairvoyant using a chipped, handleless thing of vaguely Metropolitan pattern. She turned it sharply upside down on a saucer and another chip flew off. Then she closed her eyes and rotated the cup, first clockwise, then the other way. In the greenish candle-light she looked quite dead.

'There!' she pitched forward so that her sharp nose was an inch or so from the wet tea leaves. 'Hydromancy,' she purred. 'It used to be oil or molten lead, but in a wooden caravan that's asking for trouble. One's Line of Life becomes measurably shorter just before a caravan fire, I can tell you. Of course, that does open the way for pyromancy, but it's costly in terms of caravans. My personal favourite is haruspicy.'

'Harus . . . ?'

'Muckin' about with bird entrails. I used to do that until Dr Marvo and His Miraculous Mynahs complained about it.'

'The miners complained?' Lestrade was confused. 'Were you working underground?'

'No, no,' Madame Za-Za explained, 'quite openly and above board. You can't get the entrails these days. Ooh, dear.'

'What?' Lestrade's nose-tip joined the old clairvoyant's.

'See that?'

Lestrade peered closer.

'That's a sugar lump, that is. Or what's left of one.'

'What does that prove?'

She smiled and patted his cheek, 'That you're a sweetie, sonny. But here,' the smile had gone and her left eye twitched, 'here is a wire.'

'A wire?'

'A high wire,' she nodded, 'in a circus.'

'Really?'

'I see a letter,' she whispered, 'a letter "N". Upper case.'

'Napoleon,' he muttered.

'Why do you say that?' she looked up.

'Never mind,' he answered.

'It's just that the great Mademoiselle Lenormand was imprisoned by that little corporal for cartomancy.'

'I didn't know that was illegal,' Lestrade said.

'She had a session with Napoleon's brother-in-law, the cavalryman Joachim Murat and he cut the unlucky King of Diamonds four times, one after the other. She told him he'd die by firing squad.'

'And did he?'

'Can you doubt it?' she asked.

He leaned back, 'Well, then,' he said, trying not to accept any of it, 'what of my future?'

She looked again, the eyelid flickering. 'I see two young men,' she crooned, 'one will die with a broken neck.'

'And the other?'

She looked into his anxious, dark eyes and the teeth struggled into view between her thin lips. 'No,' she said, 'better you don't know.'

He stood up sharply, old Mr Za-Za rocking as Lestrade's boot hit the table. 'How many hands have you read?' he asked.

'Thousands, sonny,' she said.

'Let me put it another way,' he leaned across the table to her, 'whose hands *haven't* you read, here in Sanger's circus?'

'Um . . . let me see. Maccomo – for all his airs and graces, he's a savage at heart. Won't let me touch him. Prefers the bone throwing, like the Aborigines. Then there's . . . Lady Pauline – old Nell's a funny one and no mistake. That vet bloke says he's a scientist and won't have any truck with it. And that American sharp-shooter's always wearing gloves or his hands are full of guns, so that's hopeless. And as for Stromboli, well . . .'

'Stromboli?'

'Aloof bugger, that one. Always the same, these augusts. Think they're something special. Live on their own. Who sees them practise for the ring? Who sees them without make-up? Who knows who they really are?'

'Who indeed?' Lestrade nodded and, picking up his bowler, the one spattered with tea-dregs, made for the door, 'who indeed?' And the long-eared owl in the caravan corner suddenly twirled his head through three hundred and sixty degrees and hooted sharply 'Who?'.

'Of course,' Madame Za-Za folded a cloth over her late husband, thereby extinguishing his flame, 'I've done the Boss's hand countless times. And every time I get the same thing. He's goin' to be hatcheted to death in 1910 as sure as my name's Za-Za.'

It was the next morning, as the late May sun crept over the green fields of Derbyshire, that they found her. She lay sprawled in the growing corn, behind a hedge, not far from the horse-lines, her face blue, her tongue protruding like some grotesque gargoyle. Around her wrinkled throat, a wire cord had bitten deep into her mottled flesh and her lips peeled back from her irregular teeth. A silver trail of saliva had trickled from the corner of her mouth to the red and black check of her clown costume.

Above her, when Lestrade arrived, still in his shirt-sleeves after a sleepless night in a kipsey-sack, her husband and her brother-in-law stood motionless, each of them lost in his thoughts. Each of them alone in his silence.

'Lister,' Lord George Sanger motioned the sergeant aside, 'we can't go on,' he said. 'I know,' he raised his hand against Lestrade's silent protest, 'but it's Mary, Mrs Whamsical Walker, the wife of the clown. The nicest, kindest soul in the circus.'

'He's panicking,' Lestrade muttered, watching as the circus folk gathered in silent horror around the cold corpse.

'Who?' Sanger asked.

'The murderer.'

'*He's* panicking?' Sanger thundered. Frightened faces turned to them. He moved Lestrade further away, where the liberty horses munched their morning hay. 'For God's sake, Lestrade, look at them. They're all terrified. I've got to stop it now.'

'One more night,' Lestrade begged. 'Make a speech, increase their wages, do what you have to, but give me one more night.'

Sanger looked at him, this green detective who had stumbled

so amateurishly into his circus all those weeks ago, bringing death with him.

'And do one thing more,' Lestrade said. 'That act you've planned – the Prince Imperial against the Zulus.'

'What of it?'

'When are you putting it on?'

'Tomorrow night. We've . . .' he glared at the body and the figures kneeling beside it, 'we were to have begun rehearsals this morning.'

'Bring it forward,' Lestrade said.

'Forward?'

'To tonight,' the sergeant nodded. 'Can you do that?'

'Well, I . . . I suppose so. Why?'

'I want the Prince Imperial caught by the Impis. I want a dramatic death in the sawdust ring. Who's playing His Highness?'

'Dakota-Bred,' Sanger told him. 'Oh, I know it won't appeal to purists, but he'll look the part in uniform with a false moustache.'

'Very well,' Lestrade nodded.

'But why . . . ?'

'Trust me, Boss,' the detective said. 'After tonight, I think all our troubles will be over.'

Whamsical Walker sat on the edge of the ring, a bouquet of feathery flowers in his hand. Across the sawdust from him, his twin brother was idly twirling a mop, dripping with soapsuds. Between them, like the ringmaster or an even more unlikely referee, stood Sergeant Sholto Lestrade, Metropolitan Police.

'This makes it all very difficult,' he shouted. 'Asking questions in public like this.'

Above him, to the odd cry of 'Hoop-la!' the Buttresses flew gracefully, twisting in mid-air as they dallied with danger and defied death (at least, that was what their poster said). A small army of aproned women clattered through the rows of seats with feather dusters, riggers hauled on wires and ropes and checked their anchorings. The Chesterfield Rose Growers Society were having a field day shovelling up elephant dung from all parts of the ring.

'We can't help that,' called Whimsical. 'We've got work to do. Mary would have wanted that.'

'Ask him,' his brother shouted, 'Ask him "How does he know what my wife would want?"'

Lestrade turned to his right, fuming. 'He says . . . . No!' he threw his bowler down in the tan, 'I'm not playing this silly game of yours any longer. This is not Joseph Lister, writing for the *Graphic*. This is Sholto Lestrade, of Scotland Yard, conducting a murder inquiry.' He closed his eyes as the pin dropped from his lapel to thud softly into the sawdust.

'Bloody 'ell,' he heard a wistful French voice above him as a Buttress flew past, his wrists bandaged.

A whistle escaped from the chief shoveller of the Rose Growers, to whom the announcement also came as something of a surprise. No one else commented, least of all the pelican that was crossing.

'At least,' Lestrade implored, 'will you move nearer to me? I shall have no choice in a minute but to arrest you both for obstructing the police in the conduct of their inquiries.'

At first neither clown moved, then Whamsical padded over on his giant shoes, fell face forward, did the splits on his way up and stood at Lestrade's elbow.

'Look at him,' sneered Whimsical, 'can't bloody help himself.'

'Always the true professional,' Whamsical countered.

'Mr Walker,' Lestrade said.

'Yes,' the brothers chorused.

'No,' he turned to his left, 'Mr *Whamsical* Walker. When did you last see your wife – alive, I mean?'

'Last night,' the clown said, not taking his eyes off his brother's. 'She lay beside me in the caravan. Like a dove taking her rest.'

'What time was this?'

'We'd been to pay our respects to Fearless Fortescue. We must have turned in just after midnight.'

'Where was 'e?' a muffled voice called as the swinging Buttress swung again. He was hanging upside-down from the safe, strong hands of the catcher, letting his fingertips brush the net above Lestrade's head.

'Who?' Lestrade shouted.

'You,' all the Buttresses and the clowns chorused.

'This is ludicrous!' Lestrade had found the end of his tether.

'No, it is not,' the Buttress assured him, 'last season we 'ad ze night off, on ze Boss. It was 'is treat. We went to see zis play at ze Ambassadors in London. In zat play, ze policeman done it.'

'What about you?' Lestrade turned his investigative attentions to Whimsical, 'when did you last see your sister-in-law?'

'Earlier than him,' he jabbed a mean finger at the loose-jacketed, battered-hatted shambles in front of him, 'on account of how I sleep *this* side of the curtain and they sleep the other.'

'Would it have been possible for her to have left the caravan without you noticing?'

'Of course,' Whamsical interrupted, 'my brother has all the observational powers of my bow tie.'

'And,' Whimsical shouted, his eyebrows leaping in all directions, 'because there is a side door. She needn't have passed me at all.'

'Everyone has passed him,' Whamsical sneered. 'Much as you and I, Mr Lestrade, pass water.'

'Ask him,' Whimsical jabbed Lestrade painfully in the chest with his index finger, 'ask him why he hasn't spoken to me in fourteen years. Go on, ask him. Go on.'

Lestrade looked resignedly at the other one. 'Well?' he sighed, 'I believe you heard the question, Mr Walker.'

'I may have,' Whamsical said, 'but it's irrelevant. He knows why.'

Lestrade found himself falling in reluctantly with the rhythm. 'He says you know why.'

'Oh, yes. Oh, yes!' Whimsical guffawed, 'I know why. But I want to hear it from his lips – via yours, of course.'

The Buttresses had stopped hoop-la-ing and flying and the dangling one just dangled, while surreptitious riggers and cleaning ladies edged closer, hoping to solve the fourteen-year-old mystery.

'All right,' Whamsical shouted, throwing his hat to the tan so that it joined Lestrade's, 'all right, I'll tell him. It's because one night in 1865 – it was a few days after Mr Lincoln was shot – I came home from a hard night in the ring to find my caravan windows steamed up.'

'I had the flu!' Whimsical bellowed, his knuckles whitening.

'You had my wife!' his brother screamed.

'Liar! She was mopping my brow.'

'Brow? Brow?' Whamsical was beside himself, as well as Lestrade. 'So! So! You were lying upside down in bed, were you?'

'Upside down! You suggestive bastard! I don't stand for innuendo of that sort!' and he swung with his left fist. The brother was faster and darted back and it caught the luckless Lestrade square on the jaw. The next thing he knew, the ring was reeling and two clowns were kicking each other with their outsize feet and rolling around in the sawdust, switches of orange and blue hair flying in all directions.

The detective toyed with breaking them up when the tears had left his eyes and his vision focused. Then he thought – why? From nowhere, Sanger's circus folk, acrobats and tumblers, poured into the ring to watch the show. Ever enterprising, George Sanger went among them with his hat held out, nobbing like a good 'un.

'Hey!' Lestrade had stepped back from the battling brothers and was calling up to the Buttresses, 'can I have a word?'

'Of course,' said the dangling one. 'Get up on the net.'

'The net?' Lestrade looked at it. The thing was head height. The thing was bouncy. The thing had great big holes in it. Such was the way with nets. He felt himself lifted on the shoulders of two hefty riggers and caught the ropes desperately. He was still teetering on the edge, trying to get his balance, when a strong pair of hands caught his wrists and he was whisked, struggling and kicking, into the air.

Terrified, he shut his eyes. His life flashed before him. The buttons flickering on his old dad's police tunic in the firelight; the kind, red hands of his mother, silver-frothed with soapsuds. The mutton-chop whiskers of Mr Poulson, he of the Academy for the Sons of Nearly Respectable Gentlefolk. The long, dangling sausages of old Mr Culloden, the Butcher who had given him his first job. And ripped corpses and eyeless men and the capital letter 'N'.

'Struggle and I will drop you,' he heard a voice say. His eyes flashed open for a second. A darkly-handsome face, surrounded by a white cap was smiling at him. But it was upside-down. In fact the whole world was upside-down. He knew he shouldn't. He knew it would be a mistake. But he did it anyway. He looked down. Miles below him, it seemed, a circle of circus folk were dithering, unsure whether to watch the kicking, gouging clowns on the floor or the dangling detective in the air. The net seemed the size of a penny red and every few seconds the wind rushed through his nostrils and dried out his eyes and his stomach bobbed level with his moustache.

'What was zis word?' the Buttress asked. 'Not *merde* by any chance, was it, Monsieur Le Strade?'

'You're French?' Lestrade was excelling at small talk, bearing in mind he was thirty feet up inside a canvas bag being supported by a man no heavier than he was whose feet were hooked precariously on a bar of wood slung from two pieces of rope. He'd never put so much faith in hemp before in all his life.

'So are all ze greatest trapeze artistes,' the man said. 'Ze great Leotard – alzo I would not personally put my trust in a man whose name is synonymous wiz vest.'

'The wire,' Lestrade gasped, 'the wire that killed Mrs Whamsical Walker.'

'What of it?'

'It is trapeze wire,' breathing was very difficult for him.

'Are you asking me or telling me?' He felt his heart jump as the Buttress let go of his left hand. Now he was the right way up again, but hanging at a precarious angle.

'Er ... given the situation,' Lestrade hissed, 'I suppose I'm asking you.'

'Louis!' the Buttress called, 'zis man 'as a question to ask you.'

'Louis?' Lestrade repeated.

'My brozzer,' the Buttress said, 'ze best catcher in ze world. When we were in Sussex last season, 'e was voted ze best catcher in Rye, but zat is doing him down.'

'Yes,' Lestrade gasped, still swinging by one arm, 'Talking of down . . .'

'All in good time. Louis is a very common French name, Monsieur Le Strade. It is a corruption of Clovis, ze ancient Frankish kings of France.'

'And he can tell me about the wire?'

''E is in sole charge of it. Now, if you want an answer to your question, bring your loose arm up, slowly.'

Lestrade did. And the Buttress caught it.

'Bon. Bon.'

The last thing Lestrade wanted now was a sweet. He just wouldn't have been able to do it justice.

'Now, I am going to accelerate. As we gazzer speed, you will feel razzer as a train must feel as it reaches top speed on its way to Brighton.'

'Really?'

'Ze object of ze exercise is to let go of my arms at ze end of ze swing and swap over to Louis.'

'Let go?' Lestrade's voice was barely audible.

'But of course. If you don't,' the Buttress warned, 'we will be strung across ze ceiling like a elastic band. Zat would not be good. You cannot change ze laws of physics. One of us would snap.'

Lestrade was sure of that and he had no doubt about which one.

'Of course,' the Buttress began to thrust with his legs so that each swing took him further, carried Lestrade faster, 'Louis will have to make a grab for your feet.'

'My feet?' Lestrade gasped.

'But of course. Unless you'd prefer to try ze somersault?'

'Somersault?' In a flash it came to Lestrade. The gypsy's warning of the night before. He saw through the red mist of panic the evil old face of Madame Za-Za and heard her chilling voice rasp out, 'I see two young men. One will die with a broken neck.'

'And the other?' Lestrade heard himself shouting.

'That's right,' the Buttress had already let go of him, 'Zat's what I told you. He's my brozzer. Over to you, Louis!'

Lestrade didn't hear the '*Merci*, Jean.' He didn't hear the horrified gasps from the ground. He didn't see the Walker brothers stop thumping each other to join in the clapping. He certainly didn't feel Louis Buttress' hands, strong and safe, catch him round the wrists, or the net as he bounced harmlessly into it. All he knew was that he couldn't walk as he was lowered gently to the sawdust. His legs had turned to jelly.

Around him a throng of excited circus people clapped and slapped his back and whistled.

'A Triple, Lister,' George Sanger was beaming, 'you've done a Triple.'

'I'm sorry,' Lestrade said, 'I'd hoped, what with these brown trousers . . .'

214

'It's only been done once before,' the showman said, taking his hat off to the detective, 'five years ago in Paris. Lulu did it.'

'But that was into a net,' Whamsical panted, 'not to a catcher.'

'Pity it doesn't count,' Whimsical was waggling a loose tooth.

'Doesn't count?' Lestrade had not known fame for many seconds. He was beginning to enjoy it.

'He's right,' Sanger nodded ruefully, 'you're not one of us, Lister.'

'Lestrade,' the entire crowd, including the still-swinging Buttresses above put him right.

'You don't have a Showman's Guild card. They'd never accept it. Of course, if you joined and tried again . . .'

'No!' a little falsetto perhaps. 'No,' Lestrade baritoned again for the sake of his honour, 'I'll ask Monsieur Louis my questions some other time.'

And then, fourteen years on, Sanger's people saw an extraordinary sight. Two clowns, two brothers, wandering from the sawdust ring arm in arm.

'Come on, Wham,' Whimsical said. 'Let's say our goodbyes to our Mary, shall we?'

'Yeah, all right, Whim.'

He would ask the eldest Buttress his questions later. When the dust had settled. When he felt stronger. Once his heart was back in place and he'd changed his trousers. It was the middle of the day. Spring had come at last, rather more in the form of summer. The circus lay dumb in the heat, the elephants and horses flicking away the flies with their tails. Chesterfield children ran barefooted through the llama straw, giggling and curious. Miss Stevens rocked gently on her chair, waiting. Always waiting.

Lestrade left his bowler on the stage where Huge Hughie had died. He took an empty paper bag one of the children had left, the one they'd brought buns in for the elephants, and he held it to him. The cages were still in the midday, the only sound the soft snoring of the cats and the only movement the languid flick of a tail. His hand trembled on the bolt. Crockett would be along in a minute to feed them. In the far corner, an adult male padded to its feet at his approach, keening the wind. It lowered its massive head, raking the huge pink tongue over the rubbery black lips. Its white whiskers curled.

A second's snick of the bolt and he was inside, wondering what was worse, this or the flying trapeze. But there were no Buttresses now. No safe, strong hands. No welcoming net. Only the naked power of the jungle. Only the breath of death. They were all watching him now. All on their feet, ears twitching. They were hungry. But this was not their feeder. Fortescue they knew, by his smell. Fortescue they had killed. And Crockett they knew, although he was a lion man and never ventured into the tiger cage alone. Maccomo, the black man, he of the red-veined eyes that never blinked, they knew him too. But this human was new. He smelt . . . different. Hostile. Strange. And he was afraid. They smelt it on his sweat. They saw it in his eyes.

He watched the big male prowl to his left, a smaller female to his right. That only left the four in the centre. And the fifth, leaner than the rest, creeping between them. One snapped at him, ears flat, eyes flaring, teeth bared. He ignored the slur but it padded forward. Forward. Towards Lestrade. The eyes were golden in the massive tawny head, ringed with white. He saw the nose, dribbling pink. The jaws gape. Desperately he tried to remember Lady Pauline's words. Stroke them. Feed them. Tickle them. Grab their noses and lips. Stick your head in their mouths. But above all, no sudden moves. No loud noises. Even as he thought it, he raised the bag in both hands, curling it softly at the open end. He blew into it, gently. So gently. Then his left hand closed it shut, trapping his breath.

The tiger in the centre was crouching now, its eyes staring into his soul. His hands parted, as though in prayer. Then he slammed them together and the bag burst. As though a shot had been fired, the centre beast sprang, leaping off the powerful hind legs and clawing for his face. There was the crash of gunfire and Lestrade went down, his world full of weight and fur and muscle and sinew. Blood trickled slowly over his face. He couldn't move his leg. A five hundred pound male tiger was lying on it, dying, its claws still deep in his calf.

The cage door clanged and Harry Masters stood there, a smoking rifle cradled on his arm. 'Now, Barabas,' he said softly as a second tiger lowered itself for the pounce, 'you *are* a rotter.' He straightened in front of Lestrade and the dying tiger, smiling like a death's head. 'Lestrade,' he said, keeping his tone level, 'can you move?'

'Er . . . I think so,' Lestrade felt as though he'd lost his leg.

'Then slide your way backwards. You're an earthworm, all right? *Lumbricus lumbricus*. Move any faster than that and you're a dead man. They can smell your blood and I've only got one shot left.'

Circus folk were hurtling from everywhere to the animal cages, checking their stride as they reached them, suddenly aware of the situation, not daring to disturb the moment.

'Jim,' Sanger was there too, 'get in there.'

'They're *tigers*, Boss,' Crockett whispered, 'I'm no good with tigers.'

'Maccomo,' the showman murmured, his arms outstretched to hold his people back. 'Where is he?'

'Still mourning, Boss,' someone told him. 'Out by the campfire. He hasn't moved a muscle in twenty-four hours.'

'Lady Pauline, then,' Sanger was desperate. 'Has anybody seen my wife?'

'Barabas,' Masters was crooning, dropping slowly to his knees, 'Barabas.' The beast could not return his stare. It blinked, licked its lips and the vet planted a huge, wet kiss on its nose. Then he rose slowly to his feet and edged backwards, still covering the crawling Lestrade with his body and his rifle.

Somehow the sergeant managed to fumble with the bolt as the cats came over to sniff and maul their dead cage-mate. Masters pushed him through the rest of the way and slammed the gate as all the living tigers launched themselves on to the dead one, ripping and clawing it to pieces. People fell around Lestrade, gripping his leg, staunching the blood, catching his tongue before it fell back into his throat.

'Harry,' Sanger caught the man's hand, 'whatever I've thought about you in the past, I take it back.'

The vet smiled.

Sanger looked at the unconscious detective and the appalling massacre that was going on in the cage. 'That's Bahadur,' he said, 'I intended to shoot him myself this morning. What with Mary Whamsical and all, it went right out of my head.'

'Talking of out of his head,' Masters said, unloading the rifle, 'what was Lister doing in that cage?'

217

'Lister?' Sanger said, 'oh no. There's something I've got to tell you, Harry.'

11

He awoke to the sound of bugles in the afternoon. From the window of Sanger's caravan he caught the lance pennons flutter and shift, saw the blue and white of the uniforms and heard the jingle of bits. Nothing unusual there. Just like Hyde Park of a Sunday afternoon. What followed however was jarring, like nothing he'd heard before. It was a distant rumble, like thunder in the mountains and a single word, muffled, deadly – 'Usuthu'.

'What's that mean, Mac?' a voice called.

'Usuthu?' Lestrade heard the black man say, 'kill – it's a Zulu word. Look, John, I'm sorry, but we're not re-staging a pygmy battle here, you know.'

'I don't have to do this,' the detective heard the accountant say, 'I'm only here because the Boss asked me to, seeing as how we're so short.'

'But you only reach the Lancers' stirrups, man. It looks so . . . well, forgive me, but amateur.'

'Oh, well, thank *you*!' the accountant threw down his assegai and zebra skin shield and walked off in a huff, the goat-hair leggings dragging on the ground as he waddled.

'OK, you black varmints!' Lestrade heard Dakota-Bred drawl, 'come 'n' get it!'

'No, no, no!' Sanger's voice carried to the caravans, 'your lines are "All right, you colonial chappies. Approach if you dare".'

'Aw, shucks, Boss. Ah thought this Imperial Prince fellah was a Frenchman. You got him soundin' like there's a plum plumb in the centre of his mouth.'

'All right,' Lestrade knew exasperation when he heard it, 'that's enough for now, everybody. Tinkerbelle, leave that idea with me, will you? You as Lord Chelmsford isn't quite working, dear.'

'Of course it isn't,' Lestrade heard Dorinda shout, 'she doesn't have the beard for it. Give me that cocked hat, you freak.'

The caravan door clicked open, and the vet stood there.

'It's not going too well, by the sound of it,' Lestrade lay back on his pillow.

'Ah, they'll be all right. "The Prince Imperial Wins Through" – that has a ring to it. What made the Boss choose that, I wonder?'

Lestrade had been wondering that, too. 'Aarrgghh!'

'How *is* the leg?' Masters asked, tossing his hat on to the stand and whipping back the eiderdown.

'Oh my God!' Lestrade turned decidedly pale at the sight of the ugly stitches criss-crossing their way up his calf.

'Well, if you will go into tigers' cages,' the vet shrugged.

'I haven't thanked you,' Lestrade winced as the pain began to recede. 'Elegant work, I'm sure.'

'Nothing to do with me,' Masters said. 'You owe your leg to the Boss.'

'Sanger did this?'

Masters poured himself a hefty one from the showman's decanter and a smaller one for Lestrade. 'Sixteen stitches,' he said.

'I don't remember any of them.'

'Just as well,' the vet observed and took a swig.

'But I understand I owe you my life.'

'Oh, my dear fellow,' Masters smiled, 'it was brute against cold reason. I've never known such a reasonable tiger as Bahadur, come to think of it. But in the scale of things, I had to let him go.'

'Well,' Lestrade said, 'I shall never forget it. Never.'

'Stuff and nonsense,' Masters was covered in confusion. 'But tell me, as one lunatic to another, Mr Lestrade, why *did* you go into the cage?'

'So,' the sergeant raised an eyebrow of discovery, 'you know too.'

'I shouldn't think there's anyone left in the circus who doesn't know you're a policeman,' Masters said, 'except they probably haven't told Miss Stevens yet.'

'Well, then,' Lestrade said, 'you don't have to ask. Fred Fortescue was killed by Bahadur, yes, but my lot as a policeman was to find out who put the tiger up to it.'

Masters smiled. 'Order, *Carnivora*,' he said softly, tilting the brandy in his glass. 'Family, *Felidae*; Genus and Species, *Panthera Tigris Tigris*. The tiger hunts by stealth at night, by choking his prey with a single bite to the throat. A full-grown male brings down thirty buffalo in a year, every one of them twice his size. And they eat from the rump first.'

'Hence my leg?' Lestrade asked.

The vet nodded.

'You know a great deal about tigers, Mr Masters.'

'I hope you do now, Mr Lestrade. They're intelligent, they're cunning, they're clever. But, thank God, they have not reached that stage of development which allows them to kill because a man asks them to.'

'Can they be trained to kill?'

The vet shrugged. 'You'd have had to have asked Fortescue,' he said. 'I personally think it's most unlikely.'

'So do I,' Lestrade watched the sunlight playing in his glass, 'but that's not how it was.'

'What?'

'The death of Fortescue.'

The vet blinked. 'But . . . that was an accident, surely?'

The sergeant shook his head slowly. 'No,' he told him, 'it was deliberate. The murderer knew a lot about tigers, too. He knew a sharp, sudden noise disturbs them. That's why I carried the bag.'

'Ah, the suitcase for Maccomo's ransom. Yes, I heard about that – the talk of the camp, in fact. Nifty bit of footwork, that.'

'No, not that bag,' Lestrade corrected him, 'the paper bag. I took an empty one into the cage with me and I burst it. The bang terrified the cats, especially the one called Bahadur. He leapt at me.'

'I heard the noise,' Masters said. 'By the time I turned the corner, you were nearly one of thirty buffalo on Bahadur's menu.'

'That was a good shot,' Lestrade said. 'You could have missed. Could have hit the bars. Me. Anything.'

'Ah, beginner's luck,' Masters chuckled. 'You're luckier than you know, Lestrade. Tell me, who's behind it all? If somebody deliberately burst a paper bag when Fortescue was in the cage, he must be a little on the insane side, wouldn't you say?'

'I'm not paid to say,' the detective told him, 'I'm just paid to catch criminals. And so far', he sighed, trying to straighten his mauled leg, 'I haven't exactly done very well.'

'You're looking for one man?' Masters asked, a curious expression on his face.

Lestrade nodded. 'One man,' he said.

Masters shook his head, 'Well, I admire you,' he said. 'I wouldn't know where to start.'

'You start with a corpse,' the sergeant told him, 'a poor unfortunate somebody who happened to be standing one day in the wrong place, whose face didn't fit. Or someone who'd seen something he shouldn't have seen.'

Masters peered into the sad, dark eyes that didn't blink. 'You know who it is, don't you?' he said. 'You've worked it out.'

'Oh, I've known for a long time,' Lestrade said. 'It's the Prince Imperial.'

'Who?' Masters missed his glass in mid-swig.

'The heir to the throne of France, the son of the late Emperor Napoleon III and his wife Eugenie.'

The vet looked at him, 'How?' he asked, 'how can that be?'

'I won't bore you with the details, Mr Masters,' Lestrade said. 'Let's just say I know that he's with the circus. I know it and yet . . .'

'Yet?'

'I can't find him.'

'The rider on the grey!' Masters clicked his fingers.

'What?'

'The pale horseman. Stromboli put me on to him. He rides on the flanks as we march. Once or twice when I've been tending to some animal or other, he's been sitting his horse on a hillside or by a stand of trees. Watching. Just watching. Could *he* be the Prince?'

'He could be,' Lestrade said, 'but I think he's closer than that. I think he enjoys the havoc he causes. Not for him long-distance death, watching the mayhem by telescope. He likes it, the bastard. He wants to be here, in the centre of things, grinning like a death's head.'

Masters' face grew dark and sullen. He stood up, suddenly different, smaller somehow. 'Mr Lestrade,' he whispered, 'I have a confession to make.'

The detective braced himself. He was a caravan's length from his knuckles and switchblade and it would take him a lifetime to reach them. 'Oh?' he said, wondering how much defence an eiderdown would be should the chips be down, should the sands have run out. Lucinda Brodie was lying nearly in this position when Fate lent a hand.

Masters looked down on him. 'My name is not Harry Masters. Neither am I a vet.'

Lestrade blinked now. Had the man who was not Masters had the animal instincts of the tiger, he'd have read the fear there for all to see.

'It's Carey. Jaheel Carey and I'm a Captain of the 97th Foot.'

'You're his ADC,' Lestrade gasped, 'the Prince Imperial's.'

Carey nodded, 'And I've been chasing a ghost for three months.'

'A ghost?'

Carey gazed out of the window where the circus folk went through their paces and Dorinda was adjusting her cocked hat for her rôle as Lord Chelmsford. 'He's cold, Lestrade,' he said quietly, 'grey. He floats like mist over a meadow – wraps wire around the throat of a woman who never did him any harm. He spikes the water bottle of the gentlest showman on earth so that he kills a little dwarf half his size. He offers love to a loveless lady, only to pin her to her bed with a Bowie knife. *And he never leaves a trace*. Now, you tell me, isn't that the mark of a ghost?'

'No,' growled Lestrade, 'it's the mark of a lucky man. So far. But I've a feeling his luck just ran out. How well do you know him?'

'That's just it,' Carey slapped his thigh, turning back to Lestrade, 'I'd only just been introduced to him the morning he went. The morning he made a bolt for it on the station platform. I wish I'd watched him more closely now.'

'They say he's very ordinary,' Lestrade nodded.

'That's what they say,' Carey agreed.

'Well, well,' Lestrade rested back, 'so you and I were working on the same case all the time.'

'Apparently,' Carey smiled.

'If you're not a vet, how the hell did you manage to remove Huge Hughie's stomach?'

'Ah, well,' Carey smiled awkwardly, 'confession number two. I was one of the first to gain a commission in the army without purchase, after Cardwell's reforms in '71. There's no silver spoon in my mouth. My dad was a slaughterman. I used to work with him as a lad.'

'How soon did you find the Prince's trail?'

Carey sat down again, 'I caught a whiff in Leicester. He'd sold his tunic to a pawnbroker, though God knows, he can hardly be short of cash.'

'But he kept his sword?'

'Oh, yes,' Carey nodded grimly, 'he used that on that poor bastard under the Cow Rock. You guessed his little game there?'

'Too easy,' Lestrade lied. 'He hoped his obvious clues would put us off the scent.'

'Precisely. Lyle must have come as a shock.'

'Because he recognized him?'

'He'd already joined the circus by then, incognito to all but those who knew him best. Willie Lyle was one of those. He had to be silenced or he'd have led them to him.'

'And my Inspector?'

'A blunderer,' Carey sighed, 'hopeless. Showing his tipstaff to anyone who cared to look. But of course, His Highness couldn't take a chance. Heneage had to die.'

'One thing I don't understand,' Lestrade said, 'if he killed Lyle to cover his tracks and Heneage because he was a copper, why hasn't he tried me?'

Carey looked at him. Too hurtful to suggest that Lestrade represented no threat at all. He shrugged. 'You've survived a Triple and a full frontal attack by a Bengal tiger. Not to mention various clashes with Dorinda and the late Lucinda Brodie. Perhaps he thinks he doesn't have to bother. Man, you've aged years in the last few weeks.'

'Perhaps you're right,' Lestrade smiled. 'Are you going?'

Carey was on his feet again, 'I must,' he said, 'I have an idea.'

'Tell me.'

The officer shook his head. 'No,' he said.

'Mr Carey,' Lestrade sat upright, 'my Inspector walked out of a door not too long ago. I asked him not to do it, but he never came back.'

'Oh, I'll be back,' Carey promised, 'I just have someone to see for one last time.'

'Who?' Lestrade shouted. 'Who is it? For God's sake, Carey, this isn't a game. This man kills people like you and I swat flies.'

'No,' Carey shook his head sadly, 'I let him go once. I won't do it again.' And he was gone.

But Captain Jaheel Carey of the 97th Foot did not come back. Not that afternoon. Not that night. The man on stilts strode through the Chesterfield mud and invited the excited, chattering crowds to 'Walk Up! Walk Up!' and to see the greatest show on earth. Lestrade forced himself up, out of the wagon, hobbling painfully to the door and then across to the Big Top. He passed the tigers turning in their cages, snarling and spitting as he limped by. The lions were altogether friendlier and Crockett soon had them in the ring, putting them through their paces to the roars of the crowd.

The Walker brothers, never happier, thumped each other with balloons filled with water and Stromboli slipped and slid his way around the tan, dodging in and out of the elephants' great feet as the Sultan urged them on. 'Back, Elvira. Up, Esmerelda. You have one of your tantrums tonight, Edna, and it's no bloody hay for a week.'

Lestrade watched it all from the ringside, steadying himself on the ropes that secured the Top. The Lipizzaners trotted past him with Angelina bouncing on their spangled backs, somersaulting over their nodding, feathered heads as the crowd cheered. Then the huge tableau wagon, drawn by six greys, lumbered into the arena and on top, resplendent in Grecian helmet and trident and Union Jack shield, sat Lady Pauline as Britannia, old Cicero the lion stretched yawning at her feet and between his paws, a new-born lamb that watched the big cat's teeth very carefully indeed. Sanger cracked his whip and roared the names of his stars, his people, his family. This was a circus of death, a bloody season. Yet the show went on and nobody knew.

Trumpets blasted the sawdust ring. Lestrade's moment had come. All day he had refused to tell Sanger why he had asked for the ending of this finale to be changed. Now, it was time to see if his plan would work. The 17th Lancers thundered into the ring, lances at the upright, pennons fluttering. They were led by a tall, rangy officer of artillery, his sword carried at the slope on his shoulder, prancing on Angelina's Blackie. It was smooth. It was slick. It stirred the blood. No one knew the agony it caused Dakota-Bred, riding a saddle that felt like a school slate under his buttocks and keeping his reins short to emulate as far as possible the seat of the British Army.

There was a gasp and then a booing as the enemy arrived. Led by a glistening Maccomo, dangling in lion skins and goat hair, an entire Impi's worth of Zulus (well, twenty blokes blacked up) ran across the tan chanting and pointing with their spears.

'So, Cetewayo!' Dakota-Bred roared, 'it's you 'n' me at last, huh? This ring ain't big enough for both of us.'

Sanger had taken up position by Lestrade and covered his face with his hand. 'It's no good,' he said, 'I'll have to get Henry Irving for next season.'

'Maccomo seems to have recovered,' Lestrade said as the lion man paced across the sawdust, thumping down his long-haired legs to make the tan jump and fly. 'I thought he'd gone very peculiar over the death of Fortescue.'

'He had,' Sanger nodded, 'I just had a word in his ear. I asked him what Sandy McPherson would have done in this situation.'

'What did he say?'

'He looked up at me and said "He'd have played the white man".'

'And so he went back to work?'

'Not immediately' – the crowd roared as the lances of the 17th came down – 'I pointed out that I actually wanted him to play the black man – Cetewayo, King of the Zulus. He said he wanted to white up to play the Prince Imperial. Having seen what a coyote's breakfast Dakota-Bred is making of it, I wish I'd let him now.'

The Lancers trotted forward, jabbing the Zulus with their lance tips.

'Look out, Bert, for Christ's sake,' one of them hissed. 'This is only make-believe, you know.'

'Come out from behind that shield, John, or you'll be crushed,' Maccomo insisted.

'Why didn't you get me a little one, then?' the accountant demanded to know. 'I can't bloody see a thing behind this. Oh, Jesus!' and he rolled clear as the squadron swept through the black ranks.

'What *are* you hoping to achieve, Lestrade?' Sanger asked for the umpteenth time out of the corner of his mouth. 'This is *my* show. I have a right to know.'

'No,' Lestrade smiled grimly. 'For the next few minutes, it's the Prince Imperial's show. All we can do is watch.'

In the next pass, the 17th did not fare as well and one by one the acrobats tumbled to the tan and lay still, their lances scattered, their charge broken. Only one white man still stood upright, his sword gleaming, unhorsed but unbowed, facing an army of black fellows.

'Well, I'll be hornswaggled,' the 'Prince Imperial' declared. 'Looks like all ma comrades is dead. The only thing ah can do is die like an Englishman ... er ... Frenchman ... er ... aw, shit! Come on, you black bastards,' and he whipped out his revolver.

Maccomo came at him, spear levelled. The zebra-skin shields came up, the assegais thrust forward. But in that great tent, one pair of eyes was not riveted on the scene centre stage. Sergeant Sholto Lestrade was looking everywhere, *anywhere* but at the ring.

As the first trick assegai struck Dakota-Bred in the chest, the American-turned-Frenchman-turned-Englishman emptied his revolver at the nearest six natives who dutifully dropped in their tracks. A second spear caught him in the ribs and he went down, the sword gone from his grasp.

It was then that Lestrade saw it. A movement out of the corner of his eye, a flash of colour by the side entrance, the blur of an orange wig and a spinning bow tie. He dashed from Sanger's side, his trouser-leg flapping as he hobbled. Mercifully he didn't hear the 'Prince's' dying speech or see him carefully drape the flag over himself before he expired. The crowd booed wildly and the triumphant Maccomo became the target of all manner of missiles, all of them infinitely more deadly than the lances of the 17th.

The Big Top's glitter and flare died away. Lestrade saw the shadow running, diving, weaving, as though following something, then doubling back. Of all the times not to have two good legs! He threw away the useless stick he was hobbling on and squelched across the llama compound. All was deserted. As he guessed, the entire company had gathered in the Big Top to watch Sanger's new spectacle. Only the animals in their cages were denied the fun.

He saw the shadow lurking near the Sparks Wagon, then cut and run across to the Freak Booths, silent in the darkness. The strains of martial music wafted from the Top. Dorinda, the Bearded Lady had arrived as Lord Chelmsford to deliver an eulogy on the dead Prince and to avenge his death, much to the delight of the crowd. But Lestrade had his own deaths to avenge.

There'd be time for eulogies later. He hobbled between the wagons that formed a circle in the night. He saw the glow of the fish tanks, the deserted caravan of the clowns and of Dakota-Bred. Then, under a canvas awning he saw him. The huge shoes, the deafening check, the baggy trousers.

'Stromboli,' Lestrade said quietly.

The figure did not move.

'It had to be you, didn't it?' the sergeant moved as stealthily as a man with a savaged leg could. 'The only one in the circus who never removed his make-up. I should have guessed sooner.'

Still, no movement from the clown.

'You were one of the three that Oliver Steele had not interviewed because augusts keep themselves to themselves, don't they? And somehow you persuaded him to sit in that damned contraption in the Sparks Wagon. Who sees augusts practise? Who knows who they really are? Nothing in the circus is what it seems. And even an ordinary-looking bastard like you couldn't take the chance of being recognized. Not *another* chance, that is. Not after William Lyle. Well, it's over. It's finished. Come out of the shadows, Stromboli. A new face in the circus. The greatest clown in the world. Quite an act. Not even George Sanger rumbled you. But now, Your Highness, the act is over. Come out and take your final bow.'

The clown shuffled forward, tottering on the great shoes, then suddenly pitched on to his face and lay in the mud, his bow tie stopped by the action of the puddle, his hair standing erect from his head. An ugly knife lay buried in the back of Stromboli, the greatest clown in the world. Behind him, another figure stood in the shadows, a revolver gleaming in his hand.

'Let's all drink to the death of a clown,' he said.

'Carey!' Lestrade whispered.

'Not exactly,' he said, 'nor Harry Masters, but Napoleon Louis Eugene Buonaparte, the Prince Imperial. Nod your head, you half-wit. You're in the presence of greatness.'

Lestrade stood where he was, the clouds scudding under the moon, the puddles pearl at his feet.

'I felt sure you'd guessed it,' the Prince grinned. 'When I got Carey's regiment wrong. He is in the 98th Foot, not the 97th. I also mentioned, somewhat carelessly, my time at Saarland. I was there of course in the late Franco-Prussian War of cursed memory.'

'Yes,' lied Lestrade, 'I thought that was odd. But I assumed a slip of the tongue . . .'

'Yes,' the Prince stepped over Stromboli and raised his revolver, 'there have been several of those recently. Over-noticing busybodies who can't keep their mouths shut.'

'Huge Hughie,' Lestrade nodded.

'Saw me coming out of Dakota-Bred's wagon having exchanged the charge in the horse pistol. The silly little freak shouldn't have been so observant.'

'Then there was Lucinda Brodie,' Lestrade was playing for time, desperate to keep this maniac's finger off the trigger.

'Ah, yes,' the Prince smiled, 'luscious and leggy. Drop her skirts for anyone, would Lucinda. Especially a gentleman like me. She saw me switch blades on that idiot husband of hers. For that of course I had to put on a clown's suit. Only she noticed. Not that she seemed to care, at first. But then she took a fancy to you – quite why, I can't imagine. That was a liaison dangereuse and I couldn't risk it.'

'Tell me about the others,' Lestrade suggested.

'What? And give the show time to finish and for the relief column to arrive? You cannot be serious, Lestrade.'

'You didn't like it, though, did you?' the sergeant blurted as the gun's muzzle came up in the moonlight, 'seeing your own death in the ring, riddled with Zulu spears. I thought I'd play Mr Disraeli's game. He – or at any rate someone in the corridors of power – has engineered this nonsense that you are serving with the army in Zululand. How does it feel to see yourself die?'

'You're about to find out, old chap,' the Prince cocked the pistol.

'But it rattled you, didn't it?' Lestrade shouted, 'I knew it would.'

The gun lowered again. 'We Buonapartes are a proud family,' the Prince murmured, 'but I have enough humility to concede that I was nettled. I didn't care to stay to watch, no. Then that idiot clown came racing after me to ask what was the matter. Something about an odd look on my face. He was next on my list anyway. I'm just sorry his end was so uninteresting. So unpoetic.

I was working on an exploding cigar. Still, needs must when the devil drives.'

Lestrade risked all by closing to him, 'And what devil drives you, Your Highness?' he asked. 'What made you duck from that train and run to Ilkley and fake your own death? What made you run away to the circus? What makes you kill?'

There was a pause. The seconds crawled by like years. 'The instincts of the tiger,' the Prince told him. 'You faced it, Lestrade. You're facing it now. The grace, the power, the poetry of death. Look into my eyes, Lestrade. You won't see me blink. You won't see me miss. I'm a crack shot, remember, even in the dark. And there's no Harry Masters now to save your life.'

'Yes,' Lestrade was grateful for any straw, 'why did you do that? Why didn't you let Bahadur have me for lunch?'

'Let's just say I didn't care to be baulked of my prey. Why let him have all the fun? I'm merely sorry that your death now will not be as painful and slow as it would have been had I let Bahadur finish his leap. Still, we can't have everything.'

'Why?' Lestrade's hand came up with his heart as the pistol levelled again. 'You still haven't told me why.'

'It's this world,' Buonaparte said, 'it's too small for me. My idiot father had an Empire and he threw it away by gambling for stakes that were too high for him. He handed over the greatest Empire in the world to an old German bastard and the rabble of Paris. *My* Empire! *My* birthright. There's nothing left for me but to avenge that.'

'On the circus?' Lestrade said, incredulous.

'On the world!' the Prince snarled. 'You know, when I was a boy, we used to play war games on Sundays at the Tuileries. There was nothing I enjoyed more. Bashing hell out of my play-mates at court. They never complained, of course. When they were bleeding and battered, they said nothing. Just like this lot, my victims here in the circus. They all went down without a word. The man at the Cow Rock didn't know what hit him. Neither did Willie Lyle, the stupid bastard. "Is it really you, Louis?" he said to me, "from The Shop? From the Alpine Club?" I killed him where he stood. Hacked him down with the cuts of the Schlägerei. He always was a useless swordsman. Then,' the Prince began to move sideways, out of the moonlight, 'when I realized how easy it all was, I decided to make it into a game. Just like those games all those years ago at the Tuileries. My English is impeccable, is it not?'

'Impeccable,' Lestrade conceded.

'I could pass for an Englishman, one whose skills would fit the circus. I was always surrounded by pets as a child and of course a Buonaparte is never afraid. I excelled in dissection in my tutor's classes, I have an encyclopaedic knowledge of fauna and so the idea of the vet was born. The Buonapartes have silver tongues too, so George Sanger fell for my story. I out-pattered the patterer. From then on, it was joy, pure joy, to kill and pass the buck. The elephant goad used on Heneage, the live ammunition on Joey Atkins, the poison on the dwarf, the knife in Linda's head, the trapeze wire on Mrs Walker. Each time I killed I pointed the finger of suspicion at somebody else. Oh, the look on all their faces. The fear. The hatred. And above all, Lestrade, the look of bafflement on yours. And there again, I have to say I wasn't brought up to do my *own* dirty work. There was always someone else on hand for that.' He drew himself up to his full height. 'They took away my Empire, took away the raison d'être of the Buonapartes. So I joined the second greatest Empire in the world – yours. Zululand offered excitement, danger.'

'A chance to kill.'

'Exactly. Only then I realized from that old buffoon the Duke of Cambridge that I wouldn't be allowed any of it. I'd spend all my time on some sunny verandah, writing despatches and letters home to Mama. That wouldn't do, Lestrade. That wouldn't do at all. Well,' he smirked like the spoiled schoolboy he still was, 'it's been jolly fun as my comrades at The Shop used to say. But I think I've had enough of the circus now. I can't say where I'll go next, but the world, of course, is my smoking oyster. Goodbye, Lestrade.'

The gun was level. Lestrade's feet, gammy and otherwise, had been sinking slowly into the mud. There was no way to turn. No chance to run. He clenched both fists, shut his eyes and waited for oblivion.

Instead there was a crash of gunfire and a snort that turned into a scream. He opened his eyes to see a massive dark shadow in mob-cap and evening gloves and a pink frock with its arms around the Prince Imperial, hugging him to her. There was a noise he had never heard before and would probably never hear again. A noise like a dry stick breaking. The noise of the snapping of another man's neck. The Prince hung in the embrace like a puppet, his feet trailing in the mud, his head hanging at a ludicrous angle. Then he slumped to the ground beside Stromboli.

Lestrade stood back and the great shadow waddled forward to him.

'Hello, Missy,' he said softly. 'Thank you.'

And the bear flopped forward on to its gloved forepaws and laid its head on his chest and licked his face with her long, pink tongue. She had waited long enough.

Lestrade packed his trunk and said goodbye to the circus. They'd all come to see him off – the Sangers, the Sultan and his elephants, Dakota-Bred, Maccomo and Jim Crockett. The Bearded Lady had fondled him as much as she dared in broad daylight at Chesterfield Station and the Lion Queen had put her scrawny arms around his neck. That was nothing however to the squeeze Tinkerbelle Watson put on him. Sanger offered him a job; looking after Missy; anything. But that was not Lestrade's road. Madame Za-Za took his hand again and patted it. 'Don't get trapped by the Bracelets of Life, sonny,' she said. The Walker brothers hugged him between them and even shy little Angelina Muffett, never very at home away from her horses, blew him a kiss as he boarded the train. Bendy Hendey uncoiled himself from the lamppost to wave as the whistle blew and the detective shunted away in the morning.

'Well, Lestrade,' the Director of Criminal Intelligence was abrasion itself three days later, the sergeant squarely on the carpet, 'what have you to say for yourself?'

'The case is closed, sir,' Lestrade told him.

'Closed? Closed? You stand by and watch some wild animal break the neck of the Prince Imperial, having . . . having, mark you, already permitted the death of your superior officer *and* disappeared undercover without so much as a kiss my . . .'

'Ah, Director,' the door crashed back and an old Jew stood there.

'Mr Prime Minister,' Howard Vincent was on his feet again.

'Tell me,' Disraeli said, looking warily around, 'is that ... reptile still here?'

'Oh, yes, sir' Howard chirped, 'having something of a siesta at the moment, behind the ottoman. Shall I . . . ?'

'No!' Disraeli screamed. He tapped his gammy way across to Lestrade, who tapped his way gammily back. 'Mr Lestrade,' he said, 'it's been too long.'

'Lord Beaconsfield,' Lestrade nodded stiffly, 'it's good of you to remember.'

'Yes, isn't it? Well, Director,' the Prime Minister slumped into a chair, 'don't let me interrupt. Carry on. Carry on.'

Vincent cleared his throat. 'As I was saying . . . your conduct in this case has been appalling, Lestrade. You have broken every rule in the book.'

'I *did* catch a murderer, sir.'

'Oh, yes, Lestrade, oh yes,' the Director growled, 'rather as I catch colds – by accident. It's the horse troughs for you, sonny. By the time I've finished the paperwork, you'll be back in blue for the rest of your natural.'

'Er . . . sir?' Lestrade had hobbled over to the window. 'Before I go and change, could you answer one question for me?'

Vincent's eyes flashed fire, but he wasn't going to appear petty in front of the Prime Minister, so he permitted the impudence. 'Very well,' he sneered, 'just one.'

'Well,' Lestrade peered down into the courtyard below where constables and detectives jostled with tethered horses, 'it's just that there's not much room here in the yard at the Yard. I was wondering where you parked your grey.'

'My what?' Vincent's face had indeed turned that colour.

'Your grey. Your pale horse. The one you rode in Yorkshire and Derbyshire when you were trailing George Sanger's circus.'

'I . . . I . . . .'

'What's this about, Vincent?' Disraeli asked, his cane outstretched.

'Well, I . . . .'

'Do I understand that you merely *followed* the circus? That you were there all the time that Sergeant Lestrade was risking his life and you did nothing?'

'I . . . I thought it best to observe. I . . .' he smiled obsequiously at his Prime Minister, 'I'm not frightfully au fait with field work. I wasn't all that sure what to do.'

'Indeed not,' Disraeli nodded, his goatee twitching. 'Mr Vincent, your political leanings – those of which we spoke not long ago . . . .'

'Oh, Conservative, Prime Minister. Through and through. They don't come any bluer – or truer – than I.'

'No,' Disraeli smiled disdainfully, 'I'm sure not. Well, then. I happen to know that there's a little seat becoming vacant shortly somewhere in the Chilterns.'

'There is?' Vincent's eyes lit up.

'Yes, some scandal is about to break concerning the present incumbent and a whole choir of boys. Oh, it'll rock the country for a few days. I shall go to the Queen, God Bless Her, and tender my resignation. She'll turn it down and we can carry on as normal. But the vacancy will be there for a man such as yourself.'

'Well, Prime Minister, Lord Beaconsfield,' Vincent gushed, 'what can I say? I'm speechless. Of course, it'll be difficult combining my constituency duties with those of the Yard.'

'Er . . . yes,' Disraeli's lower lip jutted proud of his face. 'Well, I think we can scale those duties down, don't you?'

'Scale them down?' Vincent flickered, 'I don't understand.'

'Well,' Disraeli was patience itself, 'when I say "down", I really mean "out".'

'Out?' Vincent mouthed the word. No sound came from him at all.

'Look,' Disraeli spread his arms, 'we're very grateful to you, Director, for all you've done in creating the CID, but, well, frankly, I'm afraid I shall have to let you go.'

'But sir,' Vincent had turned purple, 'Prime Minister . . . .'

'Yorkshire,' Disraeli reminded him, 'Derbyshire. You sat on your grey horse, Mr Vincent, while the Prince Imperial was killed. And you did nothing.'

'Ah,' Vincent knew defeat when he tasted it.

'Now, perhaps you could leave us alone. Take that wretched iguana for a w-a-l-k or something?'

'Thank you, sir,' Vincent stood up shakily, 'but I think I'd like to be alone for a while.'

'Of course,' Disraeli closed his fingers on his great lower lip. He waited until the door clicked behind him. 'Well, Inspector . . .'

233

'Sergeant, sir,' Lestrade said. 'Although, after today, I suspect, constable.'

'Yes,' Disraeli nodded, 'I always suspected Constable – the haywain – what a dog's breakfast. I expect that reptile could paint better pictures. But I digress – something old Gladeye's always accusing me of. Mr Lestrade, you have done your country an inestimable service.'

'Catching the Prince Imperial, you mean?'

'No, Mr Lestrade,' the old Jew's eyes narrowed, 'I mean shutting up about it.'

'I . . . .'

'You haven't? Oh, but you have, Inspector.'

'Sir,' Lestrade looked levelly at his man, 'I will not take a bribe, not even one as handsome as that.'

'Tsk, tsk,' Disraeli shook his head, 'we're not talking about bribes, Inspector. The dark days of Derby have gone for ever – "Every man has his price". No, we're talking about a professional job well done.'

'But I've written a report,' Lestrade explained.

'Ah, yes,' Disraeli frowned, 'as I came in I noticed a small conflagration on C corridor – that's where you keep your records, isn't it?'

Lestrade's face fell with a certain inevitability. 'Yes, sir,' he nodded wistfully, 'indeed we do.'

'And then, with Mr Vincent's sudden resignation from the Yard, which I received today, and his new career in politics, well, it's only your word, isn't it, Inspector? Only *your* word about the whole incident.'

Lestrade sighed. 'And the Prince Imperial?'

'Sad,' Disraeli shook his head, 'sad. The Prince Imperial was killed on 1 June of this year of our Lord 1879. He ran into a Zulu Impi in the treacherous long grass of Natal. Of course, Captain Carey, his ADC, will be court-martialled. I've sent him the transcript of his trial. Heads will roll in all directions. A pity, really – a fine officer. It would have been better had he gone north in search of the Prince rather than wasting his time in the fleshpots of London. I've already sent my deepest condolences to the little abortion's mother, the Empress, along with his bloodstained uniform and other mementoes.'

'And that's it?'

'That's it,' Disraeli struggled to his feet. 'I'll see that your promotion to Inspector is gazetted in the *Police Review*. And I think a spot of leave is in order – say, two weeks?'

'That would be . . . pleasant,' Lestrade said. He felt for the handkerchief still knotted at his wrist. 'Perhaps in Yorkshire,' he said.

'Yorkshire?' Disraeli grimaced. 'I'd have thought you'd had enough of that, already.'

'I made a promise to a lady, sir,' the Inspector said.

'Aha,' the Prime Minister patted his shoulder. 'Oh, by the by, I almost forgot. Who should call to see me yesterday but my old friend George Sanger.'

'Your . . . your old friend?'

'Why, yes. Last year, on my way back from what is, so far, the greatest triumph of my life, the Congress of Berlin, I encountered the great showman and his band played all the tunes of glory in my honour. Fine fellow. Fine fellow. He was in town planning his London season for the summer. He told me the whole bizarre story. He gave me this note for you. Good morning, Lestrade. I'll see myself out,' and he hobbled away.

The iguana slithered over the ottoman and sat basking in the morning sun, watching Lestrade through indifferent eyes. The new Inspector opened the envelope. Inside, in the Boss's immaculate copperplate, he read: 'Good roads, Lestrade, good times and merry tenting.'

He kicked the iguana on his way out.